I0613750

# Kitty's War

## by

## Barbara Whitaker

**Kitty's War**

Cover Art by *RJ Morris*

The Wild Rose Press, Inc.
PO Box 708
Adams Basin, NY 14410-0708
Visit us at www.thewildrosepress.com

Publishing History
First Vintage Rose Edition, 2016
Print ISBN 978-1-5092-1090-9
Digital ISBN 978-1-5092-1091-6

Published in the United States of America

**Still holding onto his hand,**
she reached out and touched his cheek. He shivered slightly. His skin felt cold, clammy.

He was freezing.

Desperation seized her.

She needed to get him warm. His wet clothes, the chilling wind. He could die from exposure if she didn't get help.

She released his hand and shrugged out of her sweater as she looked up and down the beach. It was deserted except for the few birds scurrying along the shore. She didn't want to leave him, but common sense told her he needed more than she could give him.

"I'll go get help."

She draped her damp sweater over his chest. His eyes flew open. He reached for her. She caught his hand and squeezed it.

His eyes pleaded for her to stay.

Her insides melted. "I won't be long, I promise." She looked into those questioning, blue eyes. "It's not far. I'll bring someone to help."

A soft smile creased the corners of his eyes, and he nodded, ever so slightly.

Her throat constricted. Her breath caught and held as if she could hold onto that moment forever simply by refusing to breathe.

Impulsively, she kissed his cold hand. The odor of burnt oil and rubber lingered on his skin. "You're safe now," she whispered. "I must go, but I'll be back. I promise."

# Dedication

To my sister, Linda,
my best friend and lifelong supporter

Chapter One

*St. Simon's Island, Georgia, April 1942*

Waves washed the sand from around her feet. Katherine wriggled her toes, enjoying the sensation of the tiny granules moving between them. Despite the chill, she couldn't resist getting her feet in the water.

She closed her eyes and absorbed the warmth of the sun, listened to the mesmerizing roar of the surf, pierced by the squawks of seagulls. The brisk wind buffeted her face, whipping the long, dark strands of her hair into curly tangles.

The one benefit of coming to Suzanne's was seeing the ocean. No, not just seeing it, experiencing it. Before coming to Georgia, the Cumberland River had been the largest body of water she'd ever seen. And it was no comparison at all to the vast sea.

Maybe someday she'd go farther, travel the world, see more—oceans, mountains, cities.

Maybe someday.

The vastness stretched before her. She glanced in both directions and then turned south, the morning sun hanging above her shoulder, glittering off the water. An occasional wave rushed up and enveloped her feet in its cool, wet grasp before sliding back into the ceaseless motion of the water.

She bent and captured a seashell tumbling in a

retreating wave. Her fingers caressed the ribbed surface as she gazed out to sea and wondered how far the shell had come.

Something dark bobbed in the swells out beyond the breakers. She shaded her eyes and focused, trying to identify the object.

It looked like a raft.

In the short time she'd been here, she'd never seen anything floating off shore. Ships occasionally appeared on the horizon, but nothing so close.

Intrigued, she moved closer, into the chilly water. A wave crashed against her legs. The wet hem of her skirt brushed against her skin as the water receded.

There it was again. It was a raft. With a man slumped over, an arm dangling in the water. He wasn't paddling or fishing. He just lay there.

Was he dead? Dear Lord, what a horrible thought!

Unable to tear her gaze away, she watched the raft float up and down with each swell. Would the incoming tide carry it toward the shore?

Waves continued to break against her legs. Without thinking, she inched toward the man in the raft.

The dark head moved; his arm flailed in a weak effort to battle the waves.

He was alive.

Her heart raced. She plunged deeper into the chilling surf, ignoring the shiver that ran through her. Cold water surged against her body. She struggled against it, toward the man.

Sand shifted beneath her feet. Her brother-in-law had warned that the powerful undercurrent would pull her out to sea if she got caught in it. How far could she go before losing her footing?

She focused on the raft, with the blue-sleeved arm flopping over its side, and willed it to float closer—close enough for her to grab hold.

A swell pushed him upward. The man turned toward her, and his eyes widened. He must have seen her because he rolled over on his stomach, his brow furrowed in concentration. He struggled to paddle toward her.

An undulating wave pulled him down out of sight. She bounced in the water, straining to find him, until he reappeared still struggling against the forces of the sea. The powerful suck of undertow tugged at her feet.

She prayed it wouldn't pull him back out to sea.

As if to answer her plea, a large wave rose up behind him and thrust him forward. Another followed, almost crashing over him. She sidestepped to get closer while fighting to maintain her footing.

She lunged and grabbed hold of a rope on the side of the raft. As she tightened her grip, her feet pushed against the moving sand. She strained with all her might, determined to tow him to shore.

Wave after wave pounded them. She let each one carry them forward, and then she used all her strength to push against the shifting bottom to keep them from being sucked back out. While she struggled in the turbulent water, he lay motionless, apparently exhausted by his brief efforts.

When they reached the shallow water, she fell to her knees, tired and triumphant. The raft with its unmoving occupant rested on the sand until another wave hit it, pushed it forward, and then tugged it backward into the surf. She scrambled to her feet and pulled the heavy load across the hard, wet surface until she reached the dry powder.

She sank into the warm sand and took a deep breath before crawling around to inspect her catch.

Dark hair, wet and matted to his head, framed a sunburned, but handsome, face. Stubble defined a strong jaw softened by a slight cleft chin. He quietly sucked air into his lungs through slightly parted, cracked lips. His dark brows were knotted in a frown, and his eyes were squeezed shut as if he was in pain.

She quickly scanned him for injuries but saw no blood or broken bones.

*How long has he been floating out there? Where did he come from? Were there others?*

She gazed out over the water. Nothing.

He groaned, and her attention jerked back to the stranger from the sea.

She placed her hand on his shoulder and gently shook him.

He winced. His eyelids fluttered and then opened. Crystal blue eyes squinted in the bright sun. He slowly raised his hand to shade his eyes and turned his head as if trying to determine where he was.

Within seconds his gaze found hers, and he smiled, an innocent, boyish smile as if he had been caught in some foolish prank.

She didn't expect the thrill that ran through her. Those blue eyes, that smile. Something deep inside her responded, as if she'd found something precious she hadn't realized she'd lost.

He reached out to her.

She grasped his hand and drew it close, mesmerized by the connection. Her breath caught. The throbbing of her pulse obliterated all sound. Her whole universe shifted.

He squeezed her hand. His smile dissolved into a grimace. His swollen lips moved, as if trying to speak, but only a pitiful groan emerged.

She shook her head. Tried to think. Perhaps the struggle had been too much for him. Too much for both of them. Perhaps her reaction stemmed from excitement and overexertion, nothing more. Yet she held his hand even more tightly.

"You're okay," she whispered. Her voice came out weak, didn't convey the reassurance she intended. So she inhaled deeply, to steady herself, and tried again. "You're safe now."

He nodded and made a feeble effort to sit up.

"No. Stay still." She urged him back. "You're safe. You'll be okay."

He slumped against the raft, closed his eyes, and sighed. His face relaxed.

Still holding onto his hand, she reached out and touched his cheek. He shivered slightly. His skin felt cold, clammy.

He was freezing.

Desperation seized her.

She needed to get him warm. His wet clothes, the chilling wind. He could die from exposure if she didn't get help.

She released his hand and shrugged out of her sweater as she looked up and down the beach. It was deserted except for the few birds scurrying along the shore. She didn't want to leave him, but common sense told her he needed more than she could give him.

"I'll go get help."

She draped her damp sweater over his chest. His

5

eyes flew open. He reached for her. She caught his hand and squeezed it.

His eyes pleaded for her to stay.

Her insides melted. "I won't be long, I promise." She looked into those questioning, blue eyes. "It's not far. I'll bring someone to help."

A soft smile creased the corners of his eyes, and he nodded, ever so slightly.

Her throat constricted. Her breath caught and held as if she could hold onto that moment forever simply by refusing to breathe.

Impulsively, she kissed his cold hand. The odor of burnt oil and rubber lingered on his skin. "You're safe now," she whispered. "I must go, but I'll be back. I promise."

She released his hand, jumped up, and dashed toward the house.

As she ran, the soaked, cotton dress clung to her body. Water dripped from the ends of her tangled hair. Her heart pounded with excitement. She had to get help for him, for the man with sparkling blue eyes and a captivating smile, the man who had stolen her heart.

She scurried on through the sea oats clinging to the flattened dune while her mind raced ahead.

*Sam will know what to do.*

Her bare feet pounded the hard-packed sand road. The gate swung open easily, and she raced across the soft, green grass.

"Sam!" she yelled for her brother-in-law before reaching the wide porch. "Sam, come quick!"

Grabbing the screen-door handle, she jerked it open, turned the knob, and the front door swung wide. She called again, "Sam!"

"What is it? What's going on?" He hurried down the stairs, already dressed for work.

Sucking air into her lungs, she held onto the door frame for support. "There's a man, on the beach," she gasped. "He was in the water...in a raft. I pulled him out onto the beach."

Her brother-in-law stood there for a second, digesting her words. "Where?"

She looked back toward the ocean. "Down that way a little." She pointed southward. "I pulled him up far enough so the waves wouldn't drag him back out."

"He's alive?" Sam glanced back up the stairway toward the sound of footsteps.

"Yes, but he looks bad. No telling how long he's been out there."

Suzanne clattered halfway down the stairs in her fancy, high-heeled slippers and pink satin robe. Katherine's princess of a sister looked like she'd just gotten out of bed.

Sam told his wife, "Get some blankets. Hurry!"

Suzanne's face lit up. She turned and ran back up the stairs.

"What can I do?" Katherine asked.

He frowned at her. "Get me some water. A bucket and dipper will do."

Sam followed Katherine into the kitchen.

"Was he conscious?"

"Yes." She slammed the bucket into the sink and turned on the faucet full blast. "I told him I'd get help and be right back."

"Probably starving." Sam took a piece of bread from the bread box, wrapped it in a dishtowel, and jammed it into his pocket. "That's enough." He lifted the half-filled bucket from the sink, then grabbed the dipper from its hook, and dropped it into the water with a splash.

"You call Dr. Spencer. Then call the sheriff's office."

An energized Suzanne appeared in the doorway, dressed in dungarees and a faded red, pullover sweater. Her arms were piled high with blankets, her feet bare and her blonde hair pulled back in a ponytail. Sam ushered his wife toward the front door.

"We'll go take care of him," he told Katherine. "You stay here and wait for the doctor. Oh, and call Mr. Jonas. Tell him I'll be late. Number's by the phone."

"And listen for the baby." Suzanne gave Katherine that superior look she used to put her little sister in her place.

Katherine followed them. "Wait! I told him I'd come back!" She caught the screen door before it slammed. "I want to help him."

"Then do what I told you." Sam wasn't one to tolerate arguments.

Katherine stood alone in the front doorway. Left behind again. Disappointment tore through her. She choked back the tears that threatened to burst forth.

*I was the one who saved him. I told him I'd come back. I promised.*

She shook her head as if the motion would erase the memory of those blue eyes, that handsome, sunburned face. The way he'd looked at her.

*Stop it,* she scolded herself. *Do what has to be done.*

She crossed the slick linoleum floor and picked up the telephone earpiece. With trembling fingers, she jiggled the metal hook up and down several times and waited for the operator to pick up.

"May I help you?" the woman's voice boomed through the receiver.

"Get me Dr. Spencer. It's an emergency."

"Is the baby all right?"

Agitated by the nosy operator's tone, Katherine bit back a smart retort. "Yes, he's fine. It's a man on the beach that needs the doctor."

"Oh…well, all right. I'll get him."

After she'd told Dr. Spencer about the man in the raft and after he'd promised to come right away, she got the operator again.

"Now I need the sheriff's office. Sam told me to call and tell them about the man on the beach."

"You just hang on, sweetie. I'll get them for you."

Katherine shivered in her wet clothes. The breeze off the ocean wafted through the still-open door. Goosebumps covered her bare arms, and she clenched her teeth to keep them from chattering.

Juggling the receiver and the telephone base in one hand, she opened the small closet door under the stairway, pulled out an old quilt, and wrapped it around her shoulders. The deputy finally came on the line, and she recounted her tale again.

After hanging up, she heard a car outside. Dr. Spencer's little coupe stopped in front of the house. She ran out to the gate and directed him toward the beach where, in the distance, Suzanne waved her arms.

Remembering the baby, Katherine eased back to the porch where she could hear his cry. She hoped he wouldn't wake so she wouldn't have to get him.

She restlessly paced just inside the front door.

Anger pulsed through her veins as she thought of Suzanne out there on the beach helping the stranger. It was so like her sister, pushing her way into the spotlight. Taking over and leaving Katherine behind.

She'd come here to help take care of her sister's new baby. She hadn't wanted to come, knew nothing about caring for a newborn, but her mother had insisted. Suzanne needed help, and Katherine was the logical choice, at least to her mother.

"Only a couple of months," her mother had said. "Your sister is more important than that old school. I don't know why you wanted to go to college, anyway."

Her mother had never understood, never even tried.

So Katherine had boarded that train and had come all the way from Tennessee to help her sister.

Suzanne hadn't changed. She still saw Katherine as the little sister who needed to be told what to do and how to do it. Maybe someday both Suzanne and their mother would accept that Katherine had grown up, that she had a mind of her own.

At the sound of an engine, Katherine ran to the doorway. The sheriff's deputy parked behind the doctor's car and set out across the dune to investigate. A few minutes later an ambulance appeared. Two men got out and hiked toward the waves. She strained to see, but they disappeared from view.

Filled with anxiety, she paced the floor and waited, wondering if the man would be okay.

Suddenly remembering Sam's other order, she picked up the telephone receiver again and asked for the number written in bold letters across the top margin of the telephone book. She left the message for Sam's boss and then quickly hung up, anxious to get off before missing something outside.

An eternity passed before the two men trudged across the dunes carrying the mysterious man on a stretcher. Her heart raced at the chance to see him again. She ran out to the road.

Just as she opened the gate, he turned his head in her direction. For a moment, before the men loaded him into the ambulance, their gazes met. He smiled, that same little boy smile, and that same warm glow filled her insides. The world stopped spinning. It was as if they were alone, the only two people on the planet.

Then, the spell snapped.

He disappeared into the ambulance. Within minutes they were gone—the mysterious man, the doctor, the deputy, and the ambulance boys, all gone. The beach stretched out beyond the dunes, peaceful and deserted.

She followed Sam and Suzanne back to the porch. Her shoulders slumped. A sense of loss engulfed her.

"Will he be okay?" she asked.

"Yeah. Doc seems to think so. Exposure mostly." Sam deposited the bucket by the door.

"Where did he come from?"

"Don't know. Probably a ship went down out there somewhere. They'll find out what happened." Impatience laced his words. "I gotta get to work."

Katherine grabbed his arm, desperate to know more. "What was his name?"

Sam frowned and pulled free. "I don't know. And, frankly, I don't care. He caused enough trouble for one day." He shifted his attention to Suzanne and planted a quick kiss on her cheek before turning toward his car.

The baby wailed, demanding someone's attention.

"You better go up and take care of little Sammy. And get out of those wet clothes." Suzanne smirked before thrusting an armload of dirty blankets at Katherine. "Good thing you're doing laundry today."

Katherine pushed through the door and dumped the blankets near the foot of the stairs. She climbed to the second floor, back to the same, boring drudgery.

Yet, today had been the most exciting day of her entire life. The mysterious man might be gone, but she would never be the same. And she would never forget him.

\*\*\*\*

His grandmother promised him that angels would watch over him, but he didn't believe her. Yet he still could see the angel with the golden halo who pulled him from the sea. After days adrift, alone and exhausted, he'd given up. Until she appeared and told him he was safe.

Grandmama had been right, after all, when she said he only had to believe and the angel would come.

He drifted off again, knowing he would live, thanks to his guardian angel.

Chapter Two

*March 1944*

*It's all part of the adventure.*

Corporal Katherine Ilene Greenlee had reminded herself all the way across the Atlantic. The thrill of exciting voyages to exotic locations had spurred her to volunteer for overseas duty. After fourteen days on a rolling ship with her stomach churning like the waves in a storm, she wasn't so sure about her decision.

She stumbled onto the gangplank. The heavy duffle bag, balanced precariously on her shoulder, toppled forward and bumped the girl in front of her. One hand went instinctively to her head to keep the steel helmet from falling as she regained her equilibrium.

"Watch it," the girl complained.

Katherine drew a deep, fortifying breath and straightened under the weight of the bag plus all her other gear. She held tighter, determined to carry it all despite her screaming muscles and roiling stomach.

If she had learned anything in this woman's army, it was to carry her own load and not ask for help. There had been times when she hadn't thought she was strong enough to make the grade, but stubborn determination kept her going. She had to prove to herself and everyone else that she could do it.

By rights she shouldn't be here at all, shouldn't

even be in the Women's Army Corps. No one knew the truth, no one except her brother, who wouldn't dare tell, and her father, who'd been so certain she'd fail that he'd let her go without a word of objection.

Her feet finally landed on the dock, but she couldn't stop and celebrate her arrival in England. Instead she trudged along behind another WAC until the sergeant pointed her to a forming line. She exhaled a sigh of relief when she reached the end of the row and manhandled her duffle bag to the ground in front of her. For a second she thought she would fall on top of it. Somehow she managed to stay on her feet.

Madge strode by as if she carried a bag of feathers and flashed a mischievous grin. The girl's hourglass figure disguised her underlying strength and stamina. Even with the Army's strenuous exercise program, Katherine could never match her friend's physical abilities or her positive, unflappable attitude. The rough voyage hadn't fazed Madge a bit.

Someone elbowed Katherine. She cut her eyes around and saw Sally, grinning ear to ear.

"We made it," Sally announced. "Jolly old England. Can't wait to write my Bill and tell him."

Katherine nodded. She didn't answer because she didn't want to get in trouble for chit-chatting in formation.

"You gonna look up your brother? He shouldn't be too hard to find. England's not that big."

"Once we get settled," Katherine muttered, glancing around for the sergeant. "Better hold it down."

She wished she had someone like Sally's Bill to write to, someone she could share her innermost thoughts with. Her brother's letters from Algiers and

Sicily had been fascinating, but that wasn't the same as corresponding with a boyfriend. The image of blue eyes and a little boy smile filled her thoughts. That's who she wanted—the man on the beach, her dream man. He'd be the perfect man who'd listen and smile and tell her he adored her.

The sergeant's shout interrupted Katherine's daydream. She stood tall and forced her mind to focus on the orders and push the image from her brain. She'd long ago given up trying to find him, the real man anyway. Instead she'd settled for a daydream, an ideal, she knew deep down would never materialize.

Once all the WACs were ashore, they marched to a loading area and climbed aboard waiting trucks. Packed like sardines, they had to pile their overstuffed duffle bags on their feet.

Katherine squirmed to get more comfortable and bit her trembling lip.

Madge leaned close. "You okay, kid?"

She nodded, but it was a lie. She fought the panic, pushed it deep inside.

"We're here. We'll be settled soon." Madge tried to reassure her, and Katherine was grateful.

"I know." She placed her hands on her midsection. "I'll feel better when my stomach calms down." Truth was she didn't like the in-between. She wanted to get there, wherever there was, and get to work. She closed her eyes, leaned her head back against the canvas cover, and willed herself not to cry. After all, she wasn't alone. Madge was here with her. She'd made it so far. This was the biggest adventure of her life. She wouldn't fall apart now.

Madge patted her hand, and Katherine realized she

had squeezed it into a tight fist. "Kitty. Relax. We'll get there, in good time."

"Are you Kitty?" a girl across from them asked.

Katherine's eyes flew open. She nodded and forced a smile. Madge had dubbed her Kitty when they'd first met. And Katherine had accepted it because she'd wanted so badly for Madge to be her friend.

"I heard you were on the ship. You're the one who got all the commendations back in Boston, aren't you?" The girl stuck her hand across the mound of duffle bags. "I'm Dallas."

Kitty nodded, unsure whether the girl meant her comment as a compliment or a jibe. She leaned forward and politely shook the girl's hand. "Nice to meet you."

Remembering her manners, she pointed toward her friend. "This is Madge."

"Oh, I know Madge. Everybody knows her." Dallas grinned, exposing a mouthful of crooked teeth. "Including all the soldiers on board."

"Not all of them," Madge quipped. "I didn't have time to meet them all."

Taking Madge's advice, Kitty relaxed listening to the girls joke. She had to learn not to get upset when she faced the unknown.

By the time they reached their destination—a sea of tents almost as vast as the ocean they crossed—she was numb from the hips down.

Thus began long days of misery. The English spring meant rain, and rain meant mud, mildew, and short tempers. Eight women crammed into a tent strained the most patient among them. The tasteless food and hours of boredom didn't help.

If the Women's Army Corps was so desperately

needed for the war effort, then why were they sitting here waiting?

To keep them busy, the brass ordered close order drill on the muddy field that passed for a parade ground. Meanwhile, the Army took its time sorting out the women's assignments.

Then one morning, out of the blue, a captain appeared bearing orders. Within hours Kitty's company boarded a train and rolled across the English countryside toward Ellingham, East Anglia, headquarters for the Second Combat Bombardment Wing of the U.S. Eighth Air Force.

\*\*\*\*

Second Lieutenant Ted Kruger watched out the side window with the same nervous tension he experienced on every mission. The waist gunner in the bomber flying beside and slightly above them waved. Their wing tips almost touched in the tight formation. One false move by an unsteady pilot could mean disaster. Ted waved back.

Above he could see more bombers. Below landmarks caught his eye, a meandering river, a town. He didn't like being at the bottom of the formation, but it beat being at the end. The "tail-end Charlie" position caught the worst of the fighter attacks.

"Flack ahead." The pilot's ominous words made his stomach constrict into a knot.

Ted's attention shifted to just ahead of him where the Plexiglas nose surrounded the bombardier, McGill. Bursts of black smoke filled the sky ahead, 88's, at their altitude, as thick as he'd seen over any target. His gut tightened even more.

"Starting Initial Point," the pilot announced.

"McGill take over."

No dodging it now. The bombardier took the controls for the bomb run.

Seconds ticked away. Ted's gloved hand clenched the pencil. He forced himself to relax before he broke another one. He couldn't plot their course on the map without a pencil.

The aircraft reeled from explosions nearby. The bumpy ride made him think of an old truck driving at top speed over a rutted, muddy road in the middle of the night. Unable to dodge the holes, even though he knew they were filled with dynamite. Unable to stop. Just straight ahead until he blew up.

*Come on, Come on. Get it over with and get out of here.*

"Bombs away." The beautiful, gorgeous words came through the intercom. The plane lurched upward at the loss of its heavy load. He let out a sigh.

"I've got it," Rollins announced. The pilot took back the controls and maneuvered away from the drop zone.

Ted marked the spot on the map and started his calculations for the return leg.

"Hang on. We're in the middle of it," the pilot warned only an instant before an explosion jarred through them. The plane bounced and shook.

Then another, louder bang.

Ted's seat collapsed, tossing him to the floor. His head hit something.

Blackness alternated with blurry, bright light.

Fiery pain burned through his thigh. His hand searched for the wound. He gasped for air. His oxygen tube must have pulled loose.

Someone hovered over him. "Kruger's hit." It was McGill's voice. Clutching his tightening throat, Ted watched as Mac stuck the tube of a walk-around bottle into Ted's mask.

He sucked in the oxygen, grateful to be able to breathe again. He reached toward the pain to make sure his leg was still there.

"Take care of him. We're almost out of it." Rollins' voice resonated with authority, as if he could control the uncontrollable situation.

Ted struggled to get up but couldn't move. He was wedged in the narrow space, pinned by something. Or was he just too weak?

He heard other voices, far away, like a dream.

"Number three's hit."

"Feathering three."

"Tony, start the put-put, or we won't have power for the auxiliary equipment."

"Will do."

Within seconds, the roar of the small motor filled the fuselage. It muffled the sounds of the flack.

After a long pause, the co-pilot's calm words came through the wire. "Everybody check in."

He heard each voice, each name. His turn came. "Kruger." He sounded funny, like a whisper. Had he even spoken? The others continued to report.

"McGill, how's Kruger?" the pilot asked.

"He's hit in the upper leg. He's bleedin' a lot, but I can't tell how bad it is with his suit and all."

The flight engineer appeared in Ted's line of sight. "Here, let's get him where we can see it." They pulled the broken seat out of the way. "Damn. Look at those holes."

Now able to move a little, Ted turned his head. Light shone through a cluster of holes right where he'd been sitting. One looked big enough to put his thumb through.

McGill rolled him on his side, tore his pants leg open, and poked around. "Get some sulfa on it. Then we'll try to slow down the bleeding."

"How bad?" Ted heard himself ask.

"Not too bad. Just be still so you don't bleed all over the place."

Ted didn't believe him. He was weak and cold.

"Almost got you in the butt. You'll get plenty of kidding for that."

McGill was trying to cheer him up. Ted forced a smile. "They better not. I'll get 'em back. You know me." He grimaced in pain.

"Fighters! One o'clock high."

The bombardier jumped up and headed for his seat in the nose. Machine gun bursts exploded from every position. The flight engineer finished wrapping Ted's upper leg and propped it up to slow the bleeding. "Hang on," he said, before returning to his gun.

Ted closed his eyes. With one engine out, they couldn't stay with the formation for long. And alone, they were dead ducks.

The whole fuselage vibrated with the roar of engines and the staccato of machine gun fire.

"The charts," he murmured. "Need course. To get back."

"Don't worry, Kruger." Rollins' steady voice boomed in his ear. "Our little friends are here. They'll get us home."

*Fighters. God bless 'em.*

Ted squeezed his eyes shut to keep the tears at bay. The image of his angel came to him, the halo of wild hair glowing in the sunlight, her sweet smile. She'd been with him since that day he'd washed ashore. And she'd come back to keep him safe in the sky, just as she'd promised.

His angel had saved him again.

\*\*\*\*

The roar of engines invaded Kitty's fitful sleep. She rolled over, half-dreaming of the train that rumbled through her small hometown at two a.m. every morning. But the roar didn't fade away. It continued, intensified. She sat up and oriented herself to the strange place, cold and damp and crude. As the cobwebs cleared from her brain, she remembered where she was. England. Air Force. Planes.

She slipped her feet from under the blanket, pulled on her shoes and her heavy jacket, and made her way outside to the latrine. They had told her, when she had volunteered for overseas duty, that the accommodations wouldn't be as good as they were in the states. Boy, was that an understatement. She had, at the least, expected indoor plumbing. Of course, technically the concrete block structure behind the row of Nissen huts was indoors. They just had to trudge outside through the mud and weather to get to it. Not much better than the tents. Would she ever get used to living like this?

On her way back, she gazed up into the pale dawn. The roar from the bomber engines continued as silhouettes of planes rose into the sky, one after another, from the nearby airfield and disappeared into the clouds. Spellbound, she stood outside the hut's door.

*Those planes are going out to drop bombs on the Germans. And I'm here in England, only a few miles away from German occupied Europe.*

The thought sent a thrill through her. She'd made it. And her brother was proud of her, even if the rest of her family frowned on her choices.

*Kawhammmmm*! The sky exploded in a ball of fire. The ground rocked. The flimsy huts rattled. Her hands flew up to shield her ears from the loudest noise she'd ever heard.

Flames boiled outward from the epicenter of the blast. A thick, black cloud rose upward as fiery debris scattered below.

She stared in disbelief, shaking like a leaf, unable to move, unable to breathe.

"What happened?" Girls pushed their way through the door of the Nissen hut.

"Oh, God!" someone exclaimed.

The flames died. Ominous, black smoke billowed against the faint dawn. Several smaller explosions followed, one after the other. Kitty jerked again with each one.

Above the distant silhouettes of low buildings, flames glowed orange. Sirens screamed in the distance. She imagined the swirl of activity on the airfield following the crash.

Whispering excitedly, her fellow WACs clustered in small groups in front of their primitive quarters.

"I wonder what happened." Madge eased closer, watching the flames die back.

"A plane, it just exploded." Kitty turned to her friend. "The roar of engines woke me. I was watching the bombers taking off when something exploded—up there." She pointed to the sky above the air field.

"Loaded with bombs?"

Kitty nodded and turned away from the awful sight, as if she could block the image of the fireball and what it meant. Those men were dead, in an instant. She reached out to steady herself. Madge caught her hand and held it.

Kitty looked up, and another image caught her eye.

The sun's earliest rays reflected on the scores of glass panes on Ellingham Castle, as if the building were ablaze from within. Its golden dome glowed. The ancient edifice came alive as it looked down, like a serene sentinel, on the sprawling conglomerate of temporary, military structures. Despite the awful crash on the airfield and the continued roar of engines, it spoke to her in Churchill's famous words "we will endure."

She shivered and rubbed her arms to quiet the chill bumps.

"Look!" someone exclaimed, and she turned back in the direction of the airfield.

A flare arched high in the lightening sky. Within seconds a bomber rose from the field and flew through the black smoke still hanging in the air. Another followed.

"How can they do that?" Madge asked.

"Do what?"

"Take off right after those poor men crashed."

"I doubt they have any choice." The sergeant stood only a few feet away. "They have a job to do, and so do we."

The truth soured in Kitty's stomach. So this was war. Death in the sky on their first day.

"Come on, girls," the sergeant called. "Show's over. Time to get dressed. We've got work to do."

Chapter Three

After chow the company marched up to the castle and halted in the gravel driveway near the main entrance. The massive, stone building's golden dome loomed above them.

Colonel Snyder, the wing's Operations Officer, delivered a cold, formal welcome that told Kitty he was not pleased to have the women under his command. He turned them over to his subordinates who quickly sorted them by military occupations and led them away to their new workplaces.

In the movies, dark wood paneling, ancient family portraits, and huge tapestries lined the walls of English castles. But not this one. When Kitty and the other girls stepped inside Ellingham Castle, they gasped almost in unison. Elaborately carved, pointed archways, oriental rugs, and colorful designs gave the impression that they'd crossed some invisible boundary into an eastern palace, perhaps in India.

The women proceeded through the ornately decorated entrance hall, past the stairway with its deeply-scalloped, pointed arches, and into the dining hall, filled with rows of typewriters, tables, and file cabinets lined up like good soldiers standing at attention and awaiting orders. Sunlight flooded through a wall of matching arched windows creating a well-lit workspace.

Several uniformed, English women reviewed their work-in-progress with Sergeant Collins while the WACs examined the equipment.

Kitty selected a typewriter at the end of a row and inserted a blank piece of paper. Her fingers tapped out a series of words and gained speed as she absorbed the feel of the machine. It worked as well as any she'd used in the states.

She sighed, pleased that finally she would be doing some useful work.

Madge plopped down at the machine facing her. "Look at this place. It's like being dropped into the Kasbah."

"Yeah, I noticed. Not exactly what I expected."

"I asked that English woman, and she said this place used to be owned by some Indian Maharaja. That's why it looks like this inside. He wanted it to look like his home in India."

Madge always managed to get the scoop. "Really. Is he the one who let the Army use the place?" Kitty wondered if they would meet the Indian royal.

"Oh, no. That was way back in the eighteen hundreds. Some old guy, an earl or count or something, owns it now. He and his wife turned it over to the English government. And the English gave it to the Americans. So here we are."

Captain Weatherby appeared. "I need volunteers to go with me to visit the men in the hospital."

"Sure. I'll go." Madge jumped to her feet.

"Don't we have work to do?" asked Kitty.

"Colonel Snyder suggested we should cheer up the wounded." Her tone made it clear the suggestion was more like an order. "I only want a handful to go with me today. But he made it plain that some of us women should visit the wounded every day. He thinks that's part of our job here—to boost the morale of the men. So we will comply." Captain Weatherby looked around. "Any other volunteers?"

Madge shot Kitty a "come on" look, but Kitty shook her head. If she'd wanted to visit a hospital, she'd have become a nurse. The smell turned her stomach, and the sight of blood made her head spin. She'd take carbon paper over bandages any day.

Madge gave a little wave and winked at Kitty as she followed the captain out the door. Madge possessed an amazing ability to get out of actual work. Yet she managed to not only stay out of trouble but to get whatever she wanted from the officers and non-coms.

Madge definitely kept life interesting. In no time she would work her charm and have all the men on the base eating out of her hand.

When they were gone, Kitty approached Sergeant Collins and asked for something to do. She preferred staying busy and getting the work done to schmoozing around the base.

\*\*\*\*

Ted stared into nothingness. He tried to picture their faces. The four officers had stuck together, had kept each other going through mission after mission. Like their pre-flight ritual.

He chuckled to himself as he saw them in his mind, he and Art Rollins and Bud Hopper and Mac McGill.

Every mission, right before boarding the plane, four grown men, four Air Corps officers had lined up and pissed off the end of the hard stand. And then they'd shook hands all around. They'd joked about it, how it was silly and didn't mean anything, but they'd done it before every single flight. Something that had started by accident somehow gave them the courage to get into that bomber believing they'd make it back.

Ted shook his head as he considered the absurdity of it. He'd been just as superstitious as the others. They'd made nineteen flights together, with their rabbit's foots, stuffed bears, and Saint Christopher's medals, before that damn piece of shrapnel grounded him.

His friends had kept going, for four more missions. Until they'd been shot down. No ritual, no lucky charms, nothing could stop the flack when your time was up.

Damn it! Why hadn't he been with them? Why had this damn wound grounded him when they had to keep flying? It wasn't right, damn it.

His fists pounded into the mattress, and he squeezed his eyes shut. But he couldn't block the truth—they were all dead. The only guys he'd ever gotten close to. Guys he could count on, like the brothers he'd never had. Gone.

And he should have been with them.

Why had she saved him? Why? Why couldn't she save them, too?

"Oh, shoot!" Newman's voice cut into his thoughts. Ted's eyes flew open, just in time to see sheets of paper scattering across the floor in the aisle between the beds.

"I'll get them." Ted slid out of bed and stooped to gather what looked like pages of a letter. His injured muscles screamed in protest.

"Thanks," Newman said. The airman had arrived a

few days ago sporting bandages around his midsection. Some kind of surgery he'd told Ted.

"Glad to help." Ted handed him the pages. "Doc says I'm supposed to move around." He grinned to keep from grimacing and retied the belt on his robe. "I wonder if a cartwheel or two would get me out of here?"

Newman's face brightened. "Better not. You might hurt yourself again and have to stay longer."

Ted nodded. "You're right."

He eased back to his own bed, rubbed his sore leg, and racked his brain for something to relieve the boredom. He didn't write letters, and he'd read the mystery novel his friends had brought him, twice. He had to get out of this place and find something to do, or he'd go crazy. Surely the doctor would give him good news today.

"Who'd you say was taking care of Butch?" Ted asked.

"That dog? Don't worry about him. He's running the place," Newman replied.

"Don't want him going hungry?" Ted remembered the mutt snuggling up beside him in the night.

Newman laughed. "Every ground crew at Allsford thought they had to feed Butch. He'll be fat by the time you see him again."

"Yeah." Ted thought of those doleful eyes and wished the pooch was here now.

A commotion at the door came as a welcome distraction. A female officer entered the ward followed by—

*Wow! Not Betty Grable!*

Had the famous movie star come to visit the

troops? He sat up straighter so he could get a better look.

The blonde knockout flashed a smile his way, and his pulse inched up a notch. She wore a WAC uniform, and boy did she fill it out in all the right places.

As he watched her ease farther into the ward, he realized she wasn't the queen of the silver screen she looked so much like. But that was better, right? Who needed a movie star? He preferred a flesh and blood woman, one he could get cozy with.

"Doll, where've you been all my life?" the guy with the bandaged hands in the first bed asked.

She laughed at the old line and shot back, "Looking for you, big boy."

After flirting with him briefly, she spoke to the kid in the next bed. The inept youngster turned beet red as the uniformed dish focused her attention on him.

*Let the boy enjoy it while he can.*

This beauty was no angel, but she came close enough. And Ted could use the comfort of a woman's company right now.

"When did the WAC arrive?" Ted asked, since the teenager was incapable of speech.

"We got here yesterday, a whole company of red-blooded American girls."

"What's your name, honey?" the boy stammered, finally able to get his head in gear.

Ignoring Ted, she gave the boy one of her pin-up girl smiles. "Madge, Madge Sorensen." She paused for effect. "And what's your name?"

The skinny kid blushed again and grinned. "Bucky."

"Bucky," she repeated, batting her eyes.

Ted watched her work the poor fellow. She was out of his league, big time. This gal needed someone to take her in hand. Give her a challenge. He folded his arms across his chest and leaned back, waiting for her to come to him.

Sure enough, she quickly bored with Bucky and eased closer to Ted's bed.

"What about you soldier? What's your name?" Her voice was soft as a feather. Her eyes twinkled as if laughing. She was in her element enjoying every moment.

"Ted," he answered and added no more.

"You don't look like you are wounded. What are you here for?"

"Just a routine check-up. The Air Corps wants to make sure we stay in shape." She arched one of her lovely brows. He could tell she didn't believe him, but he didn't care, as long as he had her full attention. "What about you? What's a pretty girl like you doing in an Army uniform?"

"We came over here to help you boys win the war."

She liked to banter. He liked that. Liked a girl who could keep up with him.

"If you're so fit, how about going dancing?" she continued, pursing her lips into a pout, her twinkling eyes betraying the tease.

He winced involuntarily. His rear end wasn't quite up to jitterbugging. "Not tonight," he quipped. "What about you and me, in the moonlight, getting to know each other?"

Her smug expression said she understood what he meant. But she shook her head. "Sorry, soldier. Just remembered, I have to wash my hair tonight. Maybe some other time."

The WAC captain called from the door, "Sorensen."

"Got to go." She turned and walked away.

"Lieutenant Ted Kruger. Remember that name," he called after her.

"What about me?" Newman called out. "I'm Lieutenant Sammy Newman. You can look me up any time."

She glanced back, then surveyed the entire ward. "Oh, I'll remember—all of you." She gave them all a killer smile as she made a dramatic exit.

"Wow! What a woman!" Newman exclaimed. "Why'd you guys have to hog her attention?"

"Aw, quit your complaining," another patient responded.

Ted agreed the pretty WAC had been a breath of fresh air. Once the pain had subsided, he'd become antsy, ready to get moving, get back up in the sky. If that wasn't a possibility, then he'd settle for a little female distraction. And Madge Sorensen would do nicely.

She didn't measure up to his angel. Not by a long shot. But she was pretty and built and looked like she'd be a lot of fun.

"Hey, Kruger. How about a friendly card game?" Newman asked.

"Sure. Why not?" It was something to fill the time until he could get out of this boring hospital. Maybe his wound would get him leave, time to find a little female companionship.

\*\*\*\*

*Little black clouds fill the sky, bursting all around.*

*There's no escape. No way to fight it. Nowhere to run. Nowhere to hide. Just wait to die.*

*The plane shakes violently.*

*We've been hit! Rollins calls.*

*Engine on fire. Flames. Black smoke trailing.*

*Another explosion.*

*Right wing hit, Bud's calm voice echoes.*

*The plane dips to the right.*

*Out the window he sees it.*

*The wing breaking apart.*

*Flames! Behind him! Deafening roar!*

*"We've got to get out!" he screams to Mac.*

*But Mac just nods. His eyes smile behind the goggles.*

*"Get out!"*

*They're spinning out of control.*

*Falling. Falling.*

*Through the sky.*

*"Art! Bud! Mac! Get out!"*

*Alone. Suspended in midair. Yet falling.*

*Falling toward the inferno below.*

*Look up, into the blinding sun.*

*There, coming out of the light, swooping down.*

*She takes his arm and draws him to her.*

*"You're safe," her soft voice assures him.*

*An angel, her face, his mermaid's face.*

*He reaches for her.*

"Wake up!" Someone shook him.

He jerked away, not wanting to leave her.

"Wake up, Kruger," the voice barked. "You're dreaming again."

Ted rolled over and covered his head with his

pillow. But she was gone. Driven away by reality.

"Come on, Ted," his fellow officer coaxed.

It was no use. He had to get up, face the day. He uncovered his head, threw back the blanket, and sat up. His sweaty undershirt clung to his body.

He ran his hands through his damp hair and sat on the side of the bed, trying to pull himself together.

He should be used to it, but he wasn't. Always the same. No use trying to shake it. The dream was his future. And his past. They'd all gone, all but him. And he would join them.

Would his angel be there when he did? Would she take him off to be with her, with all of them, in heaven? God knows he didn't deserve it.

She'd saved him before, brought him back from the edge of death. Why? Why had she saved him? What was he supposed to do? Drop bombs on Germany?

He dragged himself out through the dreary English morning, following all the other walking wounded to the showers.

The lukewarm liquid streamed over his still aching body, soothing the angry scars that marred his upper thigh and buttocks. The water relaxed him, and his head began to clear.

He joined a group of towel-wrapped men taking turns at the sinks to scrape off a day's worth of beard.

*Thank God for safety razors. Wouldn't want anyone to cut their throats and deprive the enemy.*

When had he gotten so cynical?

The man next to him caught his gaze in the mirror. "I heard you asked the colonel about going back to the bombers?"

Ted ducked his head to rinse the remaining soap

from his face and didn't answer.

"With those nightmares you have, I can't see it."

"I dunno'," Ted mumbled, scrubbing the towel over his face.

He moved into the dressing area and hoped the guy got the message. He didn't want to talk, at least not now.

The ragtag group of wounded, broken men made their way into the old manor house the English had converted into a recuperation center. The most severely wounded were waiting to be shipped home. Others suffered from exhaustion and needed a quiet place to recover. Ted was one of those who'd been wounded, but not bad enough to be out of it.

Dining tables were set up in the manor's great hall. He took a seat so the polite English women could serve him tea with milk and bread with jam. No Army food here.

"Wonder what the jam is today?" he quipped to the airman next to him.

"Rhubarb," answered the gray-haired English lady serving tea across the table. "Mistress Latham made it herself, she did."

"And I'm sure it's very tasty," Ted assured her.

He'd toned down his joking around their English hosts. Although the women understood that soldiers complained about food as a matter of course, he couldn't bring himself to joke about it in front of the polite and kindly old ladies. After all, the bread and jam tasted better than the powdered eggs he routinely gagged on.

"How much longer you goin' to be here?" asked the airman on his left.

"A few more days."

"Goin' back to the bombers, like you asked?"

Ted shook his head. "Not yet. Doc said I shouldn't be flying, not till my leg heals some more."

"Where they sending you?"

"Don't know. Haven't gotten my orders. Probably some desk job."

The guy bit into his jam-covered toast and made a face.

"Don't like rhubarb?" Ted asked, chuckling under his breath.

After forcing himself to swallow, the airman shook his head. He took a sip of tea.

"Here, take mine." Ted handed him a slice of plain toast and scooped up the offending slice slathered in jam. "I'll eat it."

"Thanks."

Ted chomped on the toast, remembering his grandmother's cooking. She'd made all kinds of jam, baked bread, canned vegetables and made it all taste good. Too bad he hadn't appreciated it at the time.

"What about you?" Ted asked. "Where will they send you? Back up there?" The wings told Ted the man was a flier.

The man shook his head. "Nope." He leaned back and patted the stump where his lower leg used to be. "That last flight took care of that. Crash landed. They said I was lucky the plane didn't catch fire, but there was nothing left but fumes." He popped the last of his toast into his mouth and sipped some tea.

Ted had forgotten about the man's disability. He'd been too caught up in his own self-pity.

"No more flying for me," the flier continued. "I'll

be headin' home, soon as they can get me on a boat."

Ted just nodded. He couldn't bring himself to congratulate the man. Maybe Rollins and Bud and the guys were lucky, going down like they did, together. At least they wouldn't go home crippled.

A pang of guilt caught in his throat, nearly choking him. He clenched his jaw, pressed his lips together, willed the food to stay down.

He should have been with them. Should have gone down with his crew.

He still saw them. Saw their faces. Waking or sleeping, it didn't matter. They were with him. Every last one. You didn't fly nineteen missions together without forming a bond, an unbreakable bond, without feeling like you were part of each other.

"Would you like some more tea?" The small, gray-haired woman smiled sweetly.

Ted nodded. "Yes, ma'am." He watched her pour and thought she would have been a real beauty in her youth.

The image of another beauty leapt into his mind. An angel with a wild halo who watched over him. Why did every pretty face always bring her to mind? Would a real woman ever make him feel the way he had that day when she smiled down on him?

Maybe he didn't deserve an angel. Maybe what he deserved was a good-time girl like the WAC that visited the hospital. She liked to flirt, and so did he. She'd look good on his arm, and that alone would cheer him up.

Maybe he'd look her up while he waited to go back to the bombers. His days were numbered, so he might as well enjoy himself while he could.

Chapter Four

*Somewhere in England*
*April 20, 1944*

*Dearest Milton,*

*We've settled into our new home with the Air Force. I'm including my new location in hopes the censor won't mark it out. The farms and rolling hills around here remind me a little of back home, even though all the houses look ancient, and the hills are much smaller. There's a bomber air field not far from here. All the noise when they're taking off—before dawn—wakes me up. Guess I'll get used to it. I'm hoping to get out and explore—when I get some time. They keep us pretty busy in the castle.*

*Yes, I said* Castle. *That's what they call it, only it's not what you would imagine. No stone walls or towers. Just a huge old country house. And I mean old as in centuries. You should see it. Hundreds of rooms and very fancy inside—not at all what you would expect in England. More like the Taj Mahal, if you can believe it. Some Indian Maharaja decorated the place like his home in India. Being old makes the place drafty. Plus bad wiring, poor lighting. Not good for the kind of work we do. The military had to set up temporary buildings for a lot of the equipment.*

*I hope your quarters are better than ours. We're sleeping in these little Nissen huts, ten girls to a hut and*

38

*the latrine in a separate building. I guess it's better than tents but not much. At least the weather's cleared up some. I remember you telling me I'd have to adjust to whatever the Army throws at me, but you know me— I like to have a little corner I can call my own. A place to escape to when everything starts getting to me. I have learned to live in close quarters. Had to or I wouldn't have survived. But part of me longs for our shelter in the woods or the little attic room. Places I could go when I needed to be alone. Get away from Suzanne and Olivia. Remember? You always knew where to find me. And you knew when to leave me be. I always loved you for that.*

*When you write, give me a hint as to where you are. I can't find out anything here. Sure wish I could see you. I was counting on us getting together once I got to England. Maybe you can arrange a meeting somewhere. You're the one who could always pull things off, so work your magic.*

*Your loving sister,*
*Katherine*
****

"What's up? Bertie said you wanted to see me."

Kitty looked up from her typing. Madge stood beside her, perfect in every way. From her neatly coiffed, blonde hair to her freshly pressed uniform, polished shoes, and nails, Madge made all the other WACs envious. Yet her infectious personality insured that everyone liked her, both men and women. All these positive qualities went a long way to make up for her less than stellar work performance.

"I proofread this report you typed, and I'm afraid some of it doesn't make sense."

"Well, I can't help it if they talk so fast. I can't get it all down. Besides, half the stuff they talk about doesn't make sense, so there's no wonder it sounds that way."

"Madge, you have to ask questions. And you have to check your spelling." Kitty studied her careless friend then drew a deep breath for strength. She tried to remember that everyone wasn't as picky as her. The other girls may call her "Miss Perfectionist," but she didn't care. When it came to work, it had to be right. She handed Marge the report. "I have marked the areas that need attention. Go talk to Lieutenant Sutton. He should be able to help you reword it."

"All right. At least he's nice and won't eat me alive like that old Lieutenant Rooker."

Kitty returned to her typing, but Madge didn't leave. Instead she leaned closer.

"I saw that dreamy guy again. The one I told you about when we first got here, from the hospital."

"You mean the wounded officer?"

"Yes, that's the one. His name is Ted, and he asked me out."

"Out! You can't go out with an officer. Besides, he's in the hospital."

"No, he's not. Not anymore. He got assigned to the Group Operations Officer, right here in the castle."

"Oh, Madge. I recognize that look. You'd better be careful." The girl had a knack for getting into precarious situations.

"Don't worry. They're not as strict over here."

Her friend slipped a mirror from her pocket and checked her perfect hair. The action made Kitty painfully aware of her own tightly-pinned mane. She'd learned to keep her wild tresses rolled tight to accomplish the neatness required by the military. Trying to remain casual, she reached up and self-consciously checked for any wayward curls.

"I don't know how you plan to date someone in a place like this. Where would you go? It's not like you could have dinner at the Officers' Club." Kitty raised an eyebrow and gave her friend a warning look.

"I know, but he said we could go to the pub in the village." From the mischievous grin on Madge's face, Kitty knew it was already too late to rein her in.

"Madge, you're asking for trouble if you go out with an officer. Surely there's some nice, equally handsome, enlisted man you could date."

"Oh, don't worry about it," Madge replied nonchalantly then eyed her carefully. "If I didn't know better, I'd think you were jealous."

Kitty balked at her friend's accusation. She might envy Madge's looks and ease around men, but she certainly wasn't jealous of Madge's new boyfriend. She hadn't even met him.

No, Kitty was the careful one, the one who didn't go out with just any Tom, Dick, or Harry. And she wouldn't dare date an officer. Madge, on the other hand, had been in and out of trouble for "bending" the rules ever since they met. Yet somehow she always managed to get by with it.

"I have to finish this," Kitty said, shaking her head.

"He said to bring a friend—for his friend. I forget his name."

"Oh, no. Not me. I'm not getting sent back to the states for improper behavior. We just got here. And I worked too hard to get here. Count me out."

"Okay." She didn't sound too disappointed. "But you'll never have any fun if you keep sticking to the rules. Life's too short to miss out. Didn't I teach you anything? Didn't you have a good time in Boston?"

"Don't remind me." Kitty wanted to forget her foray into the wild world of dancing and booze and men. She'd quickly learned to limit her drinking and be very selective about the men she danced with. Some guys moved way too fast for her taste. Thankfully, Madge watched out for her like a big sister. But right now, Kitty felt like the mature one. She looked into her friend's mischievous eyes. "Just be careful, okay?"

"Aren't I always?" Madge quipped over her shoulder as she walked away.

Kitty had to smile. She envied her friend's self-confidence with men. They made Kitty uncomfortable, tongue-tied. The only male she'd ever been able to talk to was her big brother, Milton.

A pang of loneliness struck her. She missed him, wished she could talk to him, tell him all she'd learned, all she'd accomplished, and all she wanted to do. He'd understand.

She said a quick, silent prayer for her brother. *Please God, keep him safe.* Even though he was no longer fighting in Africa or Italy, he could still be in danger. Training could be dangerous, too. In her own training, she'd seen women collapse from exhaustion in the summer heat and one who got her feet tangled in communication wires and broke a leg. Not that Milton would be careless or clumsy. Still she worried.

Despite the fact Milton was somewhere in England, she hadn't been able to find his unit. Right after her arrival in England, she had asked the captain how to find out where the First Infantry Division was stationed. That's when she had learned just how secretive the military could be. "Don't even ask," was the ma'am's advice. Kitty hadn't given up hope, though. She had to find him.

Maybe if the censors didn't cut out too much of her letter to him, he could get word to her and come up with a way for them to get together.

"Corporal." The captain's voice interrupted her thoughts.

Kitty stood. "Yes, ma'am."

"General Lake has a meeting scheduled this afternoon with officers from the entire Wing. He wants someone to take notes. From what I've been told, there will be a number of officers present, so I'm assigning two of you to insure you get everything."

"Yes, ma'am." Kitty fought to maintain her composure. The general. Wow!

"Where's Sorensen?" Captain Weatherby paused and glanced around the room. "She'll be assisting you."

"She just stepped out. I'll find her." Madge will be thrilled, too. She loved hobnobbing with the brass.

The officer nodded, her demeanor still serious and businesslike. "Both of you, be ready at thirteen fifty. I'll take you up and introduce you to General Lake before the meeting starts at fourteen hundred."

"Yes, ma'am."

As soon as the captain was out of sight, Kitty let the grin she'd been holding back explode across her face. The general. Taking notes for the general. So much more exciting than typing up dull reports.

She glanced around restlessly. She had to find Madge.

\*\*\*\*

"General Lake," Captain Weatherby addressed the Commanding General. "This is Corporal Greenlee and Corporal Sorenson. They will be taking notes during your meeting."

Resplendent in his uniform, dark hair with just enough gray at the temples to give him an air of wisdom, the officer exuded authority. "Ladies, glad to have you on board." He ushered the three women into the generous, second-floor chamber.

Kitty's fascination with history sent her mind spinning. The room had none of the main floor's oriental decor, no intricately carved arches, no white marble columns. Traditional, heavy door frames and the dark colors in the thick drapery, rug, and wall covering created a somber space. With the room stripped of its original furniture, she could only speculate as to its intended use. A sitting room, perhaps, or a spacious bedroom intended for guests—or even royalty.

An officer stood beside a long table that would have fit nicely into the dining hall downstairs. Above the table, where she imagined a portrait might have hung, a huge map of Europe covered the entire wall, dominating the room. Colorful pins marked various locations and arrowed ribbons extended across the map from England to points in Germany.

The officer looked up from the papers he held and moved closer. She recognized him as the colonel who gave the not-so-friendly welcome that first day.

"Colonel Snyder, my Operations Officer, will be running our meeting."

The three WACs saluted smartly, and the colonel returned their salute.

"We will dispense with the formalities during the meeting, ladies. Otherwise the saluting will never end." General Lake smiled as he spoke, giving an air of friendly authority. Kitty decided she liked him.

Frowning, Colonel Snyder's steely gaze pinned her. "I will introduce the officers as they arrive so you girls know who you're dealing with."

Kitty cringed at the condescending tone beneath Colonel Snyder's polite words. She'd heard it before. Officers who thought women shouldn't be wearing a uniform, thought they should be home cooking, cleaning, and having babies. She drew herself up and stood tall, determined to prove herself by doing the best job she could do. She'd earn his respect, for herself and for her fellow WACs.

"An excellent suggestion, sir." Captain Weatherby beamed. Either she hadn't detected his attitude, or she chose to ignore it. Knowing the captain, Kitty decided it was the latter. "I'll leave you to it." Weatherby eyed Kitty and Madge, giving a silent warning before she snapped a smart salute and made her exit.

General Lake casually returned the salute, then he turned back toward Kitty and Madge. "Ladies, during the meeting you will sit there." He pointed toward two straight chairs against the wall at the far end of the room.

Madge stood silent at her side while Kitty surveyed the area—the long table, the distance from one end to the other, the heavy drapes on the window at the far end that would muffle the sound. "Sir, may I suggest that one of us sit near either end of the table? That way we could hear better, not miss anything."

General Lake shot her a questioning look but

continued to listen.

"And perhaps out from the wall a bit, about here, so that we can see the map." She glanced over at Colonel Snyder, hoping he wouldn't object. "I'm assuming that the map will be part of your discussion."

He held up a manila folder. "This report is what we will be discussing." His frown made it clear he did not like her speaking up. "Your job is to take down each man's comments, verbal reports, et cetera." He glanced at Madge who stood in rigid silence beside the table. "And I'm sure it will take both of you to keep up."

"One at each end will be fine," the general interjected, his voice warm and confident. He shot Colonel Snyder a look that instantly silenced the officer.

Kitty and Madge moved quickly to grab the chairs and move them to their new positions.

"Don't let me down," Kitty murmured.

"It's a cinch," Madge whispered. "I'm better at names than you are, remember."

"I'm counting on it."

As soon as the chairs were in place, the WACs joined Colonel Snyder by the door just in time to greet the officers streaming in from the hallway.

Kitty focused on the tricks Madge taught her for remembering names as Colonel Snyder ticked off one after another. Faces, names, ranks, memory triggers. She filed it all away in her brain.

A handsome, vaguely familiar face appeared. She blinked and momentarily lost her focus.

"Kruger. Did you get it?" The colonel's voice boomed in her ear.

"Yes, sir." The good-looking lieutenant held out a

paper.

The colonel grabbed it and began reading. Without looking up he said, "Take over here, Lieutenant." He headed for the table where the general and other officers were settling in.

A grin spread across Lieutenant Kruger's face. He winked at Madge who beamed back at him.

"Corporal Sorensen," he spoke with familiarity, "Who's your friend?"

"Oh," Madge uncharacteristically stuttered. "Corporal Kitty Greenlee."

"Corporal." He acknowledged her with a smug expression. "And what exactly am I continuing?"

"Introductions." Kitty hoped her voice didn't sound too wobbly. There was something about him. Something unsettling. But two more officers appeared, and she had to force herself to focus on names and faces again.

During the meeting Lieutenant Kruger didn't sit at the table with the higher ranking officers. Instead he stood back and assisted the colonel whenever the officer beckoned.

Kitty wanted to stare, wanted to figure out what it was about this handsome lieutenant that made her ill at ease. But she had to focus on her job, focus on the words spoken and who said what in the rapid-fire discussion.

Her pencil flashed across the page creating the shorthand symbols she had perfected in training. She only allowed herself to look up when she couldn't distinguish the voice speaking. Page after page filled with notes until the meeting finally came to an end.

The general dismissed the group, and they quietly

filed from the room. A few made comments among themselves on their way out. Lieutenant Kruger gathered papers from the table, and Kitty saw him flash a discreet smile at Madge.

Kitty joined her co-worker and shot her a questioning look.

"Isn't he a dream?" Madge whispered.

Kitty followed her friend's gaze to Lieutenant Kruger who was talking to Colonel Snyder.

"Is he the one you told me about?" Kitty asked.

Madge nodded and clasped her notepad to her breast.

The two moved toward the door but were stopped by General Lake.

"Ladies, I expect to have your notes on my desk first thing in the morning." He turned to the colonel. "Snyder, make sure they have copies of everything discussed here today."

"Yes, sir. I'll have Kruger get it to them." The colonel glanced at Lieutenant Kruger who nodded in understanding.

Kitty and Madge acknowledged the officers and exited the office.

"We need to compare notes, make sure we got everything," Kitty commented to Madge in the hallway.

"Hey, girls." Lieutenant Kruger caught up to them.

Madge actually blushed when she heard his voice. Kitty stared in disbelief at her fun-loving friend. She'd never seen Madge react this way to a man.

"I'll walk you down," he continued. "We can go over the documents from the meeting."

Kitty hurried down the stairs ahead of the others, anxious to put some distance between her and the handsome officer. Glancing over her shoulder, she saw him grinning at Madge like a mischievous schoolboy.

Kitty couldn't shake the feeling that she had seen this man before. She just couldn't figure out when or where. Since joining up, she'd met so many people that she couldn't remember them all. Yet such a handsome face should trigger some memory. Maybe it was just her imagination. After all, he had shown no signs of recognizing her.

They reached her desk. The good-looking officer settled into her chair as if he belonged there, so she stood back waiting for him to realize what he'd done and relinquish her place.

Madge perched on the edge of the desk, practically in his lap, and gave Lieutenant Kruger her sweetest smile. The way he responded to her attention reminded her of the way Robert Taylor looked at Greta Garbo in *Camille*, caught in her web of beauty and charm, full of adoration. No one had ever looked at Kitty like that.

"We still on for Saturday?" He leaned forward and kept his voice at a discreet level.

"Sure," gushed Madge.

"If you can get a pass," Kitty added, unable to quell her desire to throw a wet blanket on their plans.

Lieutenant Kruger gave her a solemn look that slowly transformed into a subtle, lop-sided smile.

Instantly she was transported back to the beach, to that day. Her heart caught in her throat, her ears roared as if the surf were pounding in her head. That face…that smile… No sunburned skin. No swollen, blistered lips. But the same sparkling blue eyes, the same strong jaw line, the same little dimple in his chin. She was staring down at the mysterious man she had rescued, the man who had haunted her dreams, both waking and sleeping, since that day.

Could it be possible? Could it really be him? Her knees grew weak

"Kitty. Are you listening?" Madge asked.

"Sure. I…uh…"

"I said I've already got a pass. And since you won't go, I'm taking Bertie."

Lieutenant Kruger grinned that mischievous little boy grin she remembered. Kitty's stomach flipped. It was him, but he was looking at Madge, not her. He didn't remember her at all.

A pang of disappointment stabbed through her, just like years ago when they'd carried him away before she'd had a chance to talk to him, before she found out who he was, or anything about him. She wrapped her arms around her middle and turned away, unable to watch the man of her dreams flirting with Madge.

Chapter Five

Kitty struggled to focus on her typing. She made another mistake and stopped to tediously erase the erroneous letter from the original and two copies. Three mistakes on one letter was unacceptable for anyone, especially a stickler like her.

She never made mistakes. But for the last two days, her mind kept wandering to the image of Lieutenant Kruger sitting in this very chair flirting with Madge.

Carefully she lined up the paper so the overstrike would hit exactly the same spot she had just erased. She resumed her typing. Slower this time, she used all her powers of concentration to finish without another error.

By afternoon she could wait no longer. She found an excuse to visit the personnel office and see if Adrianne had found anything.

The day before Kitty had hesitantly approached her fellow WAC in the mess hall. She'd forced herself to push through her discomfort at asking a stranger for help. Her bravery paid off.

Adrianne proved to be a kindred spirit of sorts. She took pride in her work and understood Kitty's concern for her friend's welfare. What Kitty didn't tell Adrianne was that Kitty wanted to know about Lieutenant Kruger, not for Madge's benefit, but for her own. She had to find out if he was the man on the beach, as her instincts screamed, or if he just looked like the person she remembered.

Adrianne looked up and nodded when Kitty entered the office. She pulled a manila folder from a drawer and led Kitty to a table in the corner so no one could overhear their conversation.

"I can assure you of one thing—he's not married," Adrianne said confidently.

Kitty nodded. "Good." But the good news did not relieve her anxiety. "What else did you find?"

Adrianne opened the file and took out a single sheet of paper.

"Nothing here is confidential. I want you to know that. Just basic information, but I'd prefer you not share it with anyone. Or say where you got it. I don't want any trouble."

"I understand. I won't tell anyone." Fighting the urge to grab the page from Adrianne's hand, Kitty forced herself to breathe normally and relax. She didn't want Adrianne to question her motives.

Adrianne passed the handwritten page to Kitty. She quickly scanned the information.

*2nd Lieutenant Theodore R. Kruger II*
*Enlisted 1942—Jacksonville, Florida*
*Initial Training—Camp Blanding Florida*
*Pilot Training*
*Pre-Flight and Primary—Santa Ana, California*
*Basic—Chico, California and Advanced—Kirkland Field, New Mexico*
*Navigator Training—Hondo Field, Texas*
*Assigned to 600th Squadron of the 303rd Bombardment Group*
*Feb. 1944 Assigned to Allford Airbase, England*
*Wounded; Reassigned to 2nd Wing Headquarters*

"Was there anything about what he did before the war?" Kitty asked.

Adrianne reopened the folder and flipped through it.

"No." She shook her head as she continued to turn pages. "Oh, here's something." She placed her finger halfway down on the page. "Under next of kin he has his mother listed in Jacksonville, Florida, and he also has his grandfather listed in Nashville, Tennessee. Is that any help?"

Kitty nodded. "Yes. Thanks." She folded the paper and slipped it into her pocket.

Suzanne had written months after Kitty went home that the mystery man had been on a freighter that sank off the coast of Florida. If Kruger was from Florida, could he be the same man? A strange queasiness settled in her stomach. Maybe it wasn't him, she hedged, almost hoping Lieutenant Kruger was an entirely different person.

"Is he the one you remembered?" Adrianne's question brought her back to the present.

Kitty didn't know how to respond. "I…I don't know. But thanks for your help."

She was almost out the door before she remembered the other thing she wanted to ask Adrianne. She turned and retraced her steps in time to catch Adrianne before she settled behind her desk.

"Is there any way you can find out where the First Infantry is stationed?" Kitty kept her voice low.

A little surprised at Kitty's question, Adrianne glanced around before she responded. "That kind of info is pretty hard to come by. Why do you want to know?"

"My brother. I promised my family I'd look him up, you know, make sure he's okay."

"Doesn't he write?"

"Sure. But that's not the same as seeing him." Another WAC opened a file cabinet nearby, and both women watched her in silence. She glanced their way as she slammed the drawer shut.

When she was out of earshot, Kitty continued, "I haven't seen him for almost two years, since he went overseas. I've just got to find some way to see him."

Adrianne looked sympathetic. "Okay. I'll see what I can find out. Give me his name and outfit." She slid a piece of paper in front of Kitty. "I've got a brother in the Pacific. Last letter I got was from Australia, I think. You know how they censor stuff. He said he was 'down under,' so I took that to mean Australia."

Kitty nodded. "You're probably right." Kitty started to go but stopped herself. "Thanks again. And if I can ever do anything for you, just let me know. Okay?"

Adrianne smiled. "I will. Don't worry about that."

****

Ted looked up when the two WACs pushed through the pub's heavy wooden door and stood for a moment surveying the dim interior.

What a dish! His luck had really turned around. After all, it wasn't every day that a guy got close to a girl who looked like that.

He had almost reached her side when Madge flashed that brilliant smile. His pulse raced.

"Hi, handsome," she said.

"Hello, yourself." He grinned like a fool. No use trying to be sophisticated around this one. It would never work. "Who's your friend?"

"Bertie DeWitt. This is Ted, Ted Kruger."

The nervous girl managed a weak salute. "Lieutenant."

"Oh, don't worry about that, not here."

Someone brushed his shoulder, and Ted turned to find his friend, Marty.

"Aren't you going to introduce me?"

Ted took Madge's arm before Marty got any ideas. "Marty Wasserman. This is Madge and Bertie."

Bertie started to salute then caught herself and stuck out her hand. "Bertie DeWitt."

Marty took her hand. "Nice to meet you."

The girl flushed and giggled while she pumped Marty's hand up and down.

Good, Ted thought. Keep Marty occupied so he won't make a move on Madge.

He gave "his girl" a winning smile and grasped her arm more firmly. "We've got a table." He steered her toward the corner of the pub. Marty and Bertie followed.

Ted held the wooden chair for Madge. "Bertie, why don't you sit here, beside Madge."

Bertie smiled, and Marty shot Ted a glare before grabbing the chair for Bertie. Marty didn't miss much. He knew Ted had intentionally put the girls together so Marty wouldn't be tempted to flirt with Madge. But Marty's reaction didn't bother him. Ted had made it plain before the girls arrived that Madge was his, so hands off.

After seating the girls, Ted went over to the bar and ordered a round of drinks. Glancing back, he compared the two females. The dark-haired Bertie was tall and slender and might have held a certain attraction in the right outfit. The uniform did nothing for her looks or her figure. On the other hand, Madge's killer shape could not be hidden. In her WAC uniform, she reminded him of Betty Grable in that war movie she made with Tyrone Power, the one he'd been racking his brain trying to remember the title of since the first time he saw her. She had the actress's blonde hair, classic face, and blue eyes. And though he couldn't get a good look at her legs beneath that long skirt, the rest of her could pass for the pin-up girl's double.

The waiter appeared with a round of dark, English beer.

Ted offered a toast. "To the defeat of the Nazi's."

The others raised their glasses, and to his surprise, several of the pub's patrons joined in the toast.

"Hear, hear!" a man at the neighboring table chimed in.

"Down with Hitler!" said another patron.

They all drank to their common goal.

Bertie giggled and nudged Madge in the ribs. Madge clinked her friend's glass, and they both took another sip. Their laughter bubbled forth, and without even knowing the joke, Ted found himself laughing along.

Ted wanted to know more about the blonde beauty beside him. "You never did tell me where you have been hiding. Where's home?"

"Minneapolis," she replied. "And what about you?"

Evidently she didn't want to talk about herself. "Oh, I'm from a lot of places. But I've never made it to Minneapolis."

"Well, where were you when you joined up? I assumed you joined." She'd deftly turned the subject back to him.

"Of course, I joined. I wasn't going to wait around until they drafted me. What I wanted was to fight the Japs. But the Nazi's will have to do." He took another swig of beer.

"You didn't answer my question."

She was persistent, he'd give her that. "I was in Florida when I signed up. There was an air field near Jacksonville where I'd been working. Took some flying lessons. Figured I'd learn to fly. Might come in handy." He took another sip, and she followed suit. From the inquisitive look, he knew she was waiting for him to continue the story. He preferred to tell the abbreviated version and avoid talking about his family. "Anyway, the Japs attacked us, so I decided to sign up for the Air Corps."

"So you wanted to be a pilot?"

"Sure. Everybody wants to be a pilot. I got in to the cadet training, too." She was hanging on his every word. It was heady stuff, the way she looked at him as if fascinated by anything he said.

"Then why are you a navigator instead of a pilot?"

There it was. That tricky question. But he'd perfected his answer.

"Well, I'd had some navigation training when I was in the Merchant Marines, so they thought I'd fit better as a navigator."

Before Madge could open her mouth to ask about his time in the Merchant Marines, which is where he was steering her, Marty chimed in.

"That's not the way I heard it."

"What did you hear?" Bertie encouraged him.

Ted raised his hand in protest, but it was too late. Marty had that gleam in his eye and couldn't resist telling the tale.

"Well, as I heard it," Marty started. "Ol' Ted here was almost through pilot training when he decided to take a little joy ride."

"No." Madge gasped, but her expression told him she was dying to hear more.

"Yep. He took his plane, a big B-17 bomber, and flew it down in the gorge of the Colorado River. Flew it upstream till he came to the Hoover Dam. He was flying so low he had to pull up fast and barely cleared the dam."

"Did you get in trouble?" Bertie asked, clearly amazed at the story.

"Sure he did," Marty answered.

Ted sat back and crossed his arms over his chest. Marty didn't have to enjoy telling it so much.

"He got chewed out by his commanding officer, and when the brass found out, they kicked him out of pilot training."

"Oh, Ted. How awful." At least Madge expressed sympathy for him.

"I did it on a dare," Ted offered his only defense. "One of the other guys was supposed to go with me. He chickened out right after we dropped into the gorge."

"You mean he got smart."

"What I mean is that he wasn't good enough and he knew it."

"But what if you had hit that dam?" Bertie asked.

Since Marty started it, Ted decided to make the most of the story. "Actually, the thing showed up sooner than I expected. I was busy watching the cliffs on either side when we rounded a bend in the river, and there it was." He glanced at Madge. She was hanging on his every word. "This big block of concrete right in front of us."

"What did you do?"

"I pulled back on the stick and gunned the engines." He paused for effect. "It was close, but we cleared that dam by, oh, maybe two or three feet."

"But you could have been killed." He heard the concern in Madge's voice.

"Not a chance," he assured her.

"Problem was the whole crew could have been killed," Marty interjected. "And the plane could have been destroyed."

"Yeah. The brass was more concerned about me crashing the plane." He saw Madge's frown and knew he needed to explain further. "That was before they had the B-24. And they didn't have the production of planes up to where it is now. So the ones we were flying were precious. But we were in no real danger." He wasn't about to admit how terrified he had been.

Marty laughed. "You've got more confidence than anyone I know."

"I just knew what I could do, that's all."

"Too bad the brass didn't know what you could do. Or maybe you'd be flying bombers now instead of drawing up flight plans for the Ops Officer."

Ted saw red. His throat tightened, and his jaw clamped down hard trying to contain the anger his friend's thoughtless words aroused. He knew Marty didn't mean to provoke him. The guy was only smarting off. But the old pain still haunted him.

He should have been a pilot. It came as naturally to him as walking. But he'd taken his medicine, accepted that he wasn't going to fly planes anymore, and made up his mind to become a damn good navigator. Rollins had understood. Had let him take the controls, several times, on the longer missions. Once fighters had come at them, and he'd struggled to control his instinct to evade. He'd held to their position in formation while Rollins manned his gun. The memory brought a stab of pain. His friends were gone. And he was grounded, which was even worse. He couldn't even avenge their deaths.

"Waiter," Marty called, bringing Ted back from that dark place.

Madge must have noticed his change in mood. She placed her hand on his, but he couldn't look at her, couldn't let her see his weakness.

When the waiter arrived Marty asked, "What've you got to eat around here?"

After reciting the limited menu and hearing their choices, the man disappeared.

"Don't expect much out of the food," Ted warned them. "I've eaten here before. It's okay for English food, but you'll find out they don't cook like we're used to."

"Anything has to be better than our mess," Bertie commented.

"Just wait." Ted tried to laugh, tried to recapture his earlier cheerfulness. His gaze fell on the radio behind the bar. "After we eat, I'll turn on the radio and get some music." He turned to Madge. "Wouldn't you like to dance?"

"I'd love to."

Something about her sweet smile warmed him inside. He couldn't wait to get his arms around that luscious body. Hold her close and forget everything, at least for a little while.

****

"Can I borrow some pins?" Madge sank onto the cot, her hair still wet and about half of it twisted into numerous tight pin curls.

"Sure." Kitty stood and retrieved a small box from the shelf above her cot. She wanted to ask Madge about her "date" but wasn't sure how to approach the subject.

Madge fiddled with a curl on the back of her head. "Can you help with this?"

Knowing the answer, Madge twisted around so Kitty could get behind her.

Kitty took the strand of hair and twisted it around her finger, then pinned it tight against Madge's scalp with a bobby pin. She picked up a comb and parted off another strand, knowing her friend expected her to finish the back.

As her fingers worked, she racked her brain trying to come up with a subtle way to ask about…*him*.

Madge spoke up before Kitty had come up with something. "Ted is a fun guy. We had had a great time today."

"That's wonderful." Kitty hesitated. "What did you do?"

"Oh, we talked. Drank beer. Danced a little."

"Sounds like you had fun."

"Oh, I did." Madge turned her head and flashed her famous smile.

"Be still." Kitty tugged at her friend's hair. "Where's he from?" she asked casually.

"I'm not sure. Florida, I think. At least that's where he was when he joined up."

"So that's where his family is?"

"I don't know. We didn't talk about his family."

"What did you talk about?"

"His adventures. His buddy told a story on him, about him washing out of pilot training. I don't think Ted liked it when Marty brought it up. But since he did, Ted went on and told us all about it."

"How did he wash out?"

"Oh, he pulled some stunt with a plane, almost hit Hoover Dam."

"Wow." She'd heard of guys flying under bridges but not into dams. "So how did he get to be a navigator?"

"He said something about the Merchant Marines. I meant to ask him about it, but we got off on the dam story."

Kitty's fingers started shaking. She fumbled with the bobby pins and dropped some on the floor. As she bent over to pick them up, her mind raced. That would confirm her theory. He must be the same man. She knew it.

She started another curl and tried to sound normal. "You'd think he would have joined the Navy if he had been in the Merchant Marines."

"Yeah, you'd think. But he said he was working at an airfield and learning to fly when the war broke out. He wanted to be a pilot."

"But he didn't get his wish." Doubt clouded her mind again. It had been after Pearl Harbor when she pulled the man from the sea.

"No, I guess not. But he is flying or at least he was,

before he was wounded."

Kitty patted Madge's shoulder. "There. All finished."

"Thanks." Madge reached up and fingered the tight pin curls.

"I wish I could do that to my hair and make it look like yours."

Madge looked at her sympathetically. "You don't want hair like mine. Yours fits you perfectly. It's curly on its own. You don't have to worry with pin curls or perms."

Kitty only nodded as if she agreed. Madge would never convince her that her naturally curly mane could ever look as good as Madge's styled do.

"On its own is right. It's uncontrollable. All I can do with it is twist it up and pin it tight. That hair cream you told me about helps some, but…"

"Don't start talking about cutting it again. Remember what happened in basic."

"Oh, I won't. At least with it longer I can do something with it, even if it is pulled up tight and pinned." Kitty lay back on her cot and tried to relax, but she couldn't get Ted out of her mind. "Are you going to see him again?"

"You bet!" Madge scooted closer. "He's the kind of guy I could really get serious about."

"You, serious? I thought you were the one who told me to have a good time but never get too serious or risk getting hurt."

"That's right. But this is different. Ted's a fun guy, but he's got a strength about him. He's suffered some losses, like the pilot training and his crew going down, but he still can laugh and have a good time." Madge pulled back her blanket and slipped under it. "And he's a gentleman. A sweet-talking gentleman."

Kitty looked over at the woman who had been her closest friend, her only friend, for months. The girl who knew her way around, especially around men, had disregarded her own advice and had fallen for a man. Kitty squirmed under her own covers and rolled onto her side so Madge wouldn't see the tears stealing their way down her cheeks.

*Why did she have to fall for him? The man I've dreamed of for two years. Now he'll never see me. Why would he? Madge is perfect, and she wants him.*

Chapter Six

*Sis,*

*Got your letter. Our best bet is to try to meet in London. I will send you a wire when I get leave. I'm due for some time off. In the meantime, butter up whoever you need to so when you get my wire you can get a few days and come to London. Sounds like you're not too far out. You should be able to make it in to the city by train easy. We'll kick up our heels and have a real reunion.*

*Milton*
\*\*\*\*

"Kitty, can you proofread this for me?" Sally stood at her shoulder.

"Just put it there." She nodded toward the left of her typewriter. "I'll look at it after I finish this."

"Thanks. You're a peach."

Kitty focused on her notes. What she found most difficult was blocking out all the people, the sounds, the commotion around her. She reminded herself how their work supported the war effort. It had to be as good as the mechanics who repaired the airplanes, as accurate as the map makers, treated with as much care as the ammunition handlers. The paperwork mattered, too. Planning, strategies, reports, orders all played a vital part in winning the war.

She quickly rolled the finished pages from the

typewriter and began proofreading. She prided herself on her accuracy, yet she knew she made mistakes. The trick was to catch them herself and correct them before anyone else saw them. And she'd perfected her technique for erasures to a point that someone had to look very closely to spot any corrections she'd made, even on the carbons.

This time no corrections were needed. She smiled, pleased with herself. She loved the sense of satisfaction at having done a good job. Why didn't everyone feel the same? She picked up Sally's pages and scanned the typed words absently picking up her pencil to mark a mistake.

A male voice caught her attention. She fought the urge to look up. Instead she focused harder on the task at hand. Sixty seconds and two marks later, she laid down the pages and looked around. Lieutenant Kruger leaned over Madge's desk a short distance away. They kept their voices low until Madge giggled. Ted's deep laughter rippled across the room. Heads came up, drawn to the melodious sound.

Kitty pushed back her chair and stood. She could not stop herself from staring at the two who held the attention of the entire office. Ted basked in the attention, but Madge appeared uncharacteristically ill at ease as dozens of eyes watched her.

"You'd better go," Madge told him, "before the sergeant comes back."

"Okay, babe." Ted grinned and turned to face the room. He took a sweeping bow. "Good day, ladies." Then he waltzed from the room as if he were royalty.

*What a ham.* Kitty shook her head in disapproval.

"You're just jealous," Madge commented, as if

she'd read Kitty's mind.

"I'm not jealous. I just wish he wouldn't come in here and disrupt our work."

"Work isn't everything."

"It's what we're here for. You two can go and kid around after your shift."

Madge smiled broadly. "Don't worry. We will."

Kitty handed the papers to Sally. "I marked the errors. Only three."

"Thanks, Kitty. I'll fix them right away."

"Be careful. Don't rub a hole in the paper like you did yesterday. Do it like I showed you. Then you won't have to start over."

"I'll be careful," Sally assured her.

Kitty glanced back at Madge, who'd returned to her typing, yet she still smiled. Kitty had to admit, if only to herself, that she was envious. No man had ever paid her that kind of attention.

Somehow Ted managed to stop by every day. Some days he showed up twice. And every time he made a fuss over Madge. No wonder she absolutely glowed with happiness.

Life wasn't fair. He was my dream. He was the one who was going to come back into my life and sweep me off my feet, just like in the movies. Instead, he had reappeared and swept her best friend off her feet. Worst of all, he didn't even remember her.

She tried to shake off the bad feelings. She was happy for Madge. She really was. And she was determined not to feel sorry for herself. Someone would show up some day, and he'd love her for who she was. And she'd love him with all her heart. And they'd live happily ever after, just like in the fairy tales, just like in her dreams.

For now she'd do her job. Work to win the war so they could all go back home to start the rest of their lives.

**** 

Maps spread across the large table. Ted studied the area around Berlin, Germany, and compared the aerial photos with the map. Carefully he marked the location of the factory the bombers would target. This information would be critical. If he marked it incorrectly, then the bombs could fall on useless, non-military locations. He drove the thoughts of civilian casualties from his mind. There were always civilian casualties, but it couldn't be helped. And his guilt would not stop the bombing. He had to do his job, to the best of his abilities. Only ending the war would stop the killing.

"Lieutenant Kruger."

Ted looked up. Colonel Snyder stood in the doorway.

Ted straightened and saluted the officer. "Sir."

The colonel sauntered into the room, giving a casual salute as he moved. "Do you have the flight plans for tomorrow's target?"

"Not yet. It'll be a tough one for the bombers. Heavy flack through here"—he pointed to an area on the map—"and here." He pointed to the second area, his mind plotting alternate approaches.

"This target is critical," Colonel Snyder insisted. "We must eliminate the enemy's ability to continue. Destroy their morale. And we must control the skies." The colonel continued to move around the table, his focus on every detail.

"Yes, sir. I understand. I was just thinking about how the bombers should approach the target. We had heavy losses the last time."

"Work it out, Lieutenant. We must disrupt their production of war materials, even if we cannot completely destroy it." He looked up from the map and caught Ted's gaze. "Do what you can but remember, losses are inevitable. We must focus on destroying the target."

Ted stood straight and faced his superior officer, trying to remember how many missions the man had flown. It wasn't many. Not enough to fully understand what the men he sent on these missions had to endure. It didn't matter, not to Snyder or any of the brass. They were running this war. All he could do was follow orders.

"How many planes are we sending?" Ted asked after a few moments.

"All the available planes in the wing. Maximum effort."

Ted fought to contain his emotions. The brass used ten percent losses as acceptable. On the last mission to Germany, the losses had been over twenty percent. Too many. But Snyder didn't care.

"Perhaps if we approach from the northeast, through here." He used the pointer to show the colonel where he meant. "Maybe they wouldn't expect that. There might be less flack. Fewer fighters."

The colonel nodded. "It might work. But they'll spot us when we cross the coastline, send the fighters. Then the fighters warn the anti-aircraft batteries." He shook his head. "You know there are no surprises over Germany as long as the Luftwaffe is flying." He pointed to the map again. "Besides the city is ringed by anti-aircraft guns."

"Yes, sir. I know." Disheartened as he was, Ted had to do his job.

Colonel Snyder walked around the table and looked at the map from a different angle. "Go ahead and plot a course. Then we'll go over it and see how it works out."

"Yes, sir. Give me an hour or so to work out the details."

The officer nodded and headed for the door.

"Colonel." Ted drew a deep breath and asked the question he'd been withholding for over a week. "Have you considered my request for transfer back to the bombers?"

Colonel Snyder stopped and frowned at him. "I don't understand why you would want to put yourself in such danger. Not when you can contribute as much or more right here."

"I'm a trained navigator. I want to finish my twenty-five missions. After that I could go back to the states and train the new guys. Pass on my combat experience."

Colonel Snyder stepped closer and narrowed his gaze, looking straight into Ted's eyes. "I think there's more to it than that. I think you want to put yourself in harm's way." He hesitated a moment. "Does this request of yours have anything to do with the fact your original crew was shot down after you were wounded?"

Ted started to deny it, but he couldn't. He had to be honest with himself as well as the colonel.

"I admit that's part of it. But I was trained to fly missions, and I'm no better than anyone else. Why should I stay behind here when others are putting themselves in danger every day?"

"Well, I need you right now. So get to work." He spun on his heel and departed.

"But you'll think about it?" Ted called after him.

*Let me get back up there where I belong.*

\*\*\*\*

Ted lit a cigarette and strolled at a leisurely pace in the general direction of the castle. He was in no hurry to return to the planning office. Colonel Snyder had been deep in conversation with General Lake when he'd left the officers' mess, so he figured he had a little time to relax before tackling the night's task. Let the brass argue it out before he spent any more time on it.

He paused and looked around. A few men headed for the Officers' Club. He wouldn't mind dropping in for a beer. On second thought, he'd better not. Colonel Snyder wouldn't like it if he smelled it on his breath. Ted needed to stay on Colonel Snyder's good side so he'd approve Ted's request for a transfer.

Looking back toward the castle, he saw a WAC emerge from the building. Why would Madge be working late?

It didn't take but a minute to realize that the WAC wasn't Madge. She didn't walk with that distinctive style, almost a swagger that dared men to look. No, this girl had a different air about her. Confident, yet relaxed. Not military at all, despite the uniform.

She looked familiar. As she drew closer, he recognized Madge's friend, Kitty. The prickly one. The one who pretended she didn't like him. He'd caught her looking sideways at him more than once, so he knew it wasn't true. She probably thought with Madge around that she didn't stand a chance—which was true. Not many women could measure up to Madge. But Kitty wasn't bad. She had a sort of quiet appeal. Some guys preferred that to the flashy types like Madge. He, on the other hand, liked having the prettiest girl on base on his arm, the envy of every man around.

Before reaching the spot where he stood watching her, she took a path that cut across the once manicured lawn toward female territory. The Army believed in keeping the women separated from the men. From the warnings they'd gotten about fraternizing with the female soldiers, he half expected them to put up a fence and string barbed wire to keep them safe. But warnings hadn't deterred the red-blooded American airmen. And he was no exception.

A little female companionship tonight would make a nice distraction. He threw down his cigarette butt and strode toward her.

"Hey there," he called as he came closer. He didn't want to scare her.

She stopped and turned. Even in the dim light of dusk, he could see her body tense. She straightened to attention and saluted. "Lieutenant."

"You don't have to do that," he chided as he casually returned her salute.

"I don't want to be accused of disregarding military protocol."

Ted chuckled. "Are you always so formal?" He cocked his head sizing her up. "Don't you ever let go? Relax a little?"

She didn't reply but the tension in her body spoke volumes. She was nervous, didn't want to be alone with him. Interesting.

"Running late for supper, aren't you?" He kept his voice light, not threatening.

"I should make it…if I'm not delayed."

She wasn't very good at her attempt to get rid of him, but she'd given it a try. He wasn't about to let her off so easy.

He grasped her elbow and turned her back toward her destination. "I'll just walk with you. Make sure you get there okay."

Rather than respond, she resumed her trek at a quicker pace. He hurried along beside her, determined not to let go of her arm. She wouldn't get away that easy.

"You don't like me, do you?"

"I wouldn't say that." She glanced his way. "I'm just concerned for Madge."

"Oh, don't worry about Madge. That girl can take care of herself."

He couldn't read her thoughts, not hurrying along at this pace. Her face showed only determination.

They crossed the main road and cut between buildings to reach the road into the WAC area. Finally she spoke again. "She likes you, a lot."

Madge, she's talking about Madge. "And I like her."

"But you're not serious."

Her flat statement surprised him, and he couldn't hold back his laughter. She had no idea how ludicrous she sounded. "You've got to be kidding. Nobody's serious. Not over here."

Her brows drew together wrinkling the skin between them as she glanced up at him. Something familiar in her frowning face stifled his amusement. His throat tightened. She wasn't kidding. She really didn't get it.

"We're just having a good time, while we can," he said. "You know what it's like." He released her arm and slowed down, unsure why he needed to explain himself. "There's no point in thinking about the future. Not here. Nobody knows what's going to happen. So we just have fun while we can."

She stopped and looked him in the eye, her expression filled with concern—and something else. Anger, maybe. "Just make sure Madge understands that."

Her words, and the way she looked at him, scared him a little.

"Are you saying she's getting serious? About me?" The idea was incredible.

"Yes. I think so."

"Well, that's just nuts." He reached up and scratched the back of his head, pushing his hat forward and to one side as he did.

She turned her head, but before she did, he saw her eyes crinkle, and he realized she was trying not to smile. And he wanted to see her smile, for him, just for him.

The women's mess stood only a few feet away. She moved toward it. He jumped to her side and snatched his hat from his head.

Just before reaching the door she spoke. "Maybe so, but these things happen." She faced him and nodded. "Good night, Lieutenant."

He caught her arm again, unable to fight the urge to hold onto her. "What about you? Are you always so strait-laced? Don't you ever have any fun?"

Her gaze darted to his face. Her eyes danced in the dim light. "Sometimes." She drew a deep, ragged breath as if she were trying to calm her nerves. He watched her lips purse together and found himself wondering what she would taste like.

She tugged her arm from his grasp. An odd sense of loss crept from his fingertips, up his arm to settle in his chest. Much as he wanted to wrap his arms around her and kiss that frown from her lips, he couldn't make a scene, not here in front of the mess hall door.

"Goodnight," she whispered.

He could only nod.

She disappeared, leaving a void in her wake.

From inside the clanking of dishes and pans merged with muffled voices. The familiar aromas of greasy food and stale coffee seeped through the flimsy door of the temporary building.

He turned away and forced his feet to move. Back to the castle. Back to work. Before Colonel Snyder sent someone to look for him.

\*\*\*\*

Ted shook his head to rid his brain of Kitty's image. What had happened? What was it about her frowning face that made him want to pull her into his arms? Why had he desperately wanted her to smile at him?

Maybe it was because she shied away from him, frowned at him every time he came around. Disapproval oozed from her, fueling his need to be the clown, to act out like a kid in school taunting the teacher by entertaining the other children.

He didn't like to think of himself that way. He wasn't a kid anymore. He'd grown up. He'd had to. In some ways he'd never been a kid, not like the others. His father's death had made sure of that.

His mind returned to Kitty. Something drew him to her. Did he want her approval? She was Madge's friend. And she had made it clear she was worried that Madge might get hurt.

He disagreed. Madge knew the score. She liked a good time just like he did.

And her luscious body, that picture perfect face, provided the perfect distraction from the dark depths that lingered under the surface. He couldn't go there. Wouldn't.

He'd think about beautiful, blonde Madge.

Then why did dark-haired, prim and proper Kitty creep into this thoughts? What was it about her?

A couple of times he'd caught her looking at him, as if she were trying to see through the façade. She knew. Somehow she knew he was putting on an act, knew all his bravado covered up his fear and his pain. But he didn't sense condemnation. Her disapproval felt more like disappointment.

He wanted to fix that. Wanted her to like him. That was all it was. He just wanted Madge's friend's approval and friendship.

"There you are." The young corporal came running down the hallway.

"What's going on?" Ted asked.

"It's Colonel Snyder. He's on a rampage. Says we've got the flight path for tomorrow all wrong."

"Okay. I'll talk to him." Ted gritted his teeth. He hated working for a man who didn't care what happened to the men in those bombers.

"He's gonna' make us change it." The non-com ran

along trying to keep up with Ted's long strides. "He says it'll take too much fuel."

"He won't change it. Not if he wants enough planes to get to the target to do any damage." The route ran through his brain, the exact location of all the flack zones, the approach to the target. He'd managed to devise a route that avoided the worst of it.

Snyder hadn't flown that many missions. He didn't have to face the flack, the fighters. He preferred to stay behind and give orders rather than risk his own life.

An idea popped into Ted's head, and he smiled. It was devious but it might just work.

"What are you thinking?" the corporal asked warily.

"I'm going to talk Colonel Snyder into leading this mission."

"What!" The young man's astonishment morphed into laughter. "You devil! That'd serve him right." He patted Ted on the back. "You're a genius."

They'd almost reached their destination when the corporal asked, "How are you going to do it?"

Ted stopped and smiled down at the shorter man. "I heard Colonel Stewart led the last mission. Everybody's impressed with him. Enough to get him promoted again, maybe even give him a group." He looked toward the door and thought of the men waiting there. "If they give him one, that means a group leader gets bumped up here, to the wing. Snyder wants to be in line to take over the wing, but he's afraid of the competition."

"And if he leads a mission, it'll look good on his record. Make points with the old man."

"Exactly." Ted smiled thinking of the squirming

colonel. "Of course, it wouldn't do if he got shot down or killed, now would it?"

## Chapter Seven

*Katherine,*

*Write us when you get to England and let us know how Milton is doing. It will be nice for him to have his sister close by. Try not to embarrass him like you did when you were younger when you chased after him and his friends. Boys don't like their younger sisters running after them. Speaking of sisters, Suzanne and the children have come to live with us while Sam goes off with the Coast Guard. I think it is wrong for a married man with two children to join the service. I don't believe for a minute that they would have drafted him. But he insisted that it was for the best.*

*Olivia, of course, is the most popular girl in the senior class. Several fine young men are vying for her attention. We are urging her to keep her options open so she can make sure she chooses the one with the best prospects. Bill O'Guinn is my choice. With an athletic scholarship to the University of Tennessee, he will be a great catch for some lucky girl.*

*Your father has Andy working at the mill after school. That way he can learn the business. When Milton gets home, he will have both his sons working with him. He says he is going to change the sign to Greenlee and Sons.*

> *Give our love to Milton,*
> *Mother*

\*\*\*\*

Kitty threw her mother's letter down in disgust. *Why do I even read them?*

"Was it that bad?" Madge asked.

"It's from my mother. What do you think?" She'd let Madge read her mother's letters before so her friend understood.

"At least she's thinking about you."

"You'd never guess it from what she wrote. All about Milton and Suzanne and, of course, that beautiful and popular little sister of mine. She even mentioned Andy. Not once did she ask about me—what I'm doing, what I think if England—nothing."

"So now you know what's going on with your brothers and sisters."

"Oh, don't try to sugar coat it. She only writes me because she thinks she has to. And so she can tell all her friends about all the letters she writes." She picked up the envelope and stared at it. The only mail she'd gotten all week. Why couldn't someone else write her?

Madge moved to put her letter on the shelf above her bed.

"What about yours?" Kitty asked, not wanting to pry.

"Oh, it's from a girl I know back in Minneapolis. She'd going out with a boy I used to date. I think she wrote me just to rub it in."

"How long has it been since you heard from your father?"

Madge wouldn't look at her. Kitty cringed inside, hoping she hadn't asked the wrong question. After reaching for her nail polish, Madge finally answered. "I don't know. He's not much on writing."

Kitty knew not to say anymore. Luckily, Sally stopped at the foot of the bed and held out a box.

"Homemade cookies," she announced. "They're kind of broken up, but they taste good."

Kitty reached into the pasteboard box. She took two small pieces she guessed would have made about one cookie had they been whole.

Sally extended the box to Madge. "Go ahead. They're oatmeal. My favorite."

Madge took a large piece. "Who sent them?"

"My sister. She's a great cook." Sally moved on to share her treats with some of the other girls.

"Mmmm, they are good," Kitty commented. "And a lot better than what we got."

Madge looked up smiling and agreed. Her old cheerful self had returned.

****

*What have I done?*

Kitty could taste the sour remains of powdered eggs and spam churning in her stomach. Her thoughts raced through every task she'd performed in the last week. No obvious disaster came to mind. She must have missed something—something big for her to be summoned to General Lake's office.

After identifying herself to the general's aid, she faced the heavy, wooden door as if the executioner waited behind its deeply carved panels. She closed her eyes and drew in a deep breath. She could do this. She could face anything. She'd made it through basic, hadn't she? How much worse could this be?

Her hand trembled as she rapped her knuckles against the hard surface.

From beyond the wooden pane she heard, "Come

in."

The cold metal knob intensified the chill sweeping over her. Breathe, she reminded herself. Just remember to breathe.

Enthroned behind a heavy desk, General Lake's attention focused on the paperwork spread before him.

Kitty moved across the room as quiet as a mouse until she stood at attention before her commanding officer.

He looked up. Without thinking, she straightened even more. Her hand came up in as perfect a salute as she could muster.

"Sir. Corporal Greenlee, reporting as ordered."

"At ease, Corporal."

His warm and friendly voice eased her tension. Her breath came more naturally. Her gaze met his, and she noticed a slight crinkling around his eyes. Not quite a smile but not as threatening as she expected. She relaxed a bit more.

"Yes, sir," she heard herself murmur.

"Sit down, Greenlee."

She noted the impatience in his voice. Heat rose to her face, her heart pounded. Fighting the panic, she looked around for a chair. A pair of straight-backed, leather-covered chairs stood to one side of the desk. Reining in her emotions, she eased herself down onto the edge of the closest one.

General Lake stood and walked around the desk. As he neared, Milton's words from long ago flashed into her mind. "Look 'em straight in the eye. Don't let 'em see your fear, no matter how scared you are."

She sucked in air for strength and raised her head. The general leaned back against the heavy desk and crossed his arms. He looked at her briefly, then shifted his gaze to something behind her.

*Oh, no. This is going to be bad.*

She sat completely still. She would take whatever he dished out. She would be strong, just like Milton taught her.

"Captain Weatherby and I have been talking about you," he started.

She could feel her heart pounding, could feel the perspiration seeping through her pores. But she looked him in the eye as he continued.

"We both agree that your work is excellent. You are quick, efficient, accurate. All critical factors."

She hoped the shock didn't show in her face as she fought to appear emotionless.

"Captain Weatherby tells me you received a commendation for your work in Boston. Got you a promotion and an overseas assignment." He paused, watching her intently. "So…I've decided to have you report directly to me." He uncrossed his arms before continuing. "You will work for me exclusively."

Her mouth flew open, but she couldn't speak, couldn't believe her ears.

A hint of a smile softened his face as he recognized her disbelief. "A girl like you can help me a great deal. Be someone I can count on. Do you understand?"

"Yes, sir." Her voice came out funny, so she cleared her throat and tried again. "Yes, sir," she repeated more firmly. "I would be honored to work for you."

"Good!" He slapped both hands against his thighs and stood. "Then let's get to it." He returned to his seat behind the desk. "Sergeant Dexter will get you set up just outside my door. This place"—he waved his hand around the room—"isn't exactly set up for offices and the kind of work we do around here, but we'll make do."

She took her cue to leave and stood.

"A pretty, young thing like you—smart, hard-working—could do well in the military."

She nodded, unsure how to respond. Did he really say she was pretty?

"Oh, I almost forgot. You'll be promoted to Technical Sergeant."

Now she was in shock. A promotion. Working for the general and a promotion.

He must have seen her reaction because he smiled broadly. A warm, laughing smile. "Go on." He waved his hand toward her. "We've got work to do."

She practically flew from the room, his comments racing through her head faster than her feet skipping across the oriental carpets. Smart. Hard-working. Efficient. Accurate. And pretty. Had he really said she was pretty? She couldn't wait to tell Madge.

****

"It's not like I asked you to go to church with me," Kitty complained.

"Oh, I know. It's just that I've been to the village and you haven't," Madge replied. "There's nothing there."

"Maybe so, but it won't hurt you to look around with me."

The two moved onto the side of the narrow road as a jeep sped by.

"Ted'll be waiting for us," Madge continued.

"He said to meet him at one, right?" Kitty frowned

at her companion and checked her watch. "We've got plenty of time."

They continued their steady pace in silence.

Blooming branches of an apple tree reached across the stone wall of a small cottage set back from the road. The sweet fragrance floated in the breeze.

Kitty ducked to avoid being hit by a cluster of blossoms. She grabbed the offending branch and snapped it off. Holding the blooms to her nose, she inhaled the sweetness.

"Don't start sneezing on me," Madge joked.

Kitty grinned. "Don't worry. I'm not allergic to apple blossoms."

"Well, I remember that weekend last fall. You were sneezing so bad you had to go back to the base. Missed the bonfire and all the fun."

"That was golden rod. I should have known not to cross that field when I saw it. I knew what it would do to me."

"It was a rotten shame, too. That guy was really crazy about you."

"That guy was crazy. Period." Kitty shook her head remembering the soldier. "He was moving way too fast for me."

"So the sneezing rescued you. Is that what you're saying?"

"Something like that."

"Oh, Kitty. When will you learn? You have to work 'em. Manage their expectations."

"You're better at that than I am."

Madge patted her on the shoulder. "You'll learn. Just watch me."

Kitty laughed. "I've been watching you. It's just

that I'm not comfortable doing what you do."

"Suit yourself." Madge laughed along with her friend. "It's your loss."

They reached the heart of the village, the business district, if you wanted to call it that. A few small stores of various ages and architectural styles faced the main street. In the distance, the stone spire of a church marked the street's end. Nothing appeared to have been built within the girls' lifetime. "Quaint" was the word that came to Kitty's mind.

Through the small paned windows of one shop, Kitty noticed an assortment of china. Curious, she pushed the door open and stepped inside. Madge followed reluctantly.

The shop reminded Kitty of the dry goods store run by her neighbors in Kerrville. It smelled of oiled wood floors and freshly dyed cloth. Near the door, an ancient mannequin stood clothed in a navy blue skirt and sweater. A few bolts of dull cloth lay on a display counter. Shelves on one wall held stacks of what appeared to be shoeboxes.

Near the back wall, a white-haired lady stood behind a counter, busy cutting black cloth, probably for black-out curtains. A middle-aged, dowdy-looking woman fingered through a rack of thread nearby.

"Just 'ave a look around. I'll be with you shortly," the clerk called.

Kitty wove her way between the crowded shelves to the corner near the window where an assortment of china wear provided a colorful, if compact, display. Assorted household goods occupied this portion of the shop, lampshades, a few pots, bed sheets, and linens.

She picked up a cup covered with tiny flowers and

turned to Madge. "Isn't this pretty?"

"I guess, in an old-fashioned sort of way."

"I'll have you know I like old-fashioned, at least in some things." She replaced the cup on its saucer and continued to study the china, piece by piece, occasionally running her fingers along the smooth surface of a fragile platter or bowl.

Madge turned to a display of hats nearby. She tried one on and turned. "What do you think?"

Kitty looked up just as the clerk approached.

"You girls must be at the castle." The older woman smiled. "Haven't seen that uniform before."

"We're Americans, Women's Army Corps. And yes, we're working at Ellingham Castle, although it's not the kind of castle I expected."

The woman's light laughter danced through the air. Madge glanced up from her browsing as the native continued. "I'll wager you Yanks think a castle is all stone walls and battlements."

Kitty fought the blush of embarrassment. "Yes. I guess I expected to see something like that. "

"Oh, there's plenty of old ruins around. Just 'ave to know where to look."

"Are there really? Close by?" The woman's comment sparked Kitty's imagination.

"Of course. The old Norman fortification. Stood for centuries, till they built Ellingham Castle. Used the old stone to lay the foundation."

"Where is it?" Kitty asked eagerly.

"Just take the lane by Pemberly's. Not far, there's a track off to the right. What's left of the old place sits atop the hill."

Kitty shot a questioning glance at her friend who'd

just placed the hat back on its pedestal.

"No," Madge said flatly. "Don't even ask. We're going to the pub."

"But it's such a beautiful day. We could all go."

Madge's frown gave her answer. "Are you finished, shopping, I mean?"

"Almost." She pressed her lips together and elevated her chin just enough to let Madge know she wouldn't be pushed.

Kitty quickly returned her attention to the china display. "I was interested in your china."

The elderly lady stepped closer, self-consciously pulling her worn sweater around her thin waist as her gaze darted between the two women. "We have some lovely pieces. Are you looking for anything in particular?"

Kitty pointed to a teapot covered in tiny blossoms. "What's that pattern called?"

The clerk reached up and took the teapot down so Kitty could examine it. "It's Lord Nelson Chintz. A lovely pattern, don't you think?"

Kitty took the delicate pot, held the lid tight, and turned it over to inspect it. She then took the lid off and peered inside. There was no tag, no price anywhere.

"It's beautiful. How much is it?" Kitty asked.

"Oh, being's it's been here gathering dust and being's we don't have the cups to match, I'd say we could let you have it for ten shillings."

Kitty looked over at Madge, hoping her friend understood English money better than she did. Madge shrugged.

"What do you want that for?" Madge complained. "It'll only get broken in that hut."

"We could ship it for you," the clerk offered. "You Yanks are always shipping things back to America."

"How much to ship it?"

"Oh, another two shillings ought to do it."

"Kitty. What are you doing?" Madge protested.

"I was thinking of sending it to my grandmother. She loves things like this."

Madge rolled her eyes. "The one you're named for? The one your father doesn't get along with?"

Kitty nodded. Petty jealousies were so easily forgotten when you were far away. She studied the display again. "What about that vase?"

The clerk handed it down to her. An English rose decorated the foot-tall, flared china vase. "For a full pound, I'll add in the vase and ship it, too."

"All right. You've got a deal." Kitty beamed at Madge.

"And who's that for?" her friend asked.

"Mother. If I send her something, she can't complain about me sending this to Grandmother."

Madge shook her head smiling. "And your old man won't say anything either. Glad I don't have to keep my relatives happy."

The clerk took the teapot and vase back to the counter. Kitty slipped her arm around Madge's waist and gave her a little hug.

"Thanks for putting up with me."

"Sure. Sure."

As Kitty dug in her bag for the money, she saw Madge glance up at a clock behind the counter. Five minutes to one. "This won't take long." She hurriedly wrote out the names and addresses for the clerk.

Madge glanced impatiently toward the street and

tapped her fingers on the countertop. Kitty got the message. "I know. I know. We'll get there. Don't worry."

Madge smiled, a strange almost shy look in her eyes. "Just anxious to see him."

Madge had really fallen hard for Lieutenant Ted Kruger. And Madge never fell for any of the guys she dated. Her philosophy was to have fun, never get too attached, and never let them get too attached. Always before, if Madge thought some guy had fallen for her, she'd let him down gently, but she'd made it plain that she never got serious. Never, until now.

Kitty couldn't blame Madge. Kitty had fallen for the same guy, years ago on a deserted beach. The fact he didn't even remember her hurt, more than a little. But that wasn't Madge's fault.

Kitty just wasn't the type girl men went for, not men like Ted. No. Handsome, blue-eyed, sweet-smiling guys like Ted only went for her in her dreams, not in real life.

Kitty finished and thanked the nice English woman. She then took Madge's arm and led her out of the shop. "He'll be there waiting for you," Kitty assured her friend.

****

Ted spotted the old German trudging along, a cane in one hand and a basket swinging from his other arm.

"I'll be right back," Ted told his friend, then he hurried to cross the street.

"*Guten tag*," Ted called to the old gent.

The white-haired man stopped and turned. A smile spread across the older face at the familiar greeting. His eyes twinkled. "*Ja*, Good Day."

Ted continued in German, asking about the man's health. He knew it would please the ex-patriot's longing to hear his native tongue.

They'd met accidentally on Ted's first venture into town after leaving the hospital. He'd heard the familiar German accent, and memories of his grandparents drew him to the stranger. Despite Ted's rusty German, the aging man had been immensely pleased to hear the familiar words.

"Kruger, come on," Newman called from across the street. "The girls will be waiting for us."

"Okay." Ted waved. "I'm coming." He turned to the old gentleman. "It was good to see you again."

"Perhaps you can join me for tea one day. At number 12 Ablemare, just down the street and to the left." He held out his hand to shake. "You must come, on any day, at tea time."

Ted shook his hand. "I'd like that. Give me a chance to practice my German."

He darted across the street, between bicyclists, and turned back to wave as he reached the opposite side.

"Who's that?" Newman asked.

"Oh, just an old man I met. He reminds me of my grandfather."

When the two airmen entered the pub, they saw nothing of the WACs. "See—they're not here yet," Ted said.

They settled at a table by the large window that faced the street so they could watch for the girls and enjoy the local people going about their business.

The semblance of normalcy allowed him to pretend the war was far away, at least for a little while.

Within minutes the girls arrived. Madge greeted

them with one of her winning smiles. Kitty hung back.

"Ladies, I'd like you to meet Second Lieutenant Sammy Newman." Ted wanted to put his arm around Madge and pull her close, but he knew he'd better be on his best behavior, at least for now. "Sammy, this is Madge and her friend, Kitty."

Sammy reached out and shook Madge's hand. "Ted told me you looked like Betty Grable, and he wasn't kidding."

Madge beamed at the compliment. Beside her Kitty appeared embarrassed. Ted wasn't sure if it was because Sammy made such a big deal over Madge or because Sammy ignored her. Maybe if the girl were a little more outgoing men would pay more attention to her.

"Kitty and Madge have been friends for a long time, haven't you girls?" Ted tried to smooth over the situation with the first thing that came to his head. Something about Kitty made him sympathize with her.

"Yes," Kitty nodded quietly.

"We met when we trained at the administration school in Kentucky. Then, as luck would have it, we were both assigned to Boston, then sent over here." Madge slid into the chair Ted held for her.

"You don't sound like you're from the south," Sammy drawled, focusing his attention on Madge alone.

Ted recognized the look in Sammy's eyes. The same look he saw in the eyes of every man he'd introduced to Madge. He had to head the guy off

Ted pulled out the chair next to Madge. "Kitty, why don't you sit here." He caught her eye and tried to urge her to speak up by gesturing with his head, but she just glared at him. She disliked him, that much was clear. How much of it had to do with Madge and how much had to do with him, he wasn't sure.

Madge batted her long eyelashes in Sammy's direction. "Oh, I'm not. It's Kitty. She's from Tennessee." Madge reached out and patted Kitty on the hand. "I'm from Minneapolis."

Ted seated himself on Madge's other side before Sammy could make a move. "Sammy's from Mobile, Alabama," Ted interjected. "I thought maybe you two southerners would have something in common."

Kitty shot him an odd glance, then gave Sammy a weak smile as he sat beside her.

Somehow Ted had to get those two talking and get Sammy's attention away from Madge.

"Sammy and I were stationed at the same airbase. He's a bombardier." Ted caught Sammy's gaze and nodded toward Kitty. Thankfully the guy got the message.

"That's right. We were in the same squadron." Sammy turned to Kitty. "How long have you girls been at Ellingham?"

Chapter Eight

Ted focused all his attention on Madge. And Madge was so absorbed by Ted that she didn't know anyone else existed. This left Kitty and Sammy in an awkward position—strangers with little to talk about. Add to that the longing Kitty felt when Ted's expressive lips curved up into that infectious smile. A smile he directed at Madge, not her.

Kitty forced her attention away from the flirting man and glanced out the window. "It's a beautiful day," she commented, wishing she could escape Ted's company.

"Yeah," Sammy followed her gaze. "Makes you want to get outside."

Kitty turned to face Sammy. She had an idea, if he was willing. "You wouldn't be interested in going for a walk, would you?"

"Walk? Where?"

He actually sounded interested in her idea.

"A woman in a shop told me about some old Norman ruins just outside of town."

"Sounds interesting." He glanced over at Ted and Madge with their heads together whispering. "You think they'll want to go."

Kitty shook her head. She knew Madge. Walking into the village had been more than enough of nature for her.

Kitty touched her friend's arm to get her attention. "We're going on that walk I told you about. We'll be back later."

"That's swell." Madge barely glanced away from Ted.

When Kitty and Sammy stood, Ted got up and walked with them toward the bar. "You two have fun. We'll just stay here, listen to some music." He signaled for the bartender to bring another round.

Kitty couldn't resist staring at his sparkling blue eyes, eyes focused on Sammy, not her. She'd dreamed about those eyes, dreamed of him seeing only her, wanting only her. But he didn't even see her, barely glanced her way.

The real man was nothing like she imagined. She didn't even like him that much. He was pleasant enough, smiling, joking. Never serious, always looking for a good time. And although he focused his attention on Madge, he'd admitted that he just wanted to have fun.

On the other hand, Madge was crazy about him.

Madge loved men, loved flirting with them, loved them chasing her, loved them fighting over her. This time it was different. Madge was the one stuck on the guy. And the one time it happened, it had to be him, Kitty's dream man.

Kitty couldn't control the jealousy that crept forth from some dark place within.

It wasn't fair. Madge got all the men. Why couldn't Kitty have gotten the only man she ever wanted? The one she'd dreamed about?

She had to get out of there. Had to get away from him.

Out in the fresh air, she tried to clear her head and focus on where they were going. She recounted the directions she had been given, and Sammy nodded. The two of them strolled down the street. She glanced at him and wondered if he had noticed her desperation to get away.

Sammy remained quiet, and yet he appeared to enjoy being outside as much as she did.

For the first time in a long time, Kitty decided to let go, to enjoy her freedom. Even though she wasn't alone, she was outside, and she was doing something she enjoyed rather than following orders.

They walked along the road to the east, setting a steady but leisurely pace. Knowing Sammy was recovering from a hospital stay, she didn't want to push him too hard. She didn't want to appear nosy, so she didn't ask him about his injuries.

Instead she told him "We can stop and rest anytime you want."

"Thanks, but I'm fine. It's actually good to get out and walk. It'll get my strength up."

Kitty's thoughts returned to Ted. Maybe Sammy could fill her in. "Have you known Ted long?"

"A while, yes." He thought for a moment. "Ted's a good sort. Lots of fun."

"I've noticed." She hadn't meant to sound as sarcastic as she did.

"Don't you like him?"

"I haven't decided." She tried to offer an explanation without sounding too interested. "He's always joking. Never serious. It's like he's hiding something…or maybe himself."

He smiled and nodded. "Yeah, that's Bear. He kids

about everything. That's just how he is, uses humor to deal with everything." He gazed into the distance. "Right now he's grieving."

"I don't understand." Grieving was the last thing she would have thought of to describe Ted.

"His crew. Shot down a few days after he was wounded."

She didn't know how to respond. Ted's friends had died. Just like those men in that bomber she'd seen explode over the airfield. She couldn't imagine how painful it must have been for him.

"They came to visit him in the hospital, soon after I got there," Sammy continued. "The officers, I mean. Even through the fog of the pain killers, I remember their laughter. They were giving Ted a hard time about getting hit in the rear end. And he gave right back. He was lovin' it." Sammy paused, remembering. "He told me later the four of them were like brothers."

"How did he take it…when he found out they'd all been killed?"

"Hard." Sammy shook his head and flattened his lips in a frown. "He said he wished he'd gone with them." He glanced over at Kitty and caught her gaze. "Your friend's good for him. She's given him something to think about, to look forward to." He looked away. "Life goes on, you know."

"And what about you?"

"Me? Oh, I'm fine. Next week I go back to Allsford. Start flying again." He paused a few seconds before continuing. "Ted's lucky, getting assigned to headquarters. He might just survive this thing."

\*\*\*\*

They reached the lane the Englishwoman told her

about. It led across a pasture and up a sloping hill. Beneath the thick grass, deep indentations marked the path where, for untold years, wheeled vehicles had plodded their way up to the castle. Now only sheep grazed the hillside.

She drove thoughts of Ted from her mind. He'd chosen Madge. And it was probably for the best.

"The history books say the Normans crossed the channel and conquered this land centuries ago. To hold it, they built fortresses to withstand attacks from their enemies." Kitty relayed the story she'd read while waiting to be shipped overseas.

"It's strange how many wars have been fought over here and how old everything is," Sammy said. His pace slowed on the uneven ground.

"Are you interested in history?" she asked.

He laughed. "I always thought the Civil War was ancient history. And the Revolution, well, I guess that seemed like the beginning of time. I never thought much about anything that happened before that."

Kitty hid her disappointment in her companion's lack of interest. At least he came along, instead of sitting in a pub all afternoon. She continued her history lesson. "We fought the Revolution to get free from the English. This country was around a long time before the United States got started. Our ancestors came from over here—at least mine did."

When Sammy didn't reply, she looked back. He'd stopped to watch two lambs frolicking in the grass nearby. They were much more entertaining than her musings about the past.

The sunken road curved around the wide-spread limbs of an ancient oak that stood guard on the lower portion of the slope. Beyond it the track became steeper.

Eager to reach the top, Kitty forged ahead.

"Look," she exclaimed. "There it is. The old wall." The stones at the crest of the hill sent a thrill through her as if she'd found some lost pyramid. She glanced back at Sammy who was looking up, too. She stifled her desire to dash ahead and patiently waited for him to make his way.

The path wound around the hillside until what looked like the remains of two towers came into view. They must have flanked the entrance to the fortress.

Kitty rushed on, imagining what these still-mighty stone structures would have looked like to approaching travelers. Mounted knights would have ridden through the gate to pay homage to their lord. Flags would have flown from high up on the walls. And watchmen would have called down from their towers to identify the visitors.

Sammy reached her side, but instead of looking up at the crumbling walls, he took in the view from the hilltop.

Kitty turned around to see what those imaginary watchmen would have seen. The sight took her breath. Spread out before her were fields of different shapes and shades, like a patchwork quilt with no apparent design. Roads became mere lines dividing the shapes, interrupted by an occasional roof or cluster of trees.

Her attention returned to the wall, unable to resist the feel of the rough, hand-cut stones, stones that stood here before her ancestors came to America, before Ellingham Castle was built. The history of England lay beneath her fingertips, tangible history that didn't come from books. Touching these stones made all the stories of castles and knights of long ago real.

Kitty's gaze roamed upward. "How high do you think it is? Twenty feet?" She wondered what she could see if she climbed to the top. Could she see as far as the channel?

"I don't know," he replied, clearly tired from the steep climb. He found a spot to sit, leaning against the wall, where he could survey the surrounding countryside.

"Why don't you sit there and rest while I explore?"

He nodded. "I think I will." He pulled a pack of cigarettes and a lighter from his pocket. "Too bad we didn't think to bring something to drink." He held out the pack to offer her one.

"No. But you go ahead."

Amiably, he lit a cigarette and waved her to go on and explore.

Satisfied to leave him behind, curiosity spurred her through the undergrowth partially blocking the old gateway. Instead of an open area, or bailey, inside the wall, she found a jumble of stones with bushes and trees growing up through them.

In her mind she could see the lord's stonemasons removing stones to use as building material for his new castle. Local farmers would have scavenged for foundation stones for their homes and barns. Archeology and the preservation of history would have been far from their minds. This site probably provided much of the building materials for the surrounding area.

Kitty searched for a way to climb up to the highest remaining portion of the wall. She finally managed to pick her way from stone to stone until she stood near the top of the old ramparts. Straining her eyes, she searched the horizon for the English Channel she knew lay only a few miles to the east, but a haze obscured her view.

The panorama before her was magnificent. Far to the right, tiny, moving specks caught her eye. She guessed they were planes, bombers returning from their flights over Europe. The present intruded on the past with its subtle reminder of the violence so far away and yet so close.

The stone wobbled beneath her feet. She looked down and, for a second, envisioned herself falling from the unsteady precipice. In the blink of an eye, her beautiful day could end in tragedy. Cautiously she balanced herself and step by step retraced the route she had taken to reach the summit.

Once on the ground she relaxed. The momentary danger behind her, she smiled at her own foolishness. Milton would have taken her to task for climbing the wall. Of course, he would have led the way, telling her to remain behind where it was safe.

She ventured back through the gateway where Sammy waited.

He was content to sit and enjoy the view. She sank down beside her companion and leaned back against the aged stones to rest and absorb the sunshine.

"It's beautiful, isn't it?" He smiled and leaned toward her. For a moment she wondered if he would try to kiss her. He'd been a perfect gentleman, so far. But she'd learned that men could change very quickly.

She nodded and looked away, unsure what she wanted.

"Thanks for bringing me along."

"You're welcome. It hasn't been too much for you, has it?"

"No. It's good for me to get out and walk."

"Are you looking forward to seeing your friends when you get back to your base?"

He nodded, thoughtfully. "I guess."

With his non-committal answer, she decided to drop the subject. She pulled her knees up and rested her chin on them. Perhaps silence was safer than trying to talk.

She gazed out over the idyllic setting and made a conscious effort to preserve the moment in her memory. The fresh, clean country air filled her lungs. In the trees, leaves danced in the gentle breeze. Birds twittered among the branches. Scattered through the pasture below her, wild flowers raised their colorful faces to the sun. Sheep munched the plentiful grass. All was right with the world.

Something rumbled behind them. A dark gray, almost purple sky closed in from the north.

Sammy pushed himself to his feet. "Time to go," he announced, as if she didn't know what they had to do.

She followed him back down the winding, narrow lane.

The wind whipped around them, much cooler than moments before. They picked up their pace and made their way around the giant oak before the first raindrop hit them.

Kitty looked up. Fat splats of liquid fell all around them. One landed on her arm. Another hit her cheek. They pelted her back and shoulders.

When they reached the road, she and Sammy

exchanged a quick glance. He nodded and called to her, "Let's go."

They broke into a jog along the wet pavement.

How far was it back to the village? She tried to remember. It had seemed such a short distance when they started.

Water splashed into her shoes. Her skirt clung to her legs. The rain soon soaked through her uniform jacket. The dampness reached her arms and shoulders.

The blowing rain came down at an angle. Sammy turned up the collar of his uniform jacket and held it together at the neck. His crusher cap provided little protection.

When they rounded a curve in the road, the rain hit them smack in the face. Kitty put her hand up to shield her eyes. Water seeped down her collar. Her hair, weighed down with dampness, pulled free from its pins, and stray curls turned into wild tangles.

Finally houses appeared in the mist, and the road brought them into town. A short way up the street, the Blue Ram's sign swayed in the blowing rain. They made a final dash for what she prayed would be a warm, dry haven.

## Chapter Nine

A chilly, damp wind blew in through the open door. Heads turned. A drenched WAC stumbled through the doorway followed by an equally drowned airman. Both shivered, dripping water on the floor.

"Kitty!" Madge jumped up and ran to the soaked female.

Ted covered his mouth to hide his grin. They both looked ridiculous. Served them right. The silly girl had traipsed off with Newman in tow to explore the countryside totally unprepared for the English weather.

When the rain started, Madge had gotten worried about her friend and despite his best efforts, he hadn't been able to distract her. Why did women have to stick together? Kitty ought to be able to take care of herself. After all, she was a WAC, and WACs were supposed to be trained to survive in all kinds of situations. If they couldn't handle a little rain, how would they handle an air raid?

Madge steered her friend and the damp soldier toward the fireplace.

"Build up that fire." Madge barked the order and looked directly at him.

Ted nodded and jumped up, thankful to have something to do so he wouldn't say something smart and make Madge mad.

"Oh, you poor dears." The proprietress rushed to

their aid with towels in her arms. "Edwin, bring hot toddy's for them. Hurry now."

The waiter turned and hurried back to the bar.

Ted squatted before the flames and carefully placed two additional logs on the smoldering fire. He glanced over his shoulder and saw the shaking girl standing nearby. Madge fiddled with her hair, pulled out pins and rubbed a towel over the girl's wet head.

He returned his attention to the task at hand. He grabbed a poker and stirred the flames to life.

Newman pulled off his coat and hung it on a chair then stood near the fire trying to warm himself.

Ted looked up and the quick glance they exchanged told him his friend would survive.

The proprietress reappeared with two blankets. She draped one around the girl's shoulders. "Here you go, deary. This'll warm you up."

She handed the other to the American airman.

Aware of all the fuss around him, Ted focused his attention on the fire. He poked at it some more, just to have something to do.

"Thank you," Kitty murmured.

He looked up again. She stood close, a blanket wrapped around her shoulders, her hair loose, damp and curly, forming a sort of halo around her head.

The angel hovered over him. The surf roared in his ears. The sun burned his skin. She told him he was safe.

His throat tightened. Startled at his reaction, he choked back his thundering emotions.

Was she real? He blinked as if he could make the vision disappear. But she remained, standing over him, a knowing smile in her eyes. He wanted to reach out, to touch her, to see if she was flesh and blood.

Instinctively he raised his hand and, to his dismay, she grasped it. Her icy cold fingers almost made him shiver, not from the temperature, from the thrill of recognition.

Her sensuous lips curved up slightly. Her soft, gray, reassuring eyes caressed him. She knew. She'd always known.

A chair scraped sharply across the floor and jerked him back to reality. He released her hand as Madge spoke.

"Sit here and get warm."

He sensed Madge's eyes on him, but he couldn't meet her gaze.

"Ted's got the fire going for you." Madge hovered over her friend.

He stood, rubbed his sweating palms against his pants, and eased away. His jaw tightened. He couldn't look at either of them, not till he figured out what just happened.

He needed a drink. Something strong. His gaze roamed the room. Every eye in the place was focused on the two wet figures by the fire. The waiter emerged from behind the bar with two drinks on a tray and hurried over to the damp damsel. She took one of the glasses, and Newman grabbed the other one.

"This'll warm you up," the waiter assured them.

Ted followed the man back to the bar. "Give me a shot of whiskey, straight."

He ignored the man's wary look, watched him place a glass on the bar, and fill it. With one swift motion, Ted downed the fiery liquid.

"Again," he demanded, rubbing his fingers over his lips.

With his courage fortified, he glanced back at the

girl by the fire. The flickering light turned the edges of her wild hair into a halo like the bright sunlight had done on that day so long ago. His body tensed, his hands fisted. He turned back, grabbed the shot glass, and brought it to his lips. Again, he swallowed it in one quick gulp, then he closed his eyes and waited for the warm glow to settle over him.

Why? He'd met Kitty several times. And felt nothing. Well, not exactly nothing, but a vague attraction. He'd dismissed it as the same thing he felt every time he met a woman who was the least bit pretty or interesting or well built. So what. He liked women. But this one had been stand-off-ish. He'd accepted her attitude because he'd been much more interested in Madge. And who wouldn't be. Blonde, built, and friendly. Madge was definitely his type. Kitty had been just…just there, in the background. Until today.

"Give me another one."

He relaxed a little against the bar. The alcohol was doing its work. With his newly acquired courage, he turned to face the room.

He studied his three companions. Madge had pulled up another chair and sat facing her friend. They were talking. Or rather Madge was talking. Kitty sat with her hands extended to the fire. The blanket had slipped down exposing one shoulder. She turned her head toward him, and their gazes met.

The connection between them hummed, like an electrical current flashing across the room. She knew him, and she knew that he knew her. It had only taken an instant.

That lost, young guy welled up inside him again. The guy who'd been saved by an angel. The dream of a lost soul, crazy from an eternity floating alone on the ocean, who'd prayed to a God he barely believed in, and yet, who'd sent an angel to save him. He'd convinced himself she had been all in his head, that he had imagined her. Now he knew different. She had been real.

But what could he do about it? Ask her? How would he explain to Madge?

"There's your drink. Don't you want it?"

He turned back. "Sure." He fished a few coins out of his pocket and placed them on the bar. Then he picked up the glass and eased back to the table where he and Madge had been sitting before the sodden explorers appeared.

Madge patted Kitty on the knee, then rose and came over to him.

"She's soaked to the skin. If we don't get her out of those wet clothes, she'll catch pneumonia."

"What can I do? I don't have any extra clothes for her."

"Can you call someone? Get us a ride back to the base?"

"I don't know. I guess I can try." The strong drink made his mind sluggish and a little reluctant to do her bidding.

"Well, see what you can do." She flashed him one of her brilliant smiles, patted him on the shoulder, then returned to her friend by the fire.

He sipped his drink, absorbing its warm glow. His gaze roamed the establishment for a telephone. The proprietress appeared behind the bar. He took another sip, rose, and approached the English woman.

\*\*\*\*

Ted held the umbrella as Madge helped Kitty across the street to the waiting truck. Kitty still had the blanket wrapped around her, but it wasn't enough to ward off the chills. She couldn't remember ever being this cold. Not even when she had tagged along with Milton to play in the snow when she was ten. They'd sledded down every hill, built a snowman in the yard, and battled the neighborhood boys with snowballs. She'd been so excited that the cold had not fazed her. But now, wet from head to toe, her body ached from the lack of heat.

Her feet were so numb she struggled to walk. Even though she didn't want to, she allowed Ted to help her up into the truck. He was strong and warm. And he knew. She'd seen it in his face, the recognition, the bewilderment. The same look he'd had that day when she'd first gazed into that handsome face.

The thoughts caused her head to throb. She wanted to cry. To run and hide and pretend none of it had ever happened. But it had. She'd made a complete fool of herself. Getting drenched in the rain, then Ted recognizing her, the drowned rat.

Is that what she'd looked like that day on the beach? The thought hadn't occurred to her before, what she must have looked like. Wet, soaked to the skin from being in the water. Her wet hair blown into an unruly mass by the wind.

She hated her hair. Hated the curls that wormed their way out of the pins. She wished she could cut it off like men did. But no, girls didn't do that. Especially not nice girls. So she'd worn it in braids, pulled it back in tight buns, rolled it into a victory do like Veronica Lake. But that spring by the sea she'd let it loose, let herself be free from the ordeal of her hair. Suzanne had objected, sounding just like their mother, but Kitty's stubbornness had won out.

The truck bumped along the rutted road leading to the base. Madge scooted closer, and her body heat gave Kitty a measure of relief from the chill.

"You okay?" Madge asked.

Kitty could only nod and sniff. She raised the handkerchief to her nose and dabbed at the liquid running out onto her lip. She hadn't had a cold in ages. "Healthy as a horse" her father had called her. Another comparison to her maternal grandmother who he disliked intensely. She'd never understood why he didn't get along with his mother-in-law. She was a strong, hardworking woman who'd raised three daughters practically alone.

Thankfully, Ted sat on the opposite side of the truck bed with Sammy. Both stared out at the road behind them. Ted had been quiet, distant even. And Sammy looked like a forlorn puppy caught in a downpour. Kitty knew he'd never go out with her again. She couldn't blame him.

The truck stopped unexpectedly. Ted half-way stood, bent over so his head wouldn't hit the canvas top, and looked out.

Voices came from outside on the road.

Three soldiers appeared at the back of the truck and clambered aboard.

"Thank God you came along" one of them exclaimed.

"Yeah. We're soaked."

Sammy shifted to the girl's side of the truck and motioned for the three soldiers to take the other side.

Ted waited for them to get seated before he took up his post at the entrance.

One looked up at him, then snapped a salute.

"Sir, I didn't realize..."

Ted returned the man's salute, then the other two saluted. A sense of unease emanated from the three enlisted men.

"Relax," Ted ordered.

The three sat, eyeing him, and then shifted their gazes to Madge and herself.

The truck started to move again.

Kitty held on and tried to avoid looking at the new arrivals.

Good ol' Madge tried to break the ice. "You boys been to the village?"

"Yes 'm," one muttered. The other two nodded.

"We didn't expect it to rain like this," Madge said brightly. "Looks like you didn't either."

One gave her a wary look. The others shifted in their seats and gazed out the back. Clearly no one wanted to carry on a conversation.

They reached the gate, and the guard came around to the back of the truck. He saluted Ted and Sammy, then looked the rest over. He disappeared, and the truck started up again. They passed some buildings and other vehicles.

Soon Kitty saw Nissen huts and knew they had reached the barracks area.

"Sir, we can get out anywhere along here."

"Sit tight," Ted commanded. "We're taking the ladies to their quarters first."

The man nodded and gave her a questioning look. She stared at the floor, embarrassed at what she must look like.

The truck came to an abrupt halt. In a flash, Ted was out. Madge pulled at her arm, and Kitty willed her frozen legs to move. When she got to the edge, Ted must have seen how weak she was because he reached up and lifted her down.

His strong, warm arms wrapped around her, and she leaned her head against his shoulder. She looked up into those beautiful eyes and thought she would melt.

He quickly set her on her feet.

Madge's arm encircled her shoulder.

"Thanks," she heard Madge whisper and knew she was talking to Ted.

Madge steered her inside the hut. Kitty heard the truck pull away.

She forced herself to put one foot in front of the other, and soon she was sitting on her cot. Madge helped her peel off her clothes while several other girls hovered around helping, asking questions. All she wanted to do was crawl into bed and get warm. She'd think about everything tomorrow.

****

Ted couldn't sleep. Couldn't get her out of his head. How was it possible? How could she be here? How could his angel be here, be real? He'd been so sure that he'd imagined her. The antithesis of his mother. An angel who was everything his mother wasn't. Gentle, loving, kind.

All through his childhood he'd dreamed of having a real mother. Someone who cared for him, who wanted to take care of him, who loved him. And who loved his father.

After the sinking when he'd gone back to

Jacksonville, he'd finally accepted that his mother would never be the person he wanted her to be. Oh, she'd been upset that he'd almost died. But for the first time in his life, he'd been able to see her objectively. Everything, her whole way of thinking, revolved around herself. She really couldn't see it any other way. It was always about her.

That's why, when his father died, she'd been more concerned about what would happen to her. She'd been unable to understand his feelings, his sense of loss. She'd only seen her son as a burden, a responsibility she couldn't shoulder. So she'd left him. But she hadn't left him alone. She'd left him with his grandparents. And they had taken care of him, loved him. Even if he hadn't wanted to be there.

Out on that raft he'd thought of his grandfather and how hard the man had tried to get through to the rebellious kid he'd been. And his grandmother. Her steady, patient love. She'd laughed at his antics, covered her face to hide her smile when his grandfather tried to make him be serious.

Maybe that's why he thought the girl on the beach was an angel. Because his grandmother told him that the angels would watch over him. And he'd imagined the angels to be like her, kind and loving. And, of course, beautiful.

Kitty had that kind of beauty. The kind that shown from the inside out. Quiet and steady, kind and loving. He thought back to her concern that he would hurt Madge. Concern for someone else's feelings was nothing like his mother.

Madge was more like his mother. The thought jarred him. No. Madge wasn't near as bad as his mother. Maybe there were some similarities, but that's all. He didn't want to think he was attracted to women like his mother. Women who would hurt him. Women who cared more about themselves than anything else.

He rolled over and tried to clear his mind. He needed to get to sleep.

Unbidden, his angel came to mind. The one who'd been with him, watching over him. But this time he couldn't separate her from the one he'd seen today. The flesh and blood angel.

Chapter Ten

*"Meet me in the garden gazebo at 1600. Ted"*

She stared at the words printed on plain white paper. A wave of embarrassment, all-consuming and painful, washed over her. Mortified by the image of herself, soaked and shivering, her hair wet and wild, she struggled to control her emotions.

For two years she had fantasized about meeting this man again, dreamed of him falling head over heels in love with her. What a stupid fool she'd been.

When he finally recognized her, she'd looked worse than a drowned rat. And the way he reacted to her yesterday screamed loud and clear that he wanted nothing to do with her. If she had looked as bad on the beach that day, she didn't blame him for blocking the memory.

Then why did he want to meet her? What could he possibly have to say to her? Would he apologize for the way he acted? Would he tell her to stay away from him? And what did she want to say to him?

She stuffed the note back into the envelope and turned it over to read her name again. Neatly printed by hand, no telltale return address or identifiable handwriting. She glanced around wondering if anyone had seen the envelope or who left it on her desk. She folded it up into as small a piece as she could then slipped it in her pocket. It would definitely go into the stove when she got back to the hut.

By the end of her workday Kitty was nauseous. She wasn't sure she wanted to talk to Ted, but she had no choice.

Directly behind the enormous building, a graveled path led from a flagstone terrace into an extensive garden. On the right a high hedge shielded the garden from the sprawling stable the Americans had transformed into a motor pool. In the distance, at the far end of the garden, the "cottage" clung to the edge of a small lake. She'd been told the castle's owners had taken up residence there when the Americans took over.

Determined to see this through, Kitty strode along the path fighting the temptation to linger over a fragrant bloom or pause to watch the bees buzzing among the blossoming trees. At some other time, she might be able to relax and enjoy the formality of the garden's arrangement or investigate the variety of specimens, but not today, not with her nerves stretched to the breaking point.

Deep within the garden a vine-covered gazebo stood as an inviting retreat.

As she approached, she saw his knees and then his hands twirling his cap impatiently.

Her footsteps must have alerted him to her approach because he jumped to his feet and faced her. She glanced up at the tall figure who appeared even taller because he stood on the platform two steps above her. She grabbed for the railing and forced her gaze down to guide her feet. In her state, she did not trust her ability to climb the steps without falling. He must have sensed her nervousness because he held out his hand to help her, but she refused to accept his assistance.

"Why didn't you tell me?" his words rushed out as if he couldn't contain them any longer.

Astonished at his outburst, all she could say was "What?"

"You knew." Accusation was evident in his tone.

"What did I know?" she rebutted. "And why did you want me to meet you here?"

He looked out over the garden, where an older woman knelt digging in the dirt, his hands still fidgeted with his cap.

She stepped further into the gazebo and sat on the bench.

He turned back to her, his brow wrinkled. She thought he was going to say something. Instead he pressed his lips together, as if to silence himself, and sat on the bench facing her. After a moment he put his cap on the seat beside him and leaned forward.

"There was something familiar about you from the beginning. Then, yesterday, I knew what it was. Two years ago, on a beach, on the Georgia coast. You were there. You pulled me out of the water."

He waited for her to say something. She didn't know what to say so she just stared at him.

"I'm right, aren't I?" His insistent tone required a reply.

She released her breath and nodded.

"You knew, but you didn't say anything."

She leaned back unsure where to begin. "Why say anything? You didn't know me, didn't remember what happened, so why should I bring it up?" It sounded lame to say it out loud. She hadn't wanted to embarrass herself. But she'd been even more embarrassed by what happened yesterday. He didn't know that, she told herself. He doesn't know how much you've dreamed about him, how often you've wondered where he was and what he was doing.

"It's true. I don't remember much about that day." He looked straight at her, and she could see pain in his eyes. "It was all like a dream. You were there. You told me I was safe. And then you were gone." He looked away, back toward the garden. "I didn't think you were real. I thought you were a mermaid or an angel. Someone I'd dreamed up. Until yesterday."

Stirred by the emotion in his voice, she tried to lighten the mood. "Well, you obviously survived and recovered nicely. And by some strange twist of fate, we have met again."

"Yes." His smile looked grateful somehow. He glanced around. His hand darted out and grabbed his hat again. He tapped his finger on the bill. "I never got the chance to thank you."

"Oh," she hadn't expected that. "For…for what?"

He fidgeted with his hat. Avoided eye contact while his lips contorted. Finally his gaze rose to meet hers. "Thank you for saving my life."

Taken aback, she hesitated a moment before responding. "I…I just did what anyone would have done."

"But you were the one. You saved me."

She looked away and swallowed hard, not knowing what to say. An awkward silence stretched between them while she digested his words.

"Does Madge know?"

Her stomach twisted into a knot. "No." She shook her head and looked down at her hands. "I don't see any point in telling her. Do you?" She had tried for casual and matter-of-fact, not desperate and scared. Her gaze darted back to his face as she willed him to agree with her.

His eyes held a faraway sadness. He forced a weak smile. "All right. I don't like to talk about it anyway."

She understood not wanting to dredge up bad memories. Perhaps that was why he blocked the memory of their first encounter.

"Such lovely young people shouldn't look so sad." The older woman stood on the path beside the gazebo. In her gloved hands she held a basket of cut flowers and gardening tools.

Ted jumped to his feet. "Ma'am. We were just enjoying the garden."

"It needs more work than I can give it these days," she offered. "But it keeps me active."

Kitty rose slowly. She shot a glance at Ted and then clattered down the steps to where the English woman stood. "We were just leaving."

"You Yanks are always hurrying off to do something." The older woman eyed them more closely. "You will join me for tea, the both of you. Looks like you both need a little something." The invitation sounded more like an order than a request.

"Oh, no, ma'am. We couldn't," Ted protested as he hurried down the steps.

"You'd reject an invitation from your host and benefactor, would you?"

He put his cap on and adjusted it. "I really must go. I apologize for not joining you but…"

She nodded her understanding and dismissed him with a wave of her hand. Her frown of disapproval followed his escaping backside.

Shaking her head, she returned her attention to Kitty.

"Even though your young man had to go, you can still have a cup of tea with me."

With her sweetest smile and the most gracious voice she could muster, Kitty gave the only answer she could. "I'm sorry, but I too must go. Thank you so much for the offer." Without looking back, Kitty hurried along the same path Ted had taken.

The meeting had been private, and Ted was not her "young man." She prayed no one else had observed them together. She didn't want Madge to find out. If Madge knew about their meeting, she might guess the truth. And Kitty wasn't ready for that.

She hadn't really lied to Ted. Madge didn't know Ted was the man she pulled from the ocean. But Madge did know of the incident.

Kitty had been a little tipsy when she confided in Madge about the handsome man she had met once and dreamed of meeting again. Madge never made fun of her. She thought it was a great story, but she never told any of the other girls. That's when Kitty knew Madge was a true friend, one she could trust with her confidences.

But not this. Kitty couldn't tell Madge about this.

****

"Kruger, come on and join us. We've got room for one more."

Ted shook his head. "Sorry, fellows. Not in the mood."

He took a sip of the lousy, warm beer. He couldn't remember the last time he'd had a cold beer. Back in the states, probably. Although he'd schooled himself against remembering, the image of his last night out before they'd started the long journey to England crept into his mind.

A crowded bar filled with men clad in Air Corp uniforms, smoke hanging in the air, music from a juke box flowing around them. And lots of cold beer. Art, the natural leader, had insisted they spend their last night together. All single with no steady girlfriends, neither he nor Bud nor Mack had objected. They'd had a great time.

A pang of loneliness struck Ted. He missed them, more than he'd ever missed anyone.

A commotion caught Ted's attention. He glanced up as several officers filed into the club. For a split second, he saw them. Images so vivid he almost waved for them to come join him for a drink. Then reality slammed him in the gut. They were gone. Art, Bud, and Mack. Gone.

A sob caught in his throat, and he gulped his beer to wash it down.

"Mind if I take this chair," a young lieutenant stood next to him, hands clutching the chair back.

"No. Go ahead." Ted didn't look up. He blinked rapidly and hoped the young man didn't notice the tears threatening to betray his grief.

I've got to get a hold of myself.

Kitty's image invaded his thoughts. She wasn't bad looking. She was actually pretty in her own quiet way. And serious, way too serious. He'd always gone for the smiling, flirtatious girls. They laughed at his antics and kept him entertained. He'd never even paid attention to the quiet, serious types. If he was honest with himself, he had to admit that they intimidated him.

But Kitty intrigued him. Underneath that prim, proper, serious exterior was Kitty hiding a wilder side? He thought of that wild mass of curly hair. She always kept it tightly pinned. Yet the rain had set it free, turned her into an entirely different creature. Add in that angelic smile and he definitely wanted to get to know her.

He finished off his beer. Staring at the empty mug, he wondered what Art would advise him to do. Keep things light and fun with Madge, or find out what this was between he and Kitty?

Ted knew his dead friend well enough he could hear the advice Art would have offered. Find out what this is with Kitty. Time is short. Your orders could come through any day. Then you'd never know.

So that was it. Ted stood and carried his empty mug back to the bar. He'd break it off with Madge, and then he'd try to get to know Kitty. Maybe he'd be bored with her. Something told him that wouldn't happen. Something told him there was a lot more to Kitty that he had seen thus far.

Chapter Eleven

The Second Combat Bombardment Wing sent their planes on another raid deep into Germany. A "maximum effort" the staff called it. Tension ran high at headquarters as reports came in.

General Lake called Kitty into his office midmorning to take dictation, but every few minutes they were interrupted with an update on the mission.

Weather had been bad over many of the fields when they took off in the early morning hours. Kitty was horrified to hear that midair collisions during formation had claimed four planes. That translated to forty men gone because they couldn't see in the dense fog.

Kitty didn't normally hear about the missions until she worked on the reports. By that time, it was over. The downed planes, both bombers and fighters, were gone. The pilots and crews were either dead or presumed captured. They were just numbers, statistics, on the daily reports.

But this was different. It was happening now. They were out there, flying over Europe right now. No one knew if they would return, not even the men in the planes.

It was a big mission, an important one. General Lake and Colonel Snyder paced the office and struggled to focus on the work at hand.

A report came in of heavy flack over the target and a number of planes shot down. The general sent Colonel Snyder off to get more information.

"Sir, would you like for me to go down to the officers' mess and get you something to eat? I could bring a tray up here."

"Yes, yes. Some food might help." He got up and strode to the window. "I can't leave the office, not yet." He waved his arm. "Go ahead. And get yourself something to eat, too."

When she returned, General Lake held the phone listening intently, his face grim. "Are you sure?"

Kitty set the tray on his desk to his right.

"Yes, yes," he continued. "Send me everything you have."

Colonel Snyder entered the room. "I've just come from the map room. Everything's being updated as the information comes in."

"That was Anderson. His group had to go for the secondary target. Primary was obstructed. He said they hit heavy flack. Waiting to hear the results."

"General, you really should eat something," Kitty interjected. She'd learned General Lake liked a little mothering.

He met her gaze, and his expression softened. "You're right." He turned to Colonel Snyder. "I'll be down shortly."

The colonel left, and General Lake slid the tray over in front of him. He removed the metal dome from the plate and set it aside. "You did get something for yourself, didn't you?"

Kitty hesitated. "Uh, I wasn't really hungry."

"Nonsense."

He took a spoon and scooped some mashed potatoes and a slice of spam onto his bread plate, keeping a slice of bread for himself. He shoved the small plate in her direction.

Obediently she took it.

"Besides, I hate to eat alone." His gaze met hers and he smiled, then he looked down as he used his fork to cut the other hunk of spam.

Self-consciously, she avoided eye contact and tasted the potatoes. She could feel him watching as she ate. At times like this, she wished she were back in the steno pool where she felt safe and knew what to expect. Instead she sat here wondering what the general was thinking.

"Have you ever been to one of the air fields?" he asked out of the blue.

"No, sir."

"Well, you're going to one today."

She didn't know what he meant or what to say.

He pushed the plate away and stood. "I've been cooped up here too long. I need to get out, talk to the men." He wiped his mouth with his handkerchief. "So, we're heading over to the field, to see them come back. And you're going with us."

Kitty swallowed a bite of spam, trying not to choke on the half-chewed morsel. "Yes, sir, if that's what you want."

At his insistence, Kitty accompanied the general to the map room. Expecting to see maps on the walls, it surprised her to see men crowded around a huge table emblazoned with a map of Europe.

Curious, she moved closer so she could see what the men were doing. She easily found the English coast with colored and numbered triangles, squares, and circles that represented the air bases. Her gaze crossed the channel to the outline of the European coast. On the continent names of cities and lines representing rivers, railroads, and roads filled the space.

Soldiers, holding telephone receivers or reading from cards, moved numbered markers on the map of Europe like pieces on a game board. Some markers corresponded to the air field markings. Others she assumed were enemies.

On the far side an arm reached out to correct a young corporal's marker placement. Her gaze followed the movement, and her head jerked back when she recognized Lieutenant Kruger. The hard line of his lips and his deeply furrowed brow reminded her that this game was deadly serious business. Lives were at stake. After a few seconds, he turned his back and picked up a telephone on a table in the corner. He listened, his head nodding, his body shifting from side to side unable to contain his nervous energy, while Kitty watched, fascinated.

General Lake moved around the room and spoke with another officer. Kitty retreated to a spot near the door, sensing herself out of place in this war room. She thought of going out and waiting in the hallway until General Lake finished. Would he mind? He'd wanted her to see this, and she'd expected him to explain what was going on. Instead, he had deserted her.

She glanced at the general, deep in conversation, then back to Ted who remained on the phone. Just then, Ted turned and their gazes met. She froze.

After what seemed an eternity but could only have been seconds, he nodded in her direction. She perceived a slight wrinkling around his eyes, an ever so subtle relaxation of his tightly held lips.

She returned the nod, careful to school her expression. All he needed to see was her acknowledgement of his presence, nothing more.

She glanced back at the general still in deep discussion. Ted must have followed her gaze, for when she looked back at him, he squinted as if asking a question. The phone recaptured his attention. He leaned down and started writing. He must have been taking a message from someone on the other end of the line.

The crowded, stuffy room closed in around her. Her pulse throbbed in her head. Her skin radiated heat. She shouldn't be here, but she couldn't leave until the general finished. She backed up against the wall by the door and resigned herself to waiting.

"Greenlee," Colonel Snyder startled her.

"Yes, sir."

"See that the general's car is brought up. We will be leaving shortly."

Grateful for something to do, Kitty replied, "Yes, sir," and hurried to find the general's driver. Along the way she wondered why General Lake had ordered her to accompany him today. This was more than just secretarial duties. It was as if he wanted her companionship, wanted to share more of his work with her. Or was she imagining more than was there?

****

Kitty sat in the front with the driver while they drove the short distance to the air field just off the narrow country road that led to the village. Inside the gate the now familiar Nissen huts and hastily constructed buildings lined the well-worn dirt road.

Beyond stretched the long strips of pavement.

The driver turned and drove alongside the main runway toward a square building with a smaller square set on top of it. Windows covered three sides of the upper portion. A wooden stairway led to the roof of the main building, and a railing ran around the perimeter. Men stood atop the structure looking skyward and higher up, atop the glassed room, two soldiers searched the sky with binoculars.

Beyond the runway a group of men played baseball in the grass. Others milled around the building, restlessly waiting for something.

When the car stopped, the driver got out and opened the door for General Lake and Colonel Snyder. After the officers got out, the driver opened her door. She stepped onto the dirt road and stood next to the car, not sure what was expected of her.

"Sergeant." General Lake waved for her to join him. He took her arm and led her toward the building while Colonel Snyder moved ahead and spoke with two officers.

"Sir?" she asked as she stood by the General's side, painfully aware of heads turning in their direction.

"Stay close." He squeezed her elbow and leaned closer. "The planes will be coming in soon, and when they do, it will get busy. We don't want to get in anyone's way, but I want you to see what it's like."

Kitty nodded. She didn't understand why he wanted her here, why he wanted her to see the bombers return to base after their mission. None of the other WACs had been to the airfield, not even Captain Weatherby.

It quickly became evident to Kitty that a woman on

the field was an unusual occurrence. Men in coveralls glared at her, more out of curiosity than hostility. Some tipped their hats, others grinned sheepishly, and others whispered among themselves. If the general had not been close by, perhaps they would have been friendlier. But they kept their distance from the brass.

It struck her as odd that none of the men snapped to attention or saluted. She'd never seen such informality on a military base.

General Lake introduced her to Colonel Ashley, the air field's commander. "Brought her down to observe," the general explained.

Colonel Ashley, dressed in a leather flight jacket with no indication of his rank, eyed her curiously but kept any thoughts he had to himself. He introduced two other officers, a captain and a major also wearing leather jackets, then suggested they go up to the "tower" for a better view.

She climbed the steep steps leading to the roof of the control tower following the officers. Colonel Ashley commented to General Lake that they were in radio contact with the squadron.

Someone yelled, "There they are!"

All heads turned skyward.

She shaded her eyes against the bright sun. Specks quickly grew into airplanes. They swarmed in like trained insects circling around overhead. Colored flares streaked through the sky reminding her of a Fourth of July celebration.

A voice above urged her to come on, so she ran the rest of the way up.

General Lake half pushed, half pointed her toward the railing. She grabbed hold and returned her gaze to the field just in time to see the first plane approach for a landing. The wheels of the huge plane touched the runway about fifty yards away, and as it skidded by, the brakes screeched. The scent of burning rubber assailed her as the bomber's tires left long black streaks on the pavement.

The plane finally rolled to a stop near the end of the runway.

That's when she saw the damage so extensive she wondered how it had flown at all. One of the long wings was ripped open. Smoke poured from the engine nearest the gash. Gaping holes in the bomber's sides and tail varied from the size of a fist to ones she could have crawled through. She saw movement through the large rip in the tail and wondered how the men inside had survived.

Trucks sped down the runway. Dozens of men ran to the crippled bomber. An ambulance wailed by and pulled up beside the disabled plane. In the flurry of activity, she saw two men handed out of the belly of the bomber and loaded into the ambulance. Meanwhile a rig hitched onto the front wheel and pulled it off the main runway.

A roar caused her to jerk around. Another bomber sped by, its wheels only inches from the ground. Its wingspan almost wider than the runway. This one had more control as it slowed and rolled to a stop close behind the one being towed.

Within moments, another plane landed. Then another and another.

"I've got seventeen," someone said.

Kitty looked up to the bombers flying around above the field waiting to land. She tried to count them but kept losing track of the moving objects.

She heard General Lake ask, "How many went out?"

"Twenty-six," Colonel Ashley replied in a flat, emotionless tone.

Kitty gasped. Nine planes lost. Her brain quickly calculated—nine into twenty-seven would be three—almost a third shot down. That was too many. She'd seen loss reports but never with losses that high.

"There's two more," someone shouted.

All eyes scanned the sky to the east. Two small dots just above the horizon.

"That must be Hatton and Dempsey. Both lost engines over the target. Fell behind."

"That gets it up to nineteen," Colonel Snyder remarked, the strain evident in his voice. "Seven missing."

"Give 'em some time. There could be some more stragglers." The calm, even tone made it clear Colonel Ashley had been through this anxious waiting before.

A plane skidded by. Kitty watched it spin around and leave the runway. It tilted over on the nose and one wing. She held her breath waiting for it to burst into flames. Men tumbled out. Trucks roared to the wreck with firefighting equipment ready.

She moved to the far corner of the roof to get a better look at the crashed plane.

"Thank goodness it hasn't caught fire," she heard herself mumble.

"They were probably out of fuel." A young lieutenant stood nearby gripping a pair of binoculars.

"Oh," she replied.

"You came with the general?"

"Yes…Yes, sir." She started to salute, but he shook his head.

He looked back to the runway as another plane touched down.

"Here's O'Leary. Looks like their luck held out." Another airman nearby observed.

"Yep. Home for those lucky dogs," the lieutenant added.

The bomber rolled by. "Luck O' the Irish" adorned the nose above a naked lady holding a shamrock.

Kitty turned to the officer, curious about the comment. "What do you mean—home?"

"Finished twenty-five missions. That means they get to go home." He laughed. "You haven't been with the Air Force very long, have you?"

"A few weeks…in England." She realized she should have known about the missions. "I've been at wing headquarters. This is my first time at an airfield." She wanted to explain further, but their faces told her that she already looked foolish enough, so she decided to stop talking.

The lieutenant glanced around then leaned closer. "The way the old man watches you, I'd say he's pretty possessive." He winked. "If you know what I mean."

Heat crept from her core to her face. "No," she muttered, clinching her fist tight, "I don't know."

He looked a little startled at her response. "Okay." He held up his hand, then turned and walked away. The other airman followed him, eyeing her over his shoulder.

"Greenlee." Colonel Snyder waved for her to come.

Relieved, she followed the colonel down the stairs.

General Lake stood by the car waiting for them. She hoped they were heading back to headquarters. She'd seen enough.

The car fell in behind a truck carrying just returned airmen. Dressed in heavy clothing, the men looked exhausted. When the truck stopped beside a small building, the men climbed down like they were in their nineties and barely able to move. How long they had been flying to look so tired out?

The driver pulled the car into the narrow space between buildings and jumped out to open doors. Another truck stopped behind them to unload its passengers.

General Lake guided her inside a frame building. He directed her to sit near the door and wait for him. Uncomfortable, not as much from being the only female in the room as from feeling out of place among dog-tired men who had risked their lives, she tried to become invisible, to fade into the woodwork and not intrude in their very masculine world.

Some of the men still wore lined jackets and heavy woolen pants. She couldn't distinguish ranks from the assortment of clothing. Most had similar markings on their faces, around their eyes and mouth where they had been wearing goggles and oxygen masks during their flight. One man had a bandage on the side of his face. She wondered if he had been wounded on the mission.

Snatches of conversation reached her ears.

"Did you see any chutes?"

"When my oxygen froze up…"

"Little friends never showed up."

"Flack over Dunkirk…"

"…Confirmed kill…"

"Thought his wing was coming in my window."

"…gun jammed…"

"never had a chance."

"Can't believe they're gone."

"Tail shot off…"

"Can't send us out again tomorrow."

Some sounded unemotional, drained. Other voices were animated, almost frantic. Cigarette smoke filled the room as men chain smoked while they waited to be interrogated by the intelligence officers. Men who'd completed their interviews shouldered their way through to the outside.

Kitty soaked up their exhaustion, their anxiety, their loss. How do they do it twenty-five times? How do they cope with losing their friends? Where do they go to escape?

She thought of Ted. How many times had he gone through this ordeal? And his crew, how did he deal with their loss? Sammy said he was grieving, that he used humor to hide his feelings. Was there more to him than she had seen?

****

Kitty lay on her cot listening to the gentle rain pattering on the metal roof of the hut. She could still see the faces of the airmen. Tired, strained, grateful to be on solid ground, yet fearful knowing they would have to go back into the sky, into the danger zone above Europe.

For the first time she had really seen the war, up close and personal. Even here in England, it had been something far away, something on newsreels and in newspapers. Today she had seen it in their faces.

"Why so solemn?"

Kitty opened her eyes.

Madge stood nearby in her robe, her hair wrapped in a snood.

Kitty swung her legs around and sat up. She took a deep breath and wondered how she could explain what she'd seen.

"I was just thinking about the men I saw at the airfield today."

"Were any of them good looking?" Madge sat beside her on the cot.

"I don't know." Kitty shook her head. Her friend wouldn't understand. She hadn't been there. "They were exhausted, at least the returning crews were. The others were…I don't know…worried, anxious."

"But why? What's so disturbing about watching planes land?"

Kitty pressed her lips together. There was no point in getting angry at her friend. She hadn't been there. "One of the planes almost crashed when it landed. And there were wounded men in some of them."

"Oh." Madge's face fell.

Kitty attempted to explain further. "They sent out twenty-six planes. Only nineteen came back." She let that sink in before continuing. "You've seen the casualty figures. Seven planes lost means seventy men."

"I didn't realize," Madge murmured, her frowning face said more than her words.

"Those men saw their friends go down."

Sally and Gail heard them talking and sat on the opposite cot. Sally asked, "What did they say?"

Kitty thought about the conversations she overheard. She hadn't talked to any of them directly.

Instead she'd waited while General Lake sat in on the interrogations. She couldn't help overhearing the men talk as they waited their turn.

"Did you see Osgood get hit?"

"Our tail gunner saw it."

"Anybody get out?"

Their silence told her the answer.

"It wasn't so much what they said as how they said it," Kitty explained.

"Were they upset?"

"Some were nervous. Others were quiet, stoic. But their faces—I've never seen anything like it."

Sally and Gail exchanged a glance. Kitty could tell that they didn't really understand.

"There was one bright spot. One of the crews finished their twenty-five missions."

"What does that mean?"

"Apparently they are required to fly twenty-five missions. Then they get to go home." She looked around to see if they understood. "One of the lieutenants told me it's something we should know as part of the Air Force."

"How many make it?" Madge asked.

"I don't know. I guess we could look at the numbers. Those reports we do have all the information. I never really understood what it meant…until today."

"Geez, I guess I never thought about it either." Sally's sentimental streak made her voice crack when she got emotional.

"Didn't I hear you say you saw a plane crash?" Gail asked.

Kitty nodded. "One skidded off the runway and tipped over. It wasn't so bad. Everyone got out okay.

Another one almost didn't get stopped. It was pretty shot up, and they took two men away in the ambulance."

Sally shook her head sympathetically, then stood. "Almost time for lights out."

The others stood and moved toward their bunks. Kitty unbuttoned her blouse. No shower tonight, not with the rain. The comforting thoughts of warm water sluicing over her tired body weren't enough to send her venturing out in this steady, cold drizzle. She'd settle for washing her face in the water they kept warm on the stove.

After a cursory washing, she changed into her regulation pajamas and crawled under multiple blankets to ward off the damp air. Madge settled in the next cot as the lights went out.

"Madge," Kitty whispered.

"Yes?"

"How does General Lake look at me?"

"What do you mean?"

"Does he look at me like a soldier...or like a woman?"

Kitty could hear Madge reposition herself in the dark. "Has he made a pass?"

"No. Not really. It's just that he's so nice to me." Kitty thought about the woman's picture she'd seen in his office that first day. She hadn't seen it since.

"I thought it was kind of funny, him singling you out like he did." Madge didn't spell out her suspicions but Kitty sensed them in her voice. "You'd better be careful."

"What do you mean?"

"Colonel Snyder has made it plain he doesn't like

having us women around." She hesitated. "Something happened, before we came. Something to do with one of the British service women."

"What happened? What do you mean?"

"Oh, one of the nurses told me about it. She didn't say much. But Colonel Snyder got the girl in trouble over it. Got rid of her. If he thinks something's going on between you and General Lake, believe me, you'll be the one to take the blame."

"But nothing's going on."

"Just make sure you keep it that way. And be careful."

"You gals pipe down. Some of us are trying to sleep."

Kitty rolled over and closed her eyes. But her brain wouldn't let go. She ran every moment she'd spent with General Lake through her mind trying to figure out what his intentions were. She'd never been good at reading men. Never been able to pick up the subtle clues other girls saw. Now she feared her stupidity may have already gotten her in trouble.

Chapter Twelve

"Hey, Kruger. Colonel Snyder wants to see you."

Ted looked up from the map. "What does he want?" He looked back and drew a line. "I need to finish this."

"All I know is that he sent me to get you. Said to bring you right now."

"Okay." Ted sighed. What did he want now? The jerk would drag him away for something stupid, then chew him out because he didn't finish.

He followed the sergeant to the colonel's office.

Ted saluted crisply. "Lieutenant Kruger, reporting as ordered, sir."

"Come in, Lieutenant." Colonel Snyder waved him into the office. Two other officers stood and the colonel introduced them. "Major Carpenter, G-2, and Colonel DeMille, British Intelligence."

Ted saluted. "Sirs."

*What the hell do they want?*

"Have a seat, Lieutenant." Colonel Snyder's smug expression concerned Ted. The man loved it when someone was in trouble. And this time Ted was on the hot seat.

"Thank you, sir." Ted sat in the straight chair to the colonel's right.

"These officers have some questions for you."

Ted nodded and shifted his attention to the two

men who'd reclaimed their seats.

The American intelligence officer looked at Ted curiously. "We understand you are acquainted with Gunther Osterhagen."

Ted hesitated for a minute. It wasn't a question he expected. "Osterhagen?" It sounded familiar. "Oh, yes. He's the German man I met in Ellingham."

"How did you come to meet him?" the English officer asked. His gaze bore into Ted as if he expected Ted to concoct some elaborate story.

"I went into Ellingham—after I got out of the hospital. In one of the shops I heard him talking. His German accent caught my attention." Ted looked from the American to the Englishman. "Anyway, he reminded me of my grandfather, so I decided to go over and speak to him."

"What did you say?" the Englishman queried.

"I just introduced myself. I spoke in German and that surprised him."

"Where did you learn to speak German, Lieutenant?" The American officer must have looked in his file, and he would have seen that he spoke German. Were they trying to trap him?

"From my grandfather." Ted glanced at the colonel hoping for some support. Instead his smugness told Ted he was on his own. "My grandparents immigrated from Germany to America around the turn of the century."

"Do you have relatives in Germany?" the American continued.

"Sure, I guess so. I mean, my grandparents have relatives, but I don't know any of them."

"How many times did you meet with Osterhagen?"

Ted shifted his gaze to the Englishman. The man

was dead serious. "Twice. No, I guess you could say three times. The last time I just spoke to him on the street."

"And what did you talk about?" Ted met the Englishman's cold, hard gaze, willing the man to believe him. Finally he looked away so he could focus on his conversations with the old man.

"He asked about my grandfather...where he came from in Germany. I told him what I knew."

"Which was?"

Ted looked the man in the eye. "They came from a small town near Frankfort. They got married and then came to America."

"Why?"

"What do you mean? Why did they come to America? I guess they didn't like what was going on in Germany at the time. Thought they could do better in America." He looked to Colonel Snyder. "Colonel, what's this all about?"

Snyder just shrugged and waved his hand toward the other two officers.

The American cleared his throat and adjusted his position. "All we can tell you is that Osterhagen is under investigation by the British." He looked to his English companion who nodded slightly. "It is possible that your actions may constitute a breach in security."

"Breach in security? I never said anything to him about the base, or missions, or anything." Ted couldn't believe they were accusing him of leaking information to the enemy.

"Never the less, we must investigate."

The Englishman's attitude rubbed Ted the wrong way. "So what does this mean? Am I being accused of something?"

"You are being questioned." A forcefulness, laced with impatience, permeated the Englishman's voice. He obviously wrestled with maintaining self-control.

"So ask," Ted replied, also at the end of his patience.

"Did the German tell you anything? About himself?"

"Not much. He's from Bavaria, near Munich, I think. Said he came to England during the first war. Why would he come here to live if he supports Hitler?"

"Does he support Hitler?"

"I don't know." Ted saw the curiosity in their faces. "We didn't talk about anything like that."

"What did you talk about?" the Englishman kept pressing.

"I don't remember exactly. I was trying to speak German, and I'm pretty rusty. I tried to remember things I talked about with my grandfather so I could remember the words."

"What things?"

"About where they live. My grandfather is a butcher. I remember telling him that. And that my father is dead and my mother remarried. Stuff like that."

"This is important," the American interjected. "Did you tell him anything about what you do in the Army? About the base or the bombing missions?"

"No." Ted hesitated. "He saw the wings on my uniform. Asked about them. All I told him was that I was in the Eighth Air Force, and I'd been wounded."

"What else did he ask?"

"He asked about my wounds. I just said I was

okay. I didn't tell him how I got wounded or anything. I knew not to say anything about the bombing missions."

"When did this conversation take place? At your first meeting?"

"Yes, most of it. The second time was in the pub. He came over to me and talked for a few minutes. Said he was glad to see me, that I was doing well." Ted thought again about what he'd said. "He asked me to come to his house, for tea." Ted looked at the Englishman. "And when I saw him on the street the last time, he asked me to visit him again. Do you think that means anything?"

"He may have been trying to get you alone so he could question you further."

"Well, I didn't go. Didn't even think about it."

The major turned to address Colonel Snyder. "Until this matter is cleared up, Lieutenant Kruger must be removed from his current position."

"Hey," Ted objected.

Colonel Snyder stared him into silence. "That will not be a problem. I will assign Lieutenant Kruger to duty where he will have no contact with any sensitive information."

Ted gritted his teeth to keep from exploding in anger. What were they going to do with him? Assign him to the guard house?

"Your request to return to flying is now out of the question," Snyder continued.

The Englishman stood. Taking his cue, the others stood.

"Colonel, we will be in touch." The Englishman saluted and left the office.

Colonel Snyder nodded at the major who silently

acknowledged and followed the English officer.

Ted wasn't sure what he was supposed to do so he stood awaiting instructions.

Snyder sat behind his desk and adjusted his chair. "Lieutenant, consider yourself off duty for the remainder of the day. Report back to me in the morning. By then I am sure I will have something to keep you occupied."

"Yes, sir," Ted muttered. He managed a feeble salute before turning to leave the room. He opened the door, then looked back at the colonel. "Sir, I've done nothing wrong."

A hint of a smile crept across the officer's face. "Then you have nothing to worry about."

\*\*\*\*

"Please, just this once."

"I'm not going to the Officers' Club," Kitty said as emphatically as she could.

"Just give him a message. Tell him I've got KP and can't make our date. That's all you have to do."

Kitty would do anything for Madge. But this was too much. She didn't want to meet Ted. Not even as a favor to her best friend. She needed to stay away from him. Far away.

Madge moved closer and almost whispered. "How many favors have I done for you? What about the time I saved you from the MPs?"

Kitty cringed. Why did she have to bring that up?

"Just go over there and talk to him. His message sounded like he was upset about something. Tell him I couldn't come, but I sent you. That he can tell you what's going on, and you'll tell me later." She turned to go. "If Lois hadn't gotten sick, I wouldn't have KP, and you wouldn't have to do this. But it can't be helped." She reached the stairway and called back over her shoulder. "Thanks, you're a doll."

Kitty sat at her typewriter and sighed. How did she get into these things? Ted was Madge's boyfriend. She didn't want to be around him, and from what she could tell, he didn't want to be around her.

She thought of that night at the mess hall. Maybe it was only her. Maybe he wouldn't mind if she showed up instead of Madge.

What had she gotten herself into?

\*\*\*\*

The Officers' Club and the Enlisted Men's Club sat side by side. The two, almost-identical Nissen huts shared a graveled patio area with wooden benches and tables the patrons could use when the weather permitted.

Kitty hoped to find Ted outside waiting for Madge. No such luck. He was nowhere to be seen.

She could just leave, tell Madge he wasn't here. But Madge wouldn't believe her. So she eased over to the entrance of the Officers' Club. When a couple of lieutenants came out, she decided to take a chance and speak to them.

"Excuse me, sirs. Have you seen Lieutenant Kruger?"

The younger of the two men grinned. "Who's askin'?"

"I'm looking for him." She wasn't about to give them her name, not if she could help it.

He looked her over, leering in a way that made Kitty consider turning on her heel and leaving when the other one spoke up. "Try out back. I saw him earlier—

shooting baskets."

"Thank you." Kitty looked them in the eye and spoke clearly to let them know she wasn't intimidated.

She followed a path through the weeds to the back of the building where several men played basketball on a makeshift court. Bare chests and undershirts designated the teams. Before she could pick Ted out of the fast-moving group, one of them went for a lay-up and scored. He came down hard on his rear end. When he looked up laughing through the pain, she recognized him.

The ball bounced her way, so she grabbed it. Memories of her school days flashed through her mind as she fingered the ball's hard, nubby surface. She slowly dribbled the ball toward the two men who were pulling Ted to his feet.

When Ted's gaze met hers, her heart thudded in her chest. She caught a shallow breath when she saw his bare chest dusted with sandy hair. She held it as he limped toward her.

A bead of sweat ran down her back. She forced herself to breathe, still bouncing the ball.

"Looks like you know how to handle that pretty well." The grin spread from his expressive mouth up to his twinkling, blue eyes.

She caught the ball and held it in front of her as if it could stop the unsettling effect he had on her. "I played in high school," she heard herself say.

He took her elbow and turned her toward the goal. "Well, then, show us what you can do."

"I don't..." All she could think about was his large, strong hand clasping her arm.

"Can't hit the goal, eh?" he goaded.

Forcing herself to focus on the goal, she looked up to gauge the distance. He released his grip, and she tried to relax. She bounced the ball a couple of times and moved to where the free throw line should be. Holding the ball up, she drew a deep breath to steady herself as she set her aim. It had been a long time, but she trusted her ability, honed in long hours of practice.

She tossed the ball. It arched upwards, hit the backboard at just the right spot, and bounced downward through the hoop, just like thousands of times before.

"Wow!" she heard Ted close behind her. "I'm impressed."

She turned to face him with a little more confidence. She knew how to sink free throws.

"Good shot," the guy who caught the rebound told her.

"Yeah, that was swell," one of the others said.

"Bet you can't do it again." Ted filled the space around her, his twinkling eyes held her mesmerized. The others faded into the background.

When she didn't respond, he looked away. "I didn't think so."

"I can hit it again," she spoke before thinking. "I'll show you."

He took her challenge. "All right." He nodded to the guy with the ball.

Kitty caught it easily. She bounced it twice then with the exact same motions she sank the basket, again.

This time the ball bounced back to her. Just as she reached for it, Ted jumped in front of her and grabbed the ball. In two steps he was in the air sinking a beautiful lay-up. This time he made his landing easily.

She smiled. He reminded her of Milton. Always

had to get the last shot, score the last point, have the last word.

"You'll have to play with us sometime," the tall, dark-haired guy said to Kitty.

"Yeah. Do any of the other girls play?" the shorter one asked.

"No." She shook her head. "I mean 'no' I can't play with you, and I don't know if any of the others play basketball." She forced a smile and glanced around at the other men watching her. "Thanks for asking, but right now I need to talk to Ted...uh, Lieutenant Kruger."

She turned and walked to the edge of the court, aware that Ted followed close behind.

"Let me get my shirt," he said.

She stopped near piles of clothes, shoes, and bags and turned to watch him. He bent down to retrieve his shirt. At the sight of his bare, muscled shoulders, she drew in another quick, shallow breath. Her fingers shook so she fidgeted with the button on her jacket to keep them busy.

*Take it easy. Try to relax. He belongs to Madge.*

He shrugged into his undershirt, then grabbed his shirt and pulled it on. When he finally looked at her, his brows furrowed into a question. Before he could ask she spoke up.

"Madge sent me. She can't come. KP."

He raised his chin then nodded to convey that he understood. Then he turned back to the other men. "Gotta' go. Thanks for the game."

He rubbed his left hip, the side he favored, as he walked toward the path.

"Did you hurt yourself?"

"Naw." He shook his head as he buttoned his shirt. "Just need to work on those landings. Get back in shape."

She followed him around the hut. "I don't understand."

He placed his hand on his left buttock and looked over his shoulder at her. "Flack." He kept walking, tucking his shirt into his pants as he went. "Need the exercise to strengthen the muscles."

Kitty was glad he turned back around so he couldn't see her face because she could feel it burning. First the naked chest, then the reference to his injured butt. Not the type conversation she was used to.

## Chapter Thirteen

"You want a beer?" Ted asked when they reached the front of the building.

"Sure." She nodded, then looked around to see if anyone was watching. She didn't want any trouble for fraternizing with an officer. When she looked back, she found him smiling as if he was trying to figure her out.

"I'll bring them out. Just give me a minute."

True to his word, he returned in a few minutes with two glasses of beer. He walked past her to a bench on the edge of the gravel patio.

"Sit here." It wasn't a request, but it wasn't an order either.

She sat. He handed her one of the beers, and she took a polite sip.

He sank down beside her and winced. "Gotta' get back in shape. The boys are trying to get a couple of teams together, so we can play a real game."

When she didn't respond, he flashed her that silly, little boy grin. "Would you come watch?"

Kitty looked down at the glass of beer she held in both hands. "Madge got stuck on KP. So she sent me to come and tell you."

"You said that." He reached over and wrapped his big hand around her two small ones. The smooth glass pressed against her palms while his rough hand radiated heat into her skin. "KP. Good ol' army. Always got something for you to do, whether you want to or not."

She pulled free, avoiding eye contact, and set the glass on the bench beside her. "Yes, well, now that I've delivered the message..." Kitty started to get up, but he caught her arm and stopped her.

"Don't go. You might as well stay. We could talk a while."

"Well, if you want to." Her voice squeaked, so she cleared her throat and forced herself to relax, at least a little.

He turned up his glass and emptied it. The faint shadow of stubble on his jaw reminded her of that day on the beach. What would it hurt? A few minutes, sitting here talking to him. "Madge did say you were upset about something."

"Upset! Ha! Why would I be upset?" He waved the empty glass in the air.

She'd said the wrong thing. Now what?

He turned and glared at her. "You gonna' drink that?"

She picked up the glass and hesitated before taking another sip. He took it from her and grinned again, just before he turned it up and chugged the contents.

Kitty waited, her insides clenched tight. She hated drunks. The alcohol added a layer of uncertainty to her underlying discomfort around men, making them unpredictable.

He set the glass down beside the bench and turned back to her, his smile barely disguising a seething anger. "I've been relieved of duty." Sarcasm dripped from his words. "How's that for a laugh? I'm foot loose and fancy free." He frowned a bit, looking away. "Well, not exactly free. I'm stuck here on this base. Nothing to do. Just wait and wonder." His anger dissolved into disgust, with a hint of disappointment. He studied the empty glass for a few seconds. The muscle in his jaw flexed. "And drink."

He stood and grabbed the other empty glass. "I'm going to get another drink. And I'm going to get you one, too."

Before Kitty had a chance to say no, he was gone, without a backward glance. She thought about leaving…no, running away. But Madge would want to know what he meant by being relieved from duty. What had he done to get in that kind of trouble?

****

"Pardon me, boys." He pushed his way past several officers entering the club. A good work out and two beers still hadn't been enough to settle his seething anger. So he'd switched to something stronger.

And he had to face her.

Kitty sat waiting for him. She looked a bit lost, like she'd rather be anywhere but here, talking to him. Not that he blamed her. He hadn't handled it very well.

He made his way across the patio until he stood looking down at her. "It's just beer." He thrust the dripping glass toward her.

She took it from him and shot a wary glance his way. He sipped a little of the Old Fashioned before sinking down onto the bench beside her.

A wave of fatigue flooded over him. Some instinct told him to pull her close, to hold her warm body in his arms. Comfort. That's what he needed. And if Madge was sitting here beside him, he wouldn't hesitate. But Kitty was different.

In one sense, he barely knew her. In another, she

peered into his very soul, exposing every fault. Was she keeping him at a distance because she didn't like what she saw? Or was it because of Madge?

He'd convinced her to stay and talk. That was something. Now he just had to figure out what to say to her. He didn't really know how to talk to a nice girl. Then, maybe, she was just like any other girl.

He stretched his arm out along the back of the bench, resting on the wooden back, but close enough for him to feel the heat from her shoulders. He angled his body toward her so he could watch her, see how she reacted.

She took a sip of the beer, and her lips pursed before she forced herself to swallow. Either she didn't like beer, or she was extremely uncomfortable in his company.

"What's this about being relieved of duty?" she asked, without taking her eyes from the glass.

Her question stabbed him like a knife. His fury flared in response. He jerked his arm back, leaned forward, and clutched the drink with both hands.

"It's a bunch of crap. Just because I talked to some old German guy when I was in the village, the intelligence boys are investigating." He stared into the dark liquid and clenched his teeth as the scene in Snyder's office flashed into his mind.

"Do they think he's a spy?"

"Hell if I know. They wouldn't tell me anything. Just asked me a bunch of questions and left me sitting on my hands." He took a long drink hoping the alcohol would calm him.

Her silence hung between them. He turned to look at her, and their gazes met. In that moment he desperately needed her to believe in him. "Do you think I'm an informer?"

"I...uh, I don't know," she stammered, quickly averting her eyes. "I don't know you that well."

"You know me. You know things about me no one else knows."

His comment startled her into looking at him. "What do you mean?"

"That day on the beach. You saved me."

"But you were a stranger. I didn't even know where you came from."

"From a ship...the German's torpedoed." He leaned close, so close the faint odor of soap and something floral filled his nostrils. His eyes captured hers and refused to let her look away. "Or did you think I was a spy coming ashore to kill and destroy?"

She smiled, then. That sweet, angelic smile. "That's absurd. You were barely alive."

"Yes." Pure joy bubbled up inside him. "Exactly. That's what you will tell them." He raised his glass as if to toast her.

"Tell who?"

"The investigators."

"Why would they talk to me?"

She sounded as confused as he was. What was he thinking? He had to keep her out of his mess. He didn't want to drag anyone else into this.

He took another drink and thought about his grandparents. Were they enduring this same kind of crap just because they were German? He knew some German Americans had been interned, like the Japanese just not near as many. And although his grandfather would never write it in a letter, Ted knew they had been questioned and investigated, just as he had been when he first enlisted. Now it had started again.

"Did you tell them? About me, I mean?" she asked quietly as if afraid to interrupt his musing.

"No. Of course not. I never told anyone." His words came out flat as he gazed into the amber liquid.

"Then why do you think they would question me?"

"Oh, I don't know." He leaned back and ran his hand through his hair. "This has got me so balled up, I can't think." He drew a deep breath and turned to face her. "They won't let me go back to flying. They won't let me work planning missions. They won't let me do anything."

"They'll investigate and find you did nothing wrong. And everything will be okay."

"You really believe that?"

"Yes, I do. You have nothing to worry about."

He smiled and leaned closer, wishing he could pull her into his arms. "Are you for real?"

"Of course, I am." She pulled back, her fingers twisting a button on her jacket. Her face flushed. Something about her shyness had an endearing quality, an innocence he rarely saw.

Seconds ticked by as he soaked up her nearness. Finally he withdrew.

She released a breath and visibly relaxed. He fought the urge to gloat at the effect he had on her. The last thing he wanted was to scare her away.

He finished off his drink and placed the empty glass on the bench beside him. Then he leaned back and slid his arm behind her again, but this time he rested it around her shoulders. Using the slightest of pressure, he pulled her close, but he didn't say anything.

They sat there quietly for a few minutes until the tenseness of her body relaxed against him. It was nice sitting there together, not talking or doing anything, just being together.

"Hey, Kruger," a familiar voice called out as a lieutenant approached.

Within seconds Johnson stood over them. Another officer followed.

Kitty stiffened.

"Who's the new girl?" Lieutenant Johnson asked.

Ted straightened up, removing his arm from her shoulders. "This is Kitty…uh…Sergeant Greenlee. She's one of Madge's friends."

As he spoke, Kitty jumped to her feet and saluted the officers.

Ted joined her facing Johnson and the other officer. They casually returned her salute while looking her over, head to toe. Their superior attitude rubbed Ted the wrong way. They had no right to look at her that way.

"That Madge is a hot cookie," the second lieutenant Ted didn't recognize commented. "Mind if I move in?"

Ted's immediate instinct was to warn them to stay away from Madge. But he stopped himself. He'd intended to tell Madge today that they should start seeing other people. Instead Kitty showed up, and he couldn't very well send a message to Madge that he wanted to break up, especially not with Kitty as the messenger.

"Well, what do you say?" the officer asked.

Ted glanced over at Kitty. "You better ask Madge."

A questioning frown twisted Kitty's lovely face. He'd give her credit, though. She said nothing.

The man laughed. "All right, I will." He looked around at his companions, grinning, and then turned toward the Officers' Club.

"What did you mean by that?" Kitty asked, once they were out of ear shot.

Ted had to figure out what to say to her. It wouldn't be fair to tell Kitty he wanted to break it off with Madge and then have Kitty go and tell Madge. It wouldn't be fair to either of them. He strode back and forth trying to decide what to do, acutely aware Kitty watched him intently.

Finally, he stopped in front of her, faced her. "What time does Madge get off?"

Although surprised at his question, she maintained her composure. "About twenty-one hundred, I'd guess."

"She's at the women's mess, right?"

Kitty nodded. "It'll be lights out before she gets back to the hut."

"Okay." He turned away, trying to think what he would do.

"I don't understand. What am I supposed to tell her?"

"Nothing." He looked over his shoulder. What if Kitty saw Madge before he did? "You can say I was relieved of duty pending the investigation."

She took a step toward him, that questioning frown distorting her face.

"Don't tell her anything else." It wasn't how he wanted to handle things. He didn't want Kitty in the middle of this.

"Madge is my friend. I can't lie to her."

"I'm not asking you to lie. Just to give me a chance to talk to her." He admired Kitty's loyalty to her friend. And he didn't want to come between them. But he wanted to be free to pursue Kitty without involving Madge, without hurting her. After all, Madge was a big girl. She'd been around. She knew the score. They'd just been having fun. And it hadn't really gone that far, even though he sensed that he had been the one holding back, not Madge.

"I think I'd better go," Kitty said. "I'll give Madge your message if...when I see her." She turned and hurried away.

Ted watched her go. He could tell by the way she walked that she knew he was watching. That forced steady pace, that stiff back, head held high. He wondered if once she turned the corner onto the main road and he could no longer see her, if she would break into a run. She looked that anxious to get away from him.

Did he have a chance with her? Did she feel the same...what could he call it? Attraction? Bond? Connection? He didn't know what it was exactly. He just knew there was something there. Something different. Something he'd never felt before. And he wanted more of it.

**\*\*\*\***

In the dark outside the mess tent, Ted could hear the muffled voices of the women as they cleaned up after the evening meal. It was hard for him to imagine Madge scrubbing pans. She wasn't the type. Only try telling that to the Army. Their policy was that everyone pulled KP, every enlisted person that was. Officers like him managed to avoid the unpleasant duty.

He held his wrist up close to his face and drew deeply on the cigarette in his mouth so the ash glowed just enough to illuminate the dial. Eight-fifty, or rather twenty-fifty Army time. They ought to be finishing up.

As if on cue, the light in the tent went out, and someone emerged from the mess hall. Ted's eyes were already accustomed to the dark, so he saw them before they became aware of his presence.

A small flashlight clicked on and remained focused on the ground.

"Corporal Sorensen?" He said it loud enough for them to hear but soft enough not to startle them.

"Who wants to know," the familiar saucy voice replied.

"Lieutenant Kruger. I'd like a word." He tried to maintain an official tone, although the other women surely knew of his relationship with Madge.

"Sure." Madge's voice came from one of the shapes moving in the dark. "You girls go on. I'll catch up."

She stepped close enough for him to feel her breath on his sleeve but remained silent until the two other women disappeared down the path.

He was watching the tiny light flutter its way into the darkness when her arms slipped around his waist.

"Sorry I couldn't come earlier. I couldn't get out of this. You know how it is."

"Yes, I know." He gently peeled her hands from his midsection. "We need to talk."

Even though he couldn't see her face, he felt her body stiffen. "What's going on?"

He looked around. There was no where they could go at this time of night. Nowhere that they could go and

159

sit and talk, calmly, frankly.

"I wanted to talk to you. To explain." He took a deep breath. He had to start somewhere. He placed his hand on her shoulder and steered her down the path toward her quarters. "I've been relieved of duty."

She stopped abruptly. "What?"

He could see her face was turned up to his. "They're investigating an old German man who lives in Ellingham. I've talked to him a few times, so they are investigating me, too."

"That's ridiculous."

"Yeah, well, tell that to Colonel Snyder."

"*Humph.*"

"Right. Anyway I don't know what I'll be doing or where I'll be."

"It'll work out, sweetie. Don't you worry." She reached up and placed her palm on his cheek. She probably expected him to kiss her, but that wasn't what he'd come for. He had to finish it now, before he succumbed to her charms.

He removed her hand and almost pushed her to continue down the path. "I think we need to take a break. Not see each other for a while."

"What? Why?"

Her shock was evident in her voice, and he understood why. He'd kind of hit her out of the blue.

"I just think it would be best."

"That's no reason."

The shock had turned to irritation.

"Look, we're just having a good time here. Right? And I'm not very good company right now. So you should be free to go out and have a good time with whoever you like." He didn't want to hurt her, but he wanted to remind her what they'd said all along. Just for fun. That's all it was. And now it was over.

"You don't mean that. You're just upset. Give it a little time. It'll all work out."

"Maybe so. But for now, this is the way it has to be."

They'd stopped not far from her quarters.

"Good-bye, Madge." He turned and retreated into the darkness before she had a chance to say anything else.

He knew Madge well enough to know she wouldn't give up when she really wanted something. He'd keep his distance. After a while she'd find someone else, or a dozen someones, to have fun with.

\*\*\*\*

"What do you think you're doing?" Madge plopped down in the chair beside Kitty.

"Eating lunch," Kitty replied. "I have to grab something while the general is busy, or I wouldn't get anything. He doesn't believe in stopping for lunch." She took a bite of the thick bread, dreading what Madge would say next.

Madge had come in late last night, and Kitty had pretended to be asleep. This morning Kitty got up early and managed to get away before Madge could corner her. She'd been a coward, but she couldn't help it. She didn't want Madge mad at her.

"That's not what I mean, and you know it."

Kitty glanced at her friend while still chewing. Madge's lips were pressed together, her eyebrows furrowed in an expression of anger Kitty rarely saw. After swallowing the near-tasteless bread she asked, "What's the matter with you?"

"Ted came to the mess tent last night. He said he wanted us to stop seeing each other."

"Really!"

"Oh, don't give me that...that surprised look. You know perfectly well why." When Kitty did not reply, Madge continued "Yesterday. You met Ted at the Officers' Club. And from the stories I heard you got pretty friendly."

"Friendly. You sent me there. You said talk to him. We sat on a bench and talked. That's all."

"That's not what I heard."

"He was a little drunk. He had been relieved, and he was upset."

"I heard he had his arm around you." Madge showed no signs of calming down.

"Not exactly." Her friend's eyes flashed, and Kitty focused on the pile of mashed potatoes on her plate. "He put his arm around me...on the bench. That's all." She cut her eyes around to gauge Madge's reaction. "It was just out of habit. He didn't mean anything by it."

"Well, that's not how I heard it."

Kitty could hear the hurt in her friend's voice. "What did he tell you?"

"It's not just what he told me. It's what he told Lieutenant Carver. Ted told him that he could ask me out."

Kitty tried to remember what Ted had said to the other officers. She couldn't remember his exact words, but she had been surprised at how he had implied that Madge was available. "He was upset," she repeated.

"Sure. Upset because he's being investigated, because he's been relieved. That doesn't mean he has to break up with me."

"Did he really break up with you?" It was hard for Kitty to believe.

Tears glistened in Madge's eyes. She blinked furiously to keep them at bay. Finally she nodded.

Kitty returned her gaze to the plate of food in front of her. She no longer wanted to eat. In fact, she was nauseous. Her friend was almost in tears, and she couldn't help believing it was her fault.

Ted hadn't said it. Hadn't said that he felt anything for her. Yet she sensed the connection, just like that day on the beach. Ever since he'd recognized her, there had been something between them. Was the investigation only an excuse to stop seeing Madge? Could he really be interested in her?

Or was she only imagining it?

"Well, I'm not giving up," Madge said. "I'll give him time, if that's what he needs. But I care too much about him to let him go."

Kitty nodded, unable to respond.

Madge stood and retreated toward the entrance, zigzagging around women carrying trays, to make her way to the end of the chow line.

Kitty returned to her own dull food. Potatoes, bread, some nondescript meat. Her appetite was gone.

She took her tray to the KP line and scraped the remains into a big barrel. On the way back to her office, her thoughts drifted to her meeting with Ted the day before. He hadn't been that drunk. And he'd been nice. Easier to talk to than she expected. Since that first day when she recognized him, she'd been afraid of him. Now he seemed a little more human.

She couldn't believe he'd been accused of doing something bad just because he talked to a German in the village. It wasn't fair. She might not know him well, but she sensed his loyalty. He would never reveal military information, even by accident. She just knew it.

Chapter Fourteen

*TELEGRAM:*

*In London on Leave. STOP. Meet me at Red Cross Piccadilly Circus. STOP. Love, Milton.*

\*\*\*\*

General Lake strode into his office. "Come in and bring your book," he barked over his shoulder.

Kitty grabbed a sharpened pencil from the cup on her desk and her stenographer's pad and then followed him through the open door.

"Shall I close the door?" she asked. He'd been so busy she hoped this would be her chance to ask him.

"Yes," he replied striding to the map that covered one wall. "Take a letter."

"Yes, sir." She hurried to take her seat and open her pad. He always jumped right into whatever he was doing without waiting to see if she was ready.

He started dictating the letter. Her pencil flew across the page. She'd learned his style, the way he worded things, what he meant when he added "et cetera, et cetera." He wasn't hard to work for as long as he focused on work. But sometimes he got a little too friendly.

She watched for these times when he came closer, when he smiled a little too much, when he made jokes or when he offered her a drink. All were signs of his tendency to get too friendly. She'd managed to handle these situations when they were alone pretty well. It was when others were in the room that she got flustered and embarrassed.

That's why she'd decided on a tactic to discourage him. A tactic Madge had taught her when some soldier had gotten too interested and wouldn't give up. A fiancé. It was amazing how most men respected another man's turf. It didn't work on all of them. But she had a feeling General Lake would back off if he thought she was engaged.

"Get that typed up for me right away." It was his way of dismissing her.

She had to seize her chance. "General, may I have a word?"

He looked up, clearly surprised she wasn't leaving. His brows drew together as his dark eyes bore into her. "Go ahead."

She clutched her pad to her breast and drew a deep breath. "I got a wire…from my fiancé. He's on leave in London, and he wants me to meet him." She hoped her voice didn't sound to pitiful. She wasn't sure the general would respond to begging.

"So you want a pass to go to London." His voice was gruff and disapproving.

"Yes, sir."

"Who's this fiancé? Someone you met here?"

"Oh, no, sir. He's from back home. We've known each other for…well forever." She studied his face, fearing he would deny her request. "I haven't seen him in almost two years. He's in the First Infantry Division."

"Infantry, huh," he mused. "Probably part of the invasion force."

"Yes, sir. That's my guess. Although he's said nothing about that." She added the last bit quickly to make sure Milton wasn't suspected of leaking information.

"Well, I suppose I could spare you for a few days." His frown had transformed into a softer expression. "You never mentioned being engaged."

"I know." She struggled to control herself, to keep from blushing, or doing something else to reveal her lie. "I don't talk about it much. I guess I didn't want to jinx him." Her voice trailed off. She said a silent prayer, *Please let him believe me.*

He flipped through the calendar on his desk. "Tell Captain Weatherby I said to give you five days. That's all I can manage." He looked up, back to all business.

"Thank you, sir." She gave him a big smile and fought the urge to run around the desk and hug him. That sure wouldn't discourage him and all her efforts would have been wasted.

She hurried out, torn between running to tell Captain Weatherby and typing the general's letter. She decided she better do the typing first. Keep the general happy.

****

After a day on the English trains, Kitty took the underground to Piccadilly Circus. She had never ridden on a subway and was amazed when she got off at the right place. She had no idea what to expect of Piccadilly Circus. All she knew was that despite its name, it was not a circus, at least not the Ringling Brothers variety. The stairway from the underground emerged in a huge square or rather circle where vehicles went round a center, coming on or going off

167

the circle at the various streets. To her it was chaos . Add the hundreds of people dressed in all manner of uniforms with a few civilians scattered about, and she wondered if everyone in London gathered in this one place.

She stood on the sidewalk amidst all the people coming and going and scanned the buildings surrounding the circle. She easily spotted the big Red Cross sign. With a tight grip on her small overnight case, she headed around the circle, carefully crossing two streets before reaching her destination.

Inside she found more chaos. Military personnel everywhere. Even the Red Cross women wore uniforms. She pushed her way through the crowded lobby until she spotted a desk with a small sign "Information."

"Excuse me." Kitty leaned across the desk to get the lady's attention.

The woman smiled when she turned to greet Kitty. "Can I help you?"

"Oh, yes. I'm looking for someone. My brother. He told me to meet him here."

The woman's eyes shifted toward the crowd. "You didn't see him."

Kitty shook her head. "You don't understand. I just got to London. He's in the First Infantry Division, and he wired me to meet him here."

"In that case, he probably left a message for you." She gave Kitty a reassuring smile. "See the girl over there." She pointed to tired-looking blonde at a nearby counter. "Give her your name and ask if she has a message for you."

Someone bumped Kitty, and she had to grab the

desk to maintain her balance. "Thanks," she muttered to the woman behind the desk. Kitty then wove her way through the crowd to the counter.

Two men formed a line behind a tall officer having an animated conversation with the tired blonde. Kitty took her place at the end of the line grateful for the disinterest of the serviceman in front of her. She considered setting her overnight bag down at her feet but decided to hang onto it so she wouldn't lose it in the bustling crowd. Soon the tall officer disappeared and the two soldiers moved forward and began talking at the same time. The fatigued Red Cross worker held up her hand to silence them.

Kitty wondered at her patience. After she retrieved something for the men, they whooped with joy. The smile that spread across the woman's face dispelled any sign of fatigue as she watched them hurry away.

Kitty stepped forward and spoke to the pleased-looking woman. "Hello. I'm Sergeant Katherine Greenlee. Do you have a message for me?"

"I'll see." The woman lifted a thick folder from a shelf below the counter and leafed through its contents. Kitty gripped the handle of her bag as panic seeped into her thoughts. What if he hadn't left a message? What if she couldn't find him?

"Ah, here it is." The woman handed Kitty a small piece of paper.

Kitty grasped the note while juggling her bag. "Thank you."

She moved to one side before reading the familiar scribbling.

"Katherine—I'll check in at ten a.m. and four p.m. every day. Be at the bar in the canteen. And get yourself a place to stay. Milton."

Kitty looked up to ask the woman what their hours were, but someone else had taken her place. She checked her watch, ten after three. She compared that with the large clock hanging over the counter. Nine after three. Milton would be in the canteen at four. That didn't give her enough time to find a place to stay. She decided to go back to the information desk.

After waiting several minutes, Kitty faced the woman again. "Hi, again." Kitty forced herself to smile despite her discomfort in the crowded place. "Do you know if there is someplace for WACs to stay? A special hotel or something?"

The woman wrote an address on a piece of paper and handed it to her. "Try here. You might have to share a room, but it's a reputable place. Okayed by the WACs."

"Thanks." Kitty looked at the address and wondered how she would find it. Maybe Milton could help. She hated to ask for directions, especially since she knew nothing about London.

She slipped the paper into her pocket and headed for the canteen. Just as on every base she'd been on, there was a separate section for enlisted personnel. It wasn't as fancy as the officers' section, but it wasn't so bad. She climbed onto a stool at the bar and settled her bag between her feet before ordering a cup of coffee and a doughnut, standard fare for the Red Cross in jolly old England, or anywhere else for that matter.

At eight after four, she checked her watch for the millionth time. Her brother wouldn't stand her up, surely. How much longer would she have to wait?

The waitress asked if she wanted another cup of

coffee. Kitty shook her head. She'd already mentioned she was waiting for someone. The waitress just nodded and moved on.

Kitty occupied a seat that a buying customer could use, just like in the drugstore back home. All the popular kids hung out there. She would go in, order a soda, and sit there sipping on it, hoping someone would speak to her. Conspicuous and out of place, she'd eventually leave. Unless Milton came in. He would always stop and talk to her, even though his friends hadn't wanted to be seen with her.

"Sis, is that you?"

Kitty swung around. She almost didn't recognize him. A handsome sergeant stood before her, broad-shouldered, tan and beautiful. She slid off the stool and flung her arms around him, squealing in delight.

He lifted her off her feet and gave her a bear hug—just like old times. Then he set her down and pushed her to arm's length. "Let me look at you. Sergeant no less. That's my gal. Movin' right on up the ladder."

She smiled. "Just got the stripes. Thanks to General Lake."

"You look good. The Army must agree with you."

"I guess." Always awkward talking about herself, she shifted the conversation back to him. "Look at all those ribbons. You've been busy."

"Yeah, you could say that." A soldier standing beside him punched him in the arm. "Oh, yeah. This is Ade Carlton. He's in my outfit. My kid sister, Katherine."

Kitty stuck out her hand. "Nice to meet you."

The soldier took her hand and held it in both of his. "Likewise."

"Ade's from the mid-west, Kansas isn't it?"

"Nebraska," the soldier corrected him. "Milt can't keep anything straight."

"Okay, so I'm not so good with geography. But Katherine here, she's smart as a whip. Went to college to make a teacher."

"Thanks, Milton." She chided her brother in a friendly way. "But men don't like smart girls."

"Not true," Milton argued. "Men don't like unfriendly girls." He slipped his arm around her and steered her toward the exit. "Let's get out of here."

On the sidewalk he asked, "Did you get a place to stay?"

"Not yet. The lady inside gave me this address. Said it was for WACs."

Milton looked at the paper and nodded. "I think I can find it. We better get you over there before they get all filled up. It's not easy to find a room in London these days."

\*\*\*\*

Milton took charge. Kitty soon had a room for the next few nights shared with two other WACs on leave in London. The girls were out, but the landlady assured Kitty that they expected a roommate. She left her few belongings and memorized the address.

From the hotel Milton led them to a little Italian restaurant where a cute, pale blonde in a gray-green tweed uniform called out "Milt, my love" when she saw them.

Milton hugged the English girl then turned to introduce Kitty. "Betty Tatum, meet my sister, Katherine, and you remember Ade."

"Nice to meet 'cha," she replied in her quaint

English accent. "Milt's a great guy for a Yank. Me and my friend went out with these two blokes last night. Had quite a time of it, didn't we?"

"Swell, just swell," Milton beamed.

"How's Edwena?" Ade asked politely.

"Oh, just ducky. She's off with some RAF fliers tonight. Whole group of 'em off to Hyde Park. But I'd rather do the theatre with Milt." Betty clung to Milton's arm, and he beamed at the attention she showered on him.

"Let's go in." Milton led the way. "Betty told me about this place, and it's great. A lot better than most of these English joints."

Rationing and shortages made it hard for the restaurants to survive. Most offered a very limited menu, and what they did serve was boiled and bland. So Italian cuisine proved a pleasant surprise.

Kitty's first encounter with Italian food had been in Boston. Madge had an Italian boyfriend who'd fixed Kitty up with his friend. The soldiers took them to the Italian section of Boston where Kitty experienced the warm, friendly atmosphere and her first taste of spaghetti and ravioli.

Milton ordered for them all. The waiter served wine while they waited for the main course.

"Did you get tickets?" the English girl asked.

"You bet cha,'" replied Milton, mimicking her accent. "For that comedy you wanted to see at the Strand."

"Oooo! You're such a doll."

Kitty laughed at the girl's enthusiasm. She liked her. "I don't recognize your uniform," Kitty commented. "What service are you in?"

"Women's Voluntary Service," she replied cheerfully. "We do all sorts of things to help out. People bombed out, displaced, elderly—that sort of thing."

"Sounds like important work."

"Oh, I've seen my share. Some hair raising tales I could tell ya', during the blitz and all."

"None of that, tonight," Milton said. "We're celebrating. Katherine and me together again." He raised his glass. "How long's it been, sis? Two years."

"Not quite. You came home before you went overseas. That was in the summer of '42. I'd just come back from Suzanne's."

"Well, here's to family reunions," Ade said as he raised his glass.

They all clinked glasses and sipped the wine. Kitty beamed at her brother. He was still the same old Milton, but more. He'd matured, added some lines to his face that made him even more handsome than she remembered.

The waiter served the food, and Kitty looked around, excitement pounding in her chest. She was in London, with her brother, and in for a night on the town. What more could she ask for?

After dinner they walked to the Strand Theatre which was only a few blocks away. Milton explained that London was full of performers from all over Europe. These refugees found work in the local theatres providing excellent performances of every type. The show they saw was a light comedy. Kitty laughed until tears ran down her cheeks.

They emerged from the theatre to total blackness. The moon hid behind a cloud cover. After seeing the bustle of the city, to have it completely disappear into darkness gave Kitty the creeps.

Other people leaving the theatre jostled them along.

"Not to fear, I have my torch." Betty spoke nearby. Quickly a narrow beam of light illuminated her feet.

Other small beams appeared around them in the crowd.

"I've got one, too," announced Ade. "It didn't take me long to learn I needed a flashlight to get around in the blackout." He clicked it on and pointed it toward the sidewalk in front of Kitty's feet. She sighed, relieved to be able to see something.

"Let's see if we can find that place we went the other night. You remember, the one down below street level."

"It's getting late," Kitty interjected. "I'm beat. I think I'd better get back to my room."

"Okay, sis," Milton agreed.

Kitty thought he gave in a little too easily. Maybe he wanted to spend some time alone with Betty.

Milton acted like he knew the way, so Kitty and Ade followed him. Once she got the hang of making their way in the darkness, Kitty relaxed and held on to Ade's arm.

They turned a corner, and Milton commented they were almost there.

A shape came out of the darkness, and they came to an abrupt stop. Kitty couldn't see much with Milton and Betty ahead of her.

"Hey, watch it," Milton complained.

Betty giggled.

"Sorry, ma'am. Must have tripped on the curb. I

can't see a thing in this black out. "

She could hardly believe her ears. The familiar voice couldn't be him. "Ted?" Kitty exclaimed. "Is that you?"

Chapter Fifteen

"Kitty?" Ted's voice boomed from the darkness as he came closer.

"Who is this guy?" Ade asked.

"I could ask the same thing, Bud." Ted's irritation radiated as he faced Ade with Kitty trying to squeeze between them.

"This is Ade…" Kitty couldn't remember his last name.

"Carlton," Ade added.

"He's my escort."

"Escort, ha! I suppose he's not your fiancé," Ted said.

"My what?" Kitty exclaimed. But then the story she told General Lake flashed into her head. "Who told you that I was engaged?"

"Never mind who told me."

"What's he talking about? And who is he anyway?" Milt asked.

"He's been dating my best friend," Kitty said.

"Who are you?" Ted asked belligerently.

"That's none of your business. What are you doing here?" Milt's anger rose.

"Ted, this is my brother, Milton."

"Brother! You said you were going to meet your fiancé." The darkness couldn't hide the confusion in Ted's voice.

"What fiancé?" Ade asked.

Betty giggled.

"Oh, I just told General Lake that I was going to London to meet my fiancé so he would give me leave."

"Am I hearing you right? You told the general a lie to get leave?" Milton said. "My straight as an arrow sister lied. Again."

Kitty cringed at her brother's reaction, especially the emphasis on that last word. She'd never lied. Never. Even when it meant she or Milton got in trouble. She always told the truth. Except for that one big one that no one else knew about—except Milton.

"And how do I know this really is your brother?" Ted asked.

"Because he is," Kitty insisted.

"What I want to know is why this…this idiot followed you to London, especially if he's your 'friend's' boyfriend. What's he to you?"

"Well, I guess you could say we're friends." Kitty wondered how she could explain their relationship. "But I don't know why he's here."

"I came to make sure you were all right."

"Sounds like the bloke's sweet on you." Betty was enjoying the confusion.

"I was just afraid she might be mixed up with some unsavory character."

"I can take care of myself," Kitty insisted.

"Sounds like my little sister has grown up—at least a little. And I'm not sure I like it."

"Oh, Milton. It's a long story. And not one I want to tell right now."

"Not one you ever want to tell, apparently," Ted added.

Kitty wanted to scream at all of them. She didn't know why Ted was here. And what's more, she didn't care. She stamped her foot in frustration.

"How 'bout we leave these three to slug it out?" Ade asked Betty.

"Sounds like a good idea," Betty replied.

"Oh, no you don't. You're not stealing my girl." Milton turned on his friend as the clouds drifted overhead revealing a small portion of the almost-full moon. A soft glow engulfed the group.

"I'm not your girl, Milt. I'm not anybody's girl."

"What do you mean?"

"I mean that I decide who I go out with. I'm not one of those easy girls, you know. I like to have a few laughs, but that's as far as it goes."

"I know that, Betty. That's why I like you." Milton obviously didn't want to lose his date.

"I'll take care of Kitty. You can go on with your girlfriend," Ted offered.

Milton turned on Ted. "You stay away from my sister." His anger abruptly changed, and he froze in place.

Kitty looked from her brother to Ted. The moonlight reflected off the gold bars on Ted's collar. She realized that she'd failed to introduce Ted properly and due to the darkness her brother hadn't known Ted was an officer. But before she could say anything, Milton straightened up and saluted.

"Lieutenant," Milton said.

Out of the corner of her eye, she saw Ade snap to attention, too.

"At ease, soldiers," Ted said calmly, returning their salute. "I have no intention of pulling rank here."

"Sir, what are your intentions?" Milton asked.

"Like I said, I just wanted to check on Kitty and make sure she was okay."

"All this is my fault. I should have introduced you properly." Her gaze flew between Ted and Milton. "Lieutenant Ted Kruger. Sergeant Milton Greenlee." She motioned for them to come together, but both stood rooted in place. "Now you two can be friends," she added hopefully.

The two men continued to stare at each other. Finally, Ted broke the silence. "This officer stuff doesn't mean much as far as I'm concerned. I'm in the Air Force, and I'm an officer because I'm a navigator. It's nothing like you guys in the infantry. I'm not in command of anybody. I just navigate."

Slowly a grin spread across Milton's face. "Well, I never thought I'd hear one admit it."

"Then you two can be friends."

"Maybe. As long as he stays away from you." Milton gave Kitty a stern look then shifted his gaze back to Ted. "I don't want her getting mixed up with any officers."

Ted laughed. "I understand."

Kitty stood there wondering what to do next.

"I thought you were beat, wanted to hit the hay." Milton was back to his old self.

She nodded. "Yes. I was."

Milton looked around. The moonlight illuminated the street so they could see Kitty's quarters just a few feet from where they stood. "I'll be here to pick you up at nine in the morning, okay? We'll take in all the sites."

"Sounds wonderful." Kitty relaxed. A wave of

fatigue washed over her. She turned to Betty. "Nice to meet you," and nodded to Ade. "I had a nice time. Thank you."

Then she approached her brother and gave him a hug. "Good night." She turned toward the hotel entrance. Ted stood to one side. Unsure what to say to him, she stammered "Good night," and hurried inside.

Ted said nothing, which only added to her confusion. Everything seemed disjointed between them. Awkward. She wasn't sure why and she still didn't understand why he was here. She shook her head, convinced she'd never understand men.

****

As soon as Kitty went inside Milton faced Ted, "Now I want to know what's goin' on."

Ted took a deep breath. He wasn't sure what Kitty's brother wanted to know—or how much he already knew.

"Maybe we should go someplace where we can talk," he suggested.

Milton nodded. "Okay. I know just the place." He turned to look at Ade and Betty. "Come on. We're going to get a drink."

"Not me," Betty said. "I'm callin' it a night, too. You boys can go 'ave your drink without me."

Ade spoke up. "May I take you home?"

She flashed a smile. "That'd be just peachy." She took his arm and steered him toward a nearby subway entrance.

"Wait just a minute," Milton protested.

Ade smiled, like the cat that swallowed the canary. "You two go talk." He patted Betty's hand. "I'll see you later."

Betty waved to them and called, "Night boys."

Ted watched the two depart, leaving him to face Kitty's brother. He shouldn't have come. Had no real reason to come. Except he needed to get away from the base, from his do-nothing assignment, and it had shocked him when he learned Kitty was engaged. He should have gone to Madge and asked her about it. He could have passed it off as gossip, which is what it was. But no, he'd acted on impulse and took off to London—to face an angry brother and a confused Kitty.

Milton glared at him.

"Where's that drink you were talking about?"

Milton's frown melted into a smile. He slapped Ted on the shoulder. "Come on."

Through the blackout, glimmers of moonlight showed the way through the London streets. Foot traffic picked up with their flashlights lighting the way to a stairway down into a cellar. Milton led him through the door and blackout curtains, and into a smoky, crowded bar. Uniforms lined a bar along one wall. Others clustered around tables or shuffled their dates around the tiny dance floor to a Benny Goodman tune.

Ted and Milton pushed their way through to the bar, and Milton ordered for them both. When the bartender set the glasses in front of them, Milton handed him some coins before Ted could reach in his pocket.

"You aren't buying my drinks," Ted shouted to Milton over the din.

Milton shook his head. "You can get the next round."

Ted reluctantly agreed. He took a long swig. The warm stout tasted good. He wondered how much of the stuff it would take to get good and drunk.

"Did that general send you to check up on Katherine?"

His question caught Ted off guard.

"General Lake?"

"If that's his name."

"General Lake doesn't know anything about me coming here."

Milton took a drink. "She wrote me about him. I figured it was worse than she said, but I didn't know it had gotten so bad that she'd lie to him."

"I don't know what she told you, but I don't think the general has gotten out of line. What I mean is I think she's keeping him at bay."

"How do you know?"

"From Madge. That's Kitty's best friend."

"And your girlfriend?"

"Yes, she was, up until a couple of days ago."

"So what's…Kitty, is that what you call her? What's she to you?"

"Like she said, we're friends. We met a long time ago."

Milton's brows furrowed into an unspoken question.

"Did she ever tell you about pulling a guy out of the ocean? On the Georgia coast?" Ted asked.

Milton leaned back as if surprised. Finally, he spoke. "Yeah. She told me about it before I left the states."

Ted sighed. "That was me." How did he explain it all?

"I'm sure she would have written me if she met *that* man again." Her brother looked suspicious. "Why didn't she tell me?"

Ted ran his hand through his hair. "It's complicated. Hard to explain."

"Try me."

Milton signaled the bartender to bring another round. He pointed to a table in the corner that had just been vacated. "Come on over here where we can talk."

Milton grabbed the drinks deposited by the bartender and carried them to the table. Ted dug some coins out of his pocket and paid for the drinks before joining him.

Always cautious in places like this, Ted slid into a chair with his back against the wall. If a fight started, he wanted to be ready to get out quick, before the MPs arrived. No drunk tank for him. He was in enough trouble without being hauled in for disorderly conduct.

The infantryman settled in and sipped his drink. "Now tell me this complicated story."

Chapter Sixteen

Milton arrived at the hotel the next morning to pick her up. Ted was with him but dressed differently.

"Why are you wearing that?" Kitty asked.

"So I can go sightseeing with you and Milt," Ted replied.

"But won't you get in trouble?" Kitty looked to her brother.

"It was his idea." Milt was quick to say, a look of amusement on his face.

"You're out of uniform."

Ted laughed, and the joy in it made her feel warm inside. "I just borrowed the shirt and cap for the day. No one will notice." He grinned. "Just three non-coms out to see London."

"What if the MPs catch you?" Kitty worried.

"They're less likely to notice me this way than if I was a second luey hanging around with enlisted personnel."

Kitty frowned and looked to her brother for help.

"Don't look at me. He wanted to do it. If we're stopped, I don't know a thing—and neither do you."

"See. I'm the only one who gets in trouble. Okay?"

"Okay," she agreed, reluctantly. If he wanted to impersonate a sergeant in the infantry who was she to object?

"Besides, I'm already in trouble, so a little more

won't matter."

They turned a corner and headed to Piccadilly Circus. Milton led the way.

"Yeah, what a crock!"

"How do you know about that?" Kitty asked, uncomfortable with Ted and Milton acting so familiar.

"He filled me in last night."

"Last night?" Kitty asked. "Where did you two go last night?"

Milton grinned at Ted, who grinned back. Uneasiness pricked at her.

"Oh, we had a few drinks. Then, since Ted didn't have any place to stay, I smuggled him into my room."

Shocked, she stopped in her tracks letting the information sink in. Ted stayed with Milton last night. Incredible.

Ted turned to look at her. "Aren't you coming?"

She hurried to catch up with them.

"That's where I got the idea to become a sergeant. In Milt's room."

"What else did you two do?" She never thought about her brother making friends with Ted. She's just assumed Milton would send him on his way.

"We talked," Milton offered, glancing at Ted.

"About what?" She had to almost run to keep up with their long strides.

"Mostly about you," Ted announced. He gave her a sweet smile and slowed his pace a little so she could walk at his side.

Her unease heightened. She looked at Milton who walked ahead as if intent on reaching some unknown destination. What had he told Ted about her? Surely he wouldn't tell him embarrassing things. The sun beat down with unusual heat. Her skin crawled up her arms, her neck. A childhood memory of breaking out in hives materialized out of nowhere.

Ted stopped her by putting his hands on her shoulders and turning her to face him. "Are you all right? You look kind of funny?"

She was literally shaking in her shoes. And the feel of his strong, warm hands didn't help.

"All she needs is something to eat. I bet you haven't had breakfast, have you?"

Kitty shook her head, back and forth, unable to speak.

Her brother took her arm. He steered her into the Red Cross Canteen. "We'll get some food into you before we go a step further."

Kitty sipped the coffee and stared at the doughnuts on the plate in front of her. She thought of the letter she'd sent Milton after that dramatic day on the beach. Her account of the incident must have sounded childish. And later, in other letters, she'd shared her day dreams of someday finding the handsome mystery man.

She closed her eyes. *Please, you didn't tell him all that. Please.*

"Go ahead and eat. We're not moving until you do."

Kitty had heard that serious tone before when he'd given his kid sister orders. She picked up a doughnut and took a bite. But she didn't taste any of it.

The morning passed quickly. Ted proved a very entertaining tour guide. He regaled them with stories as if he'd lived in London all his life, but it was his knowledge of history that impressed Kitty the most.

And he was a perfect gentleman. A few times he

flashed that heart-stopping smile her way. She could not help but react. She'd stammer or catch her breath, which only made him grin like the Cheshire cat, pleased with himself.

There were none of his comic antics. Just a very pleasant, very handsome companion. Maybe her brother's presence kept him on his best behavior. Or maybe he wanted her to see him in a different light.

They walked from Piccadilly Circus to Buckingham Palace, and from there continued on to see Big Ben and the Houses of Parliament.

When Kitty delighted over the big double-decker buses, the three clambered aboard and climbed to the top. Kitty sank into the seat by her brother and slipped her arm through his.

"Now this is how it's supposed to be," she announced, squeezing his arm and smiling.

"What do you mean?" he asked.

"Oh, coming to England, finding you. Us here together." She looked around at the passing buildings. "This is what I dreamed of."

Milton glanced at Ted, who sat across the aisle. "Sis, you're crazy."

He laughed when he said it so she couldn't be mad at him. "Okay, so I'm crazy. Is it so bad? Wanting to come over here and help my big brother win this war." She turned in the seat to face him. "Now we have to figure out how we can do this more often."

"Do what?" He was still grinning at her.

"Get together like this. Wouldn't it be great if we could do this every weekend?"

He just shook his head. When his gaze shifted Ted's way, she followed it. He was laughing at her, too, like they shared a joke—a joke on her.

"I'm not kidding," she continued, a little irritated.

"I know, I know," Milton tried to calm her. "Just remember, the Army's in charge. We have to do what they say when they say it."

"Of course we do, but that doesn't mean we can't get together."

"Maybe you can talk that general of yours into giving you a pass every weekend, but I can't." He paused. His face grew more serious. "Do you know how many men are here in England? And how many of them want leave to come to London?"

Kitty stared at him. Facts and figures popped into her head. Stories about millions of men in England. The inevitable invasion. She pushed them aside, not wanting to think about what the stories meant.

"Let's just enjoy the time we have together, now," Milton continued. "Isn't that right, Ted?"

"Right," Ted agreed. He glanced ahead. "Looks like we're almost there. See the bridge." He pointed to the Tower Bridge just coming into view. He stood. "The next stop is where we get off."

Kitty tried to hide her disappointment. She'd counted on spending time with Milton. The whole reason she'd volunteered for overseas service was so she could be near him. Now she was here with him only to learn the truth. That they couldn't spend time together. They had separate jobs in different parts of the country, and the Army wasn't going to allow them time off to be together.

She descended the bus's stairs, her eyes on her brother, so strong and independent. A real soldier. He'd understood all along. Their time together would be limited.

She felt so childish. But she wouldn't be anymore. She'd be strong, too. And she'd enjoy the time they did have.

The trio toured the Tower of London where Ted entertained them with stories of Henry the Eighth's wives and the young boys King Richard held prisoner there. Afterward, the three strolled across the Tower Bridge and watched the boats on the Thames. For a quick lunch they ate fish 'n' chips on the street, then they descended into the underground and rode the subway to Hyde Park.

From their comments, Kitty realized that both Ted and Milton had been in London before. Milton knew about all the available entertainment while Ted pointed out every bar and dance hall. Ted's stories usually included some mention of his friends. A hint of sadness skittered across his face every time, quickly followed by a forced smile.

To Kitty, London was new and exciting. The famous places with their historical references were no longer words in books. They came to life with Ted's colorful narrative.

Along the way lots of American military personnel crowded the streets, many viewing the sights, too. No one noticed Ted's uniform, not even the MPs who patrolled the more crowded areas.

In Hyde Park they strolled along the main walkway. Kitty suggested they find a quiet spot where they could sit and rest. She longed to talk to her brother about small things, anything and everything, like they had talked when growing up.

A boisterous bunch of GIs blocked the path just

ahead. The group, including some English girls, appeared to have been drinking.

"Let's see if we can get around them," Milton suggested. He surveyed their options and then steered Kitty toward the grass. Their detour almost succeeded until one of the GIs called to Milton.

"Hey, Greenie. Is that you?"

"Who's the pretty girl?" another asked.

Milton waved. "Hey, fellows." Then he said quietly to Ted and Kitty, "Those two are from my company. We'll have to talk to them."

Kitty tensed, certain Ted would be found out. She glanced at him. He smiled calmly as if nothing were amiss. She hoped he could pull it off, but she doubted it.

The two soldiers eased away from the larger group. Milton confidently took charge and introduced them.

"Joe Thornton, Phil Ciccero, this is my sister, Katherine. And this is Ted Kruger."

Kitty smiled nervously. "Just call me Kitty." She tried to keep her voice friendly and sweet. "Everybody does."

Ted reached out and shook their hands. "Nice to meet you."

Joe eyed Ted. "I don't think I've seen you around. What company are you in?"

"He's been on special assignment, at Division headquarters," Milton explained.

"Hobnobbing with the brass, eh?"

"Yeah, something like that," Ted replied.

Kitty watched the two. Joe looked suspicious.

"I'm pretty good with faces. I don't remember seeing you in training or around the base."

Ted looked the man in the eye and didn't flinch. "I've been working with the intelligence boys. Top secret stuff. Can't really talk about it."

Joe nodded.

Kitty didn't know if the soldier believed Ted, but he backed off. When the two GIs returned to the group and moved along, Kitty let out a sigh.

"You handled that pretty well," Milton commented.

"I've told my share"—he looked around at Kitty—"to stay out of trouble, of course. Strictly in self-defense."

"You wouldn't have to if you didn't put yourself in these positions." Kitty knew she sounded high and mighty, but she didn't care. He could get into a lot of trouble.

"This from the girl who's engaged to her brother."

"What?"

"Okay you two. Enough. Let's find a place we can sit and relax."

They spotted a bench set away from the main walkway that faced a small pond.

Kitty sat, glad to be off her feet. Milton joined her while Ted walked to the water's edge as if he were inspecting the property.

She watched him. His tall, lean silhouette against the idyllic setting somehow brought to mind thoughts of that day and another idyllic setting—a beach and the same mysterious man. A man who fate had brought back into her life in such a strange way.

He wasn't the fantasy of a lonely girl. Just an ordinary soldier out to have a good time.

Her best friend was in love with him, she reminded

herself. And that meant she had to keep her distance, at least until Madge was ready to move on.

She turned her attention to the reason for her trip to London, her brother. "Do you get many letters from home?"

**\*\*\*\***

Milton smiled. "Mother writes. I think she forces herself to do it. She tells me what everybody is doing, especially Olivia. Sounds like our little sister's the most popular girl in Kerrville."

"Yeah, that's our little sister." Kitty couldn't contain her sarcasm, and she didn't care. "Mother's pride and joy. I'm glad someone can make her proud. Lord knows I never could."

Her brother chose to ignore her remark and continued.

"Mom says Uncle Jim is in Detroit building tanks. Rented out his farm and headed north to make some money and pay off the mortgage. Can't say as I blame him."

"Yeah, I know. Aunt Louise and the girls are staying with Grandmother until he can find a place for them to live up there. She'll probably get a defense job, too."

He looked thoughtful. "Got a postcard from Andy. Kid's growing up fast. Says Pop's got him working when he's not in school. Maybe he'll take to the business more than I did."

"You just wanted to get away from home for a while, see the world," she reassured him. "When you get back, Pop'll want you right by his side. Just like he always said."

"Yeah, I guess so. And by the time I get back

maybe I'll be ready to settle down. I still want to play baseball, though. If I can make the team." His face grew somber. He leaned forward resting his elbows on his knees and looked at his clasped hands. "This war, it wears you down, makes you think about things."

She reached over and placed her hand over his. "Will it ever be over?"

Ted sat on the grass between the bench and the pond, staring out across the water. "It'll be over when we beat them. When we pound them into dust." Bitterness laced his words.

Kitty's attention shifted to Ted. His eyes had narrowed, and a muscle in his tense jaw flexed as if he were grinding his teeth. At that moment she saw something in him she'd never seen before. A strange, smoldering anger, hatred even. She looked back at Milton, afraid she would see the same thing in her brother's eyes. Instead she saw concern, for her.

"Katherine, you know there is an invasion coming."

She nodded. "Sure, everybody knows that."

"We don't know when it's going to be, but one of these days we're going to have to invade Europe."

"By then we will have bombed them into oblivion," Ted interjected.

Milton straightened. "You fly boys can drop all the bombs you want. In the end it's the infantry that has to go in and take it."

"What are you trying to say?" Kitty asked, her insides tightened.

He drew a deep breath and leaned back so he could look at her when he spoke. "We've been here in England training for a while now. They pulled us out of

Italy. They won't tell us anything, but we all know that we'll be the ones landing in Europe. Don't know where, don't know when, but the First Division will lead the way."

Kitty could taste the fear as her mouth filled with sour saliva. She swallowed hard. Her stomach clinched. "And you'll be in danger." She barely breathed the words.

Milton nodded, his breath blowing out through his mouth as if relieved to finally speak the truth. "Yes." The word was emphatic, a confirmation of her worst fears. "That's our job, my job." He glanced over at Ted. "Like he says, we have to beat them. We have no choice."

Kitty wanted to cry, but she knew it was the wrong time for tears. She had to be strong for Milton. "With men like you, and you Ted, we can't lose."

Ted stretched out on the grass and put his hands behind his head. "You know. I almost wish I could just leave this uniform on and go with you."

"No. You've got your own job to do."

Ted looked around at Milton. "If they let me. Right now I'm useless."

"It'll work out. You've done nothing wrong," Kitty assured him. She had never been able to imagine him consorting with the enemy, no matter what they said.

"Yeah, sure. Easy for you to say, Miss Follow-the-Rules. I've been busted after being set up before. It's no fun."

Kitty ignored the jibe and thought of the story about the airplane ride that got him kicked out of pilot training. His crack told her there was more to the story and gave her a hint into what that mistake had cost him.

They all sat in silence for a few minutes. Kitty searched her mind for some cheerful topic. But it was Milton who spoke up first.

"Mother wrote that Suzanne had moved back home." Milton had always been concerned about Suzanne's marriage.

"Yes. Sam joined the Coast Guard so she and the children moved back to Kerrville."

"He didn't have to enlist. With a family and the work he was doing, he could've sat this thing out."

She detected something almost resentful in the way Milton spoke of his brother-in-law.

"Maybe he wanted to help win the war, like me."

Milton's face softened into a smile. "No. He's nothing like you." He glanced past her at Ted. "Does he know?" he asked in a whisper.

Kitty shook her head, a little embarrassed that he would mention her secret. "No. Only you. And Father, of course."

He grinned, embarrassing her more.

"You won't tell him?" Her hushed words sounded desperate even to her.

"No. You're here, and you'll be twenty-one soon. Why should I spoil it for you?"

"I don't think he'd tell, but I can't take the chance."

Milton slipped his arm around her and hugged her. "They won't send you home," he whispered in her ear.

"Big family secrets?" Ted pushed himself up to a sitting position and watched them.

"Little ones," Milton admitted, releasing his hold on her.

"You were listening?" Kitty asked.

196

"Couldn't help it. I'm right here. I can hear everything you say, except for the whispering." His stare bore into Kitty. Something told her he had heard more than he admitted.

"That's okay," Milton assured him. "It's just family stuff. I'm sure you've heard the same type things in your family."

Ted looked away, frowning. "No. I haven't. I wish I had."

Kitty wondered what planet he had come from. She couldn't imagine a family without secrets and disagreements and all that messy stuff.

"What do you mean?" Milton asked.

"I mean that I don't really have any family. No brothers, no sisters, no aunts, no uncles, no cousins. No one except my mother, who doesn't fit anyone's idea of a mother. And my grandparents, who came from Germany." He got to his feet and brushed off the seat of his pants. "So no, I don't know about all this family business." He waved his hand for emphasis. "I wish I did."

Kitty pitied him. She couldn't imagine having no family. Or next to none. Ted must have seen it in her face.

"I don't want your pity," he insisted. "I just think you should be thankful for the family you have. They're obviously well to do, businesses and all that. And they care about you in their way. I'm sure they worry about you, both of you. They wouldn't want anything to happen to either of you."

Kitty's mouth hung open. Unable to think of anything to say in reply, she clamped it shut as she watched him walk back and forth on the grass.

"And they write you, don't they?" He stopped and looked at both of them. "Every couple of months, I get a letter from my grandfather. It's mostly in German because he struggles with writing in English. My grandmother reads only German. And if I got a postcard from my mother, I'd probably faint dead away. So just be glad you have someone who's thinking about you."

"You're right. And I am grateful for them, all of them," Milton said.

"Me, too." Kitty's throat tightened, and tears threatened again.

Ted stood there a minute looking from Kitty to Milton and back.

"I'm sorry," he blurted out. "I shouldn't have said that. I don't know what I was thinking."

"It's okay."

"No. Forget it. Forget I said anything." He ran his hand through his hair. "I don't ever do that."

"Do what?" Kitty asked.

"Talk about my family."

"Maybe you should," Milton said.

Milton's voice conveyed understanding. Kitty was proud to have a brother who could listen and understand another person's pain. He'd always done that for her.

She gave Milton a hug, then beckoned Ted to come closer, so she could hug him, too. She was connected to both these men, and she wanted them both to be safe.

Chapter Seventeen

Before dinner Ted returned to Milton's quarters and changed back into his uniform. He'd had enough of masquerading as someone he wasn't. He had to face reality.

When he rejoined Milton and Kitty on the street, he lied and told them he had plans for dinner. He politely thanked them for an enjoyable day, then he promptly left, not giving them a chance to ask questions.

He was running away. He knew it. But he had to get away from them. The enormous gap between who they were and who he was had become so clear, at least to him, that he couldn't stand being with them any longer.

He ducked into a subway entrance and boarded the first train he saw. He didn't care where he went just so it was away from Kitty and Milton.

But jostling along in his own private world, he couldn't get Kitty out of his mind. She had come alive in her brother's company. Smiling, relaxed, happy. She'd even laughed at his jokes. So unlike the serious girl who cast him a disapproving eye in the middle of his entertaining routine.

Madge told him Kitty was afraid of men, afraid to get involved. But the girl he'd spent the day with had been friendly, congenial, even witty at times. She knew her history and referred to literature with a familiarity and fondness that made him want to search out Shakespeare and Chaucer. He'd read what was required in high school English but found most of it dull and irrelevant. She made them sound interesting, made him want to know more just so he could discuss them with her.

He shook off such thoughts about Kitty. He needed to stick with his own kind. He should stick with Madge. She was more his type. But when he thought of Madge, she seemed dull and superficial. All flash with no substance.

Wasn't that what he liked? Flashy, pretty, well-built dames. Women who made him the envy of all the other men. Women who looked good on his arm, who knew how to dance and make out. Women who knew how to show a guy a good time.

So why, after spending the day with a wholesome, all-American girl from a good family, did the others seem so boring, so dull, so insincere?

The train came to a halt, and the conductor announced the end of the line. Ted exited, not knowing where he was.

Above ground the world appeared surreal, filled with tumbled stone and bricks barely visible in the eerie twilight. An occasional wall stood silhouetted against the sky. Blackened timbers stuck up through the rubble and mangled iron rods projected from crumbled concrete. The short patch of street ahead ended abruptly in a pile of stone. No street signs identified the location.

He turned and watched the three people who had emerged from the underground with him hurrying off along a path toward a row of buildings standing precariously amidst the destruction.

His first instinct was to run after them. Ask them where he was and how to get back, to where? To civilization. To London.

But this was London. This is what the German bombers had done to the city.

How many had been killed? How many had been left homeless, with nothing left of their lives?

Was this what their bombers were doing to German cities? So much destruction had been wrought to satisfy Hitler's desire to rule the world. How many lives would be lost to stop the monster?

He thought of Milton and the coming invasion. Would he survive? What would Kitty do if he were killed? Would it destroy her?

Seeing them together he saw a kind of love he had never experienced. The love between a brother and a sister. He knew enough to know all siblings were not as close as Kitty and Milton. Yet it was the type of bond he had yearned for growing up. He had wanted a brother. Someone to be with, play with, cry with. He'd have settled for a sister. He just wanted someone to share his life, someone who understood, someone to keep him from feeling so alone.

He drew a deep breath and shoved the old feelings deep inside. He had to deal with now. He wasn't going to try to walk back. Not the best plan, especially in the dark. So he returned to the subway and descended into the depths of the underground chamber.

Surely another train would come. No schedule was posted. He just had to wait. So he slumped down onto a bench under the dim light of a single lamp. The shaft of light from the stairway gradually faded into complete darkness.

He chided himself for not eating. He could have had dinner with Kitty and Milton. He could be sitting right now talking and laughing in some restaurant. It would have been fun. Just watching Kitty with her brother would have been a most pleasant way to pass an evening, even if he could not talk to her himself.

He imagined watching them, as if through a window. He couldn't hear their conversation. He could just watch their faces, her face, alive, happy.

He'd done the right thing, leaving them. Putting some distance between them.

He didn't belong with people like that. Nice people.

He belonged with the drifters, the day laborers, the people who stood in bread lines, who took charity but hated themselves for it. That's who his father had been. Lost, with no job, no place for his family to live, nothing to offer them.

Although only ten at the time, the fact his father had been stealing when he was killed had been no surprise to Ted. There were times when his father brought them food and refused to say where it came from. Just before they left St. Louis, his father produced a pair of shoes for Ted, not new shoes, but ones someone had worn. Ted didn't care where they came from. They fit, and they had no holes.

Those were the dark days, the days when he had made up his mind to work hard at whatever he could so he wouldn't be hungry or homeless again.

Later, abandoned by his parents by death and desertion, his grandparents gave him stability. A home, food, clothing, regular schooling. He made a few friends, mostly boys whose families were struggling to get out of the depression. And he played basketball. Made the team on talent alone. Even so, he'd been an outsider, never included in invitations to parties, never quite good enough to hang around with the "nice" kids.

His grandparents gave him a home, but they couldn't give him social status. The immigrants were accepted in the community, to a point. But families like Kitty's would never be more than customers at the butcher shop. Those type people were several rungs up the social ladder from Ted and his German grandparents. And no uniform or gold bars would ever make up that difference.

A rumbling from far down the tunnel pulled him out of this thoughts. He straightened, hoping the sound would increase and the train would pull up in front of him.

After what seemed like an eternity, the train ground to a stop. Five or six people got off.

Ted quickly boarded. The conductor eyed him curiously.

Ted flashed him a smile and quipped. "Wrong stop."

The conductor only nodded and closed the door. Soon they were rumbling away, through the dark tunnel, toward another unknown destination.

Just like his life.

**** 

Early the next morning Ted went to Milton's quarters. He wanted to speak to Kitty's brother without her being around.

Ted informed the clerk he wanted to see Sergeant Milton Greenlee on an urgent matter. When the desk clerk hesitated, Ted flashed his lieutenant's bars and acted the part of an irate officer.

Anxious to avoid a problem with the U.S. Army, the clerk called Milton's room.

"He will be down in a few minutes."

Ted frowned.

"I woke him up. You have to give him time to get dressed."

Five minutes later Milton descended the stairs grumbling at having been roused at such an early hour.

Ted frowned back at him and ordered him outside.

"Sorry about that," Ted said as they stepped onto the sidewalk.

"What do you want?" Milton was still agitated.

"To talk to you—before I leave town."

Milton glanced around at the nearly deserted street. "What about?"

"To thank you for putting me up the other night and for letting me tag along yesterday."

Milton eyed him curiously. "No sweat. A friend of Katherine's is a friend of mine."

"Speaking of Kitty, uh, Katherine," Ted stammered. "That's the other thing I want to talk about." He hesitated, fidgeted with his hands. "She's a nice girl. And, well, uh, I want you to know that I have a lot of respect for her."

Milton only nodded, waiting for Ted to continue.

Frustrated at himself, he jerked his cap from his head to give him something to hold onto. He was never tongue-tied. Could always say what he wanted to say. Yet he struggled for the words. "What I'd like to say…like for you to tell her… Well, much as I like her, I…uh…I don't want to hurt Kitty's feelings…"

"But you don't want her to get the wrong idea."

"Right." Ted grinned, thankful Milt understood.

"Don't worry. She's a big girl. As a matter of fact, I've been pleasantly surprised at how much she's grown up. The Army's good for her."

"Yeah," Ted agreed. He looked away, his thoughts returning to the huge gap between them. "Anyway, with this war going on, all I want is to have a good time." He looked into Milton's eyes. "You understand."

"I think so." Milton nodded.

"I'll be going back to the bombers soon."

"And a lot of you fly boys get shot down."

"Exactly." Ted knew Milt would understand.

"I already told her not to get interested in anyone, not till this thing is over."

"Good advice." Ted relaxed. His gaze roamed the street. "Want a cup of coffee?"

Milton smiled. "You were the one worried about being seen with a non-com."

"Oh, that was just to avoid the MPs. I'm not really supposed to be in London." He flashed the mischievous grin that usually kept him out of trouble.

Milton shook his head but continued to smile. "Okay. I guess we can act like we're old friends."

Ted settled his cap back on his head as they walked toward a small café.

"Tell me about this friend of Katherine's."

"Madge? Oh, she's a great girl."

Inside they ordered coffee and settled at a table. "She could be a pin-up girl," Ted continued.

"Madge?" Milton's surprise meant he'd never seen Madge, not even a picture.

"Yeah. Blonde and built." Ted used his hands to trace her curves in the air. "You know the type."

Milton grinned before taking a sip of his coffee. "You like her?" He watched Ted's reaction.

"Yeah. Sure. Madge's swell." He caught Milton's gaze. "She knows the score. Strictly out for a good time, no strings."

"Unlike Katherine?"

"Kitty's the serious type. You know." Ted took a big gulp of the hot liquid.

"Yeah, I know. She's my sister."

"And you don't want her to get hurt."

Milton leaned back. "You want me to talk to her—about you." He didn't ask. He just made the statement.

Ted nodded.

"Sure. I'll talk to her. Tell her you're a swell guy but not to get mixed up with you—or anyone—till after the war. How's that?"

"That's good."

Ted was relieved. He'd accomplished his mission.

When they parted with a hand shake and "good luck" wishes, he told himself he didn't have to worry about Kitty. She'd listen to her brother.

Ted was no good for her. It was just their history and the glamour of the uniform that made her think she was interested. In the long run, she'd be glad she didn't get involved.

But he already regretted losing her. Losing the opportunity to get to know her, to find out if they had a chance together.

*No. You've made up your mind and that's that.*

\*\*\*\*

Ted got off the train, leaving behind some flyers he'd met onboard who were on their way to the airfield at Allford, his former post. He headed toward the lobby.

The local train back to Ellingham wouldn't leave for a while yet.

He wandered around the station and finally asked an Englishman if there was someplace nearby that he could get some fish 'n' chips before he caught his next train. The man gave him directions to a shop not far away.

Ted got back to the station just in time to jump onto the already moving train. Balancing the fish 'n' chips wrapped in newspaper in one hand and his small musette bag in the other, he made his way down the narrow corridor that ran down one side of the English trains. He peered into each compartment hoping to find a seat where he could eat in peace.

In one crowded compartment he saw a familiar uniform. A WAC sat staring out the window. It was Kitty. His heart raced at the sight of her, then his head kicked in telling him to get away fast before she saw him.

At that moment, a portly gentleman tried to get by him. Ted raised his arms and pressed his back against the compartment door so the man could squeeze by. Ted turned for one last glance at Kitty before he moved on and found her looking at him. Their gazes locked for a few seconds. Recognition blossomed in her face. He forced himself to smile and gave a little wave with his bag, then made his escape down the corridor.

Damn. He hadn't wanted to see her so soon. He needed time to prepare, to steel himself against what he felt for her. He couldn't deny his feelings to himself. But it wouldn't work and he had to convince himself of that fact. He had to come up with a strategy for dealing with her because he knew he would see her again. With both of them assigned to headquarters, it was inevitable.

A couple of doors down he found some airmen from the Ellingham air field. When they saw the fish 'n' chips, they pulled him into the compartment, squeezing together to make room.

Ted laughed at them and gladly shared his food. Right now he needed the camaraderie more than the nourishment.

\*\*\*\*

He hadn't ignored her. He'd smiled and waved. But no more. She hated to admit she wanted more, but she did. She'd wanted him to sit beside her the entire trip laughing and sharing small talk.

She had to stop fantasizing. He wasn't someone she imagined. He was real. And he didn't want to spend more time with her. That was pretty clear.

Her brother had tried to console her by telling her Ted wasn't the kind of guy she needed. And she wasn't the kind of girl he wanted to date.

Milton had always told her that she was the type who held back and waited till one day she would fall hard for someone. Trouble was she could fall for the wrong man. Milton had reminded her of Howard, the boy she'd fallen for in college only to find out he just wanted some "affection" before he reported for duty after being drafted. She'd been devastated when he dumped her. He'd used her and thrown her away.

It was cruel of Milton to bring up Howard. Milton was the only one she'd told the truth about her little "affair." But she knew he was just using it to warn her off Ted.

Although Milton admitted he liked Ted, a lot. They'd made friends very quickly, despite the fact they were, in her opinion, very different. And neither minded the difference in rank. It was like they had been old friends, and the Army wasn't going to separate them with their arbitrary rules. It fascinated her how men could size each other up and almost instantly become friends.

She, on the other hand, had always had trouble getting to know people, men or women, but especially men. Madge told her she had to watch for the signals. But Kitty struggled to see them. It was much easier to understand the characters in books that to read real people.

Kitty hoped to see Ted when the train arrived at Ellingham, but somehow he eluded her. Probably on purpose. Just as he'd disappeared in London.

Back at her quarters, the other girls were anxious to hear about her trip to London. She told them about her brother and the sights they'd seen, careful to avoid any mention of Ted. She reminded them all that the general thought Milton was her fiancé, so they were not to let the cat out of the bag or she would be in trouble. A couple of the girls commented on how silly she was being, but Madge spoke up to defend Kitty.

"You don't have to work for that man. He's been chasing poor Kitty ever since we got here. If he'll back off because he thinks she's engaged, then let him think it. No harm done and just maybe you'll be saving a friend."

Kitty thanked Madge for her support. Later they spoke privately.

"I dread facing him tomorrow."

"Why? Just tell him about the trip, like you told the girls, only leave out the brother part."

"I'm just not any good at lying. Somehow I always get caught."

"Well, I've done plenty of it in my time. Just stick as close to the truth as you can. That makes it easier."

Kitty was amazed at how much Madge's comment sounded like what Ted had said. Was that why they hit it off so well? Because they were a lot alike?

"What?" Madge interrupted her thoughts.

"Oh, I was just thinking of something Milton said." Kitty flashed her friend a smile. "He couldn't believe his little sister had told a lie. I've always been extremely truthful."

"Yeah, I've noticed that about you. Gets you in trouble sometimes. I hope I've taught you something about how to get along, in the Army, and with men."

"Yes." Kitty nodded. "Yes, you have."

Chapter Eighteen

*Somewhere in England*
*May 16, 1944*
*Dear Mother and Father,*
*I just got back from the big city where I spent some time with Milton. We acted like tourists and saw the sights. The palace, the tower, the bridge. Can't say where but you can guess. Milton is the same ol' brother but better. He is healthy and happy. I met some of his friends, too. Nice boys. He took me to the theater where we saw a comedy. Very entertaining. We sat in the park and talked and talked. My leave went too fast, and now I am back at the* "castle." *Tomorrow morning I'll be back at work. Just wanted to send you a quick letter to let you know I saw Milton, and he's okay.*
*Your loving daughter,*
*Katherine*
\*\*\*\*

Thirst for a beer sent Ted toward the Officers' Club. As he approached, he spotted Madge on the patio talking to two of his fellow officers. He stopped and watched them.

Much as he wanted to ignore her, his male instincts kept his eyes glued to the beauty. The perfectly stacked body, the pretty face, and blonde hair made a package that would stop any man in his tracks.

He watched her work the men. She didn't just talk

to them. She batted those big blue eyes, flashed intimate glances, moved just enough to get a guy's attention. Yet she kept them at bay, kept enough distance to maintain an air of aloofness. Like a piece of candy dangling just out of reach. He chuckled to himself. That was Madge. He could still admire her even if she wasn't his anymore.

Another girl came to mind—Kitty. She had her own kind of beauty. He'd carried the image of his angel's sweet, smiling face with him always. Now hundreds of images of a real angel crowded his thoughts. From her disapproving frown, to her melodic laughter, to the quirky raised eyebrow when she didn't quite get his joke, to the loving expression she shared with her brother, they filled his heart with a warmth he couldn't explain.

"Ted! You're back." Madge ran toward him, her face bright with excitement.

Dammit. He should have escaped when he had the chance.

She attempted to embrace him, but he resisted. He'd broken up with her, he reminded himself. So hands off. He stepped back, out of her clutches before speaking.

"Hi," he said, trying to be friendly, yet distant.

"I missed you," she cooed.

She curled her arm around his and waved "bye" to the other officers. When he saw them watching, he didn't resist her touch, didn't want to make a scene.

"Where'd you go?" she asked, pulling him away from the club.

"London," he tried to sound casual. "Only don't tell anyone. I was supposed to be in Norwich."

"Why'd you go to London?"

"Have you ever been to Norwich? Believe me, it's really dull compared to London."

She laughed. He took the opportunity to pull his arm free.

"I had to get away. This investigation thing was getting to me."

"You poor dear."

She always knew what to say. How to comfort a guy when he was down. But somehow this time she sounded a little insincere, as if she said the same thing to whoever she was with.

"I talked to some fellows stationed at Allsford. Really made me homesick for flying."

"But you're safer here. Besides they won't let you fly while they're doing all this investigating."

"I know. But that doesn't mean I don't want to be there." He stopped and turned to face her. "I want to get back in this fight. Not sit here on the sidelines."

"What's the matter with you?" She frowned at him. "You aren't going to get all serious on me, are you?"

"I don't know." He sighed. "I guess I've been doing too much thinking lately."

They continued to walk aimlessly in the fading sunlight.

"What else did you do in London?"

He wasn't sure what to say. What had Kitty told her? Better play it straight. "I did some sightseeing. Buckingham Palace, Tower of London, that sort of thing."

"Oh." She nodded, obviously expecting more.

"I ran into Kitty. Met her brother. He's a swell guy. In the infantry. Met some of his buddies." He glanced her way to see her reaction. She was quiet. Too quiet. "I heard a rumor before I left that she was engaged. Turns out she went to London to meet her brother, not her fiancé. Did you know that?"

She nodded, still looking straight ahead, her expression unreadable. "Oh, yeah. I knew about that. The general's been giving her a run for her money, so she told him she was engaged to get him to back off."

Ted acted surprised and a little outraged. "Some men can't handle you gals being around all the time, like you're all fair game. You'd think a general would be more of a gentleman."

Madge stopped and narrowed her gaze. "Where did you run into Kitty and her brother?"

He controlled his expression, breathed normally, gave nothing away. He didn't want to tell her of his interest in Kitty. After all, nothing would come of it. "As a matter of fact it was in the blackout. Darker than dark. You know how it gets on cloudy nights. Anyway, I was on the street and bumped into these people in the dark, and I recognized Kitty's voice. At least I thought it was her. Anyway, they had been to the theater."

"Kitty and her brother?"

"And an English girl, can't remember her name. Betty, maybe. And a buddy of Milt's, Ade."

"Kitty was with a friend of her brother's?"

"Yeah. Nice fellow."

She didn't say anymore. Just nodded and walked on in silence. Ted relaxed a little. She was satisfied. No need to tell her any more. After all she didn't need to know he spent the whole next day with them. Or that he enjoyed it so much. Too much.

They found themselves by the castle with the moon

rising in a dusky gray sky.

"Let's go around to the garden," she suggested. "There's a gazebo tucked away that's the perfect place to be alone."

The image of Kitty sitting across from him in that gazebo gave him an unfamiliar and uncomfortable feeling. If he didn't know better, he'd think he was afraid. Of what? Memories? Of a dream coming to life? And a life he'd never have.

"Look, Madge. Like I told you before, we need to take a break. I like you, and all that, but you need to date other guys. And I need to move on."

"What if I don't want to date other guys?"

He realized he needed to be more blunt. "I'm sorry, but I don't want to see you anymore. Understand?"

"No. I don't."

Hurt showed in her face, and guilt soured in his gut. She deserved better, but she wasn't going to get it. Not from him. "I wanted to do this nicely. Looks like you aren't going to let me. So here it is. We're done. As soon as I can, I'm going back to flying, and I'll be out of your life for good. Now do you understand."

She just stared at him. Silence wasn't Madge's thing.

He turned around and walked away from her, half expecting her to run after him. But she didn't.

Setting a steady, but aggressive pace, he strode toward his quarters. He'd call it an early night. After all, he had to report early in the morning—to the Red Cross ladies. His new assignment.

They had a meeting scheduled with some local citizens to organize some dances and social events for the Americans at the nearby airfields. Our boys needed some entertainment and the Red Cross matrons thought he could convince the local ladies groups to sponsor the events. He was dubious. But he'd play nice. He'd turn on his charm and do what he could.

Then maybe when this damn investigation was over, Colonel Snyder would let him go back to where he belonged. Flying bombers over Germany.

****

"You didn't tell me you saw Ted in London."

Madge didn't sound happy. Had she seen Ted? What did he tell her?

"Yes, we ran into him—literally. In the blackout." Maybe that was enough.

"He said you had a date with one of Milton's friends."

"Yes." Kitty's mouth went dry. She bent down to remove her shoe and hoped Madge didn't notice her hand shaking.

"Go on. Tell me. Was he cute?"

Kitty still avoided eye contact. Let Madge think her reaction was to Ade. It wasn't really lying, was it? "Oh, I guess. Well, yes. He was very nice."

"Where'd you go? Tell me everything."

"There isn't much to tell." She glanced up to judge Madge's reaction. "We went to dinner and to the theater."

"And…"

Madge clearly expected more, but there wasn't any more to tell. "And that's all…really. We ran into Lieutenant Kruger in the blackout. It's really hard to get around in the dark in a city like that."

Madge shook her head. "You've got to learn to take advantage of the situation. When you don't have much time then you have to make the most of things."

"Milton was there. What was I supposed to do?"

"Oh, sweetie. You're right. I guess a brother would cramp your style, even for me." She laughed. "Sure wish I could go to London. I'd have a great ol' time."

"I'm sure you would."

Madge gathered her things for the trek to the showers. "Ted said he liked your brother."

"Yes. They hit it off. Neither of them minded the Officer-Enlisted man difference."

"That was very democratic of your brother." Madge waved as she left the hut.

Kitty sank onto her cot. How had she gotten to be such a liar? Weren't lies of omission just as bad as outright lies? And why did she feel the need to lie about Ted? Nothing had happened between them. The truth was she wanted something to happen. She'd spent a whole day with him, and even though they'd never really been alone, she had wanted more. And he'd pulled away.

Not the kind of man you should get involved with, Milton had said. Not a good time to get interested in anyone, with the war and all.

Her brother was right, of course. And she was just dreaming again. Fantasizing about something that would never be. Her silly notion of fate bringing them together, again. That didn't mean they were meant to be together. It was just a coincidence. And the sooner she accepted that fact, the better.

Madge and several other girls returned from the showers. Madge unwrapped the towel from her head and began her nightly routine—pin curls, face cream.

Kitty finished ironing her last blouse and folded it

neatly on the make-shift shelf over her bed. As soon as she finished, Sally commandeered the ironing board.

"Did Ted tell you why he went to London?"

Madge couldn't let it go. She had to ask questions.

"No." It was the simplest answer.

"Did he say anything about the investigation?"

"He talked to Milton about it."

"He's worried. I can tell." Madge focused on getting a pin curl in place.

Kitty watched her friend, watched her face change expressions, watched the frown grow into a scowl. Madge turned to face her.

"When did he talk to Milton about it? In the blackout?"

That old sinking feeling came over Kitty, the way she always felt when she was caught in a lie. She fought it. Drew in a deep breath and told the truth, as if she had never tried to deceive.

"Ted didn't have a place to stay, so Milton let him stay in his room."

"With the enlisted men?"

Kitty nodded. "He said they sneaked him in."

Madge narrowed her eyes as if she didn't believe her.

"I told you...they hit it off. Got to talking."

"What else haven't you told me?"

Kitty couldn't meet her gaze. What should she say to her? The whole thing had been innocent. Then why did she feel so guilty?

"Well?"

"Well...he went sight-seeing with us. Just tagged along. We went to Buckingham Palace and the Tower of London, Parliament..."

"Spare me the tour. Why did Ted go with you? I thought he hung out with some flyers he knew from some air base near here."

"He probably did. I don't know what he did after he left us."

Madge leaned closer and cocked her head slightly. She studied Kitty for a few seconds before her brows arched and her lips parted. "You like him, don't you?"

Kitty could hear the accusation in her voice. It made her want to crawl under the bed. But there was no escape. She had to face her friend.

"Of course, I like him. He's a friend." She looked up and met Madge's hard stare. "Your boyfriend."

"Yeah, he was my boyfriend. Now he says he doesn't want to see me anymore." Her eyes narrowed, brows furrowed. "You'd like him to be your boyfriend. Wouldn't you?"

"No, of course not." But she could feel the lie written all over her face. She did want Ted, and no words could erase that.

Madge jumped to her feet. "I knew it. Knew something was off. The way he acted." Her voice grew louder. Girls nearby stopped to listen.

"You're lying to me," Madge continued. Her finger wagged in Kitty's face. "You stay away from him, you hear me. He's mine." She shook her head back and forth. "And if you think some wimpy little thing like you can take him away from me, you've got another think coming."

Tears welled in Kitty's eyes. "No, no. It's not like that. I don't want to take him away from you." She swiped her cheek to keep the tears from falling. She couldn't lose Madge. "You're right. He couldn't be interested in anyone like me. He's not. Really. He barely spoke to me on the train coming back."

"You were on the train together?" Fury blazed on Madge's face.

Kitty cringed, afraid her friend was going to hit her. "I just saw him, on the train. We weren't 'together'."

Madge stood there working her mouth as if trying to decide what to say next. Her mood slowly cooled. When she finally spoke, her words were dead serious. "Just stay away from him."

Kitty nodded, unable to trust herself to speak.

Madge sat back down and returned her attention to her damp hair.

The other girls, shocked by the angry exchange, whispered to each other as they resumed their activities.

Meekly, quietly, Kitty gathered her things and headed to the showers, grateful for an excuse to leave.

\*\*\*\*

The previous night's confrontation with Madge eroded Kitty's confidence in her ability to face General Lake. She wasn't sure she could pull it off. Her lies had always been so transparent.

She gave herself the same pep talk she'd rehearsed in her head since leaving London. She just had to remember to tell the truth. And avoid the one, little technicality, that Milton was her brother, not her fiancé. She also had to remember she'd given General Lake a fake last name. After all she and her fiancé couldn't have the same last name. So she'd used her mother's maiden name, Kerr, instead of Greenlee.

What a mess!

She'd lucked out yesterday. When she reported for

duty, General Lake had gone off to a meeting at Eighth Air Force headquarters. But he'd be back today. No more reprieves.

"Good morning," she greeted her boss with the brightest smile she could muster.

"Ah. Good morning, Greenlee. How was your leave?"

"Oh, wonderful, sir."

"Was your young man happy to see you?"

"Oh, yes, sir," she gushed, hoping he would be satisfied.

"Come in and bring your book," he ordered as he entered his office.

"Yes, sir," she agreed. Maybe that was the end of it. On to business.

The general settled himself behind his desk and lit a cigarette. Kitty looked around for his ashtray and moved it close to his right hand before taking her seat. He took a deep draught on the cigarette, leaned his head back, and blew out the smoke before placing the cigarette in the ash tray.

"Okay, let's get started. Send a memo to my staff."

Kitty jotted down his words as he rattled off instructions and explanations from his meeting at Air Force headquarters. When he finished, he gave her his standard instructions, "Type that up and let me read it before you send it out."

"Yes, sir." Kitty stood to leave.

"That fellow of yours, in the infantry didn't you say?"

"Yes, sir. First Infantry."

"Did he tell you anything about what they're up to?"

"Sir?"

"What's his outfit training for? Did he say?"

"Oh, no, sir. He couldn't tell me anything about that."

"Yes, of course." He lit another cigarette.

Kitty wanted to leave, but his gaze had her locked in place.

"Did he say anything about an invasion?"

"No, sir. Well," she backtracked, telling herself to tell the truth. "Everybody knows there's going to be an invasion, sometime, but nobody knows the specifics."

"Then he did talk to you about it."

"Just that there'd be one, and he'd probably be in it." She prayed she hadn't said too much. The last thing she wanted to do was to get Milton in trouble.

"Damn generals in SHAEF. They can't see that we could win this thing with bombers. Just bomb the hell out of them. Destroy all their cities. Lay the whole country to waste."

She stood there in shock. What was he talking about?

He came around the desk toward her, waving his cigarette at her. "General Spaatz has the right idea. If they'd just give us enough bombers, we could win this thing and there wouldn't have to be an invasion. Boys like that fellow of yours wouldn't have to get killed. We could get Germany to surrender by destroying their will to go on."

She didn't know what to say. Or even if he expected her to say anything. She just stood there staring at him.

He came so close she could smell the stale cigarette smoke clinging to his uniform. She trembled. Her knees weakened.

Realization softened his face. "Oh, I'm sorry, Greenlee." He turned away. "Forget what I said." He glanced back over his shoulder. "That's an order. Don't repeat any of that." He walked to the window. "Just spouting off. We all have to follow orders, you know. Even if we don't agree with them."

"Yes, sir," she murmured.

"Go ahead. Get that typed up."

She turned and ran for the door, before he said anything else.

Chapter Nineteen

To Ted's relief, the trucks pulled up in front of the English manor house near Hollingswood. He'd been watching for them over half an hour. Their arrival with American girls on board guaranteed the dance would be a success.

Air Force personnel stationed at area bases hadn't shown much interest in the Red Cross soiree until they'd announced the American WACs and nurses would attend. Friendly as the local English girls were, they didn't garner the same reaction as real American women.

Several eager airmen greeted the girls and helped them climb down from the back of the trucks. Although they wore uniforms, the skirts couldn't hide long, stocking-covered legs. And neat little hats sat atop their spruced-up hair dos. The girls had gone all out to get dolled-up for the occasion. And from the compliments he heard, he wasn't the only one who appreciated their efforts.

When several airmen gathered around to help one blonde beauty, Ted smiled. Madge always drew attention.

They'd barely seen each other lately, thanks to his new assignment. Days ago he made a point to issue a personal invitation to Captain Weatherby and her WACs. Weatherby had accepted, on the condition of

General Lake's approval.

Madge had been there, and from her reaction to the invitation, he believed she'd go AWOL if that's what it took to go dancing. She'd laid one of her killer smiles on him and had promised to come and bring her friends.

Captain Weatherby came around the side of the truck, and he let out a sigh of relief. All the girls were legit or Weatherby wouldn't have come along.

Madge pushed her way through the airmen to Ted's side.

"You look great!" he told her.

"Thanks, handsome. You don't look so bad yourself."

Ted chuckled when one of the other fellows asked, "What about me?"

"You're cute, too," Madge told him. She leaned closer to the blushing GI. "Save me a dance, okay?"

"Sure." He grinned sheepishly.

"Me, too," a burly ground crewman insisted.

She smiled easily, loving the attention. "You, too," she assured the man.

Madge turned to look back toward the truck.

"Where's Kitty?" she asked.

Ted's breath caught. Was she here? He forced himself to breathe, and as calmly as he could he turned to follow Madge's gaze. He didn't see her. A vague sense of having a weight removed from his chest allowed him to breathe more easily. He had to get hold of himself.

When Madge touched his hand and whispered "There she is," he steeled himself against any reaction before spotting the dark-haired girl with her back to them.

"Looks like she's found someone to talk to," Madge said.

Ted could feel her watching him. She must have figured out that there was something between Kitty and him. He just wasn't sure what it was.

"Kitty's really come out of her shell," Madge commented. "She used to be this shy wallflower who was afraid to talk to men."

Madge looked as if she was trying to judge his reaction to her statement. Unsure where she was going with it, he decided to go along and see. "Yeah, she is more friendly than she used to be."

"How friendly was she in London?" Anger flashed in her eyes.

He'd stepped in it now. Somehow Madge had guessed his growing feelings for Kitty. He had to make a decision—now.

He glowered down at her. "Look, I can be friendly with whoever I want to."

"So you two did get friendly in London."

Ted ran his hand through his hair. "You've got it all wrong. She's a nice girl."

"And I'm not?"

"That's not what I meant, and you know it."

"And you're interested in her. That's why you broke up with me." It wasn't a question.

"Maybe. What of it? You show plenty of interest in other guys."

"And you liked having me on your arm to show off, didn't you?"

He shook his head. "What does that have to do with it?"

"What am I to you? Do you care anything about

me? Or was I just a trophy?"

Her questions and her anger surprised him. Where had all that come from?

Before he could answer her, one of the Red Cross women interrupted them. "Lieutenant Kruger, there's some problem with the music. Would you take care of it?"

"Of course. Right away." He glanced quickly at Madge. "Excuse me."

She nodded, but he could see that she was still upset.

Talk to her later, he told himself, when you figure out what's going on.

In the grand hall the soldier he'd recruited to play the records huddled over the phonograph fiddling with the wires.

"What's the problem?" Ted asked.

"Can't get the thing to work."

"Great. Just great." Ted pushed the youngster out of the way and examined the record player they'd hauled here from headquarters. "Here's the problem. This wire's loose." Ted scanned the people slowly filing into the huge room. "Do you know Charlie Dixon?"

"Yeah, I think so. Tall, dark hair. Works on one of the ground crews."

"That's him. Find him, will you? He's pretty good with electrical stuff."

The boy rounded up Charlie, and within minutes, music filled the room. A few began to dance, then a few more.

"Keep the music going. Like I told you," Ted told the young airman. "That's what they came for, to dance."

"And for the girls."

Ted agreed with the boy. He looked over the crowd. He saw Madge near the door. It appeared several guys were arguing over who would dance with her. From the look on her face, she was loving the attention.

Someone must have won because one of the men led her onto the dance floor.

He'd keep his distance. Let her cool off for a while.

From the sidelines he watched the dancers moving around the floor. As expected, there were more men than women, but there were women, both English and American. That gave the men from the airfields a real boost after having little contact with the opposite sex for so long.

Kitty waltzed by in the arms of a private. She smiled when she saw him. And his pulse raced. Memories of London followed as she moved away. Sweet memories.

He knew he had to dance with her, talk to her. He'd avoided her for the last week. It hadn't been hard to do since he no longer worked in the castle.

He hadn't seen Madge much either. Which was good. He liked Madge a lot. She was fun, full of life. They had a good time together. But that's all it was, a good time.

He couldn't help comparing her to his mother. Madge was nicer, in a way. There toward the end, his mother had gotten pretty belligerent toward his dad. She still wanted to party and have a good time. He'd been broken, unable to cope with life. So she'd started looking for other men to give her what she wanted.

Ted was glad he'd decided to move on, before Madge found someone else. He'd made it clear. He wanted to be free to look elsewhere, free to figure out what this was with Kitty, if anything. Maybe she was just being nice to a guy she felt sorry for.

Captain Weatherby appeared at his side. "Nice dance. We appreciate your inviting us."

Ted gave her his most charming smile. "Thank you for coming." He held out his hand. "Would you care to dance?"

She nodded, barely smiling. He thought he saw the faintest blush as he took her hand and drew her close.

These serious WACs had a hidden undercurrent of emotion. His thoughts drifted from the woman in his arms to another serious female soldier. One he glimpsed in London and wanted the chance to know better.

****

Kitty kept an eye out for Ted. She watched him dance with one woman, then with another. He didn't dance with Madge, though. And she wondered why. Had they really broken up?

In the last few days, Madge had kept her distance. They hadn't really talked in several days. Hard as it was to admit, even to herself, she had avoided Madge. She hated angry confrontations. And Madge made it clear she wasn't happy with Kitty spending time with Ted in London. Even though it had been innocent sight-seeing.

When she decided to come to this dance, Kitty promised herself she would avoid Ted and make up with Madge. After all, Madge was her best friend. Madge was the one who had given her the courage to come to a dance like this, to talk to men, to dance with them, and to relax and enjoy herself. Madge had pushed her into social situations while, at the same time, building up her self-confidence and making her believe in herself. It was a gift she could never repay.

Kitty stood near the refreshment table sipping lemonade. "Have you seen Madge?" she asked Bertie.

"I just saw her going into the Powder Room." Bertie pointed toward the door. "It's down the hall on the left."

Kitty handed her empty cup to Bertie. "Take this. I'm going to talk to Madge."

She turned down several offers to dance as she made her way through the crush of the crowded ballroom. A year ago she would have run in near panic from such a scene.

The deserted hallway provided a relief. She breathed easier in the cool and quiet.

Madge emerged from the Powder Room just as Kitty approached.

"Are you having a good time?" her friend asked.

"Yes. It's a very nice party," Kitty said.

Madge walked past her, and Kitty hurried to stop her before she got away. "Can I talk to you?"

"About what?"

"I haven't seen you dancing with Ted. What's the matter?"

"I don't want to talk about it, not to you anyway."

"Do you still think something went on between Ted and me?"

"What I think is that you're trying to take him away from me."

"I could never do that. You're so pretty, and all the men love you."

"All except Ted." Madge paused and looked at Kitty as if she were examining a bug under a microscope.

"Did he kiss you?"

"No!" Kitty was horrified that Madge would even suggest such a thing.

Still watching her closely, Madge continued, "Make a pass at you?"

"A pass?" She wasn't sure she would recognize one if he had. "I don't think so. He's always joking around. You know Ted." She shook her head. "No. He didn't make any pass. He was just being friendly."

Madge visibly relaxed. "Then I can't figure out what's going on with him. He's been avoiding me. Says he wants me to date other guys."

"He's not happy—with his work, I mean. He and Milton talked about the war. Ted told my brother that he wished he were in the infantry so he could fight instead of doing silly things like organizing this dance."

"Maybe you're right. But I have a feeling I've lost him." She looked sad. Kitty felt sorry for her. Madge cared more about Ted than anyone else she'd dated, at least since Kitty had known her. She feared Madge's heart would be broken if Ted dumped her.

And where did that leave Kitty? Out in the cold. She couldn't come between Madge and Ted. If she showed her interest in Ted, it would only make it harder for Madge.

The two returned to the dance, and soon both were dancing with one GI after another. With the shortage of women, Kitty rarely danced a whole dance without another soldier cutting in.

A particularly awkward sergeant shuffled Kitty

along, while she tried to protect her toes as much as she could. Someone tapped on his shoulder producing a wave of guilty relief. Her aching feet rejoiced.

Eagerly she looked at the soldier who smoothly swept her into his arms.

"Ted," she gasped.

"Don't tell me I scared you." He laughed. "You looked like you needed rescuing. Thought I'd return the favor."

She nodded, unable to speak.

His right hand splayed across her back and pressed her into the warmth of his body, sending tingles up her spine. Her hand rested on his broad shoulder. She followed his lead around the floor as if floating.

Someone bumped into her.

"Sorry about that," she heard him say as he pulled her closer. He squeezed her hand. Their bodies pressed together, the intimacy causing heat to spread upward from the pit of her stomach to the tips of her ears. His smoldering gaze held hers.

They moved as one, turning slowly as if they had been transported to another world, far away from everyone and everything.

A slight breeze brought her back to reality. They were near the French doors that led outside. The song ended, and before she knew what was happening, Ted guided her out onto the terrace.

He inhaled deeply. "Isn't this better? Fresh air. Cooler."

She agreed wondering if he had also sensed the heat between them. She looked up at the night sky. Stars twinkled and a sliver of moon hung far above them.

Guilt at the realization Madge may have been right after all surged through her. Kitty had wanted Ted to notice her, to really see her, and maybe…maybe to want her. But her loyalty to her friend forced her to overcome her selfish desires.

"Did Madge find you?" she asked.

He took her hand and led her further out onto the terrace, away from the windows. "Why do you ask?"

Even in the dim light she could see his frown. "I saw her earlier and she…well, she acted concerned. Did something happen between you two?"

"We…we sort of argued." He tilted his head slightly.

She'd seen him do it before but hadn't figured out what it meant. Madge always said to watch how men moved, and it would tell you what they were thinking. But she still hadn't gotten the hang of it.

The direct method worked best for her. "What about?"

He smiled, that little boy grin of his. "You. At least, my trip to London and my encounter with you."

Her throat tightened. She hadn't expected him to say that. Her mind went blank. She fidgeted with her hands trying to come up with a response.

"I told her there was nothing to it. We just went sight-seeing. But she doesn't believe me. She thinks I'm interested in you."

She wanted to ask him if it was true, but the words stuck in her throat.

He moved closer and slipped his arm around her waist. Part of her wanted to pull away but part of her wanted to lean into him, feel his warmth, his strength.

"Truth is," he whispered, "I'd like to spend some

time with you, get to know you."

"But…" her voice finally returned. "But what about you and Madge?"

"Madge and I both know it's time to move on. Maybe she hasn't accepted it yet, but she knows."

She tried to keep her focus on her friend, yet the sensations radiating through her body from the presence of his arm around her waist disrupted her thoughts. "She's crazy about you," she managed.

"She thinks she is…was." He gazed into the darkness, a thoughtful expression on his handsome face. "Not any more. She doesn't trust me."

"Should she trust you?" He turned and her gaze met his.

"Are we talking about Madge or you?"

"I don't know." She pulled away and took a few steps to put some distance between them. "And before you ask, I don't know what I want either."

"Join the crowd. I'd convinced myself to stay away from you. You're a nice girl, and right now, all I know is that I don't need to get mixed up with any nice girls. I told Milt that." He came toward her, his smile spreading from his lips to the corners of his eyes. "But seeing you tonight, dancing and enjoying yourself, I had to get closer."

The music drifted out through the French doors. He took her right hand in his left, placed his other hand on her waist, pulled her close, and swept her into a waltz. They danced under the stars looking into each other's eyes, floating in a shared dream.

Laughter broke the spell. A man and a woman rushed through the doors, both near hysterics. They stopped abruptly when they saw the dancing couple.

Kitty gasped. It was Madge!

The laughter faded, and Madge's wide-eyed expression changed. Her brow furrowed and her lips drew together in a tight line.

"Sorry if we interrupted something," the soldier quipped.

"Don't worry about it," Ted said, his hand still resting on Kitty's back.

Kitty glanced at him. He watched Madge with an unusually serious expression, as if preparing himself for the onslaught he knew was coming.

Madge approached them, slowly, deliberately. "I knew it," she growled. "I knew something was going on between you two." When neither answered, she continued, "Nothing to say? No lies to feed me?"

"No one lied to you," Ted said calmly.

"Oh, yeah?" Her voice got louder. "What's all this?" She waved her hand toward them. "You're not interested in her?" She took a step toward them and faced Kitty. "And you're not interested in him?"

"Come on, Madge. Let's go." The soldier took her by the arm, but she jerked it away.

"It's over between us, Madge," Ted spoke firmly. "I told you before, but you won't listen."

Madge still stared at Kitty. "You little sneak. You've been going behind my back. Trying to steal him away from me."

"It's not like that," Kitty said. Why couldn't Madge understand?

"Sure it isn't. You weren't satisfied having the general wrapped around your little finger. No. You had to steal my boyfriend, too. Does it feel good, miss goody-two-shoes? Having a general and my lieutenant all to yourself."

"Madge, that's enough." Ted stepped between Madge and Kitty. "Go somewhere and cool off."

She looked up at him, and Kitty could see the pain in her eyes. Her loud insults hid the hurt underneath. Did Ted see it? Did he understand?

Kitty wanted to take Madge in her arms and hug her. But the time wasn't right. Madge would just push her away. Maybe later, after she calmed down.

"Come on, Madge." It was the soldier again. He took a deflated Madge by the shoulders and escorted her back inside.

Kitty stood there beside Ted, totally silent. After a few moments, he sighed and pulled a pack of cigarettes out of his pocket.

"Want one?" he asked, holding the pack out to her.

Kitty shook her head. She avoided eye contact.

He lit himself a cigarette, took a deep drag, and glanced up at the sky. Then he blew out the smoke and turned to her.

"Well, that's that." His cheerful tone sounded forced.

"Yeah. One less friend."

"But you've got me." He leaned down to be at eye level with her, forcing her to meet his gaze. "Don't I count for anything?" His eyes crinkled, his lips curved up so slightly.

"Yes, I guess so." His smile was contagious. "So you're my new friend?"

He nodded, broadening his smile. "Maybe more," he whispered.

She couldn't pull her gaze from his, not even when he reached out and cupped her face in his big hand. He leaned closer. He was going to kiss her. The thought materialized out of nowhere. For once she got it right.

His lips softly touched hers, and all rational thought dissolved. The sensation swept through her. Gently, his mouth covered hers, enveloping her in his presence.

He adjusted the angle of his mouth on hers and increased the pressure. His lips parted with a groan. Her body responded. She wanted this, wanted him. She reached out and found the fabric covering his broad chest. Her eager hands grasped the lapels of his coat as his mouth devoured hers.

She couldn't breathe, couldn't think, didn't want to think, only to feel.

His fingers slid around to hold the back of her head. His mouth retreated just enough to whisper, "Take your hair down. Please."

Eyes wide, she pushed him away and glanced around.

What had she done? What had they done?

Strains of music drifted through the open doors. He hovered nearby, still looking at her with heavy lids and that sensuous, delicious mouth.

She reached up to check the pins in her hair. "We…we better go back in."

Disappointment fluttered across his face. Then he nodded. "Yeah. sure." His chest heaved. "We'll go back."

He ushered her toward the door.

She could kick herself. What was she afraid of? Madge's anger? Or getting hurt again? Maybe she was afraid of what would happen if she ever really let go.

Chapter Twenty

*Eighth Air Force Headquarters*
*3 June 1944*
*2nd Lieutenant T. R. Kruger II:*
 *Proceed immediately to Tate Air Field. Report to commanding officer no later than 12:00, 4 June 1944. Assignment: Bomber Navigator.*
                    *P. E. Snyder, Colonel*
                    *Ops. Officer, 2nd Wing*
                          \*\*\*\*

*June 6, 1944*
   Someone stuck a flashlight in his face and shook him awake. "Lieutenant Kruger. You're flying today. Barker's crew."
   It had been a long time since he heard those words. Memories flooded back as he dragged himself out of bed.
   *Two a.m. Still dark. Dress quickly. Grab my gear and head for the latrine before the Jeep comes to drive us to the mess hall.*
   He easily fell back into the routine.
   Barker. He didn't think he'd met him. Two days wasn't enough time to meet all the pilots. And since he hadn't been assigned to a crew yet, he'd be flying relief.
   Barker's crew turned out to be an experienced crew with a dozen missions under their belt. Knowing they weren't greenhorns, relieved a little of Ted's anxiety.

He met Barker and the other officers at the briefing. It looked like a milk run to him. Just over the coastline into France. That was until the base commander spoke the word—*INVASION*!

Everyone perked up. All ears trained on his every word, all eyes on the map.

"Coast of Normandy... Armada already underway... Targets selected to deter German reinforcement to the invasion beaches."

Ted swelled with pride. What luck! To be part of the invasion. To make history. And to think he'd almost missed it.

"Good luck to you all."

The airmen burst into cheers as the briefing ended. Men filtered out of the crowded room, all grins and back slaps. Ted stayed behind with the other navigators and bombardiers to pick up their charts and flack maps.

As they were leaving a fellow lieutenant stuck his hand out. "I'm Barker's bombardier. Swarz. Glad to have you aboard."

"Thanks. Ted Kruger." They shook hands.

"How many missions have you flown?" Swarz asked.

"Nineteen."

He nodded. "Wish I only had eleven to go." They crawled onto the back of the truck for the ride to the hanger to grab their parachutes before heading to the hardstand.

Eleven. What'd he mean? They rode in silence while Ted mulled it over. Had he misunderstood?

The bombardier hopped off and selected a parachute. Ted did the same.

"What did you mean by eleven? I've only got six

more missions."

The bombardier took the cigarette from between his teeth and cocked his head to one side. "You mean nobody told you?"

"Told me what?"

"That they upped the total to thirty."

"Thirty!" Ted's gut clenched as the number and its meaning sank in. He shook his head back and forth, as if denial would change what he'd just heard.

Swarz patted him on the shoulder. "Sorry, pal. Talk to Barker—when we get to the hardstand."

Ted climbed back on the truck, still in shock.

"Hey, Barker," Swarz called when they reached the plane. "Come 'ere. Kruger wants to talk to you."

The pilot approached. "What is it?"

"Nobody told Kruger here that the total missions went to thirty."

"Yeah. They raised it the week we got here. Boy, were there some pissed off crews."

Ted fought to keep down the heavy breakfast he'd eaten. "I was at headquarters, but I didn't hear anything." He thought back. He'd been reassigned, went to London and when he came back, he was stuck working with the Red Cross. He must have been away from the action when the order came down.

"Come on. Finish the check out and get on board." Barker put his hand on Ted's shoulder. "At least you don't have to face eighteen more like we do."

Ted nodded. The pilot climbed into the plane. Ted handed him the bag containing the charts he'd gotten at the briefing and swung himself up into the B-17. Although this plane was almost new, a shiny B-17 G, once inside the familiar surroundings greeted him like an old friend. He made his way to the navigator's position and settled in.

Barker and Chernoff handled the take off like seasoned veterans. Weather made getting in formation more of a challenge. From Ted's position he could see straight ahead out through the Plexiglas surrounding the bombardier. Off to his right another bomber loomed within spitting distance. Formations were supposed to be tight and steady. Either Barker or the other pilot was having trouble maintaining his position.

On his previous missions, Ted had seen his share of midair collisions. He had trusted Rollins and Hopper with his life because he knew them well. They'd trained together, then they flew nineteen missions together. Each man knew what to expect of the other. This was different.

He didn't know Barker and Chernoff. True they had flown twelve missions. Were they good or just lucky? Could he trust them and the rest of the crew with his life? He had no choice, not now.

He forced himself to focus on the charts. He estimated flight time to the target and back would be five and a half hours.

Chernoff did his routine crew check advising they get on oxygen before they reached their cruising altitude of sixteen thousand feet. Ted adjusted his oxygen mask and cleared it so it wouldn't freeze up on him. He'd remembered to wear layers of clothing to be able to survive the below zero temperatures.

Through breaks in the clouds, he saw dozens of ships in the channel below. The invasion force. He wondered how many men would go ashore. How many would die? Milton came to mind.

*He's down there. On one of those ships. Will he survive?*

Bursts of flack greeted them as they reached the French coast. Little black clouds hung in the sky where the shells exploded, directly ahead in their flight path.

Sweat beaded on his forehead. Instinctively his hand went to his hip and leg. Memories of pain flashed through his mind. He closed his eyes trying to block the images.

The plane bounced from a near miss, and Ted fumbled his pencil with his bulky gloves. He'd almost forgotten how to manage pencil and paper in this environment.

Concentrate, he told himself.

Out of the flack, the crew settled in. Ted tried to relax.

*Milk run, remember. An easy one for your first time back.*

Chernoff came on the intercom again. "Keep your eyes peeled for fighters."

\*\*\*\*

When Kitty reported for work on June 6th, she immediately sensed something was going on. Men scurried in and out of General Lake's office. They spoke to each other in subdued but anxious tones.

She went about her normal routine. She'd worked for General Lake long enough to know he would tell her when he needed her to do something or thought she ought to know.

Sally arrived with her usual stack of reports. She eyed the activity then leaned down and whispered, "I suppose you've heard?"

Kitty shook her head, then sat very still until the

two officers who exited General Lake's office were out of earshot.

Leaning close again Sally said the word no one openly spoke of, "Invasion." She nodded her head to emphasize she knew what she was talking about. "It's on."

A thrill surged through Kitty. Finally, the Allies were invading Europe.

Another officer approached, his hands filled with manila folders.

"Got to go," Sally said brightly. She hurried away.

Kitty nodded as the man said, "He's expecting me."

She tried to return to her typing, but images of Milton filled her head. She'd seen newsreels of soldiers rushing onto beaches in North Africa and Italy. This time it was France, and her brother was one of the soldiers. Then she remembered that he'd done this before. But she hadn't. She'd been back home before. It hadn't been real. This was real.

She said a silent prayer for him and for all of the men in harm's way.

*Keep them safe and let us be successful.*

She didn't see the general for over an hour, not until one of the officers stuck his head out and said, "He wants you."

As she entered the office, her eyes immediately went to the map where clusters of pins gathered along the coast of France. She knew without asking that they must represent the invasion.

General Lake dictated a memo and instructed her to return as soon as she had it typed up. Within minutes she was back staring at the map.

Did any of the pins represent the First Infantry? Was Milton part of the invasion force as he said he would be? She knew the answer without asking.

General Lake caught her staring and placed his hand on her shoulder. "Thinking of your young man, are you?"

She nodded. "Is the First Division there?" she boldly asked.

"Don't know. None of that information is available yet." He patted her shoulder. "Right now we have to concentrate on doing *our* job."

Kitty knew he was right. Yet her stomach knotted, and it took all her concentration to keep her hands from shaking. No one had to tell her how important the invasion was. It had to succeed if there was any hope of defeating Hitler. Her brother was there, on one of those beaches. He could be killed. And if he was, how would she know?

All she could do was pray and wait.

Later in the morning when she heard words like "pill box" and "heavy resistance" and references to bombing routes for German reinforcements, she tried to imagine what it must be like for the men on the beaches. She thought of the beach on the Georgia coast where she'd seen ships far out on the horizon. She imagined smaller boats bringing men ashore, soldiers climbing out of the boats in the rough surf and making their way through the water and onto the shore.

Even for her, they would be easy targets. And all she'd ever shot was Milton's .22 rifle. He had taught her to shoot at targets he nailed to a tree. Now the Germans were shooting at him. And on the open water and bare sand, even moving, he wouldn't be that hard to hit, not for men who'd been trained to shoot. She didn't even want to think about machine guns and artillery shells.

Thousands of flights were flown that day. Many planes returned to their bases to get more fuel and ammunition, then departed for a second mission. Fighter squadrons flew multiple sorties.

She prayed for Ted, too. Back with his bomber crews, he would be flying on this day of days, like every other airman who could get aboard a plane.

Memories of that last day, the day he left, flooded back. He'd come running up the stairs all excited. She'd just gotten up from her desk, on her way to get a file for General Lake, when Ted scooped her into his arms and twirled her around.

"I'm off," he'd said. "Assigned to Tate Field." His infectious grin had made her smile, even though his news upset her.

"They cleared you?" she'd asked.

"I guess so. All I know is that I've got my orders to report right away." He stood smiling down at her, and for an instant she'd thought he was going to kiss her. But he didn't. Instead he made a promise.

"I'll write you," he paused and grew serious. "We'll get together…sometime." He'd hugged her. And she'd hugged him, breathing in his masculine scent, imprinting the feel if his strong body against hers.

Then just as quickly as he'd arrived, he was gone, bounding down the stairs and out of her life, again.

Madge had been furious when she found out. Not only was he gone, but he didn't tell her 'good-bye.' Only Kitty. Madge hadn't spoken to her since.

The momentous day went on forever. News was

sparse. Everyone was nervous, yet eerily quiet.

In the late afternoon, the anxiety on some of the faces softened. She heard snatches of conversations outside the general's office. "Men ashore" and "second wave" and "third wave" and "toe hold." No one was confident enough to use the word "success," but confidence grew as reports filtered in.

General Lake's enthusiasm finally broke through as reports from bomber missions and fighter sorties confirmed the importance of air power to the success of the invasion. Despite his theory that bombing alone could defeat the Germans, he voiced his commitment to the Air Force's support of ground troops.

In the days that followed, she heard stories of heavy fighting. The Allied troops, after landing in an area along the French coast called Normandy, moved off the beaches and slowly gained ground inland. Airborne soldiers, reportedly scattered when they dropped, fought in pockets until relieved by the landing force. The only word used to describe casualties was "heavy." That meant lots of dead and wounded.

Kitty prayed almost constantly for Milton's safety.

And she worked. Long hours. Whatever was needed. She typed, took shorthand, delivered coffee, emptied ash trays, compiled reports. She even forced herself to visit the wounded in the hospital, despite her dread of such places. It was all part of her job, she told herself. Part of what she was supposed to do to help win the war.

****

In the dark, with rain drizzling, Kitty slogged along the muddy path to the humid shelter of the Nissen hut that served as home. Exhaustion from the past week of long days, hours in meetings and at the typewriter, weighed heavily on her shoulders. Supper of cold sandwiches and lukewarm tea didn't help.

She shouldn't complain. Milton was somewhere in Normandy, and she bet he would love to have a couple of sandwiches and some lukewarm tea. She prayed he had something to eat and he wasn't sitting out in the rain.

When she got to the hut, most of the girls were getting ready for bed. Showered, clothes ironed and laid out for the next day, they quietly read and wrote letters or painted nails and curled hair.

At her bunk she sank down on the thin mattress, pulled off her shoes, and peeled the damp stockings from her legs. An unfamiliar girl stood by Madge's bed.

She gathered up a friendly smile. "Hi. I'm Kitty."

The girl looked at her kind of funny, then smiled and stuck out her hand. "I'm Charlotte. Most everybody calls me Charlie."

Kitty shook her hand. "Nice to meet you, Charlie." She glanced around. "Which bunk is yours?"

"This one." She sat on Madge's bed.

"But that's Madge's…"

"I know," the girl interrupted her. "Madge and I swapped."

"Swapped? What do you mean?"

"I guess you're the one."

"The one what?"

"She wanted to get away from."

Kitty gasped in surprise, then quickly caught hold of herself and clamped her jaw tight.

*Control yourself. Don't let her see that it upsets you.*

She drew a calming breath and glanced around. Sally and Bertie stood nearby watching. Sally whispered something to Bertie before going to her own cot.

Kitty turned her attention back to Charlie. "I don't understand. When did this happen?"

"Oh, she's been after Captain Weatherby for a week or more. I finally agreed to switch with her. No one else wanted to." She reached and pulled the blanket back so she could crawl under it. "I figured I could put up with anything."

"Thanks," Kitty murmured sarcastically under her breath.

What had Madge told her? That she was an ogre? A man thief? It was crazy. She knew Madge was mad and hurt that Ted dumped her in favor of Kitty. Was Madge mad enough to change quarters just to get away from Kitty?

She sighed in resignation. Ted was gone, transferred back to the bombers. Now Madge had moved to another hut and wouldn't speak to her. She was too tired to think about it all tonight.

She considered trudging back out through the rain to the showers but decided it wasn't worth it. She was bone tired. Her brain was exhausted from dictation and typing. All about the invasion. Men were dying, and Madge was mad over losing her boyfriend. Those men were fighting to save the world. Milton and Ade and all the others on the ground over there fighting the Germans. And Ted. He could be in a bomber somewhere over Europe by morning, in just as much danger.

Kitty undressed and slipped into bed. She refused

to think about Madge. Instead she hoped sleep would swallow her up and obliterate any thoughts of conflict—personal and physical and political.

## Chapter Twenty-One

*June 20, 1944*

Another pre-dawn wake up call. This time the mission was deep into Germany, and the crew he was flying with had only flown three missions. Their first two were flown with other crews to give them some experience and confidence. The third a short flight over the coast of France. Today would be their first long mission on their own.

For Ted it would be number twenty-three. Seven more and he could go home, if he survived.

The young pilot, Bill Webber, was cocky to the point of being arrogant. He listened to no one. At the briefing he acted like the flight deep into enemy territory would be a cake walk, like the flights along the French coast. He'd obviously never flown to Berlin or any other heavily defended German city.

Ted sat back and listened to the younger man's show of bravado. A pity all the experienced crewmen knew the new pilot was scared to death. They'd all seen the act before. All the bragging to hide the fear. In a way it was pathetic. The bad part was that Ted had to fly with the little prick.

The co-pilot, Coppacci, was quieter, comfortable letting Webber be the show-off. His demeanor gave Ted a measure of comfort. He just hoped the guy knew how to fly.

The rest of Webber's crew seemed okay. Green and scared just like they should be. They all had a long day ahead of them.

When the bomber stream crossed the Zuiderzee, heavy flack welcomed them to German-held Europe. Webber's plane, the Blonde Bombshell, flew in the middle of the formation. A position thought to protect new crews until they got the hang of formation flying and fighter attacks. Ted hoped Webber could hold formation through the flack field. A midair collision was just as deadly as the German anti-aircraft fire. And it was a long flight to Germany with lots of flack ahead and almost guaranteed fighter attacks.

Once out of the flack, Ted watched the sky for fighters. When they came, the fighters would cut through the bomber stream like a hot knife through butter. And every gunner on every B-17 waited and watched.

To make matters worse, their promised escort hadn't shown up. He'd flown with no fighter protection before. But Webber's crew hadn't. He could tell from their strained comments.

If the German fighters came, they'd attack the formation head on and scream through the gauntlet of heavily armed B-17s. With thirteen machine guns blasting away from every bomber, you'd think more of their attackers would get shot down. Some would, but most would circle and come at them again and again. Any plane that was hit, that trailed behind, became easy pickin's for the German vultures.

Ted strained to see their position in the formation. He could see the plane ahead through the bombardier's

Plexiglas nose. His view to the right side was partially blocked. Webber's inconsistent speed made it difficult to maintain visual contact with the ship on the left. He willed the little smart mouth at the controls to keep a tight formation. That and their machine guns were their only protection.

And then they came. From ahead and above.

The Blonde Bombshell sat low in the formation, so they were not the first to spot the swarm of specks descending out of the clouds. The warning came when other bombers opened fire. Within seconds the smaller, faster aircraft whizzed toward them, guns blasting.

Webber's crew had never seen a fighter attack, had never experienced the terror, the adrenalin. Machine guns blasted from every position as the ME-109s zoomed by.

Ted fired into the unknown. His limited vision made his gun less effective than the others. Yet every stream of bullets protected them from the experienced fighters who didn't want to get stung by the beast that spewed lead from every direction.

Mercifully the fighters disappeared as quickly as they arrived.

Ted knew why. Flack. So heavy, the sky ahead blackened as the formation approached. They flew straight into the deadly stuff. The fighters stayed out. They would pick up the survivors on the other side, knowing the bombers couldn't avoid it, not if they made it to the target.

The excited comments from the crew during the fighter attack faded into terrified moans as the sense of helplessness settled over them. Just sit and wait to be hit, that's all they could do.

Ted hated this part the most. The helpless feeling as the ship bounced and bumped its way to the target.

The bombardier dropped their load when he saw the planes ahead drop theirs. By the time they reached the target, explosions obscured the ground making identification of it impossible.

"Bombs away," he called.

The plane lurched upward as the bombs fell below.

"Get us out of here," the bombardier called to Webber.

"Jesus! Did you see that?"

"Oh, my God!"

A one-winged bomber slid by just below Ted's window. "Watch for chutes," he ordered.

The bomber turned on its side.

"Two, no, three," someone called.

"There go two more."

"Come on. Get out of there."

Ted couldn't see it. After a few minutes, he asked "How many got out?"

"Five," replied the ball turret gunner. "That's all I saw."

As quickly as it started the flack disappeared. The crew sat in silence, recovering from the ordeal.

Ted thought of Webber. The cocky pilot had grown silent after experiencing both fighters and flack. Maybe he'd grown up some, too.

Just as Ted expected, the fighters returned. On their first pass bullets slammed through the Plexiglas nose barely missing the bombardier.

Ted couldn't remember his name. Guilt constricted his chest. He adjusted his oxygen mask and promised himself he'd find out before they got back to England.

Maybe it was silly. He didn't know the rest of the crew either, but this guy sat right in front of him, and he almost got killed right before his eyes.

The fighters made another pass, and all guns fired at the moving targets.

"*Ughhhh*," came over the intercom.

"Coppacci's hit," Webber screamed.

The ship wavered, back and forth.

*Not good. It takes two to fly this thing.*

"Axel, get up here."

"On my way," the flight engineer replied as he climbed into the cockpit.

"Jesus!"

"Is he dead?"

"No, not yet."

Ted knew something needed to be done, and it needed to be done now.

"Webber, I had flight training. I can help you get us home."

"Who's that?" The pilot's voice shook with a combination of fear and uncertainty.

"Kruger. The navigator."

The plane lurched downward. Ted grabbed his desk to keep from hitting the deck.

"Get up here," squawked Webber.

Ted disconnected his oxygen and grabbed a walk around bottle. He then made his way up to the cockpit just as the flight engineer pulled the co-pilot from his seat. He glanced up at Ted, desperation in his eyes.

Ted helped him get Coppacci's blood covered body out of the way. If the man was alive, he wouldn't be for long.

*Focus*, Ted told himself. *Help get us out of here.*

Sliding into the bloody seat, Ted checked the controls. It had been a long time since he sat in the cockpit, and the co-pilot's position was even less familiar. He looked around to get his bearings and got a glimpse of daylight through a hole just below the side window. That must have been where the shot came through that hit Coppacci.

Webber barked orders. Ted obeyed. Together they stabilized the big bomber, but they'd lost speed. Through the blood-splattered windshield, he saw the bomber stream recede into the distance.

In addition to the wounded co-pilot, two of the four engines were damaged. They'd feathered one, and Ted's gut told him if they didn't shut down the other one it would spin out of control.

"Feathering number four," Ted informed Webber.

"I didn't order that." The younger man still desperately wanted to be in control.

"It's that, or we'll get a prop slung into our side."

"Uh, okay." Webber looked across trying to see the wing on Ted's side.

"Trust me, okay."

Webber was shaking. "We'll never catch up."

"I know." Ted drew a deep breath. "Give me the controls. Relax a minute. Catch your breath."

Webber glanced over, and for a second their gazes met. Ted recognized the terror.

"You've done a hell of a job keeping us in the air," he told the young pilot. "These damn things don't fly themselves." Ted tried to sound light, give the guy some confidence.

Webber didn't reply. Instead he stared straight ahead.

"Check on the crew," Ted suggested, hoping the pilot wouldn't lose it now.

Quietly Webber contacted each crew member. Only one reported a slight injury. Axel reported that they'd lost Coppacci. Webber sighed. Then he looked to Ted as if to ask what to do.

Ted spoke into the intercom, "Wrap him in a blanket or whatever you have. We'll take him back with us."

"Okay," responded Axel.

Ted didn't have to tell the men to watch for fighters. Flying alone at low altitude made them sitting ducks. They could only hope the Germans were busy elsewhere.

Webber resumed the pilot's duties and followed Ted's direction. At least the remaining two engines were on opposite sides, but with reduced power they had lost air speed and altitude. At ten thousand feet they took off their oxygen masks.

He'd have to look at the charts to get them back to base.

"Can you hold it…while I check the charts?"

Webber nodded. He'd gotten himself together.

The bombardier brought Ted the maps he needed. It was awkward working in the co-pilot's seat, but Ted managed to calculate a heading for England that would avoid the heavy flack zones.

He rolled up the maps and stowed them behind his seat. He and Webber changed to the new heading.

"We'll be over water most of the way."

Webber nodded.

"If we have to ditch, that water's cold, even this time of year."

"Okay. Then we won't ditch." The boy forced a grim smile. His cockiness had been replaced with sheer determination. At that moment Ted knew they'd be okay, all of them. Webber had survived the test of fire and come through it intact. He'd grown up and would make a good pilot.

Ted tried to relax. A vision of Kitty emerged from his subconscious. Hovering over him, assuring him he was okay. He still couldn't believe she wasn't an angel watching over him. She was real, flesh and blood, and he wanted to see her, wanted to hold her, wanted to feel that safety in her arms.

The memory of that one perfect kiss kept him going. She may have run away, but she had wanted him as much as he wanted her. As soon as he got leave, he'd see her again. That's why he had to get back. To see her one more time. To tell he how he felt about her. What she meant to him. Even if nothing came of it.

****

A mixed group of airmen gathered at a make-shift basketball court to pass the time and get some exercise. Ted played forward and prided himself in his abilities. He'd been offered a college scholarship, and looking back, he wished he'd taken it instead of heading off to find himself.

"Great job!" one of the guys slapped him on the back at the end of the game.

"What was the final score?" Ted asked, knowing his team had won.

"Forty-seven to twenty-eight," his teammate answered. "And you were the top scorer."

Ted beamed. He was back. "Swell," he commented, not wanting to gloat too much.

"How 'bout a cold beer?" another guy asked.

"Sounds great."

"Not me," Ted responded. "I'm gonna take a shower." He waved to the others and struck out on his own. He'd had enough for one day. Downtime sounded good to him.

After his shower he sat in the hut that served as their barracks with a good hour to kill before supper. He noticed another airman sprawling on his bed writing a letter. It occurred to Ted that he should write to Kitty. She kept popping into his mind. And he had told her he'd write, but unused to letter writing, he'd forgotten all about it. Maybe he should write her now, just a note to let her know how he was doing, that he was thinking about her.

He got up and asked the fellow if he had any extra paper. The man eyed him suspiciously.

"Don't worry. I'll get some and pay you back."

"Okay." The man handed him one sheet of paper.

"Thanks." Ted grabbed a pencil and sat down to write.

The one sheet was plenty since he had no idea what to say. Just that he was thinking of her and that he had adjusted to flying again. It was hard to start because he never wrote letters. Occasionally, he wrote a few lines to his grandparents, just to let them know he was still alive. He couldn't remember when he'd written his mother. Not that she would care. She never bothered to write him.

Guilt crept over him. What little family he had would probably be thrilled to hear from him. Even his mother. She couldn't help being the way she was. Selfish, inconsiderate. Always looking for a good time.

And his grandparents, they'd tried to straighten out a rebellious, angry kid. They'd made him go to school and church. But like his father, he'd disliked their foreign accent, their foreign ways. His friends had looked down at them, and truth be told, so had he. But now, after all he'd seen, he missed them.

He began a letter, not to Kitty, but to his grandparents. He might actually get some mail if he wrote more often. Maybe if he asked, his grandmother would send him some cookies or some of her strudel.

He jotted a few lines, folded the short letter, and returned to the airman to beg for an envelope, again promising to buy some and pay him back. In the morning, he promised himself to stock up on supplies.

And he'd write to Kitty, every day. She'd somehow become a part of his life, not just an imaginary guardian angel. A real girl—fascinating, different, beautiful in her own way, unlike anyone he'd known.

If he survived, he would see her again. He was bound to get leave, if only a few days. Ellingham wasn't that far. He'd call her, arrange to meet her somewhere. It didn't matter where, as long as he saw her again. As long as he could hold her, taste those sweet lips, just once more.

Chapter Twenty-Two

*June 10, 1944*

*Sergeant Greenlee,*

*Your brother asked me to send you this letter he wrote you. He was wounded and is at this moment in a field hospital waiting to be transferred to England. I wish I could tell you more. He is badly wounded but alive. I suspect he is out of the fighting now.*

*Pfc. J. H. Hilton, Medic*

\*\*\*\*

*June 23, 1944*

Kitty's hands shook as she reread the letter for the third time. Milton. Dear sweet Milton. Wounded.

Maybe it wasn't that serious. What did "badly wounded" mean anyway? Had he lost a leg? An arm? Her thoughts darted from one image to another. Milton in bandages on a stretcher begging for water. A hospital, like the one here at headquarters, with beds lined up in rows in the little Nissen huts. Milton as she'd last seen him, smiling, confident, strong.

She could see her mother dissolving in tears when she read the telegram. Her father, stoic and silent, would remain strong. Both her parents had such great plans for their oldest son. He would take over the family business, after years of working at his father's side. He would be a leader in the community, the church, the lodge. He would marry a beautiful, capable, young woman who would take her place in local society. Would Milton return home a hero? Or a broken man? A cripple? Would he be destroyed by his wounds?

Tears slipped from her eyes and rolled down her cheeks. She swiped them away and gritted her teeth. She wouldn't be some helpless female who cried over everything. *He is alive*, she reminded herself. *Alive.*

"Waiting to be transferred to England." She read the words again. Her thoughts raced.

Where did the infantry treat their wounded? Did they bring them from France on ships? On Planes? No air fields had been set up in Normandy. The fighting was too heavy. So they must bring them by ship. But they hadn't taken any ports so how did they get them to the ship? Rowboats? No, silly. Landing craft. That must be how.

June tenth. Almost two weeks ago. Where was he? Who was taking care of him?

Her heart ached. She needed to talk to someone, someone with more information.

The nurses. They'd know about how the wounded were handled. Maybe even know where they would be taken.

Charlie and some other girls returned from their showers and readied for bed. She turned away from them, not wanting them to see her upset.

She forced herself to put the letter away. Grabbing her things, she headed for the showers. Hard as she tried, she couldn't put it out of her mind. With Madge gone, she was all alone. It wasn't that the other girls weren't friendly. They just went about their own routine. Madge had been the only one she'd talked to, confided in. Now there was no one.

Tonight she longed for that camaraderie, longed to share the news with her friend, longed for Madge's comforting words and warm hug.

By the time she returned, the lights were out and everyone was in bed. In the darkness she let the tears flow. For Milton who lay somewhere hurt and alone. For Madge and the loss of their friendship. And even for Ted, the man she'd just begun to know, now far away at some airfield.

****

When Colonel Snyder left General Lake's office, Kitty hopped up and tapped on the office door.

"Come in," came from inside so she turned the knob and went in.

"Sir, may I speak to you a moment?" She tried to make her voice sound strong, confident, though she was anything but.

"I'm pretty busy. Can it wait?" He didn't even look up from the papers on his desk.

"No, sir." Suddenly she panicked, wondering what she should say to him. "I…uh…I just wanted to go over to the hospital. I haven't visited the wounded in a while…and…uh…Captain Weatherby said I should…"

He waved her away impatiently. "Go on, then. Just let me know when you get back."

"Thank you, sir." She turned on her heel and hurried out.

Leaning against the closed door, she took a deep breath to calm herself. She had to think about what she would tell General Lake. She'd told him Milton was her fiancé. Should she tell him her fiancé was wounded? Or should she tell him the truth? And if she did, what would he think of her? And more important, would he give her leave to go see him? If she could find him.

She jotted a note and left it on her desk for anyone who might come looking for her. Then she headed for Captain Weatherby's office downstairs to tell her where she was going. This wasn't the time to get herself caught between the general and the captain.

At the hospital Kitty searched out Lieutenant Rankin, the nurse who'd been friendly to her, unlike most who believed the lieutenant's rank meant they didn't have to speak to non-coms like her.

Lieutenant Rankin was different. She'd been a nurse before the war and put medicine ahead of the Army's caste system.

Kitty eased into Lieutenant Rankin's ward. The antiseptic smell brought instant nausea, but she tamped it down, determined to carry out her mission.

The nurse stood near her little desk reviewing a patient's chart with one of the aids. She looked up when Kitty slipped in the door.

"Sergeant Greenlee, how can we help you?"

"I…uh…I just came to visit with the wounded."

"That's nice of you. There are several in here who'd love someone to talk to."

Kitty's gaze darted around the ward, beds filled with bandaged men, some staring back at her. She fought against the dread of facing men in hospital beds. "While I'm here, if you have a minute, I…uh…want to ask you something."

Lieutenant Rankin studied Kitty, a glimmer of curiosity crossed her face. She returned her attention to the aid. "Go ahead and take care of it," she told him.

He picked up something and headed toward a

patient at the other end of the ward.

Lieutenant Rankin turned her attention back to Kitty. "So what is it you want to know?"

Guilt clenched her gut. She couldn't lie about her motives. She just couldn't. "I really came here to ask you something. But I'll stay and visit, I promise."

"It's okay, Sergeant." Lieutenant Rankin reassured her.

Kitty didn't know what to say. She started to shake. "It's…it's my brother." She managed to get out. She fidgeted with the strap on her bag, then sighed. "He's been wounded."

"I'm sorry to hear that." Lieutenant Rankin's concern was genuine. She raised her hand to get the aide's attention. "I'm going to step outside for a few minutes. Call if you need me." She took Kitty by the arm and led her outside onto the boardwalk that connected the huts.

"Now, what's this about your brother."

Kitty relaxed a little, thankful to be outside and grateful that Lieutenant Rankin would talk to her. "I got a letter saying he was wounded…in Normandy. Where would they take him?"

"Slow down. What outfit's he in?"

"The First Infantry."

"And when was he wounded?"

"The letter said June tenth."

"That's two weeks ago." She looked off into the distance as if she were thinking. Then she turned back to face Kitty. "I can make some inquiries."

"Do you think you can find out where he is?"

"I don't know." She gave Kitty a reassuring smile. "Right after the invasion, we got a request for any nurses or aids we could spare to help with the wounded. I'll start there."

"Oh, thank you so much." Kitty pulled a piece of paper from her pocket and shoved it into the nurse's hand. "Here's his information."

"Don't thank me yet. I haven't found out anything." She patted Kitty on the arm. "You look tired."

Kitty forced a smile. "I didn't sleep much." Truth was she hadn't slept at all. Her mind had raced throughout the night with all sorts of terrible thoughts. She'd tried to force herself to be positive, to not imagine the worst. But the images kept returning. The only way to fight it was to do something, stay busy and find a way to see Milton, to prove to herself that he would be okay. Then she would be able to sleep.

"I'm okay," she assured the nurse.

"Good girl." Lieutenant Rankin slipped her arm around Kitty's shoulder and gave a little squeeze. "Now you go in there and visit with those men. They're bored stiff and chompin' at the bit to get out of here."

"I will. I'll talk to every one of them."

Chapter Twenty-Three

*June 26, 1944*

The boys on the plane were swell. They dropped her off at a field near the hospital, and the pilot ordered one of the grounds crewmen to drive her to the hospital in a jeep. Having a general pulling strings worked wonders.

She waited impatiently for the hospital personnel to decide if she could see Milton. Why should it be so much fuss? After all, she was his sister, and she was in the Army, too.

As she paced, she told herself that they were busy with so many wounded from the fighting in Normandy. The place had an air of bustling activity, mostly medical, so not much time for social niceties.

Finally, an orderly came to get her. He led her down a long corridor and up three flights of stairs. Halfway down another corridor, they stopped at a double doorway.

"Wait here, Sergeant."

She nodded, wrung her hands, tried to calm her labored breathing, not from the stairs but from the excitement. She didn't know what to expect.

Images of her grandfather lying in a hospital bed sent her heart pounding. She'd been twelve, and her father reluctantly agreed she could accompany the family on a visit with his ailing father. He was supposedly better, well enough for the family visit. She remembered how her mother had pushed her forward, forced her to give the old man a hug. He'd smelled of antiseptic and something she imagined was decay. Only moments later, as the older man chastised his son for some infraction, his face had turned red, his eyes had bulged, and he'd clutched his chest. She'd watched him die, so suddenly that no one thought to push her away.

Her mother had become hysterical. Her father turned white and stood speechless. It was Milton who had pulled her away, but not before she heard her uncle ranting at the nurses. He cursed and accused them of causing his father's death. Raved at their incompetence while aids dragged him from the room. She'd sat in the hallway and waited for what seemed like hours with Milton and Suzanne.

Now she stood here, in another hospital hallway, waiting, dreading what waited just inside, fighting back the tears and panic.

The orderly opened the door and motioned for her to come in. He pointed her toward a nurse and left.

Kitty forced a smile. "I'm here to see Sergeant Greenlee, Milton Greenlee. He's my brother." She hoped her voice didn't sound as shaky to the nurse as it did to her.

"I'll take you to him, but first"—she smiled in that sympathetic way they have when they are trying to prepare you for bad news—"you must be prepared. He doesn't look like you remember him."

Kitty's anxiety must have shown on her face because the woman placed her hand on Kitty's arm.

"He's been through a lot…his wounds, surgery. He is in pain, but we cannot give him pain killer due to the head injury. Do you understand?"

Kitty shook her head. "Head injury? What happened to him? Will he be okay?"

"In time. It will take time for his injuries to heal. It will take longer for his psyche to recover."

Kitty turned her head and searched the rows of beds. Which one was he?

The nurse took her arm and led her slowly. "You can only stay a few minutes. He's weak." They passed beds on either side. "Be cheerful. Positive. He needs to believe he will recover." She stopped abruptly. "Do you understand?"

"Yes. I think so," Kitty assured her. But inside she wasn't so sure. She was terrified.

They resumed their slow walk, until they stopped at the foot of a bed. Kitty searched the bandaged head for some reminder of Milton's face. Only one eye, a cheek, a mouth, and part of a chin were visible.

The nurse stepped closer and leaned down. "Sergeant, you have a visitor, and a mighty pretty one, I might add."

Kitty stepped closer. Her whole body shook. She had to get hold of herself, for Milton.

"Hi!" She smiled brightly. "Bet you didn't expect to see me."

No sign of recognition. He stared out into nothingness.

The nurse stepped back and motioned for her to come closer. When she did, she heard a low, moaning sound.

God help me, she prayed.

Leaning down as the nurse had done, Kitty spoke more softly. "What's my big brother gone and done now?"

His eye blinked.

"Got yourself in a mess, I see."

Blinked again. Now he seemed to see her. Maybe he recognized her voice.

"Here I flew all the way here to see you, and you don't even give me a smile."

His lips moved. He tried to speak, but nothing but a moan came out.

The nurse, standing beside her, said, "Give him a sip of water."

Kitty glanced at the small table beside the bed. She picked up the glass half-filled with water and guided the glass straw to his lips.

"Take a sip. Just a little one."

His one eye bore into her as he pursed his chapped lips around the straw and drew in a few drops of water. When he released it, his tongue pushed the straw aside.

"Katherine," he whispered. His lips barely moved.

"Yes, it's me." She blinked back tears. "I had to come check on my big brother."

"Really messed up." He tried to roll his head to one side, but the bandages didn't allow for much movement.

"No. You're going to be okay." She drew in a breath to fight the choking in her throat and willed herself not to cry. "You're alive. That's what counts."

He stared at her face with his one eye. She could see the pain, the desperation, the fear.

"It's gonna take a while for you to recover. But you'll be fine. Good as new. You'll see." She sounded lame, but she took another deep breath and continued. "I was so worried about you. but now…now that I've seen you with my own eyes, well, I know you will be okay."

She touched his arm, then noticed the IV bag hanging above it, its tube attached to his arm. Bandages wrapped around his shoulder and across his midsection. Purple and yellow bruises swirled across his chest and disappeared beneath white gauze. His left arm, encased in plaster, stuck out at an angle, elbow bent, fingers barely visible.

He moved, raised his right arm ever so slightly. His face winced in pain. She grasped the hand he held out. It was cold and clammy, but it grasped tightly.

She squeezed it.

Her cheeks quivered as she forced another smile. "You'll be all right," she whispered. "You just have to be."

He closed his eye. His breath caught. He opened it again.

She thought her heart would explode in her chest. She bent down and kissed his cheek, hoping he didn't see the tear that escaped her hold. She wanted to throw her arms around him and squeeze him so tight. Like she'd done only a few weeks ago. But there was no way to do that with his injuries. So she squeezed his hand again.

When she straightened up, she forced herself to think. Talk to him. Be positive.

"You remember General Lake. Well, I explained everything to him, and he was very nice about it. He even arranged for a plane to fly me here."

She thought she could see a bit of a smile so she continued. "The boys were really very nice. I mean, they had to fly a training mission anyway, so they didn't mind flying here."

He licked his lips.

She grabbed the glass again. "Do you want some more water?"

This time he opened his mouth before the straw got to him, and he took a good strong sip. She set the glass back on the table.

"Tell the folks…" he whispered. "I…I'm sorry."

He closed his eye and frowned. She couldn't tell if he was in physical pain or struggling with expressing his thoughts.

"You don't have anything to be sorry for. You were wounded…but you survived. You're going to be okay."

"Didn't mean to…get so messed up." She could hear the struggle in him. She didn't understand it, but she knew her brother well enough to know something was eating at him.

She rubbed his arm, still holding his hand. "It's okay."

His eye roved to the ceiling. He was far away. Was he back there? In the battle when he got wounded? She wouldn't ask. Much as she wanted to, she wouldn't.

She saw the nurse approaching out of the corner of her eye. She'd tired him out. They would make her leave.

"Milton"—she leaned down close so he could hear her—"Milton, that nice nurse is going to make me leave. I don't want to go, but you need to rest."

He opened his eye and tried to smile.

She kissed his cheek again. "I love you." The tears welled up again. "You rest now, so you can get well."

The nurse tapped her shoulder, and she nodded.

"I'll come back," she whispered before standing upright. She squeezed his hand one more time before laying it gently on the bed.

She hurried away, not looking back. At the door she stopped and waited for the nurse.

"Do you know what happened to him?" She blurted out the question while swiping at the tears running down her cheeks.

The nurse eyed her sternly. Kitty wondered if she would violate some rule by telling her about his injuries.

"It looks like shrapnel to me. Some type of explosion, probably. We don't ever know what happened exactly."

"Thank you." Kitty looked down at her hands, unsure what to do next. "I'll come back...tomorrow."

**** 

The old mattress creaked when she rolled over. She couldn't sleep. Thoughts of Milton kept her awake, kept her brain racing.

How could she tell her parents? What would she tell them? That he's alive? That he would never be the same? Or would he? The nurse said he'd recover, in time. But what did recover mean?

She searched her mind for memories of him before, when they were kids and she had followed him around. The apologetic way he'd look at her when he had to tell her to go home, like he felt sorry for her, and if it was just him, she could come along. Other times he did let her tag along to town to get something for Mother, to the drug store for ice cream sodas, to the creek to catch crawdads. Sometimes he took her into the woods just to walk and explore.

When she turned fourteen, he took her hunting, but she didn't shoot anything. Later, he taught her to shoot, cans and bottles and a home-made bull's-eye. He told her he was proud of her when she hit the target. Her chest had swelled up with pride. He'd smiled at her and she knew he loved her, even if no one else did.

He even stuck up for her when their sisters made fun or criticized. Olivia, especially, disliked her and called her all sorts of names. It was hard to share a room with a younger sister who hated you, for no apparent reason except you had gotten there before her. Suzanne, on the other hand, simply ignored her, wanted nothing to do with Katherine until she needed something done, like ironing her clothes, putting her wardrobe in order, or creating hand-made cards for her many girlfriends. Even when Katherine had gone to help with the baby, Suzanne had bossed her around like a servant.

But it was her mother's frown of disapproval that hurt the worst. No matter what she did, it wasn't good enough for her mother. She couldn't sew to meet her mother's standards, couldn't cook without burning something, couldn't act like the lady Mother expected her to be.

Father only shook his head and ignored her or remarked how she was just like his hated mother-in-law. Kitty would never understand why he disliked Grandmother Kerr so much. Milton said she did something in the past that turned Father against her. And since Katherine favored her maternal grandmother, had the same unruly hair, the same gray eyes, when her father looked at her he saw Grandmother Kerr and got mad. It wasn't fair, but that's how her father was.

She sat up in the bed and wondered what time it was. She turned on the lamp and found her watch on the bedside table. Two a.m. Too early to get up. She switched off the light and stretched out on the creaky bed, knowing she wouldn't sleep.

The image of Milton's bandaged head came to her again. His one eye, his cracked lips, his cold, distant stare. He hadn't even looked like Milton.

She had to go back. She promised. She'd go sit by his bed, if they'd let her. She'd talk to him about back home or maybe she'd read to him. Did they have any books or magazines in that hospital? Maybe she could buy some. She had a little money she'd saved back.

Unable to sleep, at four she got up, bathed, and washed her hair. She'd learned that it took a long time for her hair to dry in the damp English weather. Fortunately, her room had a window that faced the waterfront. Sitting there, letting her hair dry in the breeze, she took a pencil and started drawing on a scrap of paper. She'd taken up drawing as a lonely child in search of something to pass the time. At odd times she'd take it up again, despite the fact she wasn't very good. It gave her a way to express herself.

Milton's bandaged face appeared on the paper. The rough likeness stared back at her. He looked so alone and helpless.

And what had he said. She struggled to remember. He was sorry. Why? For being wounded? For being alive? Or had he seen how upset she was and apologized for upsetting her? That was more like Milton. Dear, sweet Milton, who'd always protected her, encouraged her.

He was the only one in the family who had

encouraged her to join the WAC. She wanted to help the war effort. He was in the army, so she wanted to be, too.

Now she wondered if she had done the right thing. Maybe she should have stayed home. Taught school. Read about all this in the papers.

The tears started again. She didn't try to stop them. It was all right here where no one would see. She could let herself wallow in self-pity. Wallow in her stupidity, her failure, her inability to face her brother again, see him like that.

But she'd promised, so she had to go back. Had to put on her best smile and tell him he would be okay. But would he? Would she?

Would she be able to go on? Go back and take dictation from General Lake? Go back and face the casualty reports now she knew the pain of having someone you loved injured so badly? Did she have what it took to be a soldier…in a war?

Chapter Twenty-Four

Kitty sat in the hotel lobby drawing on the pad she purchased at the little bookstore a few blocks away. The small section of street visible through the window gradually appeared on the paper, keeping her mind focused on the page rather than on the silent telephone.

The operator had said to wait. She had not said how long. Surely she would call back if the call couldn't go through. Surely the long wait meant something good, meant he would be there when the telephone rang.

Her hands began to shake again, so she stopped and looked at her work. Not much of a subject. Old buildings facing a narrow cobblestone street. It could have been a scene from Charles Dickens or Jane Austen. Sometimes she felt like she had gone back in time into some story she'd read. Only she hadn't and this wasn't a story. It was real.

The telephone jangled. She dropped her pencil. It jangled again. For a moment she froze in place, afraid...afraid it was him, and afraid it wasn't.

"Hello." She spoke loud and clear into the mouthpiece.

"Miss Greenlee?" the woman's voice echoed in her ear. "Your call to Lieutenant Kruger has come through."

Kitty let out a breath, then nodded. "Yes. Good."

Her hands shook so that she almost dropped her bag trying to open it. She reached inside and grabbed a fist full of coins.

The voice told her how much to put in.

She forced her brain to think about the coins spread out in front of her. The crazy English money, shillings, pence, ha-pence. One after another she slipped the coins into the slots until the voice said "Go ahead."

"Hello?"

"Hello," Ted sounded odd, like he was shouting from down in a well.

"Ted, is that you?"

"Yes, it's me. What's wrong?"

"*Aughhh*!" The despair flooded out of her.

"Kitty?"

"It's Milton. He's wounded. I'm at the hospital. Oh, Ted, it's awful."

After an empty silence, his voice came through the receiver firm and gentle. "He's alive. That's what's important."

"I know, I know." She paused, unable to speak. She gasped for air, hoping she wouldn't start crying. "I just had to tell someone." Her breath hitched again. "Someone who knows him."

"I'm glad you called me. You scared me to death, you know."

"I'm sorry. Just sitting here, by myself, I had to talk to someone."

"Is he conscious? Can he talk to you?"

"Yes, he can talk a little. He asked about you."

"Do you know what happened?"

"Not really. The nurse says it looks like an explosion." She tried to laugh, but it came out more like a sob. "It was a battle, in Normandy. Lots of explosions."

"Yes. I can only imagine." His voice was soothing, calming.

"What will I tell my parents? His eye. I think he's lost his eye. And his head. All bandaged. Don't know how bad."

"You tell them he's alive. And coming home."

"Yes. They are sending him to another hospital. Tomorrow, I think."

"How long have you been there?"

"Two, no, three days. They don't let me stay very long."

"I can't get away, or I'd come, too."

A sob escaped. She wanted to see him. Wanted his familiar smile. Wanted to feel his arms around her. She didn't want to break down, didn't want to cry.

"When do you have to be back?"

She forced herself to think. "General Lake gave me a week. I'd have to think when…"

"Can you come to Norwich? After they ship Milton out."

"Norwich?"

"It's not far from my base."

It hit her what he was saying. Meet him. In Norwich. After Milton shipped out.

"You can get there by train. I could meet you."

"Yes, I guess I could."

"You don't have to. I just thought we could get together…talk about it. Before you have to go back."

"Yes. I'd like that." A calmness wrapped around her like a warm blanket.

"There's a little hotel, The Cumberland. Not far

from the train station. Take a room there, and I'll meet you."

Too soon he was gone. She'd agreed to meet him—in Norwich.

She raked the remaining coins into her bag, opened the booth's door, and stepped out into the lobby. An old man sat near the window reading a newspaper. The clerk returned to the counter from the back room. All so normal, so calm.

She checked her watch. She should be able to see Milton again today, if she hurried. Afterward she'd go to the train station and check on Norwich. She'd lost all sense of direction on the flight here. She thought she must be on the south coast of England. Norwich was north and east of London, beyond Ellingham. But close enough that she could get back to headquarters in a short time.

Her mind raced as her feet hurried toward the hospital. She had to find out for sure when they would move Milton to the other hospital.

Should she tell Milton where she was going? Would it worry him? Or would he approve? She wasn't sure. He liked Ted, but he'd warned her not to get involved with him.

\*\*\*\*

By the time she reached his floor, she had made her decision. She would not tell Milton that she was going to meet Ted. No need to worry him. Let him believe everything was just fine. She could take care of herself.

She'd already convinced Milton she had General Lake under control. All he wanted was a little female attention, some mothering from a sweet, young thing. She'd managed to avoid any physical contact beyond a pat on the shoulder or a fatherly hug. She could play the game, too. The plane ride here proved she could get what she wanted out of the old bag without compromising her principles. With luck he wouldn't demand more when she returned.

She steeled herself against the onslaught of sights and sounds and terrible smells that emanated from the wards and went in search of her brother or what was left of him.

Milton sat in a day room down the hall from his ward. From the wheel chair, he stared into nothingness, ignoring the activity around him.

Kitty touched his hand. He flinched.

"It's me," she assured him.

He wore a thick cotton robe, half on and half draped over his left side and arm, still encased in a cast. They'd removed the IV tube from his arm. Bandages still covered most of his head.

She grabbed a chair and placed it to one side, the good side, so he could see her without moving his head.

"Glad to see you out of that bed." She tried to sound cheerful.

He didn't reply, but she could tell from his face he heard her and knew who she was.

"I've been doing some sketching." She held up the unfinished street scene. "Remember when I would draw and you would critique them?"

His lips curved up slightly.

"They weren't very good, but you'd encourage me anyway."

"Good," he murmured. "Always good."

"I kept at it out of pure stubbornness." She smiled and put the sketch pad down. "Keeps me busy, out of trouble."

"You don't run and hide anymore." It wasn't a question. It was an observation.

She shook her head and smiled. "Can't run away in the Army."

"You've grown up." His weak, hoarse voice conveyed a sense of pride.

"I guess." She reached out and gently touched his good hand. He turned it over, and his fingers wrapped around hers. Her throat tightened. She fought to contain herself.

He closed his eye, his head leaned back against the high back of the chair. He looked so weak, so fragile. Her strong, muscular brother reduced to a broken man, struggling to survive.

"Can't take care of you anymore." His simple declaration broke her heart.

"You have to take care of yourself right now." She squeezed his hand. "I'm fine. I can take care of myself."

Should she tell him about Ted? That she was going to meet him? How much she wanted to see him? How she felt about him?

Her free hand drew into a fist. No, she'd made that decision, and she'd stick to it.

Milton didn't need to worry about her getting her heart broken. He'd warned her of the danger. Wait till the war's over to fall in love. Do the smart thing and wait.

Her heart hadn't waited. She hadn't expected it. Tried to stop it. Now she wanted to grab hold and never let go.

\*\*\*\*

Instead of going back to his quarters, Ted strode toward the little shack where the weather officer worked. They'd scrubbed the day's mission due to weather. He'd only halfway listened to the rest of the report, but he vaguely remembered that there was a front coming through that could ground them for a week.

He hoped so. Bad weather meant he had a good chance of getting a few days off. A pass to Norwich—to meet Kitty.

Her pain had come through the telephone and twisted his heart. His own sorrow had escaped the tight bounds where he struggled to keep it secure and had threatened to break him. He'd desperately wanted to reach across the miles and comfort her the way he needed comfort. So he'd done the next best thing. He'd asked her to come to him. And through some miracle she had agreed.

The weather officer verified that they would be grounded for a week, maybe ten days. A slow-moving front had blown in off the Atlantic, would hover over England and the continent for an unknown period of time. Not as bad as the storms back in June, but bad enough.

Ted went directly to his commanding officer and easily obtained a pass to Norwich. Then he called the Cumberland and reserved rooms.

Kitty never left his mind. Alone, facing her brother's devastating injuries, she had reached out to him. He'd honor her fragile state, he promised himself, even as he yearned to hold her, to make love to her.

A glimmer of hope glowed deep inside…that she cared for him, that she wanted him to live so they could be together. Ever since his buddies had died, he'd believed the only people who really knew him, who really cared about him, were dead. Did Kitty's call mean that had changed?

*Dear God, could this sweet angel save him— again?*

Chapter Twenty-Five

*Dear Father and Mother,*
*Milton has been wounded. I saw him in the*
*hospital, and he's...*

\*\*\*\*

On a crowded train wasn't the best place to write a letter, though she needed to tell her parents about Milton. She tucked it in her pocket and promised herself she'd finish it later, when she could focus. She didn't want to say too much. Maybe he didn't want them to know how bad it was, not yet anyway. Maybe he needed time to get himself together so he could tell them himself.

She wished she'd asked him what to do. No. He was in no shape to think about it. She had to make her own decisions, use her own judgment.

She'd start it again, tomorrow or when she returned to base.

The older man sitting beside her rose when the train stopped. He pushed his way out of the small compartment. She scooted over to sit by the window and barely noticed when someone else sat down.

"You must be American," the young woman commented.

Kitty turned to face her new traveling companion. "Yes, I am."

"I went out with a Yank, several as a matter of fact,

before the invasion, that is."

The girl reminded Kitty of Betty, Milton's date that long-ago night in London.

"These days there aren't so many left. All of 'em's gone over to France."

"What about the Air Force? They're still here."

"Oh, I don't go out with those fly boys. They's too wild. My friend went out with one, and they got into a fight in a pub. All of 'em got arrested, they did. My friend included. She swore off them fly boys and warned me off 'em, too."

Kitty laughed. "They're not all that bad."

"I went with a Yank sailor once. He was nice. Then his friend told off on him, said he had a wife and kid back home." The girl shook her head. "Gotta watch 'em."

"Yes, you do." Kitty wondered about Ted. She'd never thought about him having someone back in the states. He wasn't the type to settle down for long. The thought worried her. Would he settle down with her, or was she just another in a string of girls?

Did she want him to settle down with her? She'd called him because she was upset. She wanted someone to share her grief, her fears, her concerns. Or did she want more?

Kitty got off the train. She'd been told she'd have to change trains in London, but the station looked different from a few months earlier. When she reached the crowded main lobby, she realized that it must be a different station. She walked around looking for an information booth or someone who could tell her where to wait for her train.

"You look like you could use some help."

Kitty looked up into the friendly face. Tall, dark hair and eyes, a nice smile, and a lieutenant in the USAF.

"I am having a little trouble finding my way. Is there an information booth around somewhere?"

"Tennessee. That's where you're from."

"What?"

"Your accent. I make a study of them. I'm right aren't I?"

Kitty nodded, a little confused.

"Batting a thousand," he bragged. "Stan Applewaite." He offered his hand.

Kitty took it a little reluctantly. "Sergeant Greenlee." Something wasn't right. Alarms sounded in her innermost being. Why? He seemed okay. Polite. But something was off, maybe the way he looked at her.

"Let me take your bag." He reached for her case, and she instinctively pulled back.

"No. Uh…no, thank you. I can carry it." She glanced around to get her bearings.

He put his hand on her shoulder. "Where are you going?"

"I'm looking for someone." The lie came almost automatically.

"I see." He dropped his hand and looked around. "What does he look like?"

Kitty spotted a sign that said "Ladies" and an idea hit her. "I'd better go find my friend." She took a few steps toward the sign. He followed.

"I didn't see anyone get off the train with you." His smug expression said he was pretty sure she was lying.

"Oh, she didn't. She's meeting me here." Kitty

continued to walk toward the ladies' room.

"I'll just wait until you come out." He smiled at her as if he knew her game.

Something snapped inside her. She drew a determined breath and turned to face him. "I suggest that you get lost, sir."

He hadn't expected her fiery anger. But instead of backing off, he stepped closer, like a predator closing in on his prey.

"You're bluffing." His smug smile returned.

She glanced around, desperate to escape this man. A woman dressed in the gray-green tweed of the Women's Volunteer Army came out of the Ladies' Room.

"There you are," Kitty exclaimed as she practically ran to the woman. "I was afraid I'd missed you."

Before she could reply, Kitty threw her free arm around the stranger's shoulder and gave her a hug. "Help me," Kitty whispered.

"Not a chance, sweetie." The woman smiled and returned her hug. Then she turned to another gray-green clad woman behind her. "And Mattie's come, too."

Kitty smiled and nodded at the new face, fully aware the lieutenant was watching. "Good to see you again, Mattie."

The other woman nodded, looking a little confused, as her friend continued the ruse. "Mum'll be so glad to meet you. I've told her so much."

"I'm anxious to meet her, too." Kitty relaxed a little knowing the English women understood her predicament.

Lieutenant Applewate cleared his throat to get their attention.

"Who's your friend?" Mattie eyed the American officer with interest.

"Oh, the lieutenant was just going to help me." She shot him a stern glance. "But that won't be necessary, now that I've found you."

"Come on, Mattie." Kitty's new friend took charge. "We've got to get going. Mum's waiting." She slipped her arm around Kitty's waist and steered her away from the unhappy officer.

As they walked away, Kitty could feel his stare. After turning a corner, she glanced back to make sure he wasn't following them.

"Thank you so much," she told her new friend. "I didn't know what else to do."

"That was quick thinking," she replied. "By the way, I'm Gwen."

"Kitty." She looked back again, still fearing he would follow them.

"I've seen his type before," Gwen offered. "Trolling around for some unsuspecting woman who's all alone. No telling what he had in mind."

"Nothing good, I'm sure."

They were approaching the train platforms.

"Now I have to find the train to Norwich."

"That's where we're going," Mattie spoke up. "At least in that direction. You can sit with us."

Relief washed over her. She blinked back tears that suddenly filled her eyes. "Oh, that would be wonderful."

Sitting in the small compartment with her new English friends, she thought of Madge. How her fellow WAC had coaxed her to be more friendly to men, to talk to strangers, to make friends no matter where she was. Madge had pulled her out of her shell when everything and everyone frightened her. Yet Madge always warned her to trust her gut about people. It confused Kitty at first, but with Madge's persistent tutoring, she'd apparently learned more that she realized.

She had no idea what the lieutenant had been up to, but her sense that something wasn't right had served her well.

She wondered what Madge would think. She missed her friend, missed their talks, her teasing, her advice. How had a man come between them?

\*\*\*\*

At Norwich Kitty made her way to the hotel Ted told her about. To her pleasant surprise he had a room reserved for her.

"Has anyone been here asking for me?" she asked the clerk.

"No, ma'am." The clerk shook her head.

Kitty sighed and picked up her bag. He might not be able to come, she warned herself. She'd go up and rest, then find a place to eat. And then what? Sit alone and wait. The prospect chilled her.

Had she done the right thing—coming here? How would Ted interpret it? Would he think she was pursuing him? Would he comfort her? Or would he take advantage of her like the officer in the train station? No. Ted wasn't like that. He was her friend. And she hoped, someday, he would be more than a friend.

She'd climbed about a third of the way up the stairway when she heard the door open. She turned to look.

"Kitty!" Ted called.

She practically jumped down the stairs and into his arms.

He squeezed her tight, and she reveled in the feeling of being held in strong male arms. Safe and secure, with someone who cared.

Too soon, he pulled away.

"I must have missed you at the station." His boyish grin hinted at something mischievous. "Thought I'd be smart and surprise you. But you got by me somehow."

"I didn't expect you." She looked into his blue eyes, the eyes she vowed to never forget. "You said to wait for you here, so that's what I was going to do."

"Good girl." He pulled himself from her embrace. "Just let me check in, then we'll go find a place to eat and talk."

She watched him as he gave the clerk his name. He'd reserved a separate room. That must mean he didn't expect any more than a friendly visit. Or maybe it meant he wasn't going to push her for more, which was good since she wasn't sure what she wanted from him. For now she was just so happy to see his friendly face.

**** 

"Tell me about Milton," he asked as gently as he could. They'd successfully avoided the subject all through dinner even though it hung there right beneath the surface silently waiting.

Kitty sighed. She looked down to her hands held tightly in her lap. Sadness weighed on her face.

He thought she wasn't going to answer until he saw her draw a deep breath. Her watery eyes met his.

"He's hurt, so bad." She looked down again, as if trying to gather the words. "There was some kind of explosion." She met his gaze. "Artillery, probably. That's what the nurse said." She raised her left hand to the side of her head. "He's lost…" Her voice caught.

"His eye. You said that on the phone."

"Yes." She nodded. "And his head was all bandaged. Fractured skull, lacerations." She hurried to get it out. "And his left shoulder and arm. They're badly damaged."

She closed her eyes, and he wondered if she were imagining what Milton looked like. She drew another deep breath, looked up at Ted, and continued. "He didn't lose his arm, but he can't use it. They said something about multiple breaks and nerve damage."

She reached across the table. He grasped her hand.

"What if he loses his arm? The eye is bad enough, but his arm." She blinked back tears.

His chest tightened. Her pain pierced his heart. He had to say something, do something to help her. "He's alive. His eye or his arm won't matter." He kept his voice strong and steady. Right now that was what she needed, someone to lean on.

"Would it matter to you?"

The question hit him like a slap in the face. He squeezed her hand rather than letting go of it as he wanted to. It was his left hand. A hand and arm he didn't want to do without. Much less an eye. Not wanting her to see how much the thought scared him, he hoped his voice didn't shake with his answer. "I don't know." He met her questioning gaze. "It probably would. Of course, it would. No one wants to have his body shot up. To lose limbs."

Impulsively he got up, went around, and slid into the booth beside her. His arm encircled her shoulders, and she leaned into him. Her body felt so good pressed against him. So right. He wanted to hold her, comfort her, take her pain away.

"Milton will be all right. Just give him time. You saw him at his worst, his weakest."

"He could barely talk. And he would look away, off into nothingness."

"He needs to rest, to recover. After what he went through, you can't expect him to be the same guy he was in London." An image flashed in his mind of Milton's astonishment when Ted donned his sergeant's uniform. Not many would have gone along with Ted's antics.

She looked up at him. "I know that, but..." She looked away again. "But he's my big brother. He always looked out for me. When I saw him in that hospital, it was like he had been crushed, destroyed. Like he wasn't even there. Like he was this invalid I needed to take care of instead of him taking care of me."

"He's hurt. Someone will have to take care of him...for a while. It was good you could go see him, be there for him." Ted realized there was no one who would come to the hospital to see him if he were injured, no one he could count on to be there for him.

He jerked his mind away from such thoughts. He made himself focus on Kitty. She needed him. She was the one hurting.

The walls were closing in, the air thick with emotions. "Let's get out of here," he said.

They stepped out into a steady rain.

"I thought we'd go for a walk, but not in this." He looked down at her. "Back to the hotel?"

When she nodded her agreement, he wrapped his arm around her shoulders and gave the signal. They both leapt from the shelter of the doorway and ran for it.

By the time they reached the hotel, they were both soaking wet. Fortunately, the proprietor had a roaring fire going in the little sitting room off the lobby. Like moths to a flame, the bright fire drew them to it.

Ted took his uniform jacket off and draped it across a chair to dry out. He thought she would do the same. Instead she'd removed her little hat and fussed with her hair. The dampness had it curling out of its pins. She fingered the loose strands back into the tight roll at her nape and reinserted a pin.

"Your hair. That's how I knew it was you."

She turned to face him, a hairpin held between her teeth, her hands busy capturing stray curls. Her wrinkled brow asked the unspoken question.

He stepped closer, grasped her waist, and pulled her toward him. Holding her close, he backed up until he reached a huge wing-backed chair. He sank into it and pulled her down to sit on his knees. Her face reflected her surprise at his actions. She removed the pins from her mouth and stared at him.

"In the pub that day, your hair formed this halo around your head," he told her. "Just the way it did on the beach."

"My hair is awful, especially when it gets wet." She placed her hands on his shoulders and gazed into his eyes.

"No, it's not." He reached up and pulled out a pin she had just replaced.

"Don't." Her hand flew up to stop him.

"Let it down." It came out more of an order than a request, and she frowned in response. He switched to his most enticing voice and pleaded. "Please."

She sat there on his knees, all prim and straight, and stared at him. His throat tightened around the panic rising within him. Had he gone too far? Would she slap his face and leave? Her face was unreadable.

She turned away and watched the flames wrapping themselves around the burning logs. Slowly she raised one hand, then the other. Pins came loose, and her hair tumbled free.

His body relaxed as each curl escaped its bonds. "You should wear it down all the time."

"Not in the Army." She reached over and laid the pins on a nearby table. "I really ought to get it cut, but..." She ran her fingers up the side of her head and out through the ends of the wild mane.

Fascinated, he watched her sensual movements. He wondered if freeing her hair freed her inhibitions. "No. Don't cut it. Don't ever cut it."

"Do you know how much trouble it is trying to keep it up and neat?"

"No." His thoughts centered on running his fingers through the soft cloud, crushing it in his fist, and watching it bounce back when he released it.

She gave him an odd look. "I didn't even think about my hair that day." She paused as memories danced across her face. "I was too busy trying to get you out of the water, up on the sand so the tide wouldn't take you back out."

"I thought you were an angel." Her spell had him again, held him as if suspended in midair.

"You must have been delirious."

"Yeah...I guess." He watched her lips move as she spoke. Soft, full lips.

"Sam, my brother-in-law, wouldn't let me come back out to the beach after I went for help. He made me stay behind and call the doctor...and the sheriff." She stopped talking and looked him in the eye. "That's why I didn't come back, not because I didn't want to."

He couldn't help but laugh at her concern. "It didn't matter. You saved me." And you've been with me ever since. He didn't say the words to her, couldn't. But they were true. She'd been there, watching over him, everywhere he'd been, since that magical, miraculous day.

He pulled her close and wrapped his arms around her. She didn't resist, which pleased him. With her head resting on his shoulder, he pressed his face into her sweet-smelling hair.

It occurred to him she had no idea how beautiful she was or how seductive. Had her brother held her in his arms like this, when she was a child? Did that explain why she so easily accepted his comfort? Was she so innocent that she didn't feel the sexual undertones?

He fought the desire racing through him. He wouldn't take advantage of her, not when she was so vulnerable. He'd made that promise the minute he'd hung up the phone, and he wouldn't break it now. He owed her that much. He owed Milton that much.

Chapter Twenty-Six

She was safe in his arms. Just as she had always been safe with Milton.

Ted had held her in his arms like a brother. Then he'd left her at her door. He didn't push her, didn't try to maneuver her into some other agenda. He offered comfort, a shoulder to lean on, an ear to listen, and assurances that life would go on. That was what she needed.

But part of her wanted more, much more. Not now, not with the images of Milton's battered body so fresh, so painful. But someday.

She couldn't think. Her mind drifted, unable to focus, not on Ted, not on Milton. Just undressing took an enormous amount of energy. Through her clouded thoughts, she recognized exhaustion, bone deep, as if she'd marched for miles. She crawled into the soft bed and fell into oblivion.

When she awoke, the strange place startled her. She sat up in bed and saw her things, her uniform, her shoes, her bag, and remembered she was in Norwich. To meet Ted. She'd slept through the night, with no nightmares, no tossing, for the first time since she'd gotten the letter about Milton. Both refreshed and famished, she dressed hurriedly.

She was still pinning her hair up, when someone knocked.

Ted stood in the hallway carrying a large, black umbrella. "Good morning." He grinned, "At lease technically it's still morning."

Her hand automatically went up to her hair. "I'm sorry. I didn't realize it was so late."

She turned back toward the dresser so she could finish her hair. He followed her into the room and shut the door.

"Would you care to join me for breakfast?" His invitation may have been formal, but when she glanced at him, the smile in his eyes revealed his true, joking nature.

"Yes. I'm starving."

He stepped closer and started pulling pins from her hair.

"What?"

"Leave it down. I like it better that way." She frowned. "Don't worry; there are no WAC officers to chew you out."

"Well, okay," she reluctantly agreed. She pulled out the rest of the pins and ran her fingers through the curls.

They ventured out in search of breakfast, although the restaurants were now serving lunch. The umbrella protected them from the steady rain.

"I can't complain about the weather," he quipped. "If it weren't so bad, I'd be flying."

"How is it?" she asked. "Back flying bombers?"

From the look on his face, he hadn't intended to talk about it. She waited for his response so long she wondered if he would answer her question.

"Pretty much the same, only worse." He forced a laugh, then turned and caught her gaze. "I miss my friends. My crew. Right now I'm flying as a relief navigator, so every time it's with a different bunch of guys." They stopped to check the traffic before darting across the watery street. "Some are okay. Some are...well, let's just say I wouldn't want to fly with them all the time."

They'd reached the small restaurant. He opened the door for her and then turned to take down the dripping umbrella before following her inside.

The place was crowded with military personnel, mostly airmen. He pointed toward a table where three men appeared to be leaving.

Once they settled and ordered, her thoughts returned to what he said about flying.

"It must be frightening. Flying so high, being up there so long."

"Flying's the best part. I love it. If there weren't fighters trying to shoot us down, or flack bursting all around us, or pilots who can't stay in formation, it would be a joy."

She loved his joking, his light-heartedness, but she sensed it covered something deeper. Was it fear?

"How many more missions do you have to fly?"

His jaw clinched, and she watched a frown crease his brow. She knew she shouldn't ask, but something compelled her to plunge deeper.

"I heard before the invasion they increased the requirement to thirty. Do you have many more to fly?" she asked.

"Then the brass upped it to thirty-five." His voice dripped with sarcasm as his fist pounded the table. "Those bastards. They're determined to kill us all." He gritted out the words, struggled to contain the anger coloring his face.

She said nothing. Watched him struggle for control. He sucked in a deep breath and clenched both his fists as if he wanted desperately to hit something. She'd never seen him so upset.

His eyes flashed to catch hers. "Every mission we lose a few more," he muttered.

She nodded, trying to be understanding, yet not knowing what to say.

He looked away. He pushed his fists into his lap.

The waitress appeared carrying a tray. They silently watched as she placed the plates in front of each of them. Both stared at the unappetizing fare.

"I'm sorry." He paused as he picked up his fork. "Six more." He spat the words and then shoved a forkful of potatoes into his mouth.

"That's not many." She tried to sound positive. Doing the math in her head, she figured he'd flown twenty-nine missions.

He laughed, but it wasn't genuine. "Yeah, but one is too many if it's your last."

"You'll make it," she instinctively assured him. "I know you will."

"Yeah." He smiled at her, and this time he meant it. "Maybe I'll be lucky. Like Milton."

His comment stung, but he was right. Milton was alive. He would go home. She forced herself to return his smile. War wasn't at all what she'd expected it to be. It caused more pain than she could have imagined just a few months ago.

Despite the rain, they walked along the streets, less crowded due to the dampness. Ted got her to talk about her family. As she did, the distance of both time and space gave her a perspective she'd never had before. She realized they were people with faults and fears, strengths and weaknesses.

As she explained to Ted how her grandfather had died and left her grandmother to raise their three daughters alone, she saw how it affected her own family and her aunts' families. Kitty's mother had won the prize when she married a well-to-do businessman. Then she'd worked hard to achieve a high social status in the community. She expected her daughters to do the same—marry well and take their place in society.

Kitty's aunts had married, but neither as well as her mother. One married a farmer who'd gotten deeply in debt during the depression. Her other aunt struggled to survive and raise her children after the tragic death of her husband soon after the Great War.

That's why her mother had pushed her daughters to make a good marriage, to pick someone who would be successful.

"Mother was always trying to fix Milton up with a girl from a good family." She smiled at the memory of her brother's response. "Somehow he managed to avoid any entanglements without breaking Mother's heart." She paused. "I always admired him for that, for not hurting her feelings. Something I never could manage. Even though I didn't intend to hurt her or make her mad. I just couldn't help it."

"She tried to fix you up?"

"Oh, heavens yes. And you wouldn't believe the ones she picked for me."

"Were they that bad?"

"Horrible." She laughed. "Well, maybe not. Most of them are in uniform now. I've probably danced with boys just like them and enjoyed myself."

Ted smiled. "Yes, it's amazing what a uniform will do." His tone was light, but there was something serious lurking beneath the surface.

She looked at him and tried to imagine him without a uniform. He'd be handsome no matter what he wore. "On that ship, you were a merchant marine?"

"Yes," he responded and cocked his head as if trying to figure out where she was going with her question.

"But you didn't join the Navy."

He expelled a breath, as if relieved, and looked away. "I didn't want to have another ship sunk under me."

"Did it bother you when you came over to England? The ocean, I mean."

He laughed then, a big hearty laugh. "No. Because I flew."

Astonished she repeated, "You flew?"

He nodded. "Yes."

"In a bomber?"

"Yes. How do you think all those planes got here?"

She shook her head. "I don't know. I never really thought about it."

His arm slipped around her waist, and he hugged her. A friendly, brotherly hug. And in that instant. she knew she wanted more. She didn't want him to take Milton's place. She wanted something very different from Ted.

Did he sense it too? The change. The tension in her body. The longing.

Their gazes met and locked. They were close, beneath the umbrella, a curtain of rain surrounding them in a sort of blanket or cocoon. He leaned down and she stretched to meet him.

Their lips touched, ever so lightly. Once, then again. He tugged her closer, and her arms wrapped around his muscled warmth.

****

He held her in his arms, knowing he had to stop. He couldn't do this to her, not now, not when she was so vulnerable. He forced himself to push her away. Drawing a deep breath, he linked his arm with hers and looked around. A theater marquee caught his eye.

"How 'bout we see a movie? Get out of this rain."

"Okay." Her quiet agreement held a hint of uncertainty.

He pulled her toward the theater.

"The first feature's already started," the ticket girl warned them.

"That's okay," Ted told her as he paid for the tickets. "We just want to get out of the rain for a while."

He led Kitty inside the lobby. "You want something?" He gestured toward the small concession stand.

"No." She shook her head.

He hung the umbrella on a rack in the lobby and placed his hand on her back to direct her toward the theater. They stepped through the curtains and stood for a moment to allow their eyes to adjust to the darkness.

"Over here," he whispered as he pointed toward an empty row near the back and underneath the balcony. There weren't many people in the theater. A few couples scattered around. A group of soldiers half-way up. Some girls a couple of rows behind them.

The film was American, a western with Joel

McCrea as the famous frontiersman, Buffalo Bill. The colorful scenery provided a much needed distraction from the dreary weather outside.

Kitty sat in silence watching the movie. Ted wondered what she was thinking. About the action on the screen or about the kiss they'd shared. He had to figure out what he was doing. How to contain his raging desire. He had no future, and Kitty deserved a future. She deserved a man who could give her a life, a good life. And that wasn't him.

The last increase in missions had erased all hope he would survive this war. Before that, before he got to know Kitty, he hadn't minded. He'd thought it was just what was supposed to happen to him. His life was just one of the many that would be sacrificed to win this war. But now, now that she sat so close, now that she wanted to be with him, wanted him to comfort her, he desperately wanted to find a way to survive.

Trouble was—there was no way. There was only now. And if he followed his feelings he would only hurt her.

Gunfire on the screen made her flinch. He slipped his arm around her shoulders and she leaned into him, ever so slightly.

They watched the exciting, final scenes of the movie, with the inevitable happy ending. She smiled and he was glad the movie had been something to distract her.

He leaned over. "Good to see you smile. You must like westerns."

"I like happy endings," she told him.

"Yeah, me, too."

The black and white intro to the newsreel flashed

on the screen.

"What's on next?" she asked.

"I'm not sure. Another western, I think." A soldier passed by going to the lobby. "Do you want anything to drink?" Ted asked.

"No." She shook her head. "But you go ahead and get something if you want."

He thought about stepping out for a smoke but decided he'd rather stay here with Kitty.

The newsreel announcer barked news of the invasion force in Normandy. Images of fighting men, artillery, fighters streaking through the sky filled the screen. Stirring music accentuated the announcer's words.

Anguish showed in Kitty's face. Her eyes glistened with unshed tears. He knew she was imagining Milton wounded on the battlefield amidst all that horror.

He squeezed her shoulders, and she looked up at him with such pain that his throat contracted and he could not speak. The screen shifted to news from the Pacific front. Gigantic battleships, planes landing on carrier decks. Tears spilled down her cheeks. He couldn't stand it.

"Let's get out of here."

Before she could respond, he got to his feet and almost pulled her with him down the aisle and through the curtains into the lobby.

"I'm sorry. I should have known that the newsreel would upset you."

"No. It's all right." She wiped the tears from her face. "I'm all right." She looked around. "Why don't we just wait here until the next picture starts?"

He admired her guts. She wasn't going to give in to

it. "Okay," he agreed.

He led her across the lobby, thinking maybe they'd get a cup of coffee or maybe tea, whatever the English had to offer. Then he spotted it. One of those photo booths.

"Look." He pointed to the booth. "Let's take some pictures."

"I…I don't know." She hesitated.

"Aw, come on," he taunted. "It'll be fun."

She smiled at his attempt to cheer her up. "Okay."

He dug in his pocket for some change and slipped the coins into the slot.

He held back the curtain and pushed her into the booth. "Oh, no. It's both of us or nothing," she informed him.

"Okay." He squeezed in beside her and winked which made her laugh. He liked the sound. "You should laugh more."

"Maybe if I was around you more, I would."

His heart swelled, and he could feel himself grinning at her. "I knew you could flirt, if you just let yourself go."

She reached over and pushed the button. The camera flashed. He turned to look at her. It flashed again.

"Look at the camera," she told him.

"I'd rather look at you." It flashed again.

She reached up and took his chin and turned his face to the camera just as it flashed one last time.

"That wasn't fair."

She giggled and shook her head. "I don't care."

He knew he was lost as he bent down and captured her lips. This time he didn't just brush them lightly.

This time he kissed her for real. Tasting her, devouring her mouth with his. His pulse pounded in his head. All he knew was her. All he wanted was here in his arms. There was only now…and Kitty.

\*\*\*\*

His lips pressed hers, and hunger roared inside her like nothing she'd ever experienced. The kiss deepened, and she could taste his aching need matching hers.

When their lips finally parted, and they looked into each other's eyes in sheer amazement, she tried to sound light and cheerful. "We ought to get out of here, don't you think?"

He nodded. His eyes crinkled into a smile while his lips remained parted, as if debating whether to return to hers.

He glanced around as if he needed to get his bearings, then he pulled her from the booth. With his arm firmly around her shoulders, he herded her toward the exit.

"Wait! The pictures."

He nodded and turned around. He reached into the slot where the photos had landed and pulled them out.

Looking down, he commented "Not bad."

"Let me see." She snatched them from his hand. They were silly, but good, especially the last one where she had turned his face to the camera. That little boy grin that stole her heart on that first day gazed at her from the tiny photo, sending a thrill through her body.

"Come on." He nudged her.

In no time they stood inside the hotel lobby. Neither spoke. He stuck the dripping umbrella into the elephant-shaped umbrella stand near the door, placed his hand at the small of her back, and urged her toward the stairway.

She avoided looking around the lobby. Instead she focused on his presence, on the stairway, and on what lay ahead.

Chapter Twenty-Seven

He closed the door, leaned back against it, and pulled her close. His mouth devoured hers as if he could not get enough.

She wanted his kisses, his arms around her, holding her against his strong body.

His kisses trailed across her cheek, down her jaw line to her sensitive neck. Chills ran through her.

"I promised myself I wouldn't do this," he whispered.

"What?" She didn't want him to stop.

"Take advantage of you."

"You aren't," she insisted. "I know what I'm doing."

He stopped and looked into her eyes. There was a question, something he was trying to decide.

He swept her across the room, sat her on the bed, and sank down beside her. His arms engulfed her.

"I'm not the prize your mother wanted for you."

"I never did anything to please her, anyway."

His hand caressed her chin, pulling it up so their eyes met. "If it weren't for the war, this uniform, you wouldn't give me a second glance."

"That's not true."

"Yes, it is." His smile was dead serious.

"I saw you before. I wanted you then." She hoped she didn't sound desperate.

He smiled as he kissed her, pushing her down without leaving her mouth. Her hand ran through his hair as she held him close. The weight of his body pressed her into the mattress, his hand exploring.

"There's no future, you know," he whispered.

Was he trying to discourage her? "Don't say that."

He stopped. His gaze pinned her in place as surely as his arms held her. "I might not come back. Or I might be maimed, like your brother, or worse."

"More reason to live now." She didn't want to think of anything but now.

"Don't treat it lightly. You're not that kind of girl."

She tried to pull him closer, but he was too strong.

Tears welled in her eyes, and she fought desperately to stop them. She didn't want to be protected, like some kind of untouchable doll sitting on a shelf. She wanted someone to love her, to want her.

He watched her intently. His thumb brushed away a traitorous tear.

She drew a ragged breath. "I'm not a child. I'm a grown woman. And I've been in love with you since the first time I saw you."

"You didn't know me."

She shook her head. "But I did. I knew everything I needed to know."

"Milt told me you were prone to fantasies." His expression changed into something almost sinister. "I'm no fantasy. I'm actually a pretty sorry character. I like women, lots of women. But I've never been serious about any of them. And I don't want to get serious now." He pulled away and sat up. "I lured you here because I knew you were upset. That made you vulnerable to someone like me."

"Maybe I wanted to be lured. Maybe I wanted to be comforted." She was pleading but didn't care. "Don't pull away. Don't leave me."

He turned his back to her. "Don't. You don't know me." She could hear bitterness, and regret.

"Then let me get to know you."

He sighed, turned back to her, and a hint of a smile crept onto his handsome face. "All right." He faced her but pushed further away. He scooted to the edge of the bed as if ready to run. "I'm the son of a bum and a floozy. My father got himself killed stealing and my mother…she went from one man to another, drinking, partying…" He looked away.

"You are not your parents."

"No? Then why do I drift from place to place, try anything, dangerous, crazy. You name it." He paused. "Why didn't I do like my grandparents wanted? Go to school. Make something of myself."

"You still can."

His laugh was sarcastic and bitter. "Sure. Sure." He got up and walked across the room running his hand through his hair. Then he turned to face her. "Don't you get it? I'm a dead man. There's no way I'm going to make six more missions. Nobody's done it." He jerked away to face the tiny window. "I've watched them go down, waiting for my turn. Waiting for the flack or the fighter or the midair collision. The ball of fire. Or falling through the air, helplessly waiting to crash into the ground." His voice died down, from the weight of the pain, the anguish.

She went to him, wrapped her arms around him, praying he wouldn't push her away.

He didn't. Instead he held her, gently stroking her

back.

"You're not alone anymore," she whispered. "I'm with you. I'll always be with you."

\*\*\*\*

For the first time in his life, he belonged. She gave him that. Gave him a sense of connection to another human being, like he mattered, like someone cared, really cared.

"Let me stay with you…for a while."

She pulled back, just enough so she could look up at him, smiled and nodded.

Her soft warmth, her sweet, comforting soul melted his heart, dispelled his fear, gave him hope. Hope that maybe there could be a tomorrow. Or at least for today, hope that this beautiful woman could love him, really love him. Not like his mother, not like the others, so caught up in themselves they could care less what he needed.

Kitty was different. And she wanted to love him.

He thought of his grandmother, the strange woman he'd never understood, yet he'd always known she loved him, no matter what he did. Until now, he'd always thought that kind of love came only from old women, women who'd lived a long time and lost so much. He realized Kitty was that kind of woman. Strong, steady, unyielding. Yet she was also young and passionate.

She'd saved him once. Perhaps, now, they could save each other.

He leaned down and kissed her, gently at first, then deeper, more passionately. Her lips parted at his coaxing. He tentatively explored with his tongue until she opened to him, and he plundered her mouth with his.

The power of his desire for her shocked him. He wanted her, all of her. He wanted to show her, teach her, give her something she'd never forget. Something he'd never forget.

Her arms pulled him closer. He lifted her up and carried her back to the bed.

Neither wanted more talk. Instead they followed their instincts. Each explored the other, intoxicated by the physical presence of someone who cared.

He stopped thinking and just experienced this beautiful woman who wanted him, who loved him.

****

She awoke in a dream-like state, gradually realizing the warmth curled around her was Ted's strong, masculine body. She lay still soaking up the sensations, imprinting them on her memory. The feel of his skin. The scent of his body. The quiet sound of his breathing. All too soon he stirred and started awake as if surprised to find her there.

"Good morning," she whispered.

He rolled over and pawed at the nearby table for his wrist watch.

"What time is it?" he asked.

"Early. There's barely any light in the sky."

He settled back beside her. "Good. We don't have to hurry."

"I don't want to leave." The ache in her chest increased.

He slipped his arm around her and pulled her naked body against his. "I don't either, but we have to." His long fingers caressed her cheek, gently sliding down to lightly grasp her chin. He drew her face to his and placed a gentle kiss on her lips. "We have to go back to the real world." His eyes reflected her own sadness as his fingers continued to caress her face.

She wrapped her arms around him. "We'll see each other again...soon. Won't we?"

"Sure. In a couple of weeks. Whenever we can both get away. We can meet here, in Norwich. It's not far for you or for me."

She nodded against his bare chest. "And we'll write."

"Yes. I'll write you. I promise." He pulled back, so he could look at her face. "But don't expect too much. I'm not very good at writing letters."

She rolled her eyes.

"Just warning you." Laughter emerged from him so easily she found herself chuckling in response.

She poked his chest with her finger. "You'd better write me, mister. I don't care if they are short little notes."

"And you'd better write me long, long letters that I can read myself to sleep with." He tweaked her nose.

She responded by tickling the spot on his ribs she'd found the night before. He grabbed her hands to stop her assault, then found her mouth with his. He pressed her against the bed and rolled on top of her. Their teasing quickly progressed to more sensual activities. Activities she'd learned to enjoy, to let herself go and experience this man...this man she trusted completely...this man she loved.

Chapter Twenty-Eight

*July 6, 1944*

*Dear Father and Mother,*

*You may have gotten a telegram about Milton. I want you to know that I have seen him in the hospital. He is alive and recovering from his wounds. They brought him to a hospital in England after he was wounded in Normandy. A medic found a letter he had written to me and sent it on with a note about Milton. That is how I knew what happened to him. His wounds are serious, but he is alive and he will recover.*

*I don't know how long it will be before they can put him on a ship to the states. Depends on when a hospital ship is available, but he will be shipped to a hospital back home. I am sure he will write you when he is settled. Then maybe you can visit him.*

*You can still write to him at his overseas address, and he will get your letters eventually. I don't know if I will be able to visit him again. We have been extremely busy as you can guess from the news. As I've told you before, I cannot say anything about my work.*

*I want you to know that Milton will be okay. It will just take time.*

*Your loving daughter,*
*Katherine*
\*\*\*\*

Kitty mailed her letter, then went in search of a

new pair of stockings. She'd pulled a run in her last good pair on the train from Norwich.

Her thoughts roamed back to the platform when he'd kissed her good-bye. He'd looked so handsome in his uniform, his billed cap cocked to one side like Clark Gable. She'd wished for a camera to snap a picture. And she'd made him promise to have one made, a nice one, she could have framed. She wanted to be able to look at him every day.

Lost in her dreams, she wasn't watching where she was going. She crashed into another shopper. The other WAC grabbed the counter to keep from falling.

"Excuse me." Kitty reached for the other girl to steady her and found herself facing Madge.

Her old friend glared and said nothing.

Kitty's stomach clinched. "I'm sorry. I wasn't watching where I was going."

"I know. You practically knocked me down."

Kitty fought the urge to look away, to avoid facing Madge. Guilt drenched her in a cold sweat. She knew, to her old friend, her face was as transparent as glass.

"I'm sorry," Kitty repeated.

Madge stared at her for a moment. "Sally told me your brother was wounded."

Kitty nodded.

"I hope it wasn't too bad." Madge was truly sympathetic.

"Bad enough." Kitty could feel this enormous, unspoken thing between them. It had to be brought out into the open if she ever hoped to resurrect their friendship.

"Well, I hope he's okay."

"I've seen Ted," Kitty blurted out.

"What?"

"Ted. I saw him in Norwich."

Madge's face bloomed red with anger. "Are you trying to rub it in?"

Kitty shook her head, but Madge ignored her.

"It's bad enough you sneaked around and broke us up. To steal him for yourself. Now you're trying to gloat in triumph by telling me you've seen him. Next you'll be claiming he loves you."

"He does. And I love him."

Madge turned even redder, her eyes bulged and Kitty thought she would explode.

"You rat. You little conniving rat. You knew how I felt about him, but you went after him anyway. You meant to hurt me all along, didn't you? Show me you could steal him? After all I did for you?"

"No, no. It wasn't like that. I didn't mean for it to happen. Let me explain."

"Right! Still playing the innocent. Well, I know better."

"I knew you liked him. It's true. I tried to stop it, really I did. But…" How could she make Madge understand? "Do you remember me telling you about the man on the beach?"

"What's that got to do with anything?"

"It was him. It was Ted."

Madge inhaled sharply, then she became eerily silent. Her eyes narrowed as she absorbed the information.

"I know I should have told you. But I couldn't. You were so crazy about him. And he didn't remember me. At least not at first."

"Are you trying to tell me that Ted, my Ted, was

the man you dreamed about?" Madge's voice pierced like cold steel. "Is that why you had to have him, even though you knew I was in love with him?"

"I didn't mean to hurt you. I tried to stay away from him." She desperately wanted Madge to understand. And she desperately wanted to shed the pall of guilt hanging over her. "He pursued me. Don't you see? I tried to keep it from happening."

"I don't believe a word of it. You wanted him, and you got him." She drew a ragged breath and looked away for a few seconds. When she looked back, fury burned in her eyes. "Stay away from me. I never want to see you again." Her words ground out, full of pain and bitter anger.

Tears slid down Kitty's cheeks. She watched Madge stomp off, her fury evident in her every step.

The friend she'd counted on, clung to even, now hated her. And most of the other girls would take Madge's side, like they always did. Everybody loved Madge. And that left Kitty alone. The WACs at the castle were already cool and distant, even when they asked about her brother. When Madge got through, Kitty wouldn't have a friend left.

Madge had not only taught her about men. She had been her door to the world of girlfriends, sharing confidences, helping each other get through the tough times, celebrating the small things that made life here tolerable. When the general chose Kitty to work for him, the wedge between her and her friends had started. Several had pulled back, kept their distance. Now her love for Ted and Madge's anger would finish the job.

Could she go on like this? She'd survived as a kid with no one to talk to, no one who understood her—

except Milton. Now she had Ted. She could survive. After all, he loved her. That was all she needed.

****

Kitty focused on her typing. In her absence, General Lake had held on to his daily notes not trusting her replacements to decipher them properly. And since he insisted on everything being typed, she had returned to a mountain of paperwork. On top of that, Captain Weatherby had rotated several girls to give them experience working for the general, so the filing was a mess.

*Oh, well. I might as well work late and get caught up. No one will miss me.*

She recognized the "oh poor me" syndrome, but she couldn't shake it. Why should she? The only people who cared were Milton and Ted, and both of them were beyond her reach.

Even General Lake had been distant since her return. He was unusually preoccupied, which was unlike his usual calm, friendly manner. Even the heightened stress of the invasion had barely disturbed his steady hand. This was different. Something was going on.

His aide mentioned that he'd been called to Eighth Air Force Headquarters during her absence, and he'd come back all worked up and mysterious.

"Sergeant."

Kitty jerked. Her fingers clanked the keys, locking up her typewriter.

She looked up.

"Sorry to startle you. I thought you heard me calling you."

"No, sir. I'm sorry. I was focused on this…" She

looked down at the little arms locked together so neither could strike the ribbon. She reached into the mechanism to release them when he spoke again.

"Greenlee." Impatience added an edge of forcefulness. "Come into my office. Now."

"Oh. Yes, sir." Kitty reached for her pad and pencil, jumped up, and followed the general into his office. On the way she noticed the ink on her fingers and wished she'd grabbed her handkerchief.

Many of the officers who had streamed in and out of the general's office all morning stood or sat in various places around the office.

"Now, gentlemen, Sergeant Greenlee will take notes. I want to send out a memo to everyone under my command. But before I do, I want all of us to be in agreement."

Kitty quickly took the chair offered to her and flipped to a blank page in her pad. She headed the page with the date, General Lake's name, and began listing the other attendees. Obviously impatient to begin, the general started dictating, so she skipped a space to fill in the names later and began taking dictation.

What started out sounding routine quickly transformed into a shocking development, at least it shocked her. Apparently all the others already knew about it.

General Lake had been ordered to report to Eighth Air Force Headquarters to assume the responsibilities of another officer. The Second Combat Bombardment Wing would be turned over to Colonel Snyder who would be promoted to Lieutenant General. One of the group commanders would move into Colonel Snyder's position and various other personnel changes would be made by Colonel Snyder.

When General Lake stated he would be leaving the next day, her head jerked up. For a few seconds she lost her place. The general caught her gaze and paused long enough for her to get hold of herself.

It took a great deal of effort for Kitty to force herself to look back down at her pad and focus on her shorthand. She must capture every word. She couldn't slip up now, not when her future hung in the balance. Colonel Snyder didn't like her. He would make sure she returned to the group of stenographers. She could only pray he wouldn't retaliate against her for the general's favors. As commanding officer, he could make her life miserable.

The meeting ended, and Kitty returned to her desk to type up the notes and a draft of the general's memo. Her fingers shook as she rolled a fresh piece of paper into her machine and started to type.

"Sergeant." The general's voice was gentler this time.

She looked up. "Yes, sir."

"Come back into my office a moment."

"Yes, sir." She drew a deep breath and rose. Automatically she reached for her pad.

"You won't need that."

"Sir?"

"Just come in for a minute."

She followed him into the office. He stood by the door and closed it once she was inside. All the others had gone. A moment of panic seized her. What was he going to do?

He walked past her and waved toward a chair. "Sit down."

She sank into the chair and waited for him to speak. Maybe he would just thank her for her hard work.

"I know it was a shock to you, hearing that I'm being transferred."

She nodded, unable to speak. Somehow she knew whatever he had to say to her would be bad, very bad.

"You've worked very hard, and you've done an excellent job." He paused. "I must admit I was a little outdone with you for lying to me about your brother. Being honest is a virtue, even when it is uncomfortable."

"Yes, sir. I'm very sorry, sir." She tried to sound contrite even though she knew she would probably do the same thing again.

"Never the less, you've done an excellent job. I don't think I realized just how much you were doing until you were gone. None of the others could keep up or understand me. You always know what I'm trying to say."

"Thank you, sir."

"That's why I made some inquiries."

Kitty watched his face, tried to read his thoughts.

He placed his elbows on the desk and leaned forward until his chin rested on his fists. "I have a proposition for you."

Her heart raced. "Sir?"

"If you want, you can come with me."

"Sir?" Kitty was confused.

"To High Wycombe. Eighth Air Force Headquarters. As my secretary." He straightened up. "You don't have to give me an answer now. It's strictly voluntary. But think about it. You'd be at headquarters just outside of London. Might get another stripe out of it. Although I can't guarantee that. It'd be a great opportunity."

"I don't know what to say."

He smiled. "That's what I expected." He stood and turned to walk around the desk. "I'd like to take you with me. You'd be of enormous help. After all, that's what you're here for isn't it? To help the war effort?"

"Yes, sir." He stood by her now, and she realized she was supposed to leave.

"You'll have to give me your answer by in the morning. Sorry I can't give you more time, but the war won't wait." He laughed nervously, like he knew his joke was lame, but he said it anyway.

Still in shock, she shuffled toward the door. "Yes, sir. Tomorrow, sir."

He opened the door. "Now get those things typed up as soon as you can."

"Yes, sir." Kitty moved automatically to her desk. She sat behind her typewriter and stared straight ahead. Her mind was still trying to digest what he had said.

He wanted her to go with him to Eighth Air Force Headquarters. He was leaving tomorrow. He wanted an answer by in the morning. Help the war effort.

He was right about that. She'd come to England to do her part to help win this war. Now more than ever she wanted to do that. And if that meant going with General Lake then that's what she would do. After all, what did she have here? Ted was at the air base near Norwich. Madge hated her, and her other friends had become cool toward her. Starting over somewhere else might be the best thing. She might even be closer to Milton and be able to visit him.

Her mind raced ahead to all the changes, to what might be in her future. General Lake had been good to her. He'd actually been easy to work for. And he appreciated her work. Unlike Colonel Snyder. The decision was easy. Of course she'd go.

\*\*\*\*

Ted stared at the blank page. His supply of paper and envelopes were stacked on the table beside him, evidence of his intention to honor his promise to write to Kitty. A promise that was easier to give than to actually do. He had no idea how to write to the woman he loved.

The letters he'd written before had been brief notes. But now, things were different between Kitty and him. He wanted to tell her everything, his every thought, his every feeling. He couldn't do that. It wasn't reasonable, and he didn't have enough paper.

"Wow!" Sparky Stone plopped onto the bunk beside him. "Must be really serious. I don't believe I've ever seen you write a letter before."

"Me either," Billy chimed in. The officer stood nearby holding a mug of questionable contents.

"Lay off, fellows," Ted retorted.

"Who ya' writing?" Sparky asked.

"None of your business."

"Oh, it's gonna be that way, is it?"

"It's a girl. Okay?"

"Kruger, writing to a girl. What happened? Did one finally get her hooks into you?" Sparky persisted.

"Wouldn't be that pin-up at headquarters, would it? Thought you broke up with her." Billy had a way of getting to Ted, always jabbing him when he got the chance.

"No, it's not Madge." Ted gritted his teeth in an attempt to control his urge to blurt out Kitty's name.

"Then who? Must be hot to get you putting words on paper."

Ted gathered up his things and stood. "I think I'll go somewhere else to do this. Somewhere where I can think."

"Okay, lover boy. But keep us informed how you do. One of us might want to try her out when you're through with her."

Ted forced himself to leave before he punched someone. He couldn't bear to hear comments like that about Kitty. It had never bothered him before—joking about his girlfriends, bragging about his prowess with the ladies. But Kitty was different. She was a nice girl—his nice girl. And he wanted to protect her.

He headed for the base chapel. The one place he could count on to be quiet. He could be alone, and he could write without worry of being interrupted.

The door creaked as he entered. The room wasn't very big. Chairs lined up to face the simple altar. He hadn't been inside a church since high school when he'd gone with his grandparents. Memories of their love and the stable home they had given him flooded back. How could he have turned his back on the only people who loved him? He'd been young and rebellious, determined to make his own way with no one to hold him back. Six years and a lifetime of experience changed his perspective.

He looked at the writing materials and vowed to not only write Kitty but to also write to his grandparents. And maybe he'd write to his mother, too.

\*\*\*\*

Kitty quickly oriented herself to the office and the WAC quarters in High Wycombe. Helping General Lake settle into his new job proved more challenging. He found himself in a smaller office and one of many generals working together to coordinate the activities of a huge organization spread all over England.

This new role proved very different from running a combat wing. He had to adjust to working in committees, sitting in endless meetings, and focusing on organizational issues. Giving the orders, being the one in charge, had been easier.

To help him prepare, Kitty gathered information on everything from number of personnel and aircraft to fuel usage and supply depots. She found it fascinating.

The other WACs in the office were helpful but a little distant. Whenever Kitty asked, they provided her with assistance in a very professional and impersonal way. In the barracks the girls were friendly enough. They exchanged small talk and helped her in a more friendly fashion than in camps stateside. Yet they all kept their distance. They didn't want to get too close. After thinking about it a while, Kitty decided she preferred keeping to herself, too. She'd learned that getting close could cause problems. Right now she wanted to focus on work. After all, they were all here to help win the war.

She wrote to Ted to give him her new address. His letters would find her eventually. He'd promised to write, and in her heart she knew he wouldn't break his promise.

## Chapter Twenty-Nine

*July 7, 1944*

*Dear Grandpapa and Grandmama,*

*I've met the most wonderful girl. She is in the WAC and comes from a small town in Tennessee. Practically one of your neighbors. She's quiet and smart, just the type you would want for me. I've gone out with lots of girls, but this one is different. I met her brother, too. He is in the infantry and a real nice guy. He was wounded, can't say when or how, but I sure hope he will be okay. I'm still flying. Not too many more missions to go.*

*Sorry I haven't written more. I promised Kitty (that's her nick name) I'd write her, and so I decided I should write you more often, too. Her real name is Katherine Greenlee. Remember that name. If I make it through this thing, I'll bring her to meet you.*

*I'm enclosing a souvenir I want you to keep for me. They call it a "short snorter." Not sure why. It's a dollar bill that everyone on my crew signed after we made the flight over here. They're all gone now, all but me. So put this in a safe place for me. I don't want to lose it or accidentally spend it. Ha! Ha! It means too much to me to ever spend.*

*I think of you often even though I don't write much. Thanks for being there for me when I needed you.*

*Your grandson,*

*Ted*

\*\*\*\*

"Welcome aboard," First Lieutenant Sikes offered Ted his hand.

Ted shook it firmly. "Thanks. Glad to join you." And he really meant it. Assigned to this seasoned crew he'd already flown with made facing his last few flights a little easier. Maybe he would survive after all.

"You know everyone, I think."

"Yes." Ted shook hands with the co-pilot, "Pete" Peterson.

"Good to have you with us," the bombardier slapped him on the shoulder. "How many missions do you have left?"

"Six, counting today."

"Most of us need eight more. Sure will be glad to get it over with."

"Yeah," Ted agreed. He didn't really want to talk about it for fear they would be jinxed.

"Poor Eddie and his busted eardrums. Doc's grounded him for a least a month, maybe longer," Peterson said as they filed into the briefing room and found seats. "I told him to work it and see if he couldn't get permanently grounded."

Ted sandwiched in between Peterson and Sikes as the co-pilot continued. "Eddie just couldn't take the altitude." He reached across Ted and punched Sikes in the arm. "'Member how he screamed like a banshee when we took that dive last time out."

Ted grimaced and shook his head. "Poor guy." These men cared about each other. That would make his last few missions more tolerable.

"Pipe down," Sikes ordered. "They're getting ready to start."

The Operations Officer appeared at the front of the room and banged the podium to get their attention. Soon he unveiled the map. Their target for the day—Germany.

Ted straightened in his seat and focused on the officer's description of the mission. He had a job to do. His new crew depended on him, and he wouldn't let them down.

****

The bombardier talked incessantly until they donned their oxygen masks. Ted liked the guy but found himself grateful for the silence imposed by the need for oxygen at altitude. The co-pilot checked with each crew member regularly via the intercom so it wasn't absolute silence. Just enough to calm his nerves and let him pretend it was a routine training mission.

Since the short, but intense time he spent with Kitty, he thought more and more about what he wanted to do after the war. He loved flying. It was definitely an option. Yet it would mean being away from home a lot. Home. He'd never really thought about having a home—until now. With Kitty he could actually imagine a home, a family, settling down in one place. The question was how to make a living.

He'd read in the *Stars and Stripes* about the GI Bill Congress had passed. Maybe he could use that and go to college. Kitty went to college. She had even taught school. She'd confessed that she didn't like teaching and wanted to do something different. He was convinced she could do anything she set her mind to.

"Flack ahead," warned the co-pilot.

Ted looked through the Plexiglas surrounding the bombardier. Black puffs filled the sky ahead. The plane just above and in front of them bounced from the concussion of an explosion that just missed them.

Ted tensed. His heart pounded in his chest. No matter how many missions he flew, he'd never get used to the feeling, moving through the sky like a duck in a shooting gallery, hoping the gunners below missed their mark.

The plane shook as explosions sent shock waves through it. A memory flashed through his brain. His body tensed as if preparing for the intense pain of shrapnel ripping through his thigh. Instinctively his hand went to his leg.

*Shake it off. You've been through this lots of times. And getting hit once doesn't mean you'll get it again.*

Ted gripped his small desk to keep his charts and instruments in place. His jaw clamped so tight he expected to crack a molar. He looked around. The bombardier was holding on for dear life, too. Ted nodded to him. Knowing he wasn't alone helped get him through the terror and kept him sane.

Finally, they cleared the flack field, and the tension eased.

The pilot called to confirm their heading so Ted focused on his charts.

*Do your job. This is a good crew. As long as everyone does their job, we'll get through this okay.*

He gave the pilot the needed information. Then the co-pilot asked him to verify their position based on landmarks. With limited visibility from his small window, Ted disconnected his oxygen line and connected to a walk-around bottle so he could move forward into the bombardier's area and survey the landscape below. It didn't take long to get his bearings and confirm their position.

Ted chuckled to himself as he headed back to his seat. He'd learned why Peterson was so paranoid about their location. On a previous flight they'd blindly followed the lead plane and gotten so far off course they missed their target entirely. A flock of fighters had attacked the off-course squadron and only a few made it back to England. Peterson never wanted to be in that situation again. And Ted didn't blame him.

When he got back to his seat, his parachute caught on the back of the chair. Ted jerked it loose and started to take it off rather than sit on the uncomfortable mass. After all, he'd flown lots of missions with the parachute crammed under the seat. Something told him to keep it on. He thought of Kitty, the angel watching over him, and smiled. Was she sending him messages? Was she trying to keep him safe? What the hell! He'd wear the thing—just for her.

****

Bainbridge took control as they hit the IP and started the bomb run. Theoretically, having the entire bomber group hold a steady course approaching the target was logical. But in reality, with flack bursting all around, it was ludicrous. The anti-aircraft gunners' expertise allowed them to target the group's exact altitude. From the ground it was a turkey shoot with 88 mm cannons firing at moving, but predictable, targets.

A scream came over the intercom.

A few seconds later the left waist gunner reported the radio man had been hit. "He's bleedin' bad."

"Take care of him," Sikes ordered.

Another explosion threw the plane upward. The bombs. With the bomb bay open, if the bombs were hit, the plane would be blown to smithereens.

Peterson's voice came over the intercom. "Number three's smoking. Losing pressure."

"Okay. Bain, how much longer?" Sites asked.

"We're almost there. A few more minutes," replied the bombardier.

"McNichols, how's LaCross doing?"

No answer from the back of the plane.

"What's going on back there?" Peterson asked.

Still no reply.

"Hood, check the com lines," Sikes ordered.

"Bombs away," Bainbridge announced. At that moment the bombs jerked free. The plane lurched upward. Ted instinctively grabbed hold.

Hood mumbled something about the bombs, but Ted couldn't understand him.

A concussion rocked the bomber, again.

"Check in," Peterson said calmly, as if they were just cruising along on a routine flight.

"Bainbridge."

"Kruger."

Then silence.

"Bain, get up here and help Hood."

Ted wondered what had happened to the Flight Engineer. Bainbridge eased past and disappeared through the passage to the flight deck.

"Kruger, get back to the waist and see what's going on."

"Okay."

Ted unbuckled, disconnected his throat mike and oxygen line. He hooked up a walk-around bottle and crawled through to the bomb bay. When he opened the door, the wind from the open bomb bay doors almost sucked him out. He carefully made his way along the narrow bridge between the racks where the bombs had hung just moments before. Wind assaulted him from all sides. He focused on the hand holds and the walkway, trying to ignore the gaping empty space and the ground twenty thousand feet below.

He reached the radio compartment and forced the door shut behind him. LaCrosse lay sprawled on the floor. Blood covered his midsection, seeping through the many layers of clothing. He'd never make it back bleeding like that. McNichols knelt over the wounded man doing what he could to administer first aid.

Ted nodded to the waist gunner, then stepped around them into the waist. Colson was out of the ball turret but hung over it holding his oxygen mask to his face.

Ted grabbed another oxygen bottle. He hooked Colson to it then leaned the semi-conscious man against the bulkhead and checked him for wounds.

Blood dripped from Colson's left hand. *Probably hit in the arm.*

Ted glanced around for the other waist gunner. Movement in the tail section caught his eye. The tail gunner must have been hit.

Ted fished a knife out of his pocket. The bulky gloves caused him to fumble it. Instinctively he started to remove his glove, then he stopped himself. If his hands got frostbit, he'd be useless. He picked up the knife, cut Colson's sleeve, and peeled it back to reveal a bleeding gash in his forearm.

Ted fumbled with the first aid kit and managed to get a bandage out. He wrapped it around Colson's wounded arm as tightly as he could.

Shelton pulled the unconscious tail gunner into the waist. Ted stood, but before he could take a step the plane shuddered, knocking him off balance. He grabbed the .50 caliber gun to keep from falling.

Someone punched him in the arm. McNichols stood beside him and shouted through his mask. "Come look at LaCrosse." Ted nodded and went ahead of McNichols into the radio compartment. He knelt down to examine the wounded man. He was dead.

Ted forced himself to ignore the sick feeling in his gut. Daylight flickered through a hole big enough to put his fist through right where the radioman had been sitting.

He turned back to McNichols and shouted, "Go help the others." He nodded toward the waist. "I'm going to tell Sikes what's going on back here."

McNichols nodded.

Ted turned and pulled open the door to the bomb bay. He'd hoped the pilot had closed the bomb doors, but he hadn't.

As the cold wind whipped around Ted, he gritted his teeth and steeled himself against the temptation to look down. Instead he stood for a few seconds. Instinct told him something was wrong. He spotted a ragged hole where the hydraulics and the com lines had been ripped apart.

He had to cross the narrow bridge, had to tell Sikes about the damage, about the wounded. His mind raced ahead. Getting back, crippled, so many wounded.

An explosion rocked the plane.

Bright orange flashed around him.

He slammed into something.

Blackness. Numbness. Silence.

He floated, suspended in a surreal dream.

*Kitty.*

She came to him. Smiling, her glorious hair glowing in the sunlight.

*I'm sorry, my love. You can't save me this time.*

## Chapter Thirty

Madge sat in her hotel room staring at the words she'd typed the day before. She'd managed to get hold of the debriefing reports from Ted's last flight, and fighting tears, she'd typed up the sections describing his plane, when it was hit, when it went down.

She had wanted to know every gory detail. Everything that had happened. The report told it all, briefly, vividly. Direct from the men who'd seen it happen. Hit in the nose. Big explosion. The whole front of the plane gone. Steep nose dive. Wing came off. Two chutes spotted. Probably gunners. Jumped or thrown out just before the fuselage started to spiral.

She swiped at a tear spilling onto her cheek.

Why'd she have to fall for a guy like that? A guy who'd go and get himself killed? But she had. And he'd broken her heart. When he'd dumped her for Kitty, she'd sworn she'd hate both of them forever.

But she didn't.

When she first heard, she'd been sure the report was wrong. Mistakes were made all the time. Fear drove her to dig deeper. She'd made calls, used up favors, and she'd verified that Ted was in fact assigned to that crew. He was on the flight the day it went down. She'd talked to two airmen who'd seen him at the briefing, who'd seen the plane go down.

Second Lieutenant T. R. Kruger, NAV: Missing,

presumed dead.

His name glared at her. She couldn't change it no matter how much she wanted to.

She'd prayed he wouldn't go back to the bombers, that he'd stay at headquarters. She'd even hoped the stupid investigation would ground him. But it had only delayed the inevitable.

She sighed and slumped down on the bed. The tears came, and she didn't try to stop them.

He'd known he was going to die. His friends had died, and he'd wanted to go with them. It was crazy, but she knew it was true.

And what about Kitty?

She had been so mad at Kitty. Her anger was really wounded pride that Ted preferred Kitty to her. That's why she'd gotten so upset. That and Kitty being so stupid. The girl denied being interested in him when anyone could see the way she looked at him, the way she acted around him, how crazy she was about him.

Madge had watched Ted as some invisible force pulled him away from her and toward Kitty. Like some unexplained phenomenon in a magic act. Poof! And Ted had thrown her over for Kitty. There was nothing she could do to stop it.

Someone tapped on the door, and Madge got up to answer it.

"Aren't you coming?" the girl asked.

"I'm not hungry. You go ahead."

"What if we meet some guys and take off to a show or something?"

"Go ahead. Don't worry about me. I've got other plans."

"Okay. If that's what you want."

Madge closed the door and returned to the bed. The typed pages lay there, calling to her.

As much as she'd wanted to come to London and let off some steam, she couldn't. She had to tell Kitty. She couldn't bear the thought of the poor girl not knowing. It would be down-right cruel. The two may have fought over Ted, but now that he was gone, Madge couldn't keep it from Kitty.

She looked at her watch. One o'clock. Maybe she could get to High Wycombe before the end of the work day. She'd find Kitty and tell her the horrible news. It was the least she could do for her friend.

****

Kitty stacked the files on the table by the bank of file cabinets. After she filed them all, she would still have time to straighten up her desk before the end of the day.

With General Lake gone for the afternoon, she had used the opportunity to get his office in order. He'd become increasingly disorganized since they'd been at High Wycombe. He complained his office was too small and he had too many interruptions.

She believed he was having trouble adjusting to his new position. What would have happened to him if she hadn't agreed to come?

Subconsciously, she checked her hair to make sure no stray curls had escaped. Sure enough, some had slithered free. As she reached up with her other hand to find and adjust the pins, her thoughts strayed to Ted. She remembered how he had touched her hair, insisted she let it down. In his last letter he mentioned how much he missed caressing her hair and how he loved the way it framed her face.

Joy filled her heart. She gently caressed her curls as he would have done and relished the memory of his touch. Oh, how she wanted to see him again.

"Sergeant."

A WAC approached her.

"Yes?" Kitty straightened and assumed her most business-like pose, hoping the other woman had not noticed her daydreaming.

"You have a visitor."

Kitty's heart leapt. Could it be Ted? Had he somehow managed to come see her? She looked beyond the woman but saw no one who didn't belong.

"She's downstairs," came the explanation. "Can't let her come up without security clearance."

"Of course." Kitty fought her disappointment. "Do you know who it is?"

The woman shook her head. "A WAC from another unit." She started to turn. "I told her you'd be down shortly. When your shift ends."

"Thank you, Sergeant."

Kitty wondered who would visit her. She hadn't been here long enough to make friends. Maybe one of the girls from Ellingham Castle. But why would they come here?

When she finished the filing and straightened her desk, Kitty went downstairs. She didn't see anyone so she asked the guard on duty if there was someone waiting for her. He directed her to the little alcove under the stairway.

Madge jumped to her feet when Kitty approached.

"Madge!" Kitty was too shocked to say more.

"Hello, Kitty."

She looked strange somehow, tired and not her

usual upbeat self. But then, they hadn't parted on good terms. So why had she come here?

Madge moved closer, almost touching her shoulder. "I need to talk to you."

Kitty nodded. "Okay." What did she want? And why so serious?

"Is there somewhere we can go? Somewhere with a little privacy?"

Apprehension tightened her insides. "Sure. Would you like a cup of coffee? Or tea, maybe?"

Madge nodded.

Kitty led her out through the main entrance. They walked across the road and down the board sidewalk to the canteen.

"Maybe it won't be too crowded, and we can get a table to ourselves."

Inside they ordered coffee at the counter. Each took a steaming mug, and Kitty led the way to an empty table in the corner. Up to now they'd avoided eye contact. As they settled in their seats, Kitty decided it was time to find out what Madge wanted.

Kitty sat her mug on the table and drew a deep breath. "What do you want to talk to me about?"

Madge held her mug with both hands and stared into its depth. Finally, she looked up. Their gazes met. "It's about Ted."

Kitty froze.

Madge's face contorted. She blinked rapidly as if fighting tears. "Kitty...Ted's dead."

Kitty flinched as if Madge had slapped her. Her breath caught. Seconds passed before she could speak. "No," she murmured, shaking her head.

"It's true," Madge continued in a strong

determined voice. "His plane was shot down on the sixteenth."

"No!" She'd found her voice. "No! It can't be. I just got a letter yesterday." Her words came out loud and furious.

"It is true. I saw the reports."

"No, no, no." Kitty shook her head back and forth, wanting to escape, to run away.

Madge leaned closer and reached out to put her hand over Kitty's.

Kitty jerked away. "You're lying. You want him back so you made up this story so I would think he was..." Her voice broke. She couldn't say the words, couldn't allow herself to admit the possibility.

Madge pulled back and straightened in her chair.

Kitty glared at her old friend. She saw the tears streaming down Madge's face. At that moment, she knew. It was true.

She covered her face, trying to contain the rush of emotions. Her body convulsed, and she bent double. Madge's arm slid around her shoulders. Sobs wracked her entire being. They morphed into coughs. She struggled to breathe.

*Oh, God. Oh, God, no! No!*

Madge held her until the sobs slowed, until the numbness descended. Kitty sat in a daze. Unable to think. Unable to move.

"Drink this," Madge urged. She pressed a cup to Kitty's lips.

Kitty tasted the liquid. Coffee. She took a drink then pulled away.

Her mind tried to focus. Ted. Gone. How?

"What happened? Do you know?"

Madge had mentioned a report. What did she mean?

"They were on a mission over Germany. His plane was shot down. Anti-aircraft fire, over the target." Madge patted her hand. "Several men saw the plane go down."

"Did...did anyone get out?" She'd heard of men parachuting out of burning planes.

"They reported seeing two chutes."

She looked up into Madge's face, for a glimmer of hope. "Then... Maybe he didn't die. Maybe he got out."

Madge shook her head. "I read the debriefing reports. All of them. I even talked to two men who saw it. The whole nose was shot off the plane. The only ones who could have gotten out were the gunners in the back."

"I...I don't understand." She just couldn't wrap her mind around what Madge was saying.

"You remember, back in the states, when that nice young lieutenant took us up for a ride in a B-17?"

Kitty nodded. It had been so long ago, but for a young girl who'd never flown in an airplane, it was unforgettable. "What's that got to do with it?"

"Remember where the bombardier sat? Stuck out there with nothing but glass all around him?"

Kitty nodded. She'd ventured out there for a minute before panic set in and she'd retreated back into the body of the plane.

"The navigator sits just behind the bombardier."

She remembered. Right behind the bombardier. Right below the pilots. In the nose.

*Oh, God.*

Her head dropped. She squeezed her eyes tight.

Clenched her fists.

"He probably never knew what hit him."

Kitty wanted to curl up and die. She rocked back and forth as Madge held her. She didn't want to go on.

"I know. I know. I…I loved him, too." Madge's voice cracked.

Kitty nodded against her friend's bosom. Madge had loved him. That's why she'd been so mad. They both loved him.

\*\*\*\*

Kitty took Madge back to her quarters and arranged for her to stay the night.

A letter from Ted waited for her. She held it, unable to make herself open it. She vaguely listened as Madge explained to the girls who shared the room what had happened.

Kitty's boyfriend had been killed. B-17. Shot down.

Kitty barely knew the other girls. At that moment she couldn't even remember their names. They knew she had a man in her life because of the letters. He'd kept his promise, and once they'd started, she'd gotten a letter every day. How many more would she get before they stopped forever?

Finally, just before lights out, she gathered the courage to read his letter. With shaking fingers she tore open the envelope. At first the words swam on the page amid her tears. She blinked them away and forced herself to take deep breaths.

*Darling, Not much happening today. A training flight to get the new crews used to getting into formation. Not very exciting. I like the guys in this crew. Sikes and Peterson are good pilots, although more superstitious than most. I'll have to tell you about their pre-flight ritual. You'll laugh. Hope to see you soon. It won't be long now. When I finish up, I should get leave. Then we can get together. Till then, Love, Ted*

She felt his presence, deep inside. As if he were here beside her. She could feel his touch, his kiss, the way he ran is fingers through her hair. His arms around her, holding her close.

"When is that dated?" Madge interrupted her thoughts.

She looked at the date at the top of the page. "July 14th."

Madge sighed. "Maybe you'll get a few more."

Kitty nodded. She carefully folded the letter and returned it to its envelope. Then she opened a box beside her bed and placed it on top of the other letters. Some from Milton and some from Ted.

She gently closed the box, caressing the top. "At least I have his letters." Then a thought occurred to her. "Do you have a picture of him?" She hoped maybe Ted had given Madge a portrait, one of those shots made in his dress uniform.

Madge shook her head. "No. I wish I did."

Kitty opened the box again, shuffled through the letters until she found them. Two little, black-and-white pictures, from the photo machine. She held them, gazed at his handsome face, the grin, the little dimple in his chin.

"Can I see?" Madge asked.

Reluctantly Kitty handed the photos to Madge.

"It's all I have. These and his letters."

"One of those photo booths?"

Kitty nodded. "In a theater."

Madge stared into the distance, her eyes glistening with tears as she gave them back.

Kitty placed them in the box. She closed it and sighed. She couldn't cry any more, but the pain wouldn't stop. She wondered if it would ever stop.

Dejected, she climbed into bed. She wouldn't sleep. All she could think about was Ted. Every moment with him. Every precious moment. She'd think of him every minute for the rest of her life.

****

Madge returned to London the next day.

Kitty cancelled her plans to visit Milton. She couldn't face the train trip, hours alone, the cars filled with servicemen, airmen like Ted, who didn't know, didn't understand. Instead she worked through the weekend, taking on the continuous paperwork generated by war.

She ignored the remarks about "Lake's little darling" getting her hands dirty doing the drudge work. The other women resented how General Lake brought her in, and she'd realized early on that they wouldn't be friends. None of them knew about Ted or even Milton. And she stubbornly refused to let them see her pain.

She forced herself to focus on the endless typing and the stacks of filing. The jangling telephone grated on her nerves. A stray serviceman delivered a packet of deciphered messages, and she almost bit his head off when she saw they were for someone else. He hurried away like a puppy with his tail between his legs. She regretted her outburst but returned to her typing with no offer of explanation to her fellow workers.

Every time her mind strayed to thoughts of Ted, she harshly reprimanded herself and ordered her thoughts back to the activity at hand.

Saturday dragged into Sunday.

Guilt at letting her brother down drove her to steal a few moments to write him. After all, he was alone in a hospital, with no family, no friends. She might not get to see him again before they sent him back to the states. Should she tell him about Ted? After all, they had made friends in London. Milton deserved to know what happened.

She forced herself to write the words. Then she sat there staring at them. On paper they were so cold, so unreal, like something in a newspaper. They didn't convey her sorrow. The deep empty hole inside her so painful she feared if she dwelt on it she would dissolve into nothingness.

She'd never told Milton about Ted, how she felt about him, what he meant to her, that he was the love of her life, the one person she was meant to be with—forever. She couldn't explain in a letter. The more she tried the less sense it made.

The tears came again. She fought them back with grim determination. She would not collapse in front of the other women. She would not let them see her pain, her vulnerability. She thought of those first days in basic training, when she feared she would fail and stubbornly refused to let the others see her fear. The sergeant had called them soldiers in their own kind of trenches. She hadn't understood it then, but now she did. She was in the trenches fighting alongside soldiers who needed her to do her job, not give in to the pain of losing someone dear.

And Milton, he needed to hear something cheerful and upbeat, not more pain and sorrow. She just didn't have it in her, not now. Guilt weighed heavy on her shoulders, but grief weighed more. She could only carry so much. She wadded the letter into a ball, squeezing it tight. She wouldn't burden her brother with her loss. He had enough to endure.

General Lake remained out of sorts for the next few days. He attended meeting after meeting. When he spoke to her, he barked and grumbled, completely unaware of her somber mood. For her part, she did all she could to keep him satisfied. She typed up notes, reports, recommendations, focused on accuracy and efficiency, and kept her emotions in check.

The Eighth Air Force had been under Eisenhower's command since before the invasion. According to General Lake the change in command structure made everything more difficult. Constant consultation with SHAEF (Supreme Headquarters Allied Expeditionary Force) on every decision took its toll on everyone.

Kitty was aware of disagreements over planning of air support for an important operation in France. General Lake worked himself into a tizzy arguing with several other generals about it. Orders from SHAEF infuriated him. He didn't think the highest commanders understood air warfare at all, its strengths or its weaknesses. He ranted to Kitty and his support staff on the subject until Kitty began to worry about him.

The day of the operation reports began coming in. At first it appeared successful, then the whispers started. General Lake looked ashen but didn't say a word. He retreated to his office where he remained until General Doolittle summoned him to a meeting of the Eighth Air Force Headquarters staff.

Several WACs huddled together whispering. Kitty

needed to know what had happened. She eased into the group.

"What's going on?" she asked.

A sergeant eyed her suspiciously before speaking. "We bombed our own troops," she stated flatly.

"What?" It was unbelievable.

"It's true," another WAC added. "Reports are still coming in on casualties."

Kitty shook her head as she thought of boys like Milton on the ground being bombed.

"What makes it even worse is that supposedly orders were changed. Our flyboys didn't do what SHAEF wanted. I don't know who messed up, but heads will roll if they find out someone disobeyed orders."

"Yeah. And it would have been someone pretty high up."

"Right. The pilots and crews do what they're told."

"I just hope Doolittle doesn't get blamed."

"Yeah."

"That's for sure."

Everyone respected General Doolittle, including General Lake. The hero of the Tokyo raid had proved a capable and well-liked commander.

Kitty had no idea what would happen next. Whatever happened she firmly believed that winning the war was the most important objective, and mistakes could not be tolerated. The Allies had been fighting in Normandy for six weeks. More and more men were being killed and wounded. They had to do something to beat the Germans. How many would die? How much would it take before the Germans were driven back into their own country and forced to surrender?

Kitty focused her anger on the enemy—the Germans. They were the cause of all her pain. They'd killed Ted. They'd wounded Milton. They had to be defeated.

Chapter Thirty-One

*July 28, 1944*

*Dear Madge,*

*It's been four days since I got a letter from Ted. It was dated July 15, the day before he went down. I know there is little chance that I will get any more, but I can't help but hope that there are more, somehow lost in the process of being forwarded from Ellingham. He must not have gotten my letter telling him I'd been transferred to High Wycombe. I remember that I almost called him after I got here. Now I wish I had.*

*This small stack of letters is all I have left. And those silly little pictures. I will treasure them all the rest of my life. He was the love of my life, and there will never be anyone else. Never. I knew it that day on the beach, when I first saw him. I knew that fate or God or some unknown force brought us together and meant for us to be together, always. That's why when I saw him here in England, I couldn't help but be drawn to him. It had nothing to do with you.*

*I know you'll say that someday I'll meet someone else, but I don't think so. I loved him so much, still love him. I'll always love him.*

*I know you loved him, too. And I'm sorry you were hurt. But it wasn't the same. We had a connection from the beginning—from that day on the beach. He felt it, too. We were meant for each other. And I am so grateful that we found each other, that we had some time together, short as it was.*

*When we were in Norwich, he made me promise to always remember him. He knew that this could happen. That his plane could be shot down. I didn't want to promise because it meant that I knew he wouldn't make it, and I couldn't bear to think about it. But he made me. I promised—to remember him always, for the rest of my life. And I will. I will never forget him.*

*I try to read his letters every night. But when I do the tears start anew. The pain is unbearable. You can't know how much I want to see him again, feel his arms around me. But I know I have to accept what has happened. What else can I do? He's gone.*

*Please write to me. Please be my friend. I need a friend, and you are the only one that truly understands about Ted.*

*Kitty*

\*\*\*\*

"Greenlee, get in here."

General Lake never shouted like that. Something must be wrong. She grabbed her book and hurried into his office.

"I've…I've…" He wrung his hands and paced.

"Sir?"

"Take a letter. No, a memo. To General Doolittle. No. Dammit!"

"Sir?"

"Oh, I'm sorry, Greenlee. I'm just so frustrated."

"Can I help?"

"No…I don't know." He stopped pacing and looked at her. "They just don't understand. No matter what I say, they don't understand." He turned away again. "It was terrible about those boys. But the wind blew the signal smoke back over our troops. We dropped short. It was horrible, terrible, yes, but it had nothing to do with the flight path."

Kitty listened, unsure what he was talking about.

He turned to face her again and pounded his fist into his hand as he continued. "If our planes had gone in at that low altitude parallel to the enemy line, they would have been decimated by anti-aircraft fire. We couldn't expose them to that kind of fire." He continued to pound his fist in sync with his words. "We had to hit it on a perpendicular line, dump the bombs on the damn Germans, and get the hell out of there. There was no other way to do it."

He stopped and looked at her. "You understand, don't you?"

Instinctively, Kitty nodded. She had no idea what he meant, only that he was trying to justify something to do with the bombing.

"It was a dirty shame the bombs fell short. But it couldn't be helped. This is war. Things happen that we don't expect."

"Yes, sir," she responded. He was talking about the day we bombed our own troops. She'd seen some of the reports, the casualties, even a general had been killed. Her stomach knotted. She'd been ashamed of the Air Force. It should never have happened. There could be no excuses. Yet here was General Lake making excuses.

The telephone on his desk rang. He answered it, and his face went pale. When he hung up he turned to Kitty. "You may go, Greenlee. I have to report to General Doolittle." He came toward her and placed his hand on her arm. "You've done a good job, Sergeant. An excellent job." He left her standing there alone and wondering what was going on.

Kitty returned to her desk and her reports.

Later Captain Shelley approached Kitty's desk. "Sergeant Greenlee."

"Yes, ma'am." Kitty stopped typing and quickly got to her feet.

"Would you come to my office?"

"Yes, ma'am." Kitty grabbed her pad and pencil and followed the captain.

"Have a seat. And you won't need that." She shut the door as she spoke.

Kitty held the pad self-consciously and sank into the chair. She knew Captain Shelley didn't like her, didn't like the way General Lake had brought her into the office. After Kitty's arrival, when she discovered the many, capable secretaries at Eighth AF Headquarters, she didn't blame her. Despite the circumstances, the captain had remained professional and accepted Kitty into the organization.

The officer settled down behind her desk and clasped her hands in front of her. "I've just been informed that General Lake is being reassigned, back to the states…effective immediately."

The captain's words struck like a punch in the gut. Kitty struggled to maintain her composure, aware that Captain Shelley watched her closely.

"That leaves you in an awkward position," the officer continued.

"Yes, ma'am." Kitty focused on the wall beyond the captain, kept her body rigid. She didn't know what to say. Better to say nothing. Not ask questions.

"As you are aware," Captain Shelley continued, "we have sufficient staff. Without the general, your services will not be needed."

Kitty's heart sank. She blinked back tears and hoped the captain didn't see her hands shaking as she gripped the pad even tighter. "Yes, ma'am," she managed, then swallowed hard before continuing. "Will I be reassigned?"

"Yes." Captain Shelley paused. "Right now, I'm not exactly sure where."

Kitty fought hard as the old panic crept through her. Alone, into the unknown. Would she make it? Without Madge or Milton or…Ted? Despite her frantic blinking, a tear escaped and slid down her cheek. Much as she wanted to brush it aside, she remained still, desperately holding on.

Captain Shelley studied her. She must have seen the tear because her expression softened. "I didn't realize you were so…close to General Lake."

"Ma'am?"

"I can understand your being upset that he's been reassigned, but we're in a war, and we all must make sacrifices." Her voice was hard, unfeeling.

"Oh, I understand sacrifices!" Kitty couldn't contain her outburst. "And I don't care about General Lake."

The captain's expression showed concern—and curiosity.

Kitty turned away and swiped at the tears she couldn't stop. "I didn't mean that," she muttered. "It's…it's just been so much." She shook her head. "Too much."

"Perhaps you should explain." The sympathy in her

voice drew Kitty out.

Kitty looked up into her eyes. *Tell her,* she ordered herself. *Tell her the truth.*

"An airman, on a B-17. He was shot down." The words tumbled out. "And my brother. In the infantry. Wounded. Bad. So bad." She shook her head, fighting the pain that accompanied the memories.

"This airman. You were in love with him." She wasn't asking.

Kitty nodded.

"He didn't get out?"

Kitty shook her head.

Captain Shelley's lips pursed as if she were trying to contain her own emotions. She nodded, her eyes went to a framed photo on her desk. Kitty realized this woman had also suffered loss.

"And your brother, where is he?"

Kitty drew a ragged breath. "In a hospital, near Liverpool. They'll ship him home as soon as they can."

"Have you seen him?"

The image of Milton, bandaged and helpless, came to mind. Kitty could only nod in response, her lips trembling.

"Well," the officer sighed. "Unfortunately, it changes nothing. You will be reassigned." She paused, looking directly at her.

Kitty could feel the officer's scrutiny. "Will I remain in England?" If General Lake was going back home, would she go too?

"More than likely." Captain Shelley flipped through some papers on her desk. "You've worked hard, Sergeant. And you have a high enough security clearance. There might be a position at SHAEF. Would you be interested?"

Her spirits rose. "Of course. I'll go wherever I'm needed."

The captain looked at her warily. "Yes, you will. You will go where you are ordered to go. The job at SHAEF would be challenging, but then you do have experience dealing with difficult men."

Kitty chose not to respond. She'd learned to take the jabs about her relationship with General Lake and not let them get to her.

"That will be all, Sergeant. For now, you will continue to work in the secretarial pool. I will let you know as soon as a decision is made."

"Thank you, ma'am." Kitty quickly left the office.

Her knees went weak as what just happened sank in. She dropped into her chair and sat in a daze.

"I see you've heard." General Lake approached.

Kitty tried to stand, but he waved her to return to her seat.

"They're sending me back to the States, the Pentagon." He shook his head, resigned to his fate. "You'll be all right. They'll find a place for you."

"Yes, sir." She wouldn't tell him about SHAEF. It might not happen. "I'll be fine."

"You've done a good job, and don't you forget it." He patted her on the shoulder and disappeared into his office.

Suddenly, the tears returned. She was all alone.

*Oh, Ted. Why did you have to die? Why you? Why?*

\*\*\*\*

Her orders stated, "Report immediately."

Captain Shelley told her to pack her things and be on the afternoon train to London. By nightfall she'd be in new quarters, by morning she'd have a new job. She wouldn't know anyone. Not that it mattered.

She climbed the stairs and made her way down the hall. The room was dark so she flipped on the light. Something rustled in the corner. She'd forgotten about Caroline. The girl worked nights as a teletype operator and slept during the day. With five girls sharing the same room, one on nights relieved some of the congestion.

Kitty quietly pulled out her duffle bag and began the process of packing. She'd done it often enough to know exactly how to methodically fold and pack each item. The Army had taught her to be organized, and her many moves made packing an automatic process.

She picked up the box of letters, Ted's letters. Her fingers ran along its edges. She was tempted to open it, to read one of his letters, to gaze at the silly photos.

Her throat tightened. If she read even one word, she wouldn't be able to stop the tears.

*No, wait until later, when you are a little stronger.*

She set the box aside, saved it for last. She'd stuff them into the top of her bag after everything else.

The underthings she'd washed out the night before should be dry by now. She trekked down the hall to the bathroom to retrieve them along with her other toiletries. While there, she splashed cold water on her face to cool her emotions. She needed to get hold of herself. Be strong.

She thought of Milton's constant encouragement when she was younger. She promised herself she wouldn't let him down, as she headed back down the hall.

Suddenly, deafening noise engulfed her.

The ceiling crashed in.

Her arms went up to cover her head.

The side wall collapsed, slammed into her, pushed her down.

She slid to the floor and curled into a ball to protect herself as the roof, or maybe the whole building, collapsed on top of her.

She must have lost consciousness for a short time. When she came to, she blinked to get her bearings. She tried to get up. Her head swam. Her stomach reeled, and its contents threatened to erupt. She tightened her throat to keep it down.

She got to her knees and pushed aside broken plaster, splintered wood, wires. A large beam stood at a precarious angle, leaning against something above. It must have protected her from being crushed.

Dust and smoke assailed her nostrils. She blinked and wiped her eyes with the back of her hand to clear her vision. Her body ached, but everything seemed to function.

On her feet, she held onto the remains of one wall. Around her wood and plaster and hanging wallpaper formed a jumbled, splintered mess. Somehow the hallway floor remained intact.

She looked back toward the stairwell.

*I have to get out of here before the building collapses.*

The doorway to her room leaned awkwardly only a few steps away.

*Ted's letters. His pictures. I have to get them. They're all I have.*

Nothing else mattered. She didn't want to live without them.

She pushed herself through the dangerously angled doorway and into the room. Flames shot up through a hole where the floor and back wall had been only moments before. Beyond the fire, a green field loomed in the distance.

Straight ahead she could see them, scattered across the floor where the box had fallen. She stumbled forward, a few more feet and she could scoop them up.

A groan came from somewhere nearby.

She turned, surveyed the wreckage. Flames licked the edges. Smoke billowed into the room like a chimney that wouldn't draw.

Caroline lay on the floor, the shattered wood of a rafter on top of her.

The injured girl tried to move and moaned again. Blood stained the sheet partially wrapped around her midsection.

Kitty looked from Caroline back to the letters. Flames skittered across the floor toward them. If she didn't grab them in the next few seconds, they'd be gone.

Ted would be gone.

She had to get them. She lunged toward them reaching out.

A scream of anguish pierced the smoke.

Caroline struggled to free herself. She couldn't get out from under the debris. Without help, she would die.

Something crashed below them, and the flames leapt higher.

Kitty turned away from Ted, from his letters, from all she had left.

She tugged at the splintered board, pain stabbed her bare hands. She managed to shove the beam aside, freeing Caroline.

Kitty grabbed the injured WAC by the shoulders and pulled her to her feet.

"Hold on to me," she screamed over the growing roar of the fire.

Kitty stripped off her jacket and wrapped it around the other woman. Holding Caroline around the waist, Kitty maneuvered her toward the hallway. The scorching heat from the swirling inferno followed them.

She pushed Caroline through the angled, burning doorframe. Searing pain shot through Kitty's arm. She gritted her teeth and shoved the injured girl ahead of her, pushing aside debris as they made their way down what remained of the hallway. Smoke enveloped them, filled her lungs. Both women coughed and stumbled toward the miraculously still-intact stairwell.

Lightheaded from lack of oxygen, Kitty feared they would both tumble down the stairs. Stubborn determination kept her going. Somehow they reached the bottom.

Caroline sank to the floor coughing, unable to continue. Kitty joined her, gasping for breath.

Light shone through the broken windows of the front door.

Something inside Kitty drove her to keep going, to survive. She gathered her strength and dragged Caroline's limp body toward the light, toward safety, toward life.

****

She lay in a sterile, impersonal hospital with clean sheets, a bandaged arm, and burning pain. The antiseptic smell barely penetrated the smoke still lingering in her nostrils.

Tears stung her eyes. Then the cough returned, wracking her body as if her insides would come out.

"Here, drink this." A nurse stuck a glass straw to her lips. She sucked in the sweet, wet liquid. Weak English tea. After a few sips, she pulled back.

The nurse set the glass on the table by the bed.

"That doodlebug almost got ya'." She smiled as she tucked in the sheets. "These new ones don't give no warning. Just bam. Either they get ya' or they don't."

V-2 rockets. Kitty remembered being told about them. How they struck anytime anywhere. The old ones, the V-1's, buzzed to warn you they were coming. Buzz bombs the English called them. She remembered hearing the terrifying sound once, months before.

But there had been no warning.

The nurse moved on to the next bed. "How are you doin', miss?"

Kitty rolled her head to see the patient beside her.

Caroline had bandages on her head and neck. Her shoulder and arm were encased in plaster. The visible portion of her face was swollen and bruised.

"Okay," Caroline murmured.

The nurse tucked the sheets tightly around Caroline's waist. "Just let me know if ya' need a thing."

Caroline tried to nod.

Kitty watched the nurse walk away. Then she closed her eyes. The pain in her arm was excruciating. She had never experienced anything like it. She thought of Milton. Did he hurt like this? No wonder he'd looked so awful.

*Do I look awful? Ha!*

The small, sarcastic laugh came unbidden.

*What does it matter? There's no one to see me. No*

*Ted.*

Tears overflowed and spilled down her cheeks.

*Oh, Ted. Why did you have to leave me? Why? I'd just found you. Just started to get to know you.*

She squeezed her eyes tight, trying to stop the tears, knowing if she didn't the dam would burst and she'd never be able to stop.

"Kitty?"

She quickly blinked, tightening her throat to stop the sobs threatening to emerge. Then she drew in a deep breath and forced herself to look at Caroline. "What?"

"I just wanted…wanted to tell you… Thank you for saving my life."

The words stabbed through her, their sound penetrating her heart as surely as a sword. He had said those words, those very words, that day in the gazebo. That day he told her why he hadn't recognized her. "I thought you were an angel," he'd said. "My angel."

Her body convulsed. She doubled over as the sobs came in uncontrollable waves mixed with coughing. She gasped and sobbed and tried to scream.

*Oh, Ted. No. No. No.*

The nurse was holding her. She grasped the warm body, someone, anyone.

The needle prick barely penetrated her agony.

Finally, she lay back, the nurse still stroking her and telling her it would be all right. But Kitty knew nothing would ever be all right again.

She wanted to go home. Wanted to turn back the clock and go back to when she was safe and happy, surrounded by her family, her friends, even her sisters.

It hadn't turned out so well. This adventure of hers hadn't turned out at all.

Her thoughts drifted into the fog. She felt nothing. Darkness closed in, and she slid into oblivion.

Chapter Thirty-Two

In the days that followed, Captain Shelley visited Kitty in the hospital. The officer assured Kitty that the assignment to SHAEF had not been changed because of her unexpected hospitalization.

The surprise came when the captain announced that both Kitty and Caroline would receive medals, Purple Hearts, for their injuries. In addition, the captain would recommend Kitty for a commendation for bravery for rescuing her fellow WAC.

Kitty accepted the officer's kind words, but they did little to dispel her sense of utter devastation. She'd done nothing special. Not like Milton or Ted. Not like any of those brave men who faced death every day. She'd simply survived.

"Come and see me when you get out of the hospital," Captain Shelley told her.

So here she stood, outside the captain's office, in her newly issued uniform, her arm still bandaged.

She'd run it through her head a dozen times. The speech she planned, a confession really, would be short and to the point. She'd failed, utterly, and she wanted to go home where she belonged. She'd wanted an adventure, wanted to prove to Milton that she could do it, wanted to be a soldier and fight the enemy. But it hadn't been like that.

She'd fallen in love with a man who'd told her he

wouldn't live. He wanted to go back to the bombers and be killed like his friends. But she hadn't listened, had blocked it all out, had just wanted to love him. And she'd gotten her heart broken, beyond repair.

And Milton. Dear, precious Milton. The only person who had believed in her. She'd let him down when he needed her. She'd been so caught up in herself that she hadn't visited him when he was hurt and alone. She'd stopped writing him at the very time when he had needed her encouragement.

She'd even failed the Army. She'd gotten so caught up in working for the general that she'd lost all perspective. She'd turned her back on her training, failed to be part of the team, put her own selfish interest ahead of the service. She didn't deserve to wear this uniform and represent American women.

So she would tell the captain the truth. That she had not yet reached her twenty-first birthday. That she'd lied about her age when she'd enlisted, taking advantage of being ahead in school, of graduating high school at sixteen. It had been easy enough to say she'd been born in 1921 instead of 1923. Since she'd finished two years of college, no one ever questioned her age.

Once they knew the truth, the Army would send her home. Not just to an assignment back in the states. They'd probably give her a discharge, perhaps even a dishonorable one. She had broken the rules and deserved to be punished.

An officer came out of the office followed by Captain Shelley.

"Sergeant Greenlee." The captain smiled. Her pleasure genuine. "Good to see you out of the hospital. Come in."

She practically pulled Kitty into her office. As the captain took her seat behind the desk, Kitty reached around and shut the door. She didn't want anyone to hear what she had to say.

"Captain," she started hesitantly. "I want to go home."

"What? I don't understand."

"I've disgraced the Women's Army Corps. I have no right to be here."

"Sergeant, you've been through an ordeal. But that is no reason to give up."

"I shouldn't even be in the Army."

"Now you listen to me. I know what it is to lose someone. It's painful." Captain Shelley looked at the picture on her desk. "But it is no reason to quit."

She pushed her chair back, got up, and walked around to the front of the desk, close enough that Kitty could smell her perfume. "I'm speaking now as another woman. All right?"

Kitty nodded. An officer had never spoken to her like this before.

"What would he want you to do?"

Kitty hadn't expected that, hadn't thought of what Ted would say.

"My guess is that he would tell you to keep fighting. To help win this war. He gave his life so the rest of us could live free. Are you going to turn your back on his sacrifice?"

"I…I didn't think of it that way."

"You should." The officer smiled. "Besides, we need you. You've worked hard, got an excellent record. Why throw it away?" She touched Kitty's hand. "It'll get easier. I promise."

Kitty could only nod. She lowered her gaze, unsure what to say.

"Didn't you say you had a brother who was wounded?"

"Yes." Kitty looked back up. "Milton. He was in the First Infantry. Wounded in Normandy."

"A brave man."

"Yes, he is."

"And you don't want to disappoint him, now do you?"

"No." She was right about that. Milton would want her to keep going, to work hard, and see this war through to the end. He'd always told her not to be a quitter.

"Now that's settled." She touched Kitty's shoulder, and then she returned to the chair behind the desk.

Kitty drew a fortifying breath. Somehow she regained her strength, her determination.

"Rumor is that Eisenhower is moving his headquarters to Normandy."

"Really." Kitty's thoughts rushed ahead. "How soon?"

"Don't know. It'll take a while to move everyone. It's a big operation. But I'm sure he'll want to get closer to the front as soon as he can."

"Then I would be going to France, pretty soon, I mean."

Captain Shelley nodded, smiling. "Yes, you would."

****

Word passed down to the women huddled together below decks. Time to disembark in France. Relief filled her. Another step in the uncomfortable journey complete.

When they boarded the ship in Southampton for the short trip across the English Channel, the sweet-smelling salt air and the gentle rocking of the ship had reminded her of the voyage across the Atlantic. The memory helped her cope with her anxiety. Despite her seasickness on the longer voyage, she'd survived. She could handle a few hours of queasy stomach knowing her destination was France.

Kitty forced herself to visualize the remaining journey. Trucks across France to the new headquarters. Settling into new quarters, new workplace. Similar to those in England. Nothing drastically different. She could make it. She knew what to expect.

Again, dressed in full battle gear, Kitty felt more like a soldier than she had in basic training. And in her own way, she knew she was one. Part of the enormous military machine fighting the Germans.

When orders came for the move, she'd expected to land in Cherborg, the French deep-water port destroyed by the Germans before the American troops could capture it. Despite working frantically to repair the damage and reopen the port, it still lacked the capacity to handle all the Allies needs. When the WACs boarded the LST, word quickly spread that they would be landing on the beach, where most of the U.S. troops and materiel were still being unloaded.

She lined up and followed the others, wishing she'd been on deck to catch a glimpse of the French coast as they approached. She wondered what Milton had thought as he made this same journey months before. Had he been afraid? Had he known he'd be wounded?

A glimpse of light told her the huge doors on the front of the ship had opened. Motors cranked to life. The trucks inched forward toward the giant opening to the beach beyond.

Patiently, the women waited until the vehicles disembarked. Then came their turn. With a signal from the senior officer, the small contingent of WACs marched out of the bowels of the ship and onto the sandy shore.

Ahead was a beehive of activity—trucks, tanks, and soldiers swarming in every direction. Rows of boxes stacked high stood in random rows. Men worked diligently to unload numerous ships and move the supplies inland. A road snaked its way up the hill and away from the water.

She thought of Milton, facing gunfire as he came ashore. She glanced toward the water's edge. Huge objects that resembled giant jacks were strewn along the waterline as far as the eye could see. Her gaze drifted inland to the enormous concrete structures overlooking the beach. Damaged pillboxes, where German guns fired on the men and boats of the invasion force, stood silent.

A chill ran through her. How many men had died on this beach?

"Come on, Greenlee," someone called.

She shifted her attention to the other women, climbing aboard a deuce-n-half. She hurried her pace to catch up. An older WAC named Beulah extended her hand to help her up into the bed of the truck.

"Thanks," Kitty said, settling into the seat on the end.

Someone yelled "All aboard." The big truck jerked

into motion and took its place in the line of vehicles waiting to leave the beach.

Kitty shifted her gaze from the hulking mass of the ship to the water, sparkling in the sunlight.

Something dark bobbed in the waves.

Her heart slammed into her ribs. She gasped and clutched her chest. Without thinking she stood and almost jumped from the truck.

Beulah grabbed her. "What the…"

Kitty watched the dark object, tried to focus on it. All she could see was a raft with a man aboard. "See? See him?" she screamed, pointing toward the sea.

Beulah and another girl stood beside her. "What do you see? What are you talking about?"

"Out there. Don't you see him? The man in the raft."

"I don't see anything," the other one said.

"All I see is a hulk in the water," Beulah said. "And another one over there." She pointed to the right of the original object.

But all Kitty could see was Ted floating on a raft, too exhausted to paddle.

"Hey, Corporal," Beulah called to a passing soldier. "What are those dark objects in the water?"

He looked out over the water in the direction she pointed. "Oh, that. It's what's left of the Mulberry harbor. A bad storm broke it up about three weeks after D-Day. Couldn't be fixed." He turned to stare up at the women on the truck. "Now it's just a breakwater. Helps calm the surf."

"Thanks," Beulah said. She patted Kitty on the arm. "See, it's nothing to worry about."

Kitty blinked. Beulah was right. The object was

stationary, not floating. And no one was on it. "But I saw him," she almost sobbed, not wanting to give up the vision.

"You're seeing things," Beulah told her. "There's no man out there."

Embarrassed and sick at heart, Kitty sank down onto the hard bench. She looked at her feet, her hands, anything but the water.

In her mind's eye, she saw him still. And for a fleeting moment, she thought that she could run out there, swim to him, pull him from the water—again. Hold him in her arms—again.

But he was gone…gone forever.

The truck jerked into motion. She refused to look back. She didn't want to see the beach, the waves crashing on the shore, not ever again.

****

The French countryside gradually changed into city streets. Fields into houses into buildings. One truck followed another as they wound their way into the famous city.

Paris. She was in Paris.

But for her, there was no excitement, no joy, just gratitude the Germans had retreated. Some said the war would be over by Christmas. Oh, dear God, she hoped so. Too many had already suffered, died. It was all such a useless endeavor. Surely Hitler would realize the Germans couldn't win, that they should surrender and stop the madness.

Their truck had barely entered the city when it left the convoy and turned south. Their destination was Versailles, the new home of SHAEF, not the famous palace, but the town surrounding it. Eisenhower didn't want his staff distracted by the infamous Paris night life.

When they finally stopped, Kitty climbed out and stood on the sidewalk with eleven other WACs. They stretched their legs and surveyed the old apartment building looming before them.

An Army officer greeted the WAC lieutenant and gave instructions. Kitty overheard him say the building had been vacated by German troops the month before. The lower floors already quartered an earlier contingent of American and British women, who were currently working in the various SHAEF buildings in the area. They would occupy the empty top floor.

He waved his hand as he gave directions to the building where they would be working.

"Walking distance" she heard him say. Kitty hoped that didn't mean a mile-long hike. Judging from the hours they'd devoted in London, she didn't relish walking a long distance to her quarters after a twelve-hour shift.

Kitty and the others lugged their duffle bags up the narrow stairway. The fourth floor consisted of two apartments. The lieutenant directed Kitty and six others into a two-bedroom apartment with one small bathroom and a makeshift kitchen. The place was filthy. The smell revolting.

She and two other WACs were assigned to one of the tiny bedrooms. It contained three cots crammed side-by-side. No dresser, no chest, no closet. A board covered a broken window pane, but light filtered through the dirty glass above. No curtains softened the starkness.

Kitty deposited her bag on the cot nearest the

window and looked around in disgust. The place smelled musty, with the lingering odor of urine and unwashed bodies.

She wondered if the other apartment was as bad as this one.

Someone behind her commented that the water in both the bathroom and kitchen worked. That was good. At least they could start cleaning.

They organized themselves into teams with each pair assigned an area to clean. They found buckets and mops and soap in the cellar along with primitive wash tubs that apparently served as the laundry.

It didn't take long to discover that the water only worked part of the time. Too much demand and it cut off. They also found that it was cold. No hot water in the whole building.

The stove in the kitchen didn't work, and no one was quite sure how the place might be heated. At least the weather remained mild and clear. Open windows provided much needed fresh air and sunshine dried the freshly washed linens.

Soldiers appeared downstairs laden with K rations, enough to last a week, and essential supplies. The nearest mess hall was eight blocks away and shared with male Army personnel. The K rations would give them something to eat if they missed the limited serving schedule.

"Great!" one girl complained. "No hot food. No hot water."

"Might as well make the best of it," another encouraged.

"We signed up 'for better or worse' and this must be the 'worse'," another joked.

"And I thought the Army would be better than getting married."

"Wonder what Eisenhower's digs look like."

"A darn sight better than this."

Kitty listened but didn't join in their banter. She kept quiet and to herself these days. Maybe after a while, after they settled in, she'd try to be friendly. But right now, it took all her energy to keep going.

Instead she scrubbed the floor and walls until her hands were raw and her body ached.

She wanted to work, wanted to bury herself in the many tasks assigned to her. She didn't want to think...or feel.

She'd always hated traveling, moving from place to place, getting used to new situations. Once she settled in to working she'd be okay, she told herself. She could do this. She could survive. She had to. She couldn't let them down, not Ted, not Milton. They believed in her, so she had to do it, for them.

Chapter Thirty-Three

Flanked by guards, they straggled through the gates and into yet another fenced compound. About one-hundred and fifty men, all American officers, had traveled by train to the town of Sagan and then walked the mile or so from the wooden platform beside the tracks to this camp. Since entering the barbed-wire walls of Stalag Luft III, they'd been photographed for their POW identification cards, stripped, and issued prison clothing which consisted of an assortment of used clothing taken from previous arrivals. Despite it being mid-August, the new attire included a heavy overcoat.

Ted fingered the rough wool coat remembering his arrival in England the February before. He'd needed the wool in the cold, damp English winter. But now in the heat of August, just carrying the heavy garment made him sweat.

The reality of his situation sank in. This was a permanent camp, and he would most likely be here for a long time, long enough to need the winter coat he held. He was a prisoner—deep in Germany, a very long way from the Allied invasion front, from England and from Kitty.

Prisoners surrounded new arrivals, gawking at them as if they were strange creatures. Some recognized old friends or acquaintances and called out to them.

Ted scanned the faces, some gaunt, some hard, a few friendly. None looked familiar. No one called to him. Despite the crowd, he felt alone.

He didn't know if anyone else got out of the Sally Ann. He had a vague memory of another parachute, but it could have been from another bomber. If any others had been shot down on the same mission, they'd been scattered across the continent and could be in any one of the dozens of POW camps in German-held territory.

Other prisoners herded the newbies into a large building. Inside it looked like a crude theater with chairs and benches lined up facing a raised stage.

They'd barely relaxed in their seats when the order "Attention!" rang out.

Everyone jumped to their feet.

A full bird colonel strode to the front and climbed the stairs to the stage, his rank recognizable only by the insignia on the cap he wore. He introduced himself as Colonel Wilson Bendix, senior officer and commander of Center Compound, and he left no doubt that they were back in the Army.

"You are American soldiers, and until Germany is defeated, you will act like soldiers." The colonel's handle-bar mustache added drama to his sobering speech. "They have told you that the war is over for you, but that's a lie. They are still our enemy."

Hands on hips, the intimidating officer paced the stage and looked from man to man. "If you don't believe it, then disobey or get out of line and see how fast they shoot you. They don't give a damn about the Geneva Convention." His eyes bore into Ted as if his words were for him alone. "They may control your body, but they don't control your mind. So stay sharp. Remember who your enemy is." His gaze left Ted and moved on to another airman.

Ted released his breath. He hadn't expected to be chewed out so soon after they arrived. But the colonel's words woke him up, made him realize that even the relative safety of a Prisoner of War camp did not mean he was out of the war. His life still hung in the balance, nothing assured.

Like floating on the ocean in a life raft, he thought. He hadn't gone down with the ship, and he hadn't been killed by the civilians, but he hadn't made it to the safety of shore either. The image of an angel pulling him from the waves comforted him. She was with him, even here.

The colonel went on to explain the command structure within the camp and the rules about the warning wire. Strung thirty feet inside the fence, anyone crossing the wire could and would be shot by the guards in the "Goon Boxes," as they affectionately referred to the guard towers. He also related the story of the escape attempt the previous spring from the British compound. After the escapees were recaptured, the Germans had executed fifty men in retaliation. The colonel made his point. The Germans would kill anyone who tried to escape.

On their way out of the building, after the sobering speech, they were issued eating utensils and a single roll of toilet paper with instructions to take good care of these treasurers.

Outside, Ted stood in silence, while others milled around him.

Someone tapped him on the shoulder. "You

Theodore Kruger?"

"Yeah. I'm Kruger."

"Callahan." He frowned and made no offer to shake hands. "Come with me." His words were terse as he turned and walked away.

Ted hurried to follow him. All around him the newly arrived prisoners headed in different directions, toward different buildings.

The camp consisted of neat rows of buildings laid out with the military efficiency of the Germans. The man called Callahan led him toward two long wooden structures with doors in either end. They turned right and went between the two barracks toward a second row. Ted glanced between the structures as they passed. He estimated the distance between the buildings to be four or five feet. A barbed wire fence as tall as the rooftops with warning wire loomed beyond the second row of buildings. The warning wire, just as the colonel described it, stretched across the open area in front of the fence, knee-high and sobering.

Callahan stopped at the end of one of the buildings and pointed to the markings.

"This is block forty-seven, your new home. They're all numbered, and they call them blocks—as in cell block—not barracks. Inside there are rooms called combines. You're in combine four. Okay?"

Ted nodded, then asked, "Are there just Americans in this camp?"

"Yep. In the center compound we're all Americans. There's Brits in another. And all kinds of nationalities spread around."

"How many compounds are there?"

"Dunno. I don't get around much." A wry smile

accompanied his sarcasm.

He opened the door and led Ted inside.

Callahan pointed to a room, and Ted stepped inside. Hand-made wooden bunks stood three high. Ted counted five of them crammed into the tiny area and wondered how fifteen men would squeeze in without crushing each other. A small table and some stools filled what space there was in the center of the room.

A man who'd been sitting on one of the stools got to his feet. Ted noticed another man lying on a middle bunk.

Ted nodded to them.

"This is Kruger. Your new roommate."

Ted glanced back at the man standing in the doorway, then turned to the one standing before him, stuck out his hand and smiled. "Ted Kruger."

The airman eyed him suspiciously. Slowly he reached out and shook Ted's hand. "Lynch. Al Lynch." He pointed to the man lying on the bunk. "That's Jackson. He's not feeling so good."

A single step brought Ted to the bunk. He reached out and the man took his hand. "Jackson," Ted acknowledged him. From the black eye, busted lip, and assorted bruises, Ted understood why the man was under the weather.

"You're up there." Lynch pointed to a top bunk.

Ted looked up, then tossed his meager belongings up onto the bed. He took off the heavy overcoat while studying the structure. The boards across the end and the narrow space between each bed had him wondering how he would climb up there.

"Lynch here is the Combine Fuhrer. He can fill you in on how things work around here."

"Thanks, Callahan. I'll take it from here."

Ted jerked around and stuck out his hand, "Thanks, Callahan." He repeated the name, so he would remember it. As a youngster he'd figured out that knowing a person's name went a long way toward making a friend, even with an unfriendly type like Callahan.

The man narrowed his eyes before taking Ted's hand. A hint of a smile softened his face as their hands pumped up and down.

In the narrow hallway, several men pushed past Callahan forcing him back into the room. Ted recognized a couple as they went by, new prisoners like him who had just arrived.

"I'll be back later. Gotta see who the major wants to talk to." Callahan disappeared.

"That's our last bunk, so we're full up." Lynch commented. "The other Kriegies should wander in before mealtime then you'll meet them."

"The what?" Ted asked.

Lynch gave a little, humorless laugh. "Kriegies. It's short for the German word '*kriegsgefangener*' which means prisoner of war. So that's what we call ourselves—Kriegies."

Ted knew the German word for war—*krieg*, so it made sense.

"There's a lot to learn here. How we share our Red Cross packages, take turns cooking, cleaning up. There's a little kitchen area all the combines on this end of the block share."

"Okay," Ted agreed. "Just tell me what I need to know. I'll do my best to fit in and go along with your routine."

This was his new home. After being confined in a cell for weeks, completely alone, it would be an adjustment. But a welcome one.

\*\*\*\*

"I came down in a town. I remember the buildings were damaged. I hit hard, my chute jerked me, and I was knocked out. Next thing I know I'm being pummeled by civilians. They had me in the street, a whole bunch of them, hitting me, kicking me. Got a pitchfork or something in the ribs. Then some German soldiers showed up. I was bleeding pretty bad from the gash on my head." He lifted his too-long hair to show them the ugly, red scar. "And I must have had some busted ribs in addition to the stab wound." He could still feel the pain, like his chest was caving in. "Anyway, they took me to a hospital."

"How long were you hospitalized?" the major asked.

"I don't know. A week, maybe. A lot of it is just a blur." Ted still had headaches, but he didn't want to tell anyone. No point in it. He figured they'd go away eventually. "I do remember the day they took me out of there. There was me and two other guys who'd been wounded. A couple of guards took us to a train station. It was more like they were trying to protect us from the civilians than trying to keep us from escaping." Ted thought of the terrible sounding shouts of *"Terrorfliegers"* and "murderers of women and children." The looks of hatred in their faces needed no translation.

"Where did they take you?"

"I remember seeing a sign for Frankfort. We went through the station there and on to a place called

Oberursel." Ted noticed the officer nodded ever so slightly. Evidently he knew the place. "It's an interrogation center."

"How long were you there?"

"I counted twenty-eight days. In the cell I was in, I saw where other prisoners had marked on the wall, so I figured maybe I should do the same. I started my own set of marks." Ted remembered how the days had run together. His cell had had no window, so he'd used delivery of his meager meals as a time table. "I...I could have miscounted, but it's pretty close."

Ted didn't want to think of his stay there, didn't want to talk about it. But he knew he had to. These men were the compound's organization X. They controlled everything. They had the only direct communication with the Germans. And they had the power to make his life here miserable. Or even have him removed, put in another camp, if they didn't trust him.

When they'd brought him here, they'd told him that the two men who had given him the tour of the compound had been trying to determine if anyone could identify him. No one had. Which, to these suspicious minds, meant that he could be a spy. A German plant to feed them information about what went on among the prisoners.

"What did you tell them?"

"Nothing. Name, rank, serial number."

The officer looked skeptical. Grumbling noises from the others, hidden in the shadows, declared their disbelief.

"You were there for four weeks, kept in isolation, and yet when the German interrogator spoke with you, you said nothing."

Ted could feel the sweat sliding down his spine. "I didn't tell them anything about the military. I swear."

"But you did talk about yourself."

It wasn't a question, but Ted nodded in response. He clasped his hands together to keep them from shaking. He'd talked to the guy, all right. After days of silence, listening to the German talk, Ted had started telling stories, not from his military life, but from his life before that, growing up. And he'd told them about his German grandparents. That had probably been his mistake. Why they'd kept him so long.

"What did you talk about?" Major Burnside asked.

"I talked about growing up, playing basketball, moving around from place to place. That sort of thing."

"Did you tell them about your family?"

Ted looked into the major's eyes. Their intent stare bore into him. He had to tell them. Tell them all of it.

"Yes. You might as well know. My grandparents are German. They immigrated from Germany over forty years ago."

"And you told the Germans about them?"

"Yeah." Ted nodded. "They figured out that I spoke a little German. And my name, too, I guess. Anyway they assumed I had people from Germany."

"And they used that—to get information out of you?"

Ted nodded. "They wanted to know if I had any relatives in Germany. I told them I didn't know. And that's the truth. I'm sure my grandparents have kinfolks over here, but I don't know any of them." Ted was pleading now. He desperately wanted these men to believe him.

"This guy, this German. He tried to convince me he

was my friend," Ted continued. "He wanted me to help them. To be a stooge for them." Ted looked the major straight in the eye. "But I refused. I told him I hated Germany and all it stood for. I didn't want anything to do with them. I even told him that they could threaten to shoot me, but it wouldn't make any difference."

"So they sent you here."

"Yeah. I guess he finally gave up on me." Ted drew a deep breath and tried to calm himself. He'd done all he could to convince them.

The major pushed away from the table and stood. He moved into the shadows to join the others. Ted could hear their whispers but couldn't make out what they were saying. These men held his fate in their hands. He could only wait for their verdict.

After a few minutes, Major Burnside turned back to face Ted.

"You can stay, for now. But know that you will be watched. We don't like having men in the compound that no one knows."

Ted stood. "Thank you, sir." A wave of relief swept over him.

"Keep your nose clean."

Someone opened the door and light flooded in. Outside, Callahan waited.

"Take him back. He's okay—for now."

\*\*\*\*

Ted took up his daily routine of walking the perimeter of the compound after the morning *appell* or roll call. Twice each day the Germans lined up the prisoners in the camp's open field and counted them, by block and by combine. Only the sick were allowed to skip this daily routine. They were counted by guards who went into the blocks and located each soldier.

As he rounded the second corner, someone shouted. "Hey, Bear!"

Instinctively, Ted turned at the sound of his old nickname.

He saw a man moving slowly toward him. Each step was an effort for the pale prisoner.

"Kruger, is that you?"

The man looked vaguely familiar. "That's right. Ted Kruger."

As the Kriegie came closer Ted studied him, trying to come up with a name to match the face.

"Wynn. Paul Wynn." The man stuck his hand out. "Six hundred and third squadron. I was the navigator on the 'Special Delivery.' We went down in March. Remember?"

Ted pumped the man's hand. Memories flooded back. The barracks at Allsford. Briefings from eons ago.

"Sure, I remember you. Glad to see you." Ted had forgotten about the other crews who'd been shot down. He heard about them at the time, but he hadn't wanted to think what happened to them. They were just gone.

"Where's the rest of your crew?" Wynn asked. "Did you get separated on the way down? Mine did. Haven't seen a single one of them since they rounded us up."

Old pain stabbed through Ted's chest. His crew—gone. And a second one, gone now, too.

"I was wounded. Grounded for a while. The *Miss Bonnie* went down after that." Ted looked at the ground. He couldn't face the man, then he felt a hand on his arm.

"I get it. All of us here get it."

"I was with another crew"—Ted met his fellow airman's gaze—"when I got shot down. Don't know if anybody else got out."

"Yeah." He nodded sympathetically. "I think they intentionally do that. Separate us." He put his hand up to cover his mouth and coughed, a deep rattling cough.

"You okay?"

He tried to nod but coughed again. After a minute or two, he was able to speak. "Got this cough I can't seem to throw. Had it since last spring. It'll get better, then I'll get wet, chilled, and it comes back."

"Don't they have a doctor around this place?"

He smiled. "Not here. I've been in and out of what they call a hospital, but I've never been bad enough for them to ship me out to a real one." He patted Ted's arm. "That's good, I guess."

Ted noticed the two men who took turns shadowing him standing nearby. He called to them. "Come on over here. This man knows me. He can vouch for me."

Wynn looked around as they approached. "Sure I know him. Ted Kruger. We were stationed together at Allsford. Same group."

Relieved at finally finding someone who could identify him, Ted relaxed a bit. Maybe now he'd be accepted.

He noticed a basketball hoop mounted to the side of one of the buildings. "Do any of you guys play basketball?"

Chapter Thirty-Four

He'd been in camp almost a month before he learned about sending mail.

He stood outside one of the cook houses reading the prison newspaper tacked to the wall. The news had been transcribed from the BBC broadcasts received on secret radio sets hidden somewhere in the vast array of prison compounds. Ted hadn't been around long enough to know the secret inner-workings of the camp's news service. He only knew that at least once per week, new reports were circulated throughout the camp and posted on the cook house wall.

A couple of prisoners stood nearby talking about letters. At first Ted thought they meant letters they received. When he realized they meant they were writing letters, Ted went over and asked them.

"Someone in your combine should have told you. You can write up to four letters or cards a month, but they have to be on these special forms." He held up a postcard-like form with printing on it. "Or they have some folding letter forms you can send."

Ted went in search of these elusive forms while making a mental note to speak with Lynch about his failure to tell Ted about the mail system. He tried to tamp down his anger. He knew it would do no good. The men in his combine still didn't trust him. And getting mad at them wouldn't help the situation. But he wouldn't let it slide. Writing to Kitty and his family meant too much to him.

He assumed his grandparents and his mother had been notified by now that he was a prisoner. They knew he was alive, but Kitty didn't. She would have figured out by now that his plane was shot down. But that's all. She probably thought he was dead.

The idea of her grieving for him brought an ache to his heart. She'd been so upset when her brother was wounded. And even though he wasn't her brother, they'd been close. Very close.

It had all happened so fast. He ran the memories of those few days over and over in his head. God, how he missed her. How he wanted her, just to see her, hold her.

The memory of that day on the beach flashed before him. That beautiful face surrounded by a halo of hair. The sense of safety and belonging he'd experienced when he saw her, like he'd finally come home. For years he believed that vision and that feeling had been a dream. Until she reappeared, in the flesh. A quirky, self-conscious girl with an inner strength and a special glow about her. He'd felt the same sense of coming home when he held her in his arms.

If they only let him write one postcard, he knew it had to be to her.

And he'd keep writing her until she answered.

Guys who'd been here for a long time occasionally got mail. If he wrote her, she'd write him back. He was certain.

\*\*\*\*

In the boredom of the camp, Ted spent more time thinking than ever before. He preferred action. Action accomplished something. Action kept his mind occupied and his body fit. Thinking could creep into worry and worry accomplished nothing. It only led to obsession about things that he had no control over. So he worked to control his thinking, worked to stay in reality and focus on what he could control.

Yet he indulged himself in thoughts of Kitty. Reliving in his mind every second he had spent with her. Imagining the feel of her skin, the softness of her hair, the scent of her body.

Another prisoner warned him that he'd go crazy thinking about women. But Kitty wasn't 'women.' She was his woman, and not just that, she was his other half, the part of his soul that had been missing—until that day, the day she rescued him, not just from the water, but from being lost.

So he continued to think of her, to write to her, even though he wasn't allowed to mail the letters. He sent the short messages on post cards. Three so far.

He carefully contained the hope she would write to him. With the war progressing, mail would be disrupted. The Germans may not be mailing the cards. There was no way for him to know.

He feared most that in her grief she had turned to another. He didn't think she would, yet it was possible. She'd turned to him when her brother was wounded. Would someone comfort her the way he had? Thoughts like that were pure torture. If he let himself dwell on such thoughts, he would lose his mind.

Better to focus on action.

Early in his incarceration, he approached the compound leadership about organizing a basketball team. They in turn convinced the Germans to acquire the equipment from the International Red Cross. Two authentic balls with a hand-pump to keep them inflated and a suitable goal, net and all. When they got the new goal set up, several men signed up for the team. Ted even recruited a couple of the taller prisoners and taught them to play.

It was amazing how men with nothing to do got involved. They marked off the court boundaries. They leveled and beat the ground until the ball bounced as it should, at least in the center portion of the court. No one wanted to get more than fifteen feet from the goal. Beyond that dribbling became pretty iffy.

Every day the weather permitted, a group of men played basketball. Usually, several non-players watched and cheered them on. Even on rainy days, Ted would go out and shoot a few, just to maintain his sanity.

Basketball kept both he and the other men fit and occupied. Months passed and the weather gradually grew colder until in November it got really cold. A warning of what winter would bring. And still a few hardy fellows bounced the ball and practiced lay-ups. Only heavy rain, then snow, stopped them.

Ted became friends with several men he played with. Paul Wynn, usually among the spectators, never gained enough strength to play, but Ted taught him to shoot. Ted worried about Wynn and wondered if he would survive as winter set in.

Even when the weather was too bad to play basketball, Ted continued his daily walks around the perimeter. In December, the American commanders ordered every man to walk every day to maintain their strength and stamina. So a constant parade of men made the daily trek.

By the time the temperature hit the freezing mark, the men in his combine had thawed and become friendly. Ted had joined in their established routine of daily chores. Other combines became slack and disorderly which made him appreciate his well-disciplined roommates.

But his aching loneliness persisted. He longed for female companionship. A very specific female. And his humorous side became stale. Always a sociable guy, he found himself longing for a place to be alone. Solitude was the one thing that was never possible in this crowded environment.

****

Preparations for the upcoming Christmas holiday were well underway. The secretarial staff at SHAEF planned a dance on Christmas Eve with a real, live band. Kitty volunteered to help and found herself in the middle of planning for decorations. Versailles wasn't exactly the place to shop for the type of Christmas decorations Americans were accustomed to. So she had to improvise. Luckily, the girl helping her had loads of ideas. She'd listed all kinds of green and red items they could use.

"No OD green," Kitty insisted. "No one will think it's the least bit Christmasy."

"That narrows the list, but there are plenty of other things we can use." Nancy stepped closer and almost whispered, "Are you still planning that little trip outside the city to cut evergreens?"

Kitty smiled and nodded. "I found someone who'll take us. He also said he'd provide the ax." She spread her drawings out on her desk. "We'll put a wreath here, and here, and a big one here."

The girl grinned with glee, her feet going up and down as if she were ready to launch herself into a cheer.

Kitty had met a sergeant in the infantry who, after recovering from his wounds, was assigned to guard detail for senior staff. A casual conversation about holidays back home had turned into a conspiracy for finding the appropriate evergreen decorations. He'd located the greenery and offered to take them to gather the garlands right before the dance.

The coup pleased Kitty. Not only would the hall look festive, real evergreens would make it smell like Christmas.

"Excuse me, Sergeant." The WAC stood near her desk eyeing the crude drawings.

Self-consciously, Kitty placed her arm over her artwork and smiled up into the anxious face. "May I help you?"

"The captain wants you." She looked around. "Both of you."

"Now?"

"Yes, now." The girl disappeared almost as quickly as she had appeared.

Kitty looked at Nancy who shrugged her shoulders. Whatever it was, they had to go.

The next thing she knew, she sat at a small typing desk in a back corner typing multiple copies of reports. She'd trained herself not to read the things she typed. Instead she focused on accuracy and speed. But this was different.

Something had happened. The Germans had attacked, or rather counter-attacked, and overrun American troops. What the brass thought was a minor offensive had turned into a major battle. The reports were chilling. Many units couldn't be contacted. No one knew if they were dead, captured, or if the Germans had cut the communications wires.

"Greenlee, report to the conference room and take notes."

Kitty looked up in shock. She'd been typing for three solid days. Now suddenly they wanted her to take notes.

The girl must have seen the look on her face because she added "There's no one else available right now."

Kitty leaned down and pulled a note pad out of the stack of papers beside her desk. When she pushed the chair back and tried to stand, her legs froze in place. Slowly she pushed herself to her feet. They felt numb.

"Got to move around more," she told herself as she walked stiffly toward her next assignment. Sitting for long hours in the unheated office was taking its toll.

"Got to get the airborne in there."

"Can't fly in this weather."

"Then put 'em on trucks. Whatever it takes. We can't let the Germans take Bastogne."

Kitty had heard the names of so many places in Europe that none of them meant much to her. Somehow this one stuck. Maybe because of the importance the generals gave it.

She wondered where it was and why we had to hold it.

Back at her desk she continued to type—copies of reports, letters, memos—three carbons at a time. They appeared to be sending copies to everyone. Whatever was happening was big. She hadn't typed this much since she arrived in France.

Days later her friend from the infantry appeared at her desk.

"Here you are. I've had a time finding you."

Kitty smiled at the friendly fellow. "I'm sorry. I've just been so busy, what with everything going on and all."

"Yeah." He shook his head. "I knew we wouldn't make it home this Christmas, but I sure thought we'd get there by the next one."

"I know what you mean." Everyone was discouraged by what had turned out to be a major German offensive. They were supposed to be almost ready to surrender then they started attacking again.

"Thought I'd come by and see if you still wanted that greenery for the big dance."

"Oh. I'd forgotten all about it. I don't even know what day it is."

"December twenty-third."

"Oh. Well…" She tried to think who had been in charge of the dance. "I don't even know if we're still having it." She tried to stand, but her feet were so numb she had to catch hold of the desk to keep from falling.

The kind soldier came to her rescue and helped her sit back down. He squatted down and took one of her feet in his hand. "You're freezing."

Kitty didn't want to admit that she couldn't feel her feet.

He slid her shoe off and massaged her foot. When he looked up at her he must have realized she couldn't feel anything. "How long have they been numb?"

"I don't know. On and off for days."

He looked around. "It's too damn cold in here for you to be wearing these thin shoes and stockings. You should be wearing heavy socks—and boots—and pants." His voice rose as he spoke. "You need to see a doctor."

"Oh, no. It's nothing. I'll just rub them a little and it'll be okay."

"Ma'am, no disrespect, but I've seen frostbite and trench foot, and I know a problem when I see one."

"What? I don't understand."

He stood up. "Where's your company commander?"

She tried to take in what he was saying. When she realized he was waiting for an answer she spoke up. "The captain's down that hall at the end."

When he came back, he scooped her up in his arms and carried her down the stairs and across the street to the nurse assigned to the WAC. From there they took her to a nearby hospital.

Gradually the numbness in her feet gave way to pain. The nurses assured her it was natural in such cases. Frostbite. A mild case but nothing to ignore. If she'd been moving around more, it might not have happened. But sitting so long in a freezing cold environment had been a problem.

When she returned to work a few days later, the military had issued the women heavy pants, socks, and boots. They didn't fit well and looked worse, but the women were warmer.

The incident made Kitty think of the men at the front, in the snow, crouched in fox holes, with the Germans shooting at them. She would never complain about her living or working conditions. She had it made. They were suffering and dying. There was no comparison.

For once she was thankful that Milton was in a hospital in the states.

\*\*\*\*

The mail clerk carried her daily bundle of undeliverable mail to her sergeant.

"Here's mine for today."

"Put them there." The sergeant pointed to one of a row of baskets. "I'll get to them as soon as I can."

"From what I see that may take months."

The thin, bright-eyed woman laughed. "Weeks, maybe." She looked around her. "I've got a system. And it works."

"If you say so," the WAC private replied with skepticism.

"I'll have you know I'll have those out of here in three weeks. You mark my word."

The private laughed. "Okay. I'll be watching." She shuffled through the stack she'd just deposited in the basket and picked out a strange looking postcard. "This one. I'll keep my eye on it and see how long it takes."

The sergeant took the card and eyed it curiously. She'd seen these before.

"What is it?" the private asked.

"It's from a German Prisoner of War camp. One of our boys sending something…" She read the scrawled message. "to his girlfriend." Her voice trailed off as she remembered seeing another one almost identical addressed to the same person.

She got up and went to a box she kept on a separate table.

"What's that?"

"These are the ones I'm researching. The hard ones. The ones who've been reassigned so many times they're hard to follow."

"And what's in there?"

She shuffled through the letters careful to keep them in order. "This." She proudly held up another card with the same German printing on it and the same address written in the same hand.

"What is it? Another one?"

"Not just another one. Another card addressed to the same WAC at the same address and from the same man—Ted."

"What do they say?"

"That he's alive, and he loves her."

"Oh," her voice was soft and full of understanding. "You've got to find that one."

"I will," the sergeant answered, her face beamed with pride. "I'll make a special effort to make sure these get delivered."

Chapter Thirty-Five

The order to form up finally came. It was almost four a.m., January 28, 1945.

They stood in the bitter cold, wind-blown snow swirling around them, and waited, again.

Ted had the pack he'd made from a long-sleeved shirt slung around his neck and resting against his side. It contained his few personal possessions and what supplies he had squirreled away. His thin blankets were rolled tightly and hung from a string on the opposite side to even his load.

Others had fashioned suitcases from tin cans and cardboard or sleds from bits of wood.

Over the last few weeks, as the Russians pushed from the east, the Germans became more and more anxious. The prisoners' senior officers met with the camp commandant and returned with orders to get their gear in order and prepare to move. The Germans planned to evacuate the camp before the Russians could take it, but they would not reveal their destination or the timing of the move.

Official word had come the night before. Ted's compound had assembled in the darkness only to be told to return to their quarters and wait until the other compounds marched out. With their limited mobility, Ted and his companions had no idea how many compounds there were. The central compound housed about two thousand prisoners. If there were three or four more, then Stalag Luft III could hold ten thousand, a staggering number of men to move.

One of the men in his combine had cut an extra blanket into strips to use as scarves. Ted tied the strip of wool over his crusher cap then wrapped it around his face and neck to keep out the blowing snow and biting wind.

None of the men had real winter gear. Their uniforms were whatever they had been issued when they arrived at the camp. Like him, most had some type of overcoat, but many had worn out or inadequate shoes. Ted was grateful for the oversized boots he'd been issued. He always wore two pairs of socks, and he'd reinforced the soles by making cardboard inserts. He pitied the men whose boots were too small.

After the mandatory head count, the prisoners marched through the gate in their assorted uniforms and makeshift packs. As the ragtag bunch marched past the building where the Red Cross food packages were stored, men tossed the cardboard boxes to them.

Ted realized this might be their only food for the journey ahead. He ripped open the box and transferred its contents to his shirt-pack, grateful he would have something to eat.

Kitty came to mind, as she so often did. He pictured her sitting in front of a bright fire, her curly hair glowing in the light.

Her memory was his near-constant companion. For six months, six long months, he'd lived on the memories to survive the monotony and deprivation. He'd started imagining where she was and what she was doing. He even talked to her in his mind. He told her what he wanted to do when he saw her again, that he would hold her close and never let her go. He promised to marry her and dreamed of the children they'd have. Things he should have told her when they were together, but didn't.

*Oh God, what I would give to see her.*

Much as he despised this place, leaving meant she couldn't write him—if she ever got his cards, if she wanted to write him. He hadn't gotten a single letter in all these months. Surely she hadn't forgotten him. Even if she had a new man in her life, she would still write him. He just knew it.

Kitty kept him company as the march stretched on for hours. An all-out blizzard combined with the bitter cold slowed their progress. Men with frozen feet stumbled along. The stronger ones helped the weaker. More and more men collapsed from fatigue, from the freezing cold.

Ted focused on staying with the men in his combine. Traveling in a group, with each man looking out for the others, made sense. He'd never become close friends with any of these men. But they'd learned that life was better if they worked together.

The guards, many of them older men, struggled alongside the prisoners. Loaded with their own supplies plus the weight of their rifles and ammunition, their impatient threats to shoot slackers and anyone trying to escape rang hollow. Instead of shooting those unable to go on, the guards loaded them into the few, overcrowded trucks following the long procession.

They marched all day with only short breaks to rest. The snow continued.

Well after dark they entered a small village and

stopped outside a church. Ted's group shuffled inside the unheated structure before every inch filled with exhausted prisoners. The unlucky huddled outside against the walls or broke into mausoleums in the nearby cemetery.

On the second day the snowfall slowed, but the temperature fell below zero. The Germans gave each man a cup of warm water and a thin slice of their horrible black bread for their breakfast. After eating, the men formed up and walked on, following those in front, into the unknown.

Ted could barely feel his feet as he trudged along the snow packed road pounded hard by the thousands of feet that had gone before him. He gritted his teeth and resolved to survive. Even if he lost both feet, he would survive. And he would find Kitty and never let her go.

In the early afternoon, Ted saw a familiar figure standing like a statue in a snow bank beside the road. He faced a Christmas card scene of sparkling white stretching across a field to a cluster of evergreens at the foot of a small hill.

Ted stopped when the man coughed. The small, hacking sound could only come from his friend, Paul Wynn. Ted joined him. Beneath the snow-covered wool scarf that covered most of his face, Paul coughed again.

"Paul."

Wynn turned his head just enough to see who was beside him. His eyes crinkled in a smile. "The ol' bear." He returned his gaze to the far hills.

"Why are you standing here, Paul? You need to keep moving."

Another cough answered him. After a few moments, Paul spoke. "You go on. I can't…"

Ted saw the man waver and grabbed him. "Don't give up. You can make it."

"Leave me here, where it's peaceful."

"No," cried Ted. "I won't leave you." He wrapped his arm around his friend's waist and pulled him back onto the road.

Jackson had stopped to see what Ted was up to. When he saw Ted wrestling with the near-frozen man, he grabbed Paul's other arm. "Come on, ol' man. Move your feet."

Paul responded to their coaxing and started to walk with the two men holding him upright.

Ted had to do something to keep his friend moving, so he started talking. He told stories of his training days, his near-miss at Hoover Dam, his adventures in pursuit of the ladies. Anything to keep them going and their minds off the terrible cold.

Ted didn't know how long he could keep it up. With only short breaks, they continued into the night. Finally they stumbled into a village. Someone directed them into a barn. Although it was unheated, they were out of the wind.

Ted found a spot on the crushed straw and settled his friend beside him. Paul, still coughing, fell into a restless sleep. But Ted couldn't relax, couldn't rest.

The smell of damp, moldy straw invoked a feeling of impending doom. He tried to shake it and make himself sleep. His body ached for rest, yet he waited for the disaster he knew was coming.

A vision flashed before him. He bolted upright and sat trembling from the impact of the vivid memory.

"Your father is dead!" His mother screeched as she shook him awake. "They shot him," she screamed.

"Caught him stealing and shot him."

The memories flooded back.

They'd found an abandoned shed, half-fallen in. Old straw covered the floor where someone had slept there before.

His father had lost all their money. His mother angrily berated the man for his stupidity, for allowing thieves to assault and rob him. What could he have done? Yet she went on with her incessant harping.

When she'd finally run out of steam, his father told her to wait for him in the shed. He'd walk to the nearest town and send another wire to his father. The old man would send the train fare to get them to Nashville. They'd only have to wait until it arrived.

Ted remembered complaining of being hungry. The old guilt washed over him. Maybe if he hadn't complained…maybe his father wouldn't have tried to steal the food…maybe he would still be alive.

Ted forced himself to look around at the men lying and sitting on every inch of space in the barn. They reminded him of the hobos camped near the railroad tracks. Some were suspicious, some friendly. But by that time his father trusted no one. He'd led them away, until they'd found the shed.

He told himself his father had tried to protect him, had tried to feed him, take care of him. His mother, on the other hand, had come apart. Always demanding and selfish, the woman became distraught when her husband lost his job, then their home. She hated his immigrant parents and never wanted to ask them for help, but she finally saw it as their only hope.

The wire brought money for the trip from St. Louis east to Nashville. Had his father not been robbed, had they not been thrown off the train, his life might have been very different.

But no, after that fateful night, his life changed forever.

Looking back, he knew he'd been better off living with his grandparents. He'd been ashamed of their accents and strange ways. But they'd given him stability, a home...and their love. As a rebellious teenager he'd resented their rules, their advice, and when he graduated, he'd lit out, determined to find his mother.

He found her. The same flighty woman, making selfish demands on her new husband just as she had done years before. Age had accentuated her faults while stealing her looks. No longer the beautiful woman he remembered from childhood, she let him know she didn't want a grown son hanging around, revealing her true age, something no layers of makeup could hide.

Hurt and unwanted, Ted impulsively signed on to the crew of a freighter and set out to see the world.

Then the Japanese attacked.

After the freighter went down, he'd returned to Jacksonville, to the mother who didn't want him. The man at the airfield encouraged him to join the Army, fight the Japs.

And here he sat, a prisoner of the Germans, marching through the snow to some unknown prison camp, where he may or may not survive.

His father had hoped for the best and tried to do what he thought he needed to do to survive. Except he hadn't. He'd died. And more than likely, Ted would, too.

Ted lay back on the hay, certain he would not

sleep. He forced his thoughts to Kitty, the one bright spot in his miserable life.

That bright, sunshiny day, she'd smiled and told him he was safe. He had to believe he would be and he would see her again. It was all he had.

\*\*\*\*

The third day's march blurred into the cold, white landscape. After a short rest stop, Paul couldn't get to his feet. A POW officer got the Germans to load him into one of their trucks. Paul was so weak and hopeless. Ted bid him good-bye and wondered if his friend would make it.

Well after sun up the next morning, they shuffled through another village and stopped at a tile factory on the edge of town. After days of bitter cold, the heat from the kiln shocked Ted's body. He and his combine mates climbed up into the loft above the furnace and collapsed. The fires helped thaw frozen feet, hands, and bodies. Pain replaced numbness. Despite his aching feet, for the first time since leaving Stalag Luft III, Ted fell into a deep sleep.

The Krauts allowed them to rest in the factory for two days. The food they gave the Kriegies was barely edible: weak soup, hard tasteless bread, and lumps of white margarine.

When they returned to the road, the temperature had warmed enough to turn the snow to slush. Ted's feet, now thawed, got wet. He began to cough, a dry hack that failed to clear the phlegm from his chest. And his insides churned into the beginnings of diarrhea.

After another seemingly endless day, they reached a railroad yard on the edge of a town. Tough, new guards loaded the Kriegies into boxcars, like cattle, and locked them inside. Fifty men overcrowded the dark, closed space. Body heat provided the only warmth. Shelter from the wind meant little air to breathe. No toilet facilities meant the stench grew worse as time passed. Lack of water added to the misery.

Only a few could sit while the others stood on painful, tired feet. Ted clung tenaciously to the spot he'd found near a wide crack where a whiff of air penetrated the putrid atmosphere. He found himself longing for the open road and the long march.

The train sat on the track for hours.

Ted's cough grew worse. A heavy weight pressed on his chest. When his painfully churning bowels betrayed him, misery overtook him. Men grumbled and cursed around him. He pressed his face to the crack and forced himself to inhale. His thoughts went to Kitty, wondering where she was and grateful she could not see him in this unbearable condition.

When the train finally jerked into motion, the man next to him pulled himself up to his feet. He shoved Ted to one side. The guy he fell against shoved back. Lightheaded and weak kneed, Ted slid down to the soiled floor. His weakened body sank into the sea of misery that surrounded him. He gasped for air but damp stench brought on a spell of coughing.

The joke was on him after all. He told her he was a dead man. But he didn't die when the plane exploded. No, that was too good for him. This special hellish fate better suited his worthless soul. He wanted it to be over. He understood Paul's need to give up, to lie down in the clean, white snow and gaze out on the peaceful landscape.

But Ted Kruger, the arrogant SOB he was, told him

to keep going. For what? His friend was probably lying beside the road, dead. And smart ass Ted Kruger sat in his own excrement at the bottom of a locked boxcar filled with sick, dirty, exhausted men.

*Just let me die and be done with it.*

Kitty couldn't save him from this. She would be better off. With him gone, she'd find some nice, decent guy.

He leaned his head back against the wooden wall and listened to the train rumbling along the track. If he could only see her one more time. See her beautiful face surrounded by that halo of curly hair, telling him he was safe, that she loved him. He'd die happy.

****

Finally the doors slid open. Bright light and a gust of fresh air swept into the boxcar.

Men shuffled around him. Ted couldn't move, couldn't get to his feet. He closed his eyes and wondered if they would just leave him.

Men, other prisoners, pulled him to the door. They lifted him from the train and carried him away.

They had arrived at Stalag 7A outside Mooseburg.

Jackson and a couple of other men deposited Ted on a bunk in a cold, damp barrack. His combine crowded into an already occupied building. They complained loudly about the too small stove, no kitchen, no indoor toilets, and too many prisoners.

*At least the march is over. At least we can rest. And maybe get warm.*

Word came from the Kriegie commanders that the Germans had consolidated many POW camps into this one enormous facility. All nationalities and military types were thrown together. Stalag Luft III had been luxurious compared to this place.

After a few days Ted's fever rose. They moved him from the barracks to the prison hospital, as it was. With no medicine and no doctor, little could be done except to keep him warm and force feed him warm soup and water.

He clung to Kitty, talked to her in his delirium, held her in his dreams. The image of her hovering over him, hair wild in the wind, and love in her eyes kept him struggling to hang on.

Chapter Thirty-Six

*January 30, 1945*

"Hurry and change. We don't want to be late."

"Okay," Kitty answered, starting up the four flights of stairs.

"I'll grab the mail. You go on. I'll get yours, too."

"Thanks, Betty."

Kitty tackled the stairs and tried to convince herself that going to this shindig was a good idea. A banquet meant a decent meal. Live music would be a treat, for her anyway. She'd stayed in most nights when the other girls went out. Nothing interested her anymore.

She reached the final landing trying to figure out how Betty had talked her into going. It wasn't the possibility that General Eisenhower and General Bailey would attend. More likely it was the prospect of seeing General Doolittle again. She'd met him once, or more correctly she'd been taking notes in a meeting he attended. Nevertheless, she was impressed. Maybe it was her soft spot for the Air Force. She'd been away from it for months, yet she still felt connected to the fly boys.

Memories of Ted and shot up planes skidding off the runway combined and caused her to catch her breath. No. It was just the climb. Four flights always took her breath.

She entered the room she shared with three other WACs and headed for the makeshift closet where they hung their uniforms. Her section was on the far left where everything got smashed against the wall.

She pulled out her uniform dress and held it up to her. It had been months since she had tried on the dress, and she could tell it would hang loose on her now. She'd lost so much weight, and she hadn't bothered to take it up. She never wore it anyway.

That meant her good uniform would have to do. At least she'd ironed her best blouse the last time she did laundry. Problem was she didn't have a decent pair of stockings.

She heard Betty coming in.

"Betty, can I borrow a pair of stockings?"

"Sure," the girl replied. She threw a bundle on Kitty's bed. "Looks like the mail is catching up again. We both got a bunch."

"Thanks for bringing it up." Kitty laid out her skirt to determine if it needed to be pressed. She grabbed the bulky bundle by the string and placed it on the table out of her way.

Betty dug through her foot locker. She pulled out a small paper bag and tossed it at Kitty. "That's my emergency pair." She went to the closet to get out her clothes for the evening. "You owe me one," she said over her shoulder.

"Thanks." Kitty smiled, glad to have Betty for a roommate.

Kitty thought of Madge. Her last letter said she had been transferred to Belgium. At least that's how Kitty had interpreted the 'code.' She glanced over at the bundle of letters and wondered if she'd gotten one from

Madge.

Betty went to the bathroom, and Kitty took advantage of the moments alone to undo the bundle. She spread the letters out on the bed looking only at the return addresses. One from home, two from Milton. She picked up one of Milton's and started to open it when something else caught her eye.

It looked like a post card. She reached out and moved it with the tips of her fingers. That was strange. It had German printing on it. She picked it up. The original hand-printed address was to Second Wing Headquarters in Ellingham. It was marked through as was High Wycombe and London.

When had this been mailed? And who was it from?

She turned it over and saw the signature.

Her breath caught. Her heart stopped.

She froze.

Ted.

She blinked, again, then again. She gasped, trying to catch her breath.

It can't be. It can't…

A chill ran up her spine.

She sank down on the edge of the bed. Her eyes flew to the words written on the small card.

"I'm alive… I love you…"

She couldn't see through the tears. She blinked frantically. She gasped for breath again.

"How?" she heard herself ask.

"What?" Betty stood over her.

Kitty looked up. The shock must have been evident on her face.

"What's wrong?" Betty asked.

She couldn't speak. She just looked at the card. It

was like holding a message from the grave. From a ghost...

Betty took the card from her hand and looked it over. She read the message aloud.

*Sept. 12, 1944*

*Kitty,*

*I am alive and thinking of you. I'm here in this camp and making it okay. It is a miracle that I am here, but no more miracle than the day we met. The angel that pulled me from the waves threw me out of that plane and saw that I landed safely. Remember that I love you and that I will see you again. In the meantime, watch over me, my Angel.*

*Ted*

Kitty's heart began to pound. Tears rolled down her cheeks. Could he be alive? Could it be real?

Betty turned the card over and read the return address.

*Second Lieutenant T. R. Kruger*

*Gefangenennummer: 7213*

*Lager-Bezeichnung: Stalag Luft 3*

*Deutschland (Allemange)*

"It's from Germany. That's a POW camp. Who is this guy?"

"Ted," Kitty murmured. "He's..." She couldn't talk, couldn't explain. Her body shook uncontrollably.

"He's your boyfriend, isn't he?"

Kitty nodded. My boyfriend. My love. She didn't even try to stop the tears.

Betty sank down on the bed and put her arm around Kitty's shoulders. "You thought he was dead."

Kitty nodded, even though it hadn't been a question. She leaned into Betty's shoulder, covered her

411

face with her hands, and sobbed. "He's alive. He's really alive."

Betty held her and patted her on the back to comfort her. Kitty realized she was squeezing the card so tight she might damage it, so she laid it on the bed with the rest of her mail. She wiped away the tears with the back of her hand and looked down at his careful printing.

The corner of another card peeked out from underneath a letter. She pulled it out and realized it was a second card, almost identical to the first one. She quickly read his words and choked up again.

*October 8, 1944*

*Kitty,*

*I am still here in this camp and still thinking of you. Life is easier somehow when I think of you waiting for me. This is the second card I've sent. I hope you get it so you know I am alive and well. I don't know how long it will be but know that one of these days I will see you again. I love you and miss you. Please write. I don't know if I will get your letters but send them and maybe some will get through. Watch over me, my angel.*

*Ted*

She picked up both cards and compared the dates. September 12, 1944, and October 8, 1944. It was the thirtieth of January. Almost four months ago he'd mailed the last one. Four months for the cards to reach her.

Time stood still as she held them. A lifeline to Ted, so far away in a prisoner of war camp. He must have been there since last summer—and still there through the horrible winter. Fear gripped her.

*Oh God, let him be okay. Let him still be alive.*

Betty left her sitting on the bed, lost in memories.

Sometime later Betty returned. "Come on, Kitty. We've got to get going." Betty shook her as if trying to wake her from a deep sleep. "The boys are downstairs waiting."

"I don't..."

Betty pulled her to her feet. "You are going. No argument. Now let's get you dressed."

In a few minutes they were descending the stairs, Ted's cards in her bag. She'd keep them with her always. They were her connection to him, to life, to the future, to any hope of happiness.

She drifted through the evening wanting to tell everyone she met that he was alive. She didn't, of course. Only in her mind. But that night, for the first time in ages, her smile was real. She laughed and chatted and, yes, even danced.

*He's alive!*

She had to celebrate, even if she and Betty were the only ones who knew why.

****

By March the Allies had fought their way into Germany all along the front. The Germans stubbornly refused to surrender and defended their homeland like madmen.

Kitty typed reports, hundreds of them. She found herself reading more, trying to understand what was going on in the war. She especially watched for anything related to POWs.

On a short leave in Paris, she went to the displaced persons section hoping to learn something about prison camps and their liberation. Other than learning the locations of the various POW camps, she gleaned little.

All the information coming out of Germany was confused and inconsistent. Only a few freed French slave laborers had made their way back to Paris.

Near the beginning of the month, Patton's army crossed the Rhine on a bridge the Germans forgot to blow up. Soon pontoon bridges stretched across Germany's last line of defense, and Allied troops poured into the heart of Germany.

By April horrible, unbelievable reports poured in of concentration camps and their emaciated, mistreated occupants. After reading one report, she got sick and ran for the bathroom where she threw up her breakfast. A fear gripped her. Fear like she had never known. The report told of prisoners being executed by their guards only hours before the Americans arrived. It described the guards as desperate and brutal and merciless.

She prayed for God to keep Ted safe.

Surely there was some sanity left. Surely there were men who knew they were beaten, who wanted to live even if they had to surrender. Surely they wouldn't kill the prisoners of war.

Kitty's only consolation was that most of the camps she read about were not military, not Air Force or Luftwaffe run camps. She hoped desperately that it made a difference.

****

"I still can't believe you're here." Kitty reached across the table and squeezed Madge's hand.

"Me either. At the last minute, Colonel Kessler gave in, and I was out of there before he could change his mind." Madge flashed her signature smile, guaranteed to melt hearts.

The two women sat in the sunshine at a table in a

side-walk café in Paris.

"How did you arrange to fly?"

Madge gave a sly wink. "Oh, you know me. Used the old charm and in no time those boys were falling all over themselves to get me on board."

Kitty heard herself chuckle and realized it was the first time in a long time she'd really laughed. "I'm glad you came."

Madge straightened and turned to look in one direction then another. "A girl can't come to Europe and not see Paris. It's just not done." Her voice mimicked a hoity-toity heiress from an old movie.

Kitty laughed again. "You're crazy."

"I know. But someone has to entertain you." Her face turned serious. "You look good, Kitty. Too thin and too serious. In a way, you're the same old Kitty. And in another way, you're more grown up, more confident."

"I had to grow up. No one could be exposed to all this and not."

"And you're happier because he's alive."

Kitty nodded. Mentioning Ted still brought tears, but she choked them back. "Just knowing he's alive. We were so sure he was dead. And now, well, it's like he was reborn. Or maybe I was."

"Have you heard any more? How he got out of the plane?"

Kitty shook her head. "No. Nothing. I got one more letter since I wrote you. But it says pretty much the same thing. That he's okay and…well, I'm sure the mail is censored, so he can't really say what it's like. It was so cold back in the winter. And all these horrible reports."

"I know." Madge took a sip of what passed for coffee, looking thoughtful. "I don't suppose you'd let me see them. What he wrote, I mean." She glanced at Kitty from under her long lashes.

Kitty saw a glimpse of sadness, loneliness even. She looked away, hesitating. She didn't want to share them, not with anyone. They were all she had. Yet she remembered how upset Madge had been, how they'd cried together. Madge had loved Ted, too. And she'd accepted that Ted loved Kitty. So maybe it wouldn't hurt, just to let her see them.

She reached for her bag hanging at her side. She opened it, slid out a brown envelope, and handed the envelope to Madge.

"Oh, Kitty." Madge's voice almost broke when she took the envelope. She stared at it for a moment, then looked back at Kitty. "Are you sure?"

Kitty nodded, her throat tight with emotion.

The two cards and a folded letter slipped easily out of the envelope and into her friend's hand. One by one she read them. Her face contorted as she fought the tears. "Oh, he does love you, a lot. I can hear it in his words." A tear slid down her cheek, and she brushed it away. "You are the luckiest girl in the world."

"I know."

"And look. He sent them to Ellingham. No wonder it took so long for you to get them."

"Yes. I've written to him and given him my new address. But I don't know if he's gotten any of my letters. You see what he says."

"Those beasts. They may be prisoners, but they deserve to get mail. It's hard enough not getting mail when you aren't a prisoner."

Suddenly Kitty pitied Madge. She remembered that Madge never heard much from her family. Sometimes she went months without a letter. Madge may have had lots of boyfriends, but she didn't have anyone who really cared about her.

Madge put the cards back in the envelope and handed it back to Kitty. She had a far-away look about her. After a moment she reached into her pocket and pulled out her compact. As she checked her makeup and hair, the sadness melted away and the confident beauty returned.

"Well, my friend, if we're going to see Paris while we're here, we better get started." Kitty tucked Ted's cards away in her bag and stood.

"Are you going to be my tour guide?"

"To tell you the truth, I haven't seen much since I've been here. It's only been a little over a week since my transfer to Displaced Persons." Slinging her bag over her shoulder and adjusting her cap, Kitty smiled at her friend. "I guess we'll have to explore together."

Madge slipped her arm through Kitty's and grinned. "Let's go. I'm sure we can find some nice boys to show us around."

Kitty laughed. Madge saw everything as an opportunity to meet men.

## Chapter Thirty-Seven

*April 29, 1945*

Ted stood among the crowd of prisoners as a line of Sherman tanks separated from the main body and slowly drove down the road beside the camp. His height allowed him to see more than some of the others.

"What's happening?" a shorter man asked.

"They're American tanks. Trucks and jeeps following them."

"Why don't they hurry up?"

"Probably making sure nobody is going to start shooting."

"Are they getting closer?"

"Yeah." Ted started when the lead tank crashed through the main gate and drove into the camp. "Damn!"

"What? What?" the shorter man shouted.

"They just plowed through the gate."

"They're really here, aren't they?" the man's voice broke with emotion.

"Yeah, they're here. They're finally here." Ted's throat tightened. He didn't want to start coughing again. He'd been in and out of the hell-hole they called a hospital, and he sure didn't want to go back. The damp spring weather with mud everywhere hadn't helped.

The officers tried to control the men as they surged

toward their liberators. Emotions ran high. Men climbed up on the tanks and trucks. Others cheered.

Ted hung back. His mind raced into the future, to a future he believed he would have. He'd find Kitty. And he'd hold her in his arms. He'd never let her out of his sight. They'd go home together. He'd take her to meet his grandparents. And he'd go to her hometown to meet her family. Then they'd have a big wedding. No. The wedding would come first. He'd marry her as soon as they could find someone to marry them. He had no doubt that she'd marry him, not after the time they'd spent together. She had to marry him. She'd kept him going, kept him alive.

The celebration continued with hugs and cheers and spontaneous singing. The Americans distributed some food, mostly K-rations. And the medic's checked out the prisoners who were in bad shape. The officers assured the prisoners that they would be evacuated as soon as possible. In the meantime they were told to stay put, within the camp, so they would be safe and could be processed. A matter of days, they said. After so long, it was unbelievable.

Artillery fire came from the nearby town. Someone said the Germans had destroyed the river bridge and were firing from the opposite bank of the river. American troops continued to arrive. They stopped and rested outside the camp until they could continue their pursuit of the enemy.

The next day, General George S. Patton himself arrived at the camp. He got out of his jeep and walked in the mud among the newly liberated men. Everyone cheered the famous general.

Patton assured the prisoners he would continue the

fight and beat the Russians to Vienna. To do that he needed supplies and that meant delaying their evacuation so his men could fight on. Of course, the men cheered him. They wouldn't stall the war effort, not now when the Germans were on the run.

Medical personnel arrived and set up an aid station. They examined many of the prisoners, including Ted. With his chronic cough, he was tagged for early evacuation to a hospital. The doctor recommended he rest, but Ted disagreed. He'd rested in the prison hospital long enough. Fearing that lying in bed would only make him weaker, he'd forced himself to get out of bed and move around. He'd walked and walked.

As a freed prisoner, he did the same. He walked. He watched others play basketball and toss a baseball back and forth. He didn't have the strength to join in, but he enjoyed watching and dreaming of the day when he could return to the basketball court.

After a few days, three American nurses arrived. Ted decided to check them out. It had been months since he'd seen an American woman.

"Hi, beautiful. Where've you been all my life?"

The nurse stood with her fist on her hip and smiled at him. "There's nothing wrong with you, soldier."

Ted grinned, feeling more like his old self than he had in months. "So let me out of this place." He crooked his finger, bidding her to come closer. When she approached cautiously, he whispered, "I'm needed in England."

"England? For what?" She eyed him curiously.

"My girl. She needs me." His smile faded into a plea. "And I need her."

"How'd you get involved with an English girl?"

"Oh, she'd not English. She's a WAC, with the Eighth Air Force."

Her expression changed to one of understanding. "How long have you been here?"

"I was shot down last summer, July."

"You know, a lot has happened since then. The Army and the Air Force have moved onto the continent. France, Belgium. She may not be in England now."

The information hit him like a blow to the gut. It hadn't occurred to him that Kitty might not be in England, at Ellingham, where she'd been when he left. He closed his eyes imagining Kitty in the Castle.

"She was in England when I left." He slowly opened his eyes. "She may think I'm dead." He coughed, his hand covering his mouth. "I wrote her." He looked into the woman's face, desperately needing someone to understand. "I don't know if she got my letters. I never got any back."

The nurse patted his hand. She didn't say anything, sensing that he needed to talk.

"The damn Germans moved us to this place so even if she did write…" Ted fought back tears. "I…I have to see her."

"You will, soldier. You will."

****

*May 9, 1945*

*Dear Milton,*

*You should have seen the big celebration in Paris. It was unbelievable. So many people in the streets, so much wine and laughter. After five years of war, the French really celebrated. And of course all the Allies joined in. You would have loved it.*

*Glad to hear you're making progress in the rehab*

*program. You can take me out dancing when I get home. Don't know when that will be. Rumor is that us WACs are low priority. The fighting men will go home first. But that's okay. They did the hard part.*

*I guess I can tell you what I'm working on now that the war is over and no more censorship. I'm working with the various countries accounting for displaced persons. It's unbelievable how many people Hitler took out of France and the low countries to use for slave labor and how many he put in prison. As the Allied armies moved into Germany, these people were freed. People are trying to find their loved ones. It's heartbreaking. Sometimes they learn from a released prisoner that their family member died. Even that sad news is better than never knowing.*

*I can relate to these people because of Ted. I've never been able to verify his location after the camp at Sagan was moved. I pray every day he is still alive. You are the only one who knows about Ted, except for Madge. So you understand. I don't mind staying here for a while if it means I find him.*

*Write me soon.*

*Your sister,*
*Katherine*
****

After a truck ride to a nearby air field, Ted and a group of ex-POWs met the crew of the B-17 that would carry them to a processing center near Le Havre, France. Before climbing aboard, Ted asked if any of them knew a WAC named Kitty Greenlee.

"Nope. Never heard of her," the co-pilot replied.

Others shook their heads.

"She was stationed at Ellingham. Worked for

General Lake."

"Sorry, Buddy. I never even heard of a General Lake."

The navigator spoke up. "How long have you been a POW?"

"Almost ten months," Ted replied. It felt longer. A lifetime almost.

"We've only been in ETO since last December," the pilot told him. "We've been flying missions out of England, but a lot of bombers and fighters were moved to fields in France and Belgium."

Ted's heart sank. How would he find her? Then he had an idea. "What about Madge Sorensen? She's a WAC, too. Blonde, built, looks like Betty Grable."

"Nope, but I'd sure like to meet her."

The others shook their heads.

Discouraged, Ted climbed aboard the bomber. Instinctively he moved toward the navigator's seat.

"You boys'll have to sit on the floor in the waist," the navigator said.

"Sure. It's just that I'm a navigator, and I'm used to sitting up front."

"Well, in that case, come on." He motioned for Ted to follow him into the nose. "We're flying with just a five-man crew. You can sit up there in the bombardier's seat."

Ted grinned. "Not dropping any bombs this run, huh?"

"Right."

Not only were there no bombs, there was no need for oxygen. They flew across Europe at about five thousand feet, so Ted got a view of the countryside below.

Ted thought that this might be the last time he would fly in a B-17. At least this time he wasn't being shot at, and he could enjoy it. He fought to suppress the painful memories of his last fight and the men who would never go home.

He could see the English Channel not far ahead when the pilot began his approach to an air field near the coast. The big plane came in for a smooth landing and taxied to a hard stand where the pilot welcomed them to Camp Lucky Strike.

By then Ted was determined to ask everyone he met about Kitty and Madge. Surely someone knew one or both of them.

Instead of boarding the waiting truck, Ted approached the ground crew. He then walked the short distance to the next hard stand and asked the crew who'd landed minutes after them.

The truck carrying the other POWs drove by. Ted decided that they couldn't do anything worse to him than he'd already been through. Finding Kitty was more important than following orders.

After questioning the second crew, Ted hitched a ride back to the officers' quarters.

He approached a group of airmen. "Does anybody here know a WAC named Madge Sorensen? She's a real looker. Blonde, great figure, friendly, looks like a pin-up girl."

He looked around as men shook their heads. "She was assigned to the Eighth Air Force in England. Has a friend named Kitty Greenlee."

Still nothing.

Ted sighed. He racked his brain for ideas.

A guy approached from the back of the group. "I

met a Madge a few months back. Pretty blonde. Might be her."

"Where?"

"I flew in to a base in Belgium. It was back in the winter. I got snowed in. Had to stay until it cleared. There was a pretty blonde WAC in the Officers' Club. I think her name was Madge."

"You said Belgium." Ted was excited. Maybe if he found Madge she could tell him where Kitty was. Maybe she was in Belgium, too. "Can you write that down for me?"

"Sure." The man found a piece of paper and pencil and wrote down the name of the base.

Ted thanked the men. He left the Officers' Club and continued to ask everyone he met about Madge and Kitty. He was taking no chances. Maybe the Belgium lead was good, or maybe it wasn't. He'd keep asking until he found them.

Before nightfall he made his way to the tents where the POWs were being processed. As he suspected, other than chewing him out for wandering off, they did nothing but assign him to a bed for the night.

The next few days were spent being processed, examined, de-loused, outfitted with new uniforms and boots, and fed. All the ex-prisoners delighted in the hot showers. They lingered under the warm spray and lathered up with more than generous amounts of soap. Meals provided another joy. In the past Ted had barely tolerated Army food. Now it tasted delicious. The staff warned them not to eat too much. Their digestive systems weren't used to this type of food and might rebel. Sure enough, most of them suffered from upset stomachs and had to revert to soup for several days.

During processing the ex-POWs were told that they had priority for shipment to the states. They would get their orders as soon as transports arrived at Le Havre.

Desperate, Ted located a telephone and had the operator place a call to Madge Sorensen at the base in Belgium. Within minutes, the operator told Ted to wait while the WAC could be located and brought to the phone. A thrill ran through him. Madge would know how to find Kitty. They might have been fighting when he left, but they wouldn't have lost touch, At least he hoped so.

**\*\*\*\***

"Hello."

"Madge, it's Ted. Ted Kruger."

Silence from the other end of the line.

"Madge, are you there? Can you hear me?"

"Ted," the voice sputtered. "Ted, is it really you?"

"Yes. I'm at Camp Lucky Strike, near Le Havre."

"Then you're safe?"

"Yes, thanks to the Germans. I've been in a POW camp."

"I can't believe it. Can't believe it."

"Madge, where is Kitty? Is she there in Belgium with you?"

There was a short pause. "No. Kitty's in Paris."

"Paris." He blinked back tears. He'd found her. "Where?"

"She's working for SHAEF. With displaced persons. Hang on. I just got a letter from her."

Ted heard her rustling papers. Then she read off an address in Paris. Ted grabbed a pencil from the operator and jotted it down.

"That's where she lives, not where she works."

"How come she's working for SHAEF?"

"Oh, it's a long story. I'll let her tell you."

"Oh, thank you for this, Madge. You don't know what this means to me."

"I think I do. I saw the letters you wrote her."

"She got them?"

"Yes. Two cards and a letter from a prison camp. Before that she thought you were dead. We both did."

"Did she write me? I never got any letters from her."

"She wrote. Lots of them. She loves you, you know."

"Oh, Madge. I've got to find her. They're going to send me back to the states, but I have to find her first."

"Tell the chaplain. See if he'll help you get a pass."

"I will. And thanks again, Madge. You're swell."

"Just look me up when we all get back home. I've got Kitty's folks address. I'll let them know where I am. Looks like it will be a while before us girls get to go home."

"Bye, Madge. And thanks."

Ted hung up. Now all he had to do was get a pass to Paris and Kitty would be in his arms. His throat tightened. He could feel the cough coming on. He didn't even try to stop it. Just let it hide his tears.

## Chapter Thirty-Eight

He leaned against the stone building, lit a cigarette, and waited. He'd gotten good at waiting. Only this time he knew he didn't have to wait long. Kitty would come home soon enough. He'd hold her in his arms, kiss her, and tell her how much he loved her.

How many times had he imagined the scene? Hundreds? Thousands?

This time it would be real. Or would it? What if she didn't feel the same? What if she'd found someone else? Forgotten him?

No. Don't think that. Madge said she loved him.

So he'd wait. Wait to see her for himself. See how she reacted. See if she'd agree to his plan. They'd get married. Right here in Paris. The chaplain said it might be possible.

He watched the busy street. This whole part of the city was filled with military. American, British, French, Canadian. He even saw a New Zealander. But he was watching for an American WAC.

Since he didn't know where she worked, he carefully scanned every woman coming from any direction.

He remembered how hard Kitty worked when they were in Ellingham. She'd stay late to finish something. But not today. Don't work late today.

He wondered if General Lake had been transferred

to SHAEF. Was that why Kitty was working for them instead of the Air Force? He hoped not. He didn't trust General Lake. The man had been way too friendly toward Kitty. The officer's reputation had started to influence people's opinion of Kitty. Yet she had appeared oblivious to the rumors and innuendos. Maybe something had happened, and she'd transferred. He hoped she hadn't been hurt.

So much time had passed. What had she done all these months?

Two WACs approached. He quickly realized that neither was Kitty—just by the way they walked, before he saw their faces.

When they turned to enter the building, he stepped out of the shadows and spoke to them.

"Excuse me, Ladies. Do you know Kitty Greenlee?"

They looked him over, curious about his sudden appearance.

"Who wants to know?" one asked.

Ted stepped closer. "Second Lieutenant Ted Kruger. I'm a friend of hers."

"Haven't seen you around. Where'd you get that uniform?"

He glanced down, suddenly aware of his unusual appearance. "Oh, this." He flashed them one of his best smiles. "They gave us these uniforms at Camp Lucky Strike. It's all they had."

"You look like a buck private with lieutenant's bars pinned to your collar." The WAC may have been kidding, but he got her point.

"Like I said, it's all they had. You see, I've been in a prison camp and...well, our uniforms got kind of messed up."

"Prison camp?"

"Yeah. In Germany."

Realization swept across their faces quickly followed by a look of horror.

Did he look that bad?

"Oh, you poor dear," one cooed.

"And you said you were looking for Kitty?" the other asked.

He nodded and smiled again, hoping they would tell him something.

"She lives upstairs. Fourth floor, I think." She reached out and took his hand. The other girl gently grasped his other arm, as if she thought he would collapse.

"When do you think she'll get here?" he asked.

"Come inside. You can wait in the little vestibule."

"I'd rather wait out here," he protested. "How long do you think it will be?"

"I don't know. She might not come home right after work. She might stop somewhere and get something to eat."

"But how will I find her?" Panic clutched at his stomach. He tried to control it. He could wait, as long as it took.

"I tell you what. We can go check the canteen. That's probably where she'd eat."

"That would be nice of you," he told them. "I'll wait right here."

The two women hurried off in the direction they'd just come from. One turned and waved before they crossed the street and disappeared.

Ted sighed. He fished another cigarette out of his

pocket and lit it before slipping back into the lengthening shadows.

Again he leaned against the building. At least he knew this was the right address, that she'd come eventually.

He took a deep drag on the cigarette and scanned from one direction to the other, careful to examine every pedestrian on the street.

A woman emerged from the others. She was alone. With each step she became clearer. Dark green WAC uniform. That silly hat perched on her head. She took long, confident strides as she came closer and closer. Until finally he knew.

It was her. It was Kitty.

\*\*\*\*

Kitty headed to her room, too exhausted to eat. Maybe later. Right now she just wanted to lie down and rest.

She'd dealt with so many people in the last few days. Since the surrender, everyone thought their loved one would instantly appear. But it didn't work that way. They hadn't gotten any names from the newly liberated camps. They were still processing the ones who'd been freed in early March. Yet she could understand their frustration, their anxiety. She wanted word, too. She'd tried to get away, get over to the office that handled prisoners of war. But she'd been so busy.

Maybe tomorrow.

She crossed the street. Her block. Just a little ways yet.

She noticed a soldier emerging from the deepening, afternoon shadows. He stood in front of her building for a minute then started walking toward her. There was something vaguely familiar about him. He was thin, but his height, the way he moved…

He came closer.

She froze, unable to move.

It couldn't be. It couldn't be him. She must be imagining…

"Kitty."

"Oh, Ted!" She launched herself into his arms. "Ted! Ted! Ted!"

She couldn't stop saying his name as she wrapped herself around him, holding him as tight as she could.

He was real. She could feel him. His arms were around her.

She pulled away just enough to look up into his face, the most handsome face in the world. "How?"

He grinned down at her, eyes glistening. "Kitty," he whispered. "My Kitty."

His face was thin, gaunt, with dark shadows circling his eyes. The body she held so tightly was thin. She could feel his ribs beneath the shirt that hung loosely from his shoulders.

"How did you get here? How did you find me?" She had so many questions.

"Train, plane, taxi." He leaned down and brushed his lips across her cheek. "I got hold of Madge. She told me where you were."

The longing in his eyes told her he wanted to kiss her, wanted her to kiss him. Why was she waiting? She shook off the questions, the doubts, and stretched up on her tip-toes so she could reach him. He understood instantly. His lips met hers. Nothing else mattered but the taste of him, the feel of him. He pulled her closer and deepened the kiss.

She floated on a cloud of joy.

*He's home, safe, in my arms.*

When he finally released her he was grinning, laughing. She laughed, too. Free from all the worry, all the anxiety.

They rocked back and forth in each other's arms. People stood nearby watching. But she didn't care. They understood. They'd all been through this war. No one was untouched.

"Looks like he found her," a familiar voice nearby commented.

"You two better get off the street. You're drawing a crowd."

Kitty looked around and saw two familiar faces. WACs who lived in her building. They had names, but her brain couldn't come up with them.

"Hi, girls." Ted greeted them. "I found her."

She looked up into his smiling face. He was looking at the other women, but he still held her tightly, as if he thought she might slip away.

With the women on either side, they pushed through the crowd toward their building.

As they reached the door, Ted pointed to something by the wall. "My bag."

"Oh, I'll get it." One of the girls darted to the side and grabbed the small ditty bag, then followed them inside.

"Men aren't supposed to go upstairs," one girl commented.

Kitty steered him to a cushioned bench in the little alcove beside the stairs. They both sank down to sit beside each other. Ted grasped her hands and stared at them. He was in as much a state of shock as she was.

"Can we get you anything?" one of the girls asked.

"No," Kitty answered. "Just let us sit here a minute."

The two faded away, their voices and footsteps echoing on the stairway.

"Oh, Ted," she sighed.

He drew a deep breath, then stifled a cough. "I…I have to ask you." His gaze met hers.

"What?"

"If you'll marry me?" His voice pleaded, his face desperate.

She hadn't expected him to ask her, not yet. He'd only just appeared out of nowhere.

"I know it's sudden, but I don't have much time."

"What do you mean?"

"They're shipping me home." He forced a smile. "I've got a three-day pass. And the name of a chaplain who'll help us."

"Three days." Her throat contracted. She fought back the tears. "But you just got here."

He nodded. "I know. I know."

He looked so pitiful. Nothing like the strong confident man she'd known in England. She pulled him into her arms.

He held her tightly. "You're the only thing that kept me going. Thinking of you. Holding you again." His hand reached up and touched her hair. She knew what he wanted. For her to take it down so he could run his fingers through it.

"I know it's sudden," he continued. "But I love you. And I want to marry you. Before we're separated again."

"Oh, Ted." She couldn't think, couldn't imagine.

Get married. Three days. After months of waiting, not knowing if he were alive or dead.

He pulled away so he could look at her face. Doubt clouded his. "There's someone else."

"No! Oh, no." She couldn't believe he thought such a thing. "It's just…just so sudden."

He relaxed a little but still gripped her shoulders. "I can't lose you."

She shook her head. "You won't lose me. Not ever."

A smile crept from his lips to his eyes.

Her gaze took in his handsome face. She reached up and ran the tips of her fingers down his smooth cheek to his strong jaw line. "I love you," she whispered.

Tears welled in his eyes. "I love you, too."

His lips touched hers in a gentle caress.

Someone opened the door, startling them.

Kitty looked around, aware they were being watched. "Okay, now." She pulled him to his feet. "First things first. Have you eaten?"

He shook his head.

"Then let's get something to eat." she said. "After that, we'll see if we can find this chaplain of yours."

\*\*\*\*

They stood in the chapel waiting. The captain and a small group of WACs stood in the back while the chaplain paced.

"If she doesn't get here soon, we'll have to go ahead without her." Kitty squeezed Ted's hand. "The captain won't wait much longer."

He faced her, holding both her hands. "And my ride won't wait either." He smiled. "Do you mind too much if she doesn't make it?"

She shook her head. "She'll understand."

Ted turned and motioned to get the chaplain's attention.

"Are you ready?" the chaplain asked.

"Looks like we'll have to go ahead with it. No maid of honor. But then there's no best man either. Just the two of us."

There was a sad finality in his words. She wished some of his friends were here to witness the ceremony, but from what he'd said, most were dead, and he didn't know where any of the others were, except for Milton, who was thousands of miles away.

The chaplain signaled to the group of WACs who moved toward their seats. Then he turned to Ted and Kitty.

"You understand, this is just…well, a sort of pledge. It's not legal. With all the formalities and paperwork the French require, it just wasn't possible in such a short time."

Ted nodded impatiently. "We know, we know." He turned to Kitty and smiled. "The ceremony is for us. It means…" His voice broke. "It means a lot to us."

Kitty blinked back the tears. He was so determined to marry her. So determined they'd never be separated. He'd insisted they go through the motions, have the ceremony even if it wasn't legal.

A commotion outside the chapel drew her attention away from her fiancé. She knew before the door burst open who was causing the uproar. Madge. She'd made it, at last.

"There you are!" Madge rushed into the chapel and up to them. "Sorry I'm late. We had a little trouble at the airfield."

Kitty noticed an Air Force officer who quietly followed Madge into the room. He came closer. "Sammy!" she exclaimed. "Sammy Newman."

The airman stepped closer.

Ted grabbed his hand and shook. "Newman, you son of a gun. Where'd you come from?"

"Madge here, she told me I had to come. Said you two were getting married."

"That's right." Ted beamed.

"Can we get started?" the chaplain interrupted.

"Sure, Sure," Ted replied.

"Sammy, you stand there by Ted," Madge said in her take charge way. "And I'll stand by Kitty. I mean Katherine."

Kitty hugged her friend. "Thank you."

When she released her, Kitty saw tears glistening in Madge's eyes.

"I just had to be at my best friend's wedding."

One of the girls handed Kitty a little bunch of flowers to serve as her bouquet.

"Do you have the ring?" the chaplain asked.

Ted fished a gold band from his pocket and held it up.

"If this young man is to serve as your best man, then he should hold the ring."

Ted turned to Sammy. "Would you?"

"I'd be honored."

Ted handed the ring to Sammy, then turned to Kitty. He stifled a cough, and she feared he'd have another uncontrollable coughing spell. They came on when he got emotional. Like when they went to her captain to ask for the time off and she'd refused, at first.

After he told her he'd been a POW and only had a few days, he'd succumbed to a spell of coughing and almost collapsed right there in her office. He'd managed to gain her sympathy to the point where the captain had helped with the arrangements.

But no matter what the captain or the chaplain had done, it hadn't been enough to budge the formidable French bureaucracy.

So they'd settled for a ceremony that held no legal value. But it meant a great deal to Ted and Kitty.

One of the WACs stepped forward and handed Ted a glass of water. He took a sip and gave it back to her.

"Thanks," he murmured.

Kitty hoped that was enough to prevent any further coughing.

"Join hands," the chaplain instructed.

Kitty clasped Ted's hand and the ceremony began.

Within minutes they'd both said "I do," and the chaplain said, "Within the power vested in my by God and these witnesses, I pronounce you man and wife."

He paused, then with a small smile continued. "You may kiss the bride."

Ted grinned at her before he leaned down, pulled her close, and kissed her.

She clung to him, never wanting to let go.

The shouts of congratulations from the little group drew them apart. Madge hugged Ted while Sammy hugged Kitty. Then Sammy shook Ted's hand and congratulated him.

"I'm really glad you're here. How'd you do it?"

"Madge, of course. She ordered me to come."

"I did not. I just suggested it," Madge replied.

"We'd almost given up on you," Kitty interjected.

"We had to catch a plane," Madge explained.

"You mean I had to arrange it." Sammy grinned. "Of course, Madge here can talk anyone into anything."

Ted gave the beaming blonde a big smile. "Oh, I know. She can be very persuasive."

The WACs produced a bottle of champagne and some glasses. When everyone had a filled glass, the captain proposed a toast. "To the happy couple."

Ted put his arm around Kitty's shoulders and squeezed as the others drank. Then he held up his glass and spoke. "To all of you. And you're all invited to the big wedding"—he smiled down at Kitty—"strictly to make it legal, you understand, when we all get back home."

He taped his glass against Kitty's, and they both drank.

He handed his glass to Sammy. "And you'll have to forgive us, but we don't have much time to celebrate. I'm due back, and I have to catch a train."

"No, you don't," Madge said.

"What?" Kitty exclaimed.

"You have to catch a plane." Madge winked at Sammy. "That'll buy you a few hours for a honeymoon."

"Oh, Madge." Kitty hugged her.

Madge reached out and touched Ted's arm. "It's the least we can do for my two best friends."

## A word about the author...

Barbara Whitaker writes historical romances with a focus on the World War II era. Originally from a small town in Tennessee, she currently calls Florida home.
http://www.barbarawhitaker.com/